A SECOND CHANCE

A SECOND CHANCE

An Amish Romance

LINDA BYLER

New York, New York

The characters and events in this book are the creation of the author, and any resemblance to actual persons or events is coincidental.

A SECOND CHANCE

Copyright © 2019 by Linda Byler

Good Books books may be purchased in bulk at special discounts for sales promotion, corporate gifts, fund-raising, or educational purposes. Special editions can also be created to specifications. For details, contact the Special Sales Department, Good Books, 307 West 36th Street, 11th Floor, New York, NY 10018 or info@skyhorsepublishing.com.

Good Books is an imprint of Skyhorse Publishing, Inc.®, a Delaware corporation.

Visit our website at www.goodbooks.com.

10 9 8 7 6 5 4 3 2 1

Library of Congress Cataloging-in-Publication Data is available on file.

ISBN: 978-1-68099-447-6
eBook ISBN: 978-1-68099-450-6

Cover design by Jenny Zemanek

Printed in Canada

TABLE OF CONTENTS

A SECOND CHANCE

CHAPTER 1

THE INDOOR-OUTDOOR THERMOMETER ON THE HIGH SHELF IN THE kitchen registered minus four. The sun had not yet broken the frigid, creaking darkness as Edna snapped the cheap cotton sheets, threw them across the line, and tugged, arranging them hurriedly before they turned into stiff unmanageable fabric crusted with ice. As she reached into the clothespin bag tied snugly about her waist, her red, chilled fingers fumbled for one wooden clothespin out of the dozens all rolled together along the bottom. She found one and clipped it expertly to the already hardening sheet.

Icy wind was the best thing for getting rid of any germs that clung to the sheets used in childbirth. They had been washed in scalding water with a glug of Clorox, rinsed in sweet-scented Downy, and now frozen stiff in the merciless, battering wind that roared across the Indiana landscape, as level as a cookie sheet.

Jutting her chin forward, she yanked at the ends of the soft black kerchief tied around her head. Cold. It was seriously cold. Steam swirled around her as she opened the washhouse door, closing it quickly behind her, shivering slightly.

She may as well get used to it. Winter was here and laundry took up a large portion of her life, being a *maud*, or maid, for any young couple blessed with a squalling newborn, in need of a housekeeper, housecleaner, babysitter, cook, dishwasher, or anything that included the care of the new mother, the older children, and the husband.

Edna Miller was twenty-nine. She would turn thirty in July. All her life, from the age of fifteen, she had been hired out to any Amish family that needed her, whether at childbirth, for spring or fall housecleaning, or for keeping the home fires burning when someone went away for a vacation or to visit an ailing relative.

Short, dark-haired and dark-eyed, soft and round and capable, Edna was crackling with a zest for life. There was no job too mountainous for her. She had no husband or children, and had never had a date in her life.

She was Edna, take her or leave her.

The wringer washer chugged along with its air-powered motor undulating beneath it, the agitator jerking back and forth, creating a distinct waving motion as it scoured the whites.

She wanted a mug of steaming coffee, but knew she wouldn't have time to drink it. Besides, she didn't want to risk waking the sleeping, exhausted mother, or the newborn snuggled on the recliner with the grandmother who slept in her dress and black knee socks, her feet encased in men's lined moccasins.

Poor thing. The grandmother was too old for this; covered haphazardly with an insufficient throw, her mouth hanging open as she eclipsed all the snores Edna had the misfortune to encounter.

She had a feeling this one was a *bupp*. The *buppa* were the babies whose eyebrows were raised in anxiety, who whimpered and gasped at the slightest discomfort, whose mother spent more than one long night trying to soothe them to sleep, whose father hovered with monumental attempts at fixing everything, but eventually slunk out of the house in bewildered defeat.

Edna fished a steaming towel out of the swirling, sudsy water and fed it into the wringer, then another. She hummed beneath her breath, remnants of songs heard at the New Year's Eve hymn-singing at Atlee Rabers. Now that had been some serious party mix. She'd have to ask Atlee Katie for the recipe, perhaps make a batch. Maybe it would help to cheer up this brand-new mother, so tired and overwhelmed. Edna had been watching the rapidly receding euphoria that was the sure-fire harbinger of a grand display of baby blues, that unexplained quagmire of hormones and self-exhaustion and negative thoughts. She would do everything she could to help pull her out of it.

Leona Mast had been a beautiful highflier who had driven around with the more disobedient boys in their flashy cars or trucks and finally married her match in a wedding that had been the talk of the town. Spoiled, protected from most of life's prickliness, this was a real waker-upper, Edna knew. Pushing any judgmental thoughts away, she resumed her humming, carried the basket of wet towels out the door, a wave of steam immediately obscuring her view.

Edna hung up the last of the towels, hurried back into the welcoming warmth of the washhouse, and decided to let the white underwear wash for fifteen or twenty minutes while she snuck around the kitchen to make a pot of coffee. Coffee was a necessary pleasure in life. Edna preferred hers with a dollop of flavored creamer, but she would settle for milk and sugar. She never drank it black.

She carried the yellow and black DeWalt battery lamp, checked to make sure it was on the lowest setting, and pushed up on the "on" button. A dim white glow bathed the kitchen in its white light and Edna began opening doors close to the gas range, fumbling to find the familiar handle of the Lifetime drip coffee maker. Ah. There it was. She drew it out slowly, careful to hold it level so it would not slide noisily, or knock the lid off. She opened the top cupboard doors, searching for the familiar blue Maxwell House container. Or the red Folgers. If she were really lucky, she'd find Starbucks or Dunkin' Donuts. Maybe Green Mountain.

"The coffee is in the green canister with the cork lid," came the gravelly voice from the grandmother on the recliner.

Edna jumped, thoroughly startled.

"Didn't mean to wake you."

"It's alright, as long as Leona gets her rest."

She poured the water into the top portion of the coffee maker and set it to drip, checking the time as she did so. Six-thirty. The sun would be painting white streaks on the black horizon soon. Good. Made it easier to finish hanging out the laundry. Quietly, she opened the refrigerator door, searched for the anticipated red and blue bottle of Coffeemate, discovered there was none.

From the recliner, "Leona doesn't use creamer."

Again, Edna jumped. Didn't the woman miss anything? The disgruntled irk in her throat kept her from a reply.

Ah well, time to push back the irritation. She couldn't allow it. She was here for two weeks, so Christian love was in order.

Oh God, hear my prayer. Give me a sweet, loving heart.

She went back to the washing machine, disgusted by the milk that was as bland as chalkwater, that 1% crap. Watching the figure, Leona was.

Hear my prayer, Heavenly Father.

Edna mopped the floor and rinsed the washing machine, glancing out at the clothes on the line, stiff as armor in the steady gale as winter's icy fingers spread across the land. The wind would freeze all except a few stubborn corners of the heavy towels. Socks would need to be hung from the PVC ring in a warm corner of the washhouse, but that was normal in winter.

She flung open the kitchen door, the sunrise washing the beige walls in an orange glow, the double windows above the sink on fire with the brilliance of it. Edna surveyed the perfectly crafted oak cabinets, faux ceramic tile linoleum in a blended shade of brown, the best hutch and matching table and chairs. It was every new mother's dream kitchen. She was grateful for the toasty warmth as she set out to prepare breakfast. New mothers needed fiber, so she began preparing a dish of baked rolled oats with apples and raisins, making only a minimum of noise.

She heard the recliner's soft release, turned to see the grandmother sitting upright, holding the swaddled newborn.

"Can you hold her a while, till I go to the bathroom?" she asked, her voice thick with fatigue. Edna knew she had barely slept for the second night in a row and felt a dash of sympathy.

"Just lay her down, she'll be fine," Edna replied with all the confidence acquired from years of working with mothers and babies.

"She'll wake up, I'm afraid. Come take her."

So Edna went, lifted the baby carefully, and lay the sleeping baby on its side, drawing the blankets up to cover her ears.

This one was a cutie, with all that dark hair and round face. Of course, both parents were nothing to sneeze at, so you could expect a cute one from this couple.

But all babies were cute, every one. Innocent little gifts of God, for sure.

Edna loved the babies, loved to bathe and cuddle and swaddle them. It was a joy to hand them, clean and fresh, to the appreciative mothers, the benevolent fathers.

Most of the time.

As with many other jobs, this one had its downsides, which she figured was completely normal, so her ambition never wavered. Her enthusiasm to meet another family, another newborn, another washing machine, was what kept life interesting.

Edna was the youngest of six children. Her three brothers and two sisters were all married and lived in Indiana, in various homes with various children in various stages of finances and acquisitions. Edna had worked as *maud* for all of them at various times. The sisters-in-law were good friends, all of them amiable, easy to accommodate, and her nieces and nephews were like bright flowers dotting her existence. There were seventeen of them—eight girls and nine boys.

Her aging parents were a growing cause for concern. They were in their seventies, with health problems cropping up like unwanted dandelions in an otherwise well-kept garden. But there was no time to think of all that now. The toast was done, eggs scrambled, juice poured. The table was set with yellow Fiestaware, like individual spots of sunshine on the snowy tablecloth, the orange juice in the glasses reflecting more of the golden glow. She placed the steaming casserole of baked oatmeal on a cast-iron trivet near the butter dish and a tiny pot of strawberry jam.

Edna stood back, pleased.

"Breakfast!" she sang out, the old elation rolling over her as she waited to see the happy faces, the appreciative words. It was what she loved to do.

The grandmother scuttled into view, a forefinger to her thick, chapped lips, her eyes bright with warning.

"Shh. Don't wake Leona."

"I thought she was awake."

"She was. But the baby is sleeping so I told her to get her rest. She's not going to sit up at the table yet. She'll need a tray."

She lifted her chin to peer through her bifocals at the baked oatmeal.

"Do I see raisins?" she asked in a churlish tone.

"You do. You do see raisins," Edna replied, a stiff smile drawing her lips away from her teeth.

"Leona won't eat raisins. You'll have to eat it yourself."

"Oh. Well, I can. What about you? Will you join me?"

"I don't eat raisins."

"Oh. Will you eat the toast and scrambled eggs with me?"

"White or wheat?"

Edna thought she was trying to be funny, making up a bird tune, "whit a wheet, whit a wheet." She laughed, her faced wreathed in happiness, so glad to find a rare spot of humor in this serious, careful house.

She finished laughing, said "Uh, Huh! Yeah," and was pinned to the wall with angry darts from the grandmother's eyes.

"I fail to see what's so funny. I asked if the toast was made with white bread or whole wheat. I don't eat whole wheat."

"I see. Actually, it's white."

"Then I'll eat."

"Good."

They slid into chairs simultaneously, bowed their heads with unspoken agreement born of years of tradition, and prayed in silence to thank God for the food. Edna added a plea of deliverance from judgmental thoughts.

Being the soft, round little person she was, Edna needed sustenance after hanging all those wet clothes out in the arctic chill, so she heaped a sizable portion of fluffy scrambled eggs onto her smooth yellow plate. She reached for a slice of toast and proceeded to spread it thickly with butter, while the grandmother picked at the crust on her toast, then lifted a cup of black coffee to her lips with one pinkie held at a fashionable angle.

"I don't care much for scrambled eggs. I eat mine poached."

"Is that right?"

"You don't need to use sarcasm."

"Oh, of course not. Didn't mean to sound sarcastic at all. I have never heard of anyone who doesn't eat scrambled eggs."

She held up a finger. "Leona?"

There was a weak wail from the bedroom, and the grandmother knocked over her chair to get to her long-suffering daughter quickly. Edna glanced at the sleeping baby as the grandmother sailed past on small, tapping feet.

She shrugged, figured this was a good time to dispatch of the scrambled eggs, which were absolutely wonderful with a glug of homemade ketchup and a slice of buttered and jellied toast. She paid no heed to the low murmurings from the bedroom. She reveled in every bite, washing it all down with copious amounts of orange juice.

"Edna!" came the grandmother's panicked voice from down the hall.

"Yes?"

"We need your help."

"Coming."

Two pale faces greeted her entrance, one with fatigue, the other with anxiety.

"She needs help. There. Lift her from the other side. Careful now, she has a sore shoulder. Ready, Leona?"

A weak gasp escaped Leona's lips before she sagged back on the bed.

"It's alright, Leona. Take your time."

To Edna, "She's been through so much."

Edna tried to stop the thoughts, but they barged right through and made themselves known.

Oh for crying out loud. Did she now? No worse than thousands of other women before her and no doubt thousands after.

The baby grunted and began a high-pitched yowl of hunger, sending Leona back against the pillows with a shuddering sigh. Fat, glistening tears of hopelessness slid down her porcelain cheeks, sending the grandmother shuffling off to the recliner, shaking her hands as if ridding herself of an ant invasion.

Disaster Alert. All units deployed. Edna hid a maniacal grin and went to relieve the grandmother of the howling infant, sending her hurrying back to her despondent daughter. She took the baby to the adjacent nursery, decorated in beige and turquoise.

She unwrapped the little girl and changed the tiny Pamper, a chore she never tired of. The tiny, delicate, perfectly formed limbs, the rounded velvety stomach, the ten fingers and ten toes. Miraculous. Truly angelic.

With sure fingers, she zipped up the warm sleeper with the

purple giraffes all over it, tucked her back in the soft blanket, and carried her to Leona.

"Time to eat, Mama!" she trilled brightly, her intention of lifting some spirits falling flat as Leona glared and the grandmother scowled.

"I can't nurse her now. I need to eat first."

Unbelievable.

A hot thrust of outrage thrust through Edna. Never one to mince her words for the sake of others, she could not help herself, opening her mouth to deliver a firm, well-meaning lecture that folded itself like plastic wrap around mother and daughter.

"You can and you will, Leona. You have just brought this innocent angel into the world, and now it is your duty to provide for her to the best of your ability. Your life is no longer your own. You will make sacrifices for this child, and you may as well start now."

They both looked as if they might suffocate, but Leona dried her tears and sat up while Edna arranged pillows behind her back, brought a snowy white burp cloth, and helped her get the baby situated and latched on.

"Now sit back, try to relax."

Turning to the weary, harried grandmother, Edna said she was going to make arrangements for her departure, hushing Leona's protests.

"No. Nope. Time Momma leaves now. After three days visitors stink like fish."

The grandmother's mouth opened and closed like a fish, but no words came forth.

After the baby was settled, Edna made a perfect cup of poached eggs for Leona. She delivered them with freshly buttered toast and sat watching with pity as Leona suppressed her ravenous appetite by taking small, careful mouthfuls under the watchful eye of her mother. Edna dug into the baked oatmeal, heaping a cereal bowl with it. She washed it down with a cup of coffee laced with sugar and more of the thin, chalky milk.

"I hurt," Leona moaned.

"Normal thing to do. I'll put a clean sheet on the recliner and you can rest. Time you got out of that bedroom, O.K.?"

Her mother opened her mouth to protest, but Edna waved her away.

"Call a driver. Time for you to go."

Edna could tell there was no love wasted between them, but that was alright. She'd seen it too many times. Overprotective mothers only enhanced the daughter's symptoms, besides robbing them of the ability to draw on their own reserves of confidence.

Time to go, Momma Bear, she thought.

The pretty house was bright with winter sunshine. The wind hummed around the eaves, sending snow spray cascading down from the spouting, whirling it away in a diaphanous curtain across the front lawn.

The wooden bird feeder swung crazily, emptied of birdseed, the bewildered winter birds twittering in the white pine by the tall fence.

Edna softly hummed and whistled as she washed dishes, polished the stove, then swept the kitchen floor. She found a yellow can of Lemon Pledge and sprayed it liberally on a rag cut from a T-shirt, dusted the furniture, and Swiffered the hardwood floor in the living room. She searched every closet, every drawer, for birdseed or suet cakes, but came up empty.

She saw Leona crack open an eye from where she lay on the couch.

"Good. You're awake. The birdfeeder is empty."

"Who cares?"

Alrighty, then. Edna said nothing and turned away to hide her rush of annoyance. She ironed two shirts she found in a basket, sewed a button on a pair of trousers, then tiptoed past the resting Leona and went to her room upstairs. Edna tucked her hands under her cheek and fell asleep for a much-needed midafternoon nap.

It was the cold that awakened her, so she sat up, yawned, smoothed her hair that was pinned to the stiff, white bowl-shaped covering to her head, and slid quietly down the stairs.

Leona opened one eye.

"I'm thirsty."

"Certainly. You will be."

She returned with an insulated tumbler of ice water.

"It's 32 ounces. You can drink three or four of these, and it will do you good. It'll increase your milk supply, keep you hydrated. . ."

"I know all that."

"Of course you do."

"I'm hungry."

Edna sat on the sofa, crossed her arms, and observed Leona like a bright-eyed little bird; her head shifted to one side.

"You know this is not a time to watch your weight. You need the calories to help your milk supply."

"That's not what Mam says."

"Really? What does she say?"

"If I'm careful now, the weight will drop off easily, the hormones helping me to regain my figure. But I'm so hungry."

Her voice ended high, in a little girl wail of pleading.

"Then you shall eat. What your mother doesn't know won't hurt her. You need your strength."

With that, she marched to the kitchen, whipped up milk, eggs, and cinnamon, dipped stale sourdough bread in the mixture, and toasted it in a skillet with a tablespoon of butter.

She made a brown sugar and corn syrup mixture to drizzle across it, sliced a banana over the top, and served it on a tray.

Leona's eyes flew open in surprise.

"Oh my goodness!"

And she ate. There was no extension of the pinkie, no minced chewing, and small bites. She ate without reserve and washed it all down with gulps of ice water. Edna watched her eyes brighten and her cheeks flush. Leona even laughed a little as she started to tell Edna about how the midwife had gotten confused with directions and almost didn't make it in time for the birth.

When the baby cried that jarring yowl of indignity, Leona smiled hesitantly, but reached for her and looked down into her face with something like motherly concern.

It was a beginning. Just as Edna had predicted. It worked every time, didn't it? Get rid of the sticky tack visitors and give the new mother some good food, plenty of water, a little rest, and she starts to perk up.

"I'm still worried about the birdies. It's fierce out there."

Leona looked up.

"Oh, yeah. You said something. Did you check the basement?"

So Edna was filling the feeders, half hidden by the looming white pine, when Leona's husband came home early. She finished squeezing suet cakes into the cages before wading through the powdery snow and into the washhouse.

Keith, Leona's husband, had already shucked his outerwear and was kneeling beside the recliner, his arms around his wife and sleeping daughter.

It was a scene straight from Heaven, and Edna turned away to hide the quick tears that sprang to her dark eyes.

Oh indeed. She'd passed judgment quickly and without tenderness on this selfish, spoiled young woman and her exacting mother, but here was love in its purest form. Keith loved his wife, spoiled or not.

Edna sniffed and wiped her eyes with a corner of her white apron.

Edna had been a *maud* for so long, to so many families, that she knew how to handle nearly every situation that could come up. Yes, she had done the right thing by kicking Leona's mother out, and now she could bask in the joy of seeing this young couple step into the world of parenting together, unfettered by the mother's critical eye. Edna wasn't a proud woman, but she knew she was good at this job and she loved it. It was a huge reward to give of yourself over and over to these families, to let the blessings pile up like sacks of coin in a bank vault.

She was blessed, she told herself, over and over to the point of becoming like a broken record stuck in a groove. *Blessed, blessed, blessed. Happy, happy, always happy.* She was always looking forward to the next house and the next mountain of dirty diapers and sour-smelling bibs and socks. *The next frigid morning, hanging the frozen sheets with purple fingers that will never know the feeling of my own newborn, never grip the hand of my husband.*

She caught herself, shaking her head. *One moment I rejoice in a family's perfect circle of love, the next I slide down the ravine of self-pity.* She would not allow herself to wallow in the swamp of "what ifs" and "why nots?"

She was satisfyingly single. Happily unattached. A leftover blessing. There were so many well-meaning names for the single ladies. Wasn't there a song about "all the single ladies"? She'd heard it once.

She grabbed the Swiffer, dipped her head, squeezed her eyes tightly, and prayed to God for a new and right heart, and none of these selfish thoughts.

She started thinking about Leona's mother again. A rare bird, for sure. She was attentive, but she could hardly qualify as a nurturing mother. Leona was probably doing very well, considering what she'd grown up with. Keith was a treasure.

They'd named the baby Lucinda. Poor thing. What was wrong with them? Lucinda Raquel.

Ah well, none of her business. None at all.

She set to work peeling potatoes, hoping Keith was among the ranks of the ninety and nine who loved a heaping mound of mashed potatoes with a glob of thick chicken gravy sliding down around it.

CHAPTER 2

THE TWO WEEKS WITH KEITH AND LEONA PROVED TO BE WHAT SHE could honestly label "good." There were ups and downs, but all in all, given Leona's liberal upbringing, Edna decided little Lucinda was off to a good start in a mostly well-adjusted home.

Edna left the young family and headed home on a cold, starlit night, as still as death and about as bright. Going home meant the usual headshake, a rattling of all her mental capacities, a rearrangement of her thoughts and responsibilities.

It was always good to see her parents, even though their aging bodies demanded a new and strong perspective from Edna.

She paid the surly minivan driver, waited till he pressed the button to release the back door, and swung her luggage out in one powerful swoop. She shouted "Thanks" back over her shoulder as she headed toward the low front porch built along the front of the white stucco ranch house.

The smell of peroxide and Pepto-Bismol assaulted her nose. Without thinking, her hands came up to wave at the air.

Her father, round-faced with a white beard and matching cap of silvery hair, smiled at her from his deep seat in his chair. His stomach was a perfect imitation of a well-stuffed sausage, his broadfall denims stretched to the limit.

"Home again, Edna. Like a well-trained homing pigeon, you

always return. And if you didn't, Mam and I would surely miss it."

Edna smiled, and thought that was a nice way of saying he was the one who benefited from having an unmarried daughter, but knew, too, that he spoke the truth. There was never a doubt that she was loved and cherished.

Her mother made an appearance from the bedroom door, tying a clean apron around her own ample waistline.

"Oh, it's you, Edna. I heard Dat talking to someone. How was your stay with the young couple?"

Edna nodded, said it was good.

Did she ever say anything otherwise? Why burden them unnecessarily with tacky accounts of the selfishness of youth?

"I baked bread," her mother said, "so there will be a fresh loaf for our evening meal. We haven't eaten yet. Have you?"

"No. I put a casserole in the oven for Keith and Leona, but I left before it was done. I'll take care of my luggage and then join you."

The long hallway ended in a spacious bedroom complete with a seating area, a large kneehole desk with a marble top, a bookcase groaning under the weight of her many novels, a cherry four-poster bed stacked with pillows on an eiderdown quilt, a tall chest of drawers, and a low dresser with a tall mirror. The walls were decorated with pictures of country landscapes, done in muted colors of gray, beige, and white, and a bulletin board containing homemade cards from various young nieces and nephews who mostly thought she was awesome.

She shivered, then turned the gas wall unit to the highest setting and was rewarded by the familiar whoosh of the sharp line of blue flame.

She glanced in the mirror as she threw her luggage on the tufted gray sofa. *Ugh. What a bleached potato.*

She needed some sun, which she knew was not possible in winter unless she spent an entire day sled riding. Perhaps she should consider skipping church to find some slope and turn her face to the sun.

Ah well, it was what it was.

She left the door of her room ajar, carrying an armful of soiled clothing to be distributed in piles by the washing machine. She'd take care of it on Monday morning.

She found the source of the strange odor, an oversized bottle of pink Pepto-Bismol, the black cap askew, sticky rivulets drooping from the top, like sweet, pink mucus. Beside it, on the windowsill loaded down with Campbell's soup cans and Maxwell House coffee cans containing geranium cuttings in different stages of growth, was a white plastic lid filled with a clear liquid. Edna knew instinctively that was the odor of peroxide. Her mother's pharmacist told her a capful of peroxide among geraniums would keep pests away, which was now her mother's undisputed law.

Every time her mother made a trip to Henry's Pharmacy in Odin, she came away with another truth written in stone, the laws by which she lived. Grimacing, Edna picked up the pink bottle, grabbed a dishcloth, started wiping up the gooey mess.

Ugh. Disgusting. She quietly took the cloth to the washhouse door and threw it in the general direction of the soiled laundry. She wiped down the bottle, replaced the cap, asked who had an upset stomach.

"Why, me. You know how my lower intestines fizz like a can of pop," her father answered. "Nothing beats that pink stuff."

Her mother nodded in agreement.

"Good stuff. Harry from the pharmacy says it's the best."

Edna moved every tin can to wipe the scattered dirt and curled brown leaves, the dead, dehydrated houseflies upended with legs like waxed thread. She chased a stinkbug into a corner with an edge of a paper towel, then flushed him down the commode.

"Oh now, he wasn't hurting anything," Her mother commented, inserting an arthritic finger in the potato soup to check the temperature, then licking it thoroughly.

"Mom, use a spoon," Edna said, suddenly weary.

Her parents were so old and senile, like overgrown children. She needed to be here for them; to clean, monitor blood pressure and heart rates, keep tabs on her father's diabetes.

A quick irritation zigzagged through her veins. Where were her sisters? Her sisters-in-law? The minute she stepped in the door, there was everything to be done at once.

"Wasn't Fannie here this week?" she asked.

"No. I don't believe she was. Sadie stopped in to borrow my pinking shears on her way to town. Come, Edna, leave that now. Put your dishcloth away. We want to eat."

The tablecloth was peppered with food, dried to rough flakes. It smelled worse than the dishcloth. The Melmac soup bowls were stained and scratched, with the spoons and forks thrown haphazardly across them.

Edna compared this table to the one she had left earlier, then berated herself for the comparison. These soup bowls held many childhood memories, of fresh blueberry pie in summer, homemade strawberry ice cream in winter. Spoons clattering, children laughing and talking at the dinner table when it still held four leaves to accommodate eight of them.

No, this was fine, this sour tablecloth with watery potato soup her mother had forgotten to thicken.

After her mother had carefully ladled it into their bowls, she looked puzzled, then asked what was wrong with the soup.

"It's fine," her father said.

"It's good," Edna told her.

Satisfied, her mother smiled happily and ate the thin potato soup and served the crusty homemade bread with the same wide smile of satisfaction she always had at mealtime.

"Good bread, Mam," her father commented, buttering his fourth slice.

"Your sugar," she warned, pointing with her fork.

"Ah, I'll be careful tomorrow."

All of the normal everyday chatter crashed down around Edna with a tightening sense of portent. In the two weeks she had been gone, they had seemed to age years.

But in the morning, after a long winter's night of deep sleep beneath layers of quilts, Edna felt a renewed sense of optimism, sniffing the familiar smell of frying cornmeal mush and strong coffee, her father singing some off-key version of plainsong as he clattered the lid on the cookstove.

Edna washed, brushed her teeth, and combed the heavy dark hair up and away from her face and secured it with clip barrettes. She shrugged into a dress of deep burgundy, arranged her white covering on her head, and went forth to address the day.

"Morning, Edna!"

"Morning."

"How was your night?"

"Slept like a log. Hardly a dent in the covers."

"Good, good. Nothing like your own bed."

Edna smiled at her father. Clean, his face shaved, beard trimmed, he was still a handsome old man.

"Message for you. Dave Chupp's wife had their baby. Another son."

"Really? Alright, then. I'll go there tomorrow morning. Church today, though, and thought maybe we could visit Chip and Fannie this afternoon."

It was another bright day in January, the air sharp with the cold, the sky a deep shade of blue with puffy gray clouds woven through.

Old Dob, their faithful horse, stood with his neck outstretched, his eyes half-closed as he waited till everyone was safely tucked into the buggy, blankets wrapped securely, gloves pulled on, reins taken up. Then he was off on a reluctant two-step as the steel wheels squeaked and crunched across the frozen snow.

"Close the window now," her mother said. It was what she always said in winter. In the heat of summer it was, "Can't we open both windows, Dat?" In the back seat, Edna smiled before tucking the plaid buggy robe more securely around her legs.

Yes, her parents were alright. And they would be for another ten years. The next job had already presented itself, which meant more money in her already sizable bank account. Edna felt satisfied, accomplished.

When they arrived, they joined the other women in the kitchen where there was already a lively discussion about all the latest happenings in the community. She wished someone would ask her about her own life, but no one ever did.

They were discussing vacations. Florida. Pinecraft. Who was leaving, who was staying for months. The bus schedule and travel mishaps. Edna pursed her lips, lowered her eyelids to half mast, and let her chest heave with disapproval. Plain people frittering away their hard-earned money on worthless pleasure should be *verboten*. Why the ministers allowed these rampant travels was beyond her. Everyone knew the things that went on in Florida.

Her nostrils flared, quivered with anger. These folks chased after Florida's sun, spent their money in expensive restaurants and on pricey bus fares, stayed in luxurious houses with killer rent.

Well, it wasn't for her, that was sure. She would do the right thing, sock her money away in the fashion of her forefathers, then disperse it to some charitable cause as she saw fit. All this senseless spending to go on vacation would rip the Amish church straight down the seams.

Pleased at her own steadfastness, she walked lightly, with sanctimonious tread, following Verna to her place on the varnished wooden bench. She picked up the heavy, black *Ausbund*, the book of German songs, and laid it carefully across her lap. Yes, she would take up her cross and carry it, be a follower of Jesus by denial of the flesh. She would be a true disciple in serving her Lord. Let others follow the frivolous paths of pleasure. Her lot in life was a glad sacrifice, to travel alone, but not alone, with Christ by her side.

Verna smoothed the pleats in her skirt and leaned over to ask if she'd heard about Orva Schlabach's wife's cancer?

Edna bent her head to catch the words, shook her head, then drew back, wide-eyed, when Verna said it had spread to her liver.

"It's nothing but a death sentence," she whispered.

"How old is she?" Edna breathed.

"In her thirties, I think."

Edna made the expected sympathetic sounds, then opened her songbook, carefully leafing through it to find the announced page.

She opened her mouth and sang, knowing she was contributing to the health and well-being of the Old Order Amish church. A single girl, doing what she could to make life easier for others, being a *maud*, a good example to the young mothers like Leona. The world tried its best to push and shove its way into the homes of those who instilled time-honored traditions into their children.

Take this practice of having a *maud*. Many of the young mothers had a sister helping out a few days a week, and that was it. They did not "take care" after a baby arrived the way their mothers had. It was a shame. But *mauds* were an expense, so many young women did without.

She let her thoughts wander, the way they tended to do in church. Everyone was married, bore children, and belonged to a bearded man who was concerned for his wife and children. Good men who followed the ways of our Lord and fulfilled

His will, marrying one woman and staying faithful till death parted them. Having been in so many homes, Edna knew there were many men who truthfully gave their lives for their families. Praise God.

Edna felt downright pious this morning. Filled with a sense of accomplishment and righteousness. But not self-righteous, she hoped. She shouldn't have been so judgmental about folks taking vacations. She bowed her head to pray for a better heart.

As always, she watched mothers hand over *griddlich*, fussy babies to adoring fathers, caught the look of love and caring between the parents, and wondered for the thousandth time why no young man had ever chosen her.

No matter how many times she assured herself that God saw the need for a *maud* in the community, it was still a Band-Aid over the wound that never quite healed.

It hurt.

There were single ladies who chose to be without a man, perfectly content to live their life alone, and they were the ones who had been asked by many young men. They could saunter down life's path secure in the knowledge they were attractive to someone. They had been looked upon as desirable in some man's eyes, even though they chose to stay single.

But not Edna Miller. Not once.

She shrugged her shoulders to relieve the stiffness in her back, as if to rid herself of the encroaching stabs of self-pity. No sense in it, she knew, but still. Sometimes it was downright hard.

There was a resounding clunk, followed by the outraged wail of the small child who had been unruly and fell backward off the bench. A rustle as hands reached for the little one, the shrieks drowning out the voice of the minister for a short time. An older child made her way along the benches with a snack sent by the mother to console the little one.

Young girls bent their heads and giggled, traded hard candies, and acted as if they couldn't sit still for one second. Edna was momentarily annoyed, but then remembered her own youth.

This was her church, her way of life, a dear place. She was seated among those she loved. She could not imagine anything other than the traditions with which she had been brought up. Looking around at all the dear faces, the elderly, the middle-aged, the pillars of trust and example, she felt a deep gratitude.

Would she grow old, with snow-white hair, an increase in her already ample girth, her cape pinned only a bit haphazardly, a larger white covering, still alone, still making her own way financially? She pushed back the foreboding, the undisclosed, frightening future of being encumbered with health problems of her own, saddled with fading parents, unable to work.

Well, only God knew, so there was no reason to live in a state of anxiety. She turned her head to the minister, her face a smooth mask of devout observance, glad to be able to conceal the inner workings of her mind.

She wondered if most women really appreciated their husbands. She had seen plenty in her work as a *maud*. Appreciation for the husband's paycheck was often sadly lacking, but then, she tried to be fair in all her judgment, so she smoothed over the outrage to understanding. For how could these women know, if they never had to make their own way? She pursed her lips, finding contentment with her calling, glad she could feel a sense of elevation.

In the buggy with her parents, a warm lap robe tucked around her legs; she had a clear view of the road, the oncoming traffic, so she took it on herself to be her father's eyes and ears.

It was cold and windy, but clear and bright. Edna looked forward to being at Fannie's house, warm and comfortable, with children dashing through the rooms in every stage of growth and development. Nine of them, cherubic, blond, and red-cheeked, flowing with good health and happiness, encouraged to speak their mind, every opinion considered carefully by loving parents, especially their father, Johnny Troyer, who had always been known as Chip.

"Dat, there's a tractor-trailer coming this way," Edna offered.

"As if old Dob would notice," her father stated drily.

"Well, you never know what might scare him in his old age."

"Now, Edna, you sit back and relax. I am perfectly capable of driving my own team."

Edna crossed her arms and thought, *But for how long?*

As she had anticipated, a cloud of warm air scented with the rich smell of popcorn, coffee, and ham in the oven enveloped their chilled noses. Children flung themselves into her welcoming arms, shrieking her name.

Fannie, flushed and bright-eyed, hurried to the door with an arm going around her mother's rounded shoulders.

"Well, hello! It is wonderful seeing you again. You've waited too long to come for a visit."

Edna smiled and nodded as she tugged at her bonnet strings.

"Hello yourself, Fannie."

Chip greeted them from the laundry room door, where he stood buttoning his denim overcoat, a wide smile wrinkling his pleasant blue eyes.

"Chip, how are you?" Mam responded.

"Couldn't be better. How are you, Mother?"

"Oh, I'm good. Still able to do for Dat and myself, which is a blessing," she answered, sliding the heavy woolen shawl off her shoulders, handing it to Fannie's outstretched hand.

"We have baby bunnies," yelled Cindy, the rotund little four-year-old who spoke with a lisp, her straight blond hair tucked into her small black covering.

"Seriously? We'll have to go see them," Edna responded.

"Now? Can we go now?" five-year-old Delbert shouted, jumping up and down as if his legs were on springs.

"Let Edna warm herself, Delbert. O.K.?"

They moved to the warmth of the coal stove in the living room, holding out their hands to the cheery glow from the glass door. Edna rubbed her hands, shivered, then turned her back to the stove to chase away the goosebumps. Fannie drew up a glider rocker, helped her mother into it, then hurried away to bring a fleece throw to cover her legs.

"Can't have you catching a cold, Mam."

"Oh, this feels so good."

Her mother gazed up at her eldest daughter with the light of adoration in her eyes. Fannie returned the smile, patted her shoulder, asked whether she would like coffee or tea. Edna lifted the smallest child, a little boy of eighteen months, and asked what he received for Christmas. He looked into her face, thinking for a few moments before his face lit up and he wriggled himself out of her grasp, onto the floor, and toddled away to bring a stick horse wearing a bridle. He pressed a button, and the horse whinnied and made galloping sounds.

"Horse!" he announced proudly. "A horse!"

Dolls, doll beds, a distribution of puzzles and games, skates and trucks were all brought for Edna's approval by a ring of eager, blond-haired, blue-eyed children who were all talking at once. Her father and Chip entered with gray mugs of steaming coffee and bowls of popcorn seasoned with brewer's yeast and plenty of melted butter.

Edna watched her sister upend the sugar pourer into her father's coffee mug, hand him a bowl of popcorn along with the salt shaker, then watched the liberal scattering of salt into the already salted dish.

Blood pressure, she thought. She opened her mouth to ask him to stop, then closed it, decided to stop being a worrywart.

"You do make the best popcorn, Fannie," he chortled, the glistening of melted butter on his well-rounded cheeks, already staining his white beard.

"Nothing like popcorn on a cold Sunday afternoon, right, Dat?" Chip boomed.

"Oh, absolutely. You didn't grow this, did you?"

Ach, Dat, Edna thought. *You know he did. You know he gets top price for his six different varieties of popcorn. You just want to hear it again, the huge success old Chip has, selling the stuff to buyers who will, in turn, sell it to higher-up companies like Williams Sonoma.* She'd seen the Amish popcorn in the *Martha Stewart Living* magazine, for an exorbitant price, too.

Her mother beamed her approval from her rocker, a handful of popcorn thrown in her gaping mouth, half of it dribbling onto the fleece across her lap, a few kernels rolling onto the floor at her feet.

Mam, one kernel at a time.

Edna turned away, trying not to supervise her mother's popcorn inhalation. She didn't eat popcorn the way normal people enjoyed it. That mouth was like a vacuum, sucking up kernels on high speed, after which she'd sit and pick her teeth with a straight pin taken from her belt, complete with a few appreciative belches before hitching herself up and replacing the pin. Then she'd crack "old maids," the unpopped kernels, with her teeth until the bowl was empty. That was when she'd hold the bowl out to Fannie with a compliment and request for a refill.

Chip launched into a lively account of neighbor Myron's frozen water pipes in his hog barn and the ensuing flood which turned into a sea of ice.

"They were in Geauga for the weekend. I guess her brother got married that Thursday, the way I heard it."

"Geauga?" her mother asked, her words tangled around a mouthful of fresh popcorn. "I didn't know she had *freundshaft* in Geauga."

"Yeah, a couple of brothers. They had to get the hogs into another barn. Couple broken legs, them fat things sliding all over the place. You know those hogs don't have strong leg muscles to begin with, stuck in those feeder pens. You couldn't pay me enough to raise them things," Chip laughed, leaning back in his chair, plying a toothpick between his teeth.

Irritation raked itself across Edna's mind, but she caught herself just in time, shut her mouth after a deep breath.

What was wrong with her today? Chip was the most likable of the two brothers-in-law, so why would his description of his neighbor's hog barn bring on this narrow-eyed meanness?

Her father laughed, his mouth open wide, with wet, chewed kernels strewn across his tongue.

"Not much profit for those poor hog farmers. I saw in the *Farm Journal* that the prices hit the lowest mark in five and a half years."

Edna was relieved when it was time to see the bunnies. She helped the little ones bundle up, bending over to tug sturdy little Muck Boots on resisting feet, buttoning coats, tying scarves, and pulling little gray beanies onto tousled heads. There was relief in the fresh air, the lisping voice of four-year-old Cindy laughing at Delbert's antics, and in holding mittened little hands as they slipped and slid to the barn.

"You can't put your hand in the cage," Cindy warned.

"She bites and scratches," Delbert agreed, puffed up with his own wisdom.

The bunnies truly were the most adorable creatures, mere ounces of fluff with almond-shaped eyes and velvety ears, their noses twitching.

"Aww, they're hardly even real. They look like stuffed animals," Edna gushed, and was rewarded with avid agreement.

"Dat said this one, over here, this white one?"

"Yes?"

"He said she's going to have babies in a few weeks. You'll have to come see them when they're born. You will, right?"

Edna nodded. "I will try!"

But she knew she likely wouldn't be able to since soon she'd be firmly entrenched in the Dave Chupp household, which held six boys and one girl under the age of ten. It certainly wasn't her first time at the Chupp home, so she knew that the mother insisted on cloth diapers and Gerber plastic pull-ups, the elastic slightly acrid no matter how often they swirled around in steaming hot water with a cupful of cheap liquid detergent.

Edna's heart sank in spite of herself.

CHAPTER 3

The smell of unwashed clothes, dirty diaper pails, and slop buckets under the sink greeted Edna when she arrived at the Chupp home the following morning. She felt the rush of adrenaline as her eyes took in the unbelievable mountain of dirty dishes stacked any old way in the sink, all over the countertops, spilling onto the floor and scattered across the table. A very young child was crying inconsolably somewhere in the region of the bathroom, followed by gruff commands from none other than Dave Chupp himself, who made a wild-eyed appearance from the doorway.

"Oh, it's you. Well, praise the Lord!" he called out happily. "This mess is out of control."

Edna waved a hand as she set her duffel bag on a stack of newspapers.

"It's alright," she trilled, a smile widening her tight features. "This is to be expected. We'll have everything set right in a few days. No problem."

Dave raked a hand through his messy hair. *Hasn't showered in a while, now has he?* Edna thought. But she kept her smile in place as she shook hands with the pale Emma sagging on the recliner, holding the newborn baby.

Her dress was open, revealing a tattered slip, the baby wrapped in a blanket that must have been handed down seven times, the satin binding in loose slivers, the color somewhere between pink and green.

Edna lifted the sleeping infant, turned him on his back, exclaimed at the thick thatch of dark brown hair, the button nose, saying he was the cutest one yet, the same thing she always said.

She'd been here for every one. All seven of them.

Emma smiled up at Edna. "You think so?"

"Oh, definitely."

Emma fairly shone with pride. Dave emerged from the bathroom, a squalling one-year-old tucked beneath one arm, for all the world like a twenty-pound sack of sunflower seeds, crimped in the middle.

"Sorry, Edna, there's a messy diaper beside the commode. I don't wash them out. I can change a baby, but that commode part, I don't do."

"I'll get it," Edna chirped, and handed the baby back.

She hurried to the bathroom, bent over the commode and thought, *oh no.* Her search for a bottle of toilet cleaner produced nothing, so she upended the green container of powdered Comet into the water, grabbed the stained toilet brush from its container in the corner, and proceeded to slosh it around as furiously as if she was killing a rodent, followed by a yank on the lever to flush. She bent to pick up the messy diaper, lifted it by two corners, and brought it up and down to rid it of its contents, flushed again, rinsed, wrung it out and looked around for a diaper pail. None at all. Only a heap of soiled diapers in the corner. Edna wished she could curl her fists and roar her frustrations, but she knew that was not what this situation required. It was their refusal to change that was the hardest to take. She could work her fingers raw, whip the place into shape, and without fail, a year or so later she'd come back, and everything would be a wreck again. If anything, this time it was even worse than before.

She went to the built-on lean-to that served as a room for the rusting Maytag wringer washer, galvanized rinse tubs, and a green shelf (or one that had been green years ago) containing an odd assortment of mismatched Tingley rubbers, old green hunting boots, and children's sneakers encrusted with last fall's mud and manure. Puddles of melted snow contained flecks of straw and jagged mats of yet more manure like smashed stinkbugs. She surveyed broken plastic buckets, empty fly spray containers, bags of garden dust closed and clamped shut with wooden clothespins, trowels and graying cardboard strawberry boxes, a shoebox with black banana peels hanging over the side as if an octopus had somehow died in there. There was a torn halter hung from a broken shovel handle and various bits of blue baler twine scattered amid green tennis balls and worn-out baseball gloves.

Edna stood, her hands on her hips, and let out a long slow expulsion of air before rocking on her heels. She wanted to bring in a contractor's garbage bag, hang it from a doorknob, and throw everything into it, including the washing machine and wobbly rinse tubs. Then she would take a pressure washer to this disgusting lean-to and watch it turn to ice, like the neighbor Myron's hog barn. If only she could.

She found an unused five-gallon plastic bucket, peered inside, and recoiled. It was half full of rancid lard peppered with mouse droppings.

Looks like cookies and cream ice cream, she thought sourly, before turning to a chipped granite dishpan containing only dust. She whacked it against the side of her leg to empty it.

Good enough.

She carried it to the bathroom, flung the diapers into it, and marched back out, then returned to start moving dishes out of the sink. Thank goodness for a large sink, and yes, plenty of Dawn dish detergent. She filled it, picked out all the plastic tumblers and coffee cups first, then the utensils, the dinner plates, various bowls and quart jars rimmed with applesauce or bits of deer meat.

Children yelled, ran, screeched, and whined like little cars on a private interstate highway, the exhausted mother in their midst; her eyes closed, her face like a pale moon, and the baby asleep on her chest. Edna turned to start on the kitchen table, startled to find Dave Chupp stretched out on the couch, his work boots propped on a limp frayed pillow.

Emma opened one eye and discovered Edna staring. "He's tired," she said apologetically. "Didn't get much sleep."

Edna nodded, smiled, assured Emma she understood, though she didn't. Was he really so tired that he couldn't wash a few dishes? He thought he was worn out. Huh. What about Emma? Eight children in ten years.

Outwardly, she remained the good and faithful *maud*, speaking only what was expected, working with flying hands, strong arms, and a kind expression she had mastered over the years. She had a highly polished veneer, beautiful to behold, but she was beginning to realize there was a knothole of bitterness underneath, weakening the structure of her life. She prayed to God on a daily basis, knowing the irritation could be mastered with His help, and yet, it always crept up.

Did Emma know the day she was a blushing bride? Did she ever suspect her handsome groom would turn into . . . well . . . into that lump on the couch? Could anyone know, or did poverty and laziness simply creep up on a couple like the changing seasons, and suddenly they looked, and everything was rusty or loose or broken or filthy?

Edna remembered both of them as single young people, clean, well-respected, soft-spoken. They always had a circle of friends, and they dated three years which was no longer than some other couples.

Well, stop, Edna. None of your business. You can't figure out the whole world.

So she worked, finished those dishes, swept and scoured, yanked the rope on the wheezing gas engine till she thought she'd popped a hernia in her stomach, hung out the three loads of yellowed prefold diapers with rows of plastic pants like little shower caps, her fingers red from the damp and the cold.

She cooked a mishmash of macaroni, peas, and deer meat and served it with applesauce and a jar of limp dill pickles she found amid the unmentionables on the bottom shelf of the refrigerator. The family ate with relish, Dave smacking his lips as he spooned in the good, hot food, Emma with her white face bent over her plate, the baby lying on a pillow on the corner of the couch.

Dave asked for jelly bread. Edna's first impulse was to blurt out, "Get it yourself." But she didn't. She pushed back her chair, found a loaf of sliced store-bought bread (as white as snow and about as nutritious) and set it on the table, with a smile, asking the children if they would like jelly bread, too.

She spread the dark purple grape preserve, the cheapest brand and in an enormous jar, halved the slices, and handed them out, while Dave spread two slices for himself and wolfed them down.

After everyone was finished, he hooked his thumbs in the right belt of his trousers and praised her cooking warmly.

"We do appreciate you, Edna. You deserve a gold medal as the best *maud* in all of Indiana."

"Why thank you. I try my best, but you know as well as I do, I'm not perfect."

"Very close, Edna. Very close."

Edna swallowed self-consciously. What if a banner unfurled from her tongue, with all her thoughts written on them for everyone to read? He would never praise her then. There was not one thing in her thoughts worthy of praise.

She looked up and smiled. He returned her smile, followed by a slow, meaningful wink. Shock spread from her fingertips to her toes.

She blinked furiously, her face red with suffusing heat. She rose to her feet, pushed back her chair, and busied herself at the sink.

Emma's whining voice cut into her confusion.

"I'd love some dessert, Edna. Why don't you bake this afternoon and let the cleaning go? I need my coverings washed, too, and there's a basket of ironing. Ach my, come here, Joshua. Yes, he's poopy. Edna would you clean him? I don't believe there are any clean diapers, so maybe you can just use a tea towel for now."

Edna obeyed immediately, welcoming the distraction. Her hands shook as she went about her business, trying to convince herself it was nothing, it was only Dave's way. She had been here many times before, every year, in fact, and he had never given her a reason to distrust him. He never once came across as creepy.

Ugh.

That was her own unspoken rule. If there were even a hint of questionable conduct, she'd walk right out, no matter what. But she had never thought herself attractive, never had a problem, or remotely expected one. Perhaps it was her smile. She should have been more circumspect.

She put the incident out of her mind and busied herself baking with the ingredients she was able to find. A greasy plastic pail with a lid proved to be half full of flour; another contained a spattering of damp, lumpy sugar. There were a few bags of confectioners' sugar half full with a wire twisty keeping the contents in the bag and brown sugar spilling out of a "Yoder's Bulk Foods" bag. In the chaotic drawers, she found coconut and a sticky bottle of vanilla, and there was plenty of Blue Bonnet margarine in the door of the refrigerator.

She mixed a batch of Grandpa cookies, a brown sugar and cinnamon cookie with a vanilla frosting. She cooked cornstarch pudding, after finding an immense container of cornstarch. Milk seemed to be plentiful as well.

Halfway through her rummaging and baking, Emma made her limp appearance at the kitchen table, draping her thin, despaired form into a kitchen chair. Edna tried to paste the kind smile in place, but couldn't help comparing her to Gumby, the rubber stick man you could bend in any pose.

Emma ate three cookies, licking the vanilla frosting from her fingers, which seemed to perk her up.

Eyeing Edna with a malevolent glint, she remarked on her ample figure. "You work so hard. I don't see how you can be fat."

"I'm lined with sheep's wool," Edna fired back.

Emma raised her face and let out two sharp barks, like a beagle, then smiled, her face taking on a distant remembering of prettiness.

"Good joke, Edna. You're funny. No, you're not really fat. Just curvy."

Then, "Did you hear about Orva Schlabach's wife? I think her name is Sadie, or Sarah. Sarah. I think."

The one-year-old stood at her side, his nose running, his matted hair like a bottlebrush in the back where he'd lain on it.

"Here, Ivan. Here, hold still."

She swiped at the child's greenish mucus with a corner of the tablecloth.

Edna's eyes popped, but she swallowed her dismay, shoveling cookies off a tray as one possessed.

Emma slid little Ivan onto her lap, gave him a cookie, and reached for another one for herself.

"Yes, her name is Sarah. She has cancer. And now they say she has spots on her liver. You know she won't last long. It's so terribly sad, with those three children. They only ever had three as she's always had health problems."

Emma paused, shook her head from side to side.

"Sometimes I wonder, though. Would it be so bad, to leave this old world? Some would say there's something wrong with me talking this way, but they wouldn't understand the constant need for me to keep my head above water. It's all just over-whelming, and every year, there are more babies. I know God wants us to have children, they are a gift from the Lord, we all know, but it brings an almost frightening workload. I'm so dreadfully tired and worn out."

She continued, the words suddenly tumbling out like they'd been pent up a long while. "I wasn't raised this way, believe it or not. I know things have spun out of control. Dave is very devout in his beliefs, and he says each baby is the will of God, but I can hardly do it anymore."

She got up to go to the sink for a drink of water, sliding Ivan off in the process, resulting in an immediate howling, echoed by a high-pitched wail from the newborn on the couch.

The kitchen door was flung open as four boys burst through, red and white lunch buckets clattering on the countertop.

"Cookies! We got cookies!"

Handfuls of cookies disappeared in grabbing, filthy hands. The boys barely noticed Edna as they cast her sideways glances, then tore through the kitchen to shuck their coats and stocking caps between puddles of melted snow and dirt. It was only after they had clomped upstairs that Edna realized they had com-pletely ignored their mother, and she them.

"It's too much, Edna. Look at that. Those cookies will barely make it into the pantry. I know it's because I never have time to bake."

Edna took a deep breath. Her back ached from the tension of frosting the cookies, a pain between her shoulder blades like a knife, and it was already late afternoon, time for the eve-ning meal. Suddenly, the whole situation irked her so much she couldn't hold back.

"You need to talk to your doctor or midwife. You need a break. Tell them you're depressed. They can give you something for it. Get yourself some Geritol with iron. These kids need rules. Those boys shouldn't be allowed all those cookies before supper. Wake up and look around you. You have all these kids, now help yourself. If you don't take care of yourself, no one else will."

Edna spoke in short, clipped sentences.

"Where are your mother and sisters? Don't you have anyone who can come in to give you a lift? Oh, and another thing? Disposable diapers."

Emma gasped, shook her head. "No, no, we can never afford it."

Edna pressed on.

"Where does Dave work?"

"The RV factory. You know, where everyone else does."

"He makes enough for you to buy Pampers. Buy the cheap brand. This house smells so strongly of dirty diapers it burns your eyes."

She was horrified to find Emma weeping softly; her long, bony fingers held up over her face. Her first reaction was to apologize but quickly decided to let well enough alone. Perhaps Emma wasping around the house like an unwelcome silent shadow, carrying her huge basket of depression on top of her head was half the problem. She needed to stop floating and start paddling, even if Dave was less than ambitious. She married him, and now it was up to her to make the best of it.

The remainder of the day, Edna was watched with a hooded gaze from the wan woman on the recliner. Children of all ages clattered through the house, doing exactly as they pleased. Boys snapped rubber bands like missiles that whizzed across the room, hit walls and windows, their younger siblings. The final straw was one in the gas burner, where it slowly melted, setting up an awful stink.

She grabbed the offender by the sleeve, shoved her face into his grinning one and ground out, "You do that one more time, and you'll go to your room."

He drew back, his bold gaze never wavering.

"Good. I like it in my room. Go ahead."

There were snickers all around from the watchful brothers.

"Alright. Your Dat will be home in an hour. We'll see if he agrees."

They leaped out of the kitchen, into their winter clothes, and outside, yelling insults about the fat, angry *maud*.

Edna mashed the potatoes, fried inexpensive ground beef, and made a milk gravy. She sliced Velveeta cheese into elbow macaroni and dished up canned green beans as Dave walked through the door, surrounded by his entourage of grinning schoolboys.

"Smells wonderful in here," he said, jovial and red-faced.

Edna kept a low profile, the wink still fresh in her mind. Dave joked with the boys, held the lone little girl while Edna finished putting the food on the table. He bent over to wipe the smallest one's nose, then drew him up to sit beside his sister.

They sat down to eat, Emma sliding quietly into her chair on her husband's left, her eyes raised to his, the cowed expression downright piteous.

"How are you feeling, Emma?"

"Not good. I'm awful weak."

Dave didn't offer a reply, merely bowed his head for the silent prayer that was practiced before every Amish meal.

It was complete bedlam after that.

The boys all talked at once, reached across each other's plates, grabbed utensils, and dug into mounds of potatoes and gravy. The toothless first grader squirted elbow macaroni through the gap in his line of teeth, while his little sister caught the noodles and promptly swallowed them.

There were simply no rules or discipline. Dave was too preoccupied, and the poor mother was awash in her own river of despair.

Edna ate, becoming steadily more disgruntled.

When she finally got to her assigned room, she was too weary to care if the room was cold or the mattress was beyond help. She was alone and it was dark and blessedly, luxuriously quiet.

She fell into a deep sleep, the kind where the night passes in a moment. She woke refreshed, immediately ready to tackle the immensity of her day. She had lunchboxes packed, breakfast made, and Dave out the door by six. The children who went to school ate at seven and were out the door by a quarter to eight. She had a quick slice of toast, a cup of coffee, and then brought the old wringer washer buzzing to life. She washed mountains of soiled clothes, washed dishes, straightened the kitchen between loads. She cleaned the lean-to, sorted through the junk, filled a garbage bag and threw it in the dumpster.

If they could afford a dumpster, they could afford Pampers, too, she thought. She baked five fruit pies, then a shoofly cake, and scrubbed the kitchen floor after lunch.

Emma faded into her recliner and offered not one word. This went on until Edna realized she was pouting, wanting her to feel bad about the day before. Well, two could play at this game, and she wasn't going to lose.

She brought in the freeze-dried clothes, the fluffy towels and sheets and tablecloths, folded them, and put them away. Then she tackled the pantry.

She found unused plastic containers, labeled them, and stored oatmeal, raisins, coconut, baking cocoa, everything in neat rows, after scouring the shelves with Pine-Sol water that was steaming hot.

"I hope you know I won't be able to find my things when you leave," came the high whine from the recliner.

"That's O.K. At least I'll be able to while I'm here."

After a rubber band hit the back of her neck, she caught Emery, the second of the boys, around the waist and got down at his level. "You do that again and you'll be sorry," she hissed in a low, deadly voice.

After that, the rowdy group circled her with something akin to respect, which kept those rubber bands in their pockets. Mealtimes were more normal, with Edna giving swift discipline to anyone misbehaving. Dave approved, Emma sulked.

"Now you listen to Edna, boys. She doesn't put up with your shenanigans the way Mam and I do." There was another slow wink in Edna's direction, accompanied by a wide grin that fell just short of leering.

Well, as long as he keeps his distance, Edna thought. *Maybe he's just friendly like that. Hasn't he always been jovial?*

Winter evenings were long, the children all rowdy, romping around the small house with nothing to interest them. So Edna brought out the Monopoly game.

"No. Pieces lost. I hate Monopoly."

"Money's not all there."

"We don't like games."

Emma's voice came from the chair, "Edna, come get Beth. I have a headache."

Edna hurried over to retrieve the crying child and placed her on her lap to soothe her. A sour smell came from the top of her head, so she asked Beth if she wanted to have a bath. She nodded.

Edna let her play in the tub with measuring cups and spoons, adding a dash of her own bath soap for bubbles. Then she put in Beth's little brother, Ivan. She scrubbed their hair with plenty of shampoo, dressed them in clean faded pajamas, and sent them to their mother, like scented flowers, their faces shining.

"*Ach* my. Here comes my Bethey. Don't you smell nice!"

With that, the languid, disinterested mother cuddled her sweet-smelling daughter, her face in the gleaming wet hair. Softly, her voice wavering, she began to sing, one of the old hymns Edna remembered from school.

Edna was surprised to find quick tears stinging her eyelids.

Perhaps it wouldn't take much to give Emma new hope and energy. She'd ask to go to town, and she'd buy Geritol vitamins with her own money.

Emma's mother banged the lean-to door, letting in a blast of frigid air, before tugging the door closed behind her. She was a tall, thin woman clad in a coat and scarf, her square face resembling her daughter's. She thrust out a calloused hand, greeted Edna with more warmth than Emma or Dave had shown.

"My, Edna, you're a wonder. Like a magic fairy, you come in here and spit shine everything, even the children. God must have a special place for you in Heaven."

"Oh now, you are only flattering me," Edna replied, sliding a pan of rolls into the oven. She'd known Emma's mother was coming, so she'd set the sour cream rolls to rise first thing. She had a bowl of caramel frosting on the side, ready to spread. Coffee waited in the Lifetime drip coffee maker, the sun sparkling on the snow through the polished kitchen window. The floors were swept, the toys put away, Beth's hair freshly braided, the baby asleep in his crib.

"Hello, Mam." Emma said quietly.

"Oh, there you are. How are you?"

She examined her daughter with the knowing eyes of a mother, then turned to Edna. "Can't you teach her how to manage a household the way you do?"

Edna knew the words were like falling bricks on Emma's head, each one cutting deeply. Edna saw the slump of the shoulders, the drawing inward on herself, watched her return with shuffling gait to the recliner, to gaze unseeing into space.

Edna turned to the mother, raising a forefinger to her lips as if to stop the flow of vicious words.

"What?"

The mother looked bewildered. She had done nothing wrong.

Everyone knew Emma was a slob, dragging herself around her house making half-hearted attempts at order and cleanliness. She took after her husband's side of the family, not hers.

The sweet rolls were light, the caramel frosting divine, the coffee just right, steam curling up from the dark liquid. Everything was perfect, but the morning had been effectively ruined by the mother's lofty attitude, holding herself far above her despairing daughter without realizing there was anything wrong.

Oh, of course she loved her daughter from her perch on Superior Mountain. But Edna knew she had no clue how to lower herself to be a help to Emma. She could have come in amid the mess, lent a hand, praised the small number of abilities Emma did possess. It was called nurturing, like spading and watering a garden.

Edna listened to the mother describe the many accomplishments she had achieved over the years and watched the daughter wither away. She walked around the rest of the day with a sour stomach that churned around the rolls she had consumed too quickly.

CHAPTER 4

A WARM WIND SPRANG UP IN SOME SOUTHERN STATE AND ADVANCED on the state of Indiana, set the snowdrifts and icicles into steady decline, revealing tufts of wet brown weeds, pieces of lumber, broken plastic pails, the bleached rib cage of some small animal, a cracked Cool Whip container that steadily filled with water from the broken spouting. Blue skies were peppered with white puffy clouds, which made Edna stop the hanging of laundry and gaze skyward, shaking her head at the unusual formations above her. She thought a January thaw was just what she needed to strip the stale beds and wash everything in hot water and the secret drop of Clorox she had started to add. If she had to use the Dollar General's most inexpensive soap powder, then she could at least be assured the germs were gone.

All those stained yellow diapers worked to dispel her good humor. For one thing, it was hard on her pride, hanging them on the line, and for another, she could not persuade Emma to consider buying disposable diapers.

She gritted her teeth and held her breath to fish out the soiled diapers, wring them out by twisting in either direction as hard as possible, before throwing them in the sputtering washing machine. One of these days that thing was going to breathe its last breath, and that was the truth.

She filled every line with threadbare sheets and torn blankets, then caught sight of the boys leaving for school. Her mouth flattened to a grim, determined slash as she prepared her speech for those two oldest.

She'd supply the garbage bags and give them orders to start picking up outside; there was no sense in any of this debris laying around as if no one lived here. On Sunday visitors would begin to arrive, well-meaning friends and neighbors bringing baby gifts and food, so if she was the *maud* they'd listen to her. If Dave would support her, see to it that things got done, it would make all the difference.

She finished hanging the last blanket, carried the clothes basket and clothespin bag to the washhouse, rinsed the machine and the tubs, swept the chipped concrete floor, picked up an array of children's clothes, and went to the kitchen to heat leftover coffee. If there were any shoofly cake left, she'd have a nice chunk of it in a bowl, with milk.

She found Emma seated at the kitchen table with something in a bowl, her head bent over it as she spooned it up, the clicking of the spoon hitting her teeth the only sound in the kitchen.

"Oh, you're up. Good morning. I hope you've slept well," Edna remarked, hoping she sounded cheery enough. Her eyes slid sideways to the battered aluminum cake pan containing only crumbs and smudges of shoofly goo.

Sure enough, she'd eaten the last of it.

Emma put down the spoon, belched, lifted the tablecloth to wipe her mouth, fixed a penetrating stare at Edna and asked why she had to settle for shoofly cake when she should have something hot for breakfast, and no, she had not slept well, the baby didn't settle, which was due to the tomato sauce in the spaghetti they had for supper, which had made her milk acidic.

Edna took a deep cleansing breath, turned the burner on under the stained, battered coffeepot, and apologized for not having her breakfast ready.

"It's alright, I'm used to looking out for myself."

"Would you like an egg sandwich if I make one for myself?"

"No. I want three fried eggs with mush."

"The cornmeal is all gone. I fried the last of the mush yesterday morning."

"Well, you'll have to go to the store, then. I guess."

They ate their eggs together, Edna making small talk, attempts at lifting the poor woman's spirits with a description of the clouds, the melting snow, and the arrival of spring in a few months, but there was no response.

"Emma, would you like for me to buy a few boxes of Pampers for you? I'd think it would certainly help your workload considerably."

Emma shook her head.

"Mam would have a fit."

"You're a grown woman, Emma. If Dave wants you to use them, I think you should. What your mother doesn't know doesn't hurt her."

"But I can just hear her. She'll think I'm lazy."

Edna sat back and rolled her eyes at no one in particular. It was the only way she could keep from saying things she'd regret later. Honestly, this situation was beyond decency.

"I'll get some. What size would Ivan take? And Atlee isn't trained yet." Emma sighed, a deep and weary sound that reached Edna's soft heart.

"Three diaper babies. I have three again. I don't know how I'll ever manage after you leave. I should potty train Atlee, but he's just not ready. He doesn't want to sit on the potty chair."

None of your children want to do anything you say, Edna thought. *You're like an old dishrag someone threw in the corner.*

She had no answer to the whining, the cry for help from this woman who lacked even one ounce of energy and optimism. Part of Edna felt a deep sympathy, Emma having gotten herself into a situation that was simply unmanageable through doing what her husband felt was right. As she had done all her life, swimming along on the current of her mother's views, never quite coming up to her golden standards. There was no thinking for herself, no rebellion, simply this washed-out existence where her husband and children took up everything she had to give until there was nothing left.

In her own eyes, she was submitting to her husband, the exact thing she was supposed to do, slowly spinning the cocoon of righteous martyrdom around herself until her surroundings were mostly hidden from view. The chaos, the filth, simply wasn't there, or if some of it penetrated her conscience, she immediately justified her lack of concern with exhaustion.

Emma was exhausted and had ample reason to be drained of energy. But these children were here, by the will of God and her husband's convictions, and they could no more help being born than someone could keep from breathing. And by all appearances, they would grow up wild and undisciplined, lacking the guidance from either parent.

Dave Chupp was a good person, easygoing, jovial, the whole world his playground, with goodwill coming out of his ears. Edna believed he loved his wife, his children, his cup running over with his own sense of accomplishment, so who was she to stick a pin into his balloon?

She looked across the table at the languid Emma and felt a decided sense of urgency. Something had to be done. Could be done.

"Emma, would you consider seeing a doctor about your . . ." just say it, she thought.

"Depression?"

She hurried on, without giving her time to answer.

"You know you're feeling overwhelmed. Tell your doctor how you feel. He'll explain it to you, and give you a small dose of an antidepressant, just enough to restore the brightness in your world."

Emma's eyes narrowed.

"No. Oh no. No. Not those pills. They're only for crazy people. It will mess with my brain and well . . . you know, I'll do something. People do if they're on them things."

"But you'll never make it on your own. Your children will get you down, and Dave doesn't see it. You need help."

"No. Not medical pills, I'll take more vitamins, build myself up."

Edna pressed on, relating other cases where women suffered from terrible depression after the birth of a baby, and the difference one pill could make in their life.

"I've been doing this for fourteen years, Emma, and have seen so much. Why wouldn't you go for help if it's available? For your children's sake? They need a mother, not just a helpless shadow."

"No. No. I will not see a doctor. We don't even have a family doctor. My mother raised me to depend on natural alternatives. We don't take antibiotics."

"This is not an antibiotic," Edna said firmly.

"Worse. It's worse."

"Would you consider going for counseling then?"

Edna thought a counselor would persuade her, perhaps. Or get Dave to see this was not a normal family life.

"Counseling? What for? My mother wouldn't want me to do that. She says counseling is overrated. People just need to get a grip."

The mother again.

Edna sighed. "Well, I'll call a driver. Get the groceries you need. And I'm buying Pampers. You need them."

Emma said nothing, merely watched Edna pull on a sweater and go to the phone, housed in a shack built on to the washhouse.

Edna stepped into a fresh mound of dog doo, then into an icy puddle, wiped her shoes on a sunken pile of slush, yanked open the door to the telephone, and dialed the number with shaking fingers.

She bought bulk foods. Comet cleaner and Clorox. She bought the largest box of Tide with bleach she could find, two boxes of the cheapest disposable diapers, each box containing one hundred and twenty diapers.

If they only lasted for the time she was helping them, it would ease her own workload. If Dave did not approve, well, then, it was time that man had a talking-to, a genuine addressing of the situation he called home.

She sang as she organized her purchases in the pantry, whistled under her breath as she pulled Pampers from boxes and stacked them on the baby's changing table, the larger size in the sink by the bathtub in the downstairs bathroom, with Emma hovering over her, wringing her hands in agitation, saying over and over she didn't know what Dave would say.

What he did say was what Edna figured he would. He approved of purchasing the disposable diapers, if that is what she wanted, which led Edna to believe Emma's fear of her husband was embedded deeply from her childhood, the mother's overreaching views and constant belittling were what Emma now expected from all adults in authority.

So here was a beginning. A first step, and a small one perhaps, but at least the house would no longer reek of the acrid stench of old wet diapers thrown into corners. She caught Emma at the baby's changing table, gingerly picking up a disposable diaper with one thumb and forefinger, as if it might be alive and would deliver a bite.

She unfolded it, turned it first one way, then another, before figuring out which side went beneath the baby's bottom. Her eyes held a light of newfound optimism when she met Edna's eyes.

"Just imagine, Emma. No more diaper pins and plastic pants. No more safety pins. But . . . after you leave?"

"After I leave you'll go right on using these Pampers. Dave has agreed one hundred percent."

"Really? You're sure?"

"Absolutely. I told him your diaper washing is ridiculous. You can afford to buy these diapers."

Emma dipped her head to hide her smile.

"Ach. Well. Alright then."

Edna stirred cornmeal and water into boiling, salted water, turned the gas burner to low and let it cook for forty-five minutes, savoring the rich smell of roasted corn. She put on the kettle for boiling water, measured two cups of molasses and a teaspoon of baking soda into a large bowl, and began measuring brown sugar and flour for the crumb topping on a shoofly cake. She'd likely be making another one tomorrow, the way this family ate anything homemade.

She set the molasses and boiling water to cool, then began a double batch of chocolate chip cookies. She whistled low under her breath and whirled around the kitchen stocked well with adrenaline. There was something about providing food for a large family that filled up her heart and supplied deep inner happiness.

She knew she had never experienced romantic love or the affections of a man, but could not imagine it was much different, or better, than this.

Being a *maud* meant she had the best of both worlds. She could do what she loved, which was the domestic work of keeping a household running smoothly, then retire after two weeks to her own domain; the full and ongoing responsibility would rest on someone else's shoulders.

Now, here, if she were the mother, her first priority would be to instill some values in these children. Teach them to pick up clothes, toys, make beds, wipe shoes or boots, wash hands, improve table manners, and have absolutely no talking back. She knew she could do it.

But after two weeks, she'd be gone.

Her baking finished, she wiped down the counters, the front

of the kitchen cupboards, then filled a bucket with hot water and a generous splash of Pine-Sol, before getting on her hands and knees with a large rag and setting to work on the kitchen floor.

She met the school-age children at the door, one hand propped on the doorframe, the other on her hip.

"Shoes off," she said loudly.

"Naw."

"We never hafta take off our shoes."

"Take them off," Edna barked, hoping she sounded like a German Shepard. The boys gave her an exasperated look, she heard snatches of "stupid," "bossy," and "*maud*," but they kicked off their wet shoes.

"Now pick up your shoes and carry them to the washhouse. I just cleaned the kitchen floor."

"Duh. It's just gonna get dirty again."

"Not if I have my way. Your mother is going to need help after I'm gone, and there are ways you can help. This is one of them."

Baleful looks, but they bent, retrieved their shoes and tiptoed through the kitchen, the smallest one sniffing, "Cookies?"

Edna reached out to touch his straight blond hair.

"That's right. Fresh chocolate chip cookies. But first, I need to have a meeting with all of you, O.K.?"

An arrogant look, a tossing of his long, unkempt bangs, but they didn't say anything. They simply slid into kitchen chairs after hanging their clothes on the hooks Edna had supplied for them.

She joined them, searched each one's face for signs of outward anger or rebellion, found only resigned patience.

"O.K., good. Now you know this is my last week, and then your mother will be in charge again."

Raised eyebrows, snickers.

"And you're thinking, 'Good.' Well, that's as it may be, but you will have to change your ways. You're old enough to help your mother wherever you can."

"She doesn't make us work, so you can't, either," from the oldest.

"Oh yes, I can. And she will, too. So will your father."

Edna delivered a rousing sermon, quite proud of her ability to make them take notice, to sit up and listen. The mother in the bedroom for a nap, she kept her voice modulated, but let them know their mother was in no condition to carry on herself, that she was depressed and needed them all to shoulder some of the responsibilities. They could wash dishes, make beds, take out the trash.

"She doesn't ever make us do that stuff."

"She will after today. A new day is starting for you guys."

She received a few stares of unbelief, but plodded on, saying children could be a blessing to their parents, and this is what God wanted them to do, that He looks down from Heaven and loves little children, expects them to be kind and helpful.

She produced the garbage bag with instructions to pick up all the trash, find a rake and gather the loose hay and straw, also the clumps of manure and wood chips, then put it in the garbage tote.

"We never did this kinda stuff."

"Do it." Edna said, without hesitation.

She watched from the kitchen window as they all stood together in a huddle, the garbage bag hanging like a deflated balloon between them. The oldest one did most of the talking, his thumb jerking in the general direction of the house, with some serious nodding of agreement from the younger ones.

But they accomplished their task, then piled into the washhouse, hung up their coats and, unbelievably, kicked off their sneakers, came into the kitchen, and sat expectantly.

Edna praised their fast work, brought mugs of hot chocolate and a plate of cookies, and then sat and listened to them talk about their day at school. Emma appeared at the bedroom door, rubbing the sleep from her eyes, her dress hanging open, stained with milk and the baby's vomit, her hair greasy and uncombed, the *dichly* on her head sliding off toward the back.

The boys all turned in her direction, but said nothing.

Emma came to the table, sat beside the smallest one, reached for a cookie, stuffed half into her mouth.

"Did you sleep well?" Edna inquired.

"I did." She answered. "Feel like a new person."

She smiled at the boys.

"How was school?"

"O.K. Good." Shrugs

"They picked up the trash outside." Edna said.

"They did? Snow melting so much?"

Emma got up to stand by the window, then turned to reveal another smile appearing on her gray, drawn face.

"It's like spring, isn't it?"

Edna sat alone with Dave after everyone had retired for the night. She kept her voice low, knew the bedroom door was kept ajar, for the heat, but told Dave in her no-nonsense way that things had to change.

"Emma needs your help. You have to shoulder more of the responsibility. It doesn't hurt you to wash dishes, take out the trash when you see the can is full. The most important thing you can do is teach the children to do the same. You know this place is a dump."

She felt bad when she saw the cringe, the embarrassment on his unlined, good-natured face. But she pressed on, stating her argument, saying how cleanliness was next to godliness, and that company would be arriving, and it was time this family got their act together and changed their slovenly ways.

"Boy, you're really hitting me here," he remarked.

"Sorry, but if things don't improve, your wife is going to go from bad to worse. I'm serious. I want her to see her doctor, but she won't."

Dave sat up straight, fixed her with a penetrating stare. "She's not that bad, is she?"

"She sure is. If she'd see her doctor, I guarantee she'd be diagnosed as having a severe case of postpartum depression."

"You're serious?"

"Of course I am. She's not well. Is it any wonder? One woman alone can do only so much, and that's it."

Then she threw all caution to the wind and suggested eight children were enough. She did not add, "for now," either. Enough.

Dave eyed her with suspicion.

"Now. Now in that category, Edna, you will not tell me what to do. No sir. My quiver isn't near full, and God clearly instructed us in the Bible. Children are a blessing around our table."

A shot of anger.

"Your table, maybe. But not Emma's."

Dave recoiled. His eyes narrowed. "What do you mean by that?"

"Exactly what I said. She is overwhelmed. If she were a hardy woman, it would be entirely different. A whole other ball game. She's not. If you don't start taking care of her, you might not have a wife."

There. She'd dropped that bomb.

Dave's chair scraped the floor as he got to his feet. He stood behind his chair, then, his hands like paws on the back, his blue eyes boring into hers.

"You know, I used to admire you a lot. I would have recommended you to everyone, but no more. You have meddled into affairs that are none of your business whatsoever."

With that he stomped off toward the bedroom and disappeared through the door, closing it firmly behind him. Edna remained seated at the table, her cupped hand scraping cookie crumbs from the tablecloth, her back bent like a much older woman's.

Was it true what he said?

Perhaps she had overstepped her boundaries. But she would not apologize. He could chew on her words a few days, choose to spit them out or swallow and digest them, and make an honest effort. About time.

On Sunday morning Dave and the four oldest went to church, so Edna cooked a large breakfast for Emma and the little ones, straightened the house, put on a clean apron, and waited for company to begin arriving.

The windows gleamed, every fingerprint wiped, the floor was swept and scrubbed, the furniture dusted. There were cookies, cupcakes, and pumpkin pies in the pantry, and a large container of beef stew cooling in the refrigerator. She made sure the beds were made, the coats and shoes hung up or placed on the shelf, and the washhouse swept clean.

Emma seemed to take a new interest in changing diapers, a job that had fallen to Edna before, so that was a most encouraging sign. Now for the mother's arrival and continuing support.

Of course, they were the first to arrive, the usual greetings, the ensuing fuss about the new baby, mostly by Emma's father, who hadn't seen him yet. Emma smiled, pleased to receive praise from her "Dat," but her mother wiped the smile away sufficiently by eyeing the stack of disposable diapers with a withering glance in Edna's direction.

"I hope Emma had nothing to do with this."

"She didn't," Edna said sweetly. "Dave thought she seemed a bit overwhelmed with the three little ones all in diapers."

"Oh? He did?"

"Yes. He's very caring of his wife. Emma does so well, you know, but with Atlee and Ivan still both in diapers, Dave thought she should switch to disposables." Edna leaned close, gave her an intimate wink. "He makes good money, so it isn't as if they couldn't afford it."

A deep breath and straightening of the shoulders from the mother, a look of fresh appreciation to her daughter.

"Well. That's nice. Yes. I know he provides well."

Edna nodded. She served coffee, accepted praise for the house's appearance, and thought gleefully, "She's eating out of my hand. Flattery did get me somewhere."

James and Ivan Hoschtetler arrived, followed by Dave's grandparents. The living room was filling up, so Edna made more coffee, refilled cups, served cookies on a tray with napkins. She watched Emma closely for signs of fatigue, but there were none. She appeared a changed person, smiling, talking, sharing glances with her husband, showing off the new baby as if it was the first one.

The transformation was nothing short of amazing.

The third couple was Orva Schlabach and his thin, pale wife, whom Edna and Emma had discussed earlier. Her eyes were sunken in sharp cheekbones, but alert and bright with interest. Edna invited the couple in, and her heart swelled with pity for this small woman so obviously carrying on a brave battle for her life, knowing the dreaded disease was slowly spreading through her vital organs.

Orva was of medium height, much wider than his wife, but that was all Edna could remember afterward, hurrying ahead of them to place a few more folding chairs, make sure there was enough coffee.

All afternoon, she helped with the company, her thoughts distracted with the cancer patient's courage, and the light of love in her bright eyes as she held the newborn. She kept him the entire time, repeatedly gazing into the small face as he slept.

Edna's emotions simply got the best of her. She stayed in the kitchen, catching mewling little sobs that kept forming in her chest, traveling up through her throat. Did Orva know her time on earth was short? Or was it only the innocence of the new baby, the undisclosed amount of time this sweet child would be given to spend its days on earth?

She measured coffee into the coffee maker, blew her nose with a wad of Kleenex, and stood gazing out of the kitchen window, seeing nothing.

Death and life. Disease and good health. Who knew?

God called the shots, that was all there was to it. Life was like an immense orchestra, the maestro directing every swelling sound. Either down to the depths, or up to the heights, everything from sickness, accidents, unexplained suffering, to the opposite.

Which was the opposite? What were the heights? A child born, or a person released from a disease-riddled body?

Well, either way, she was no philosopher. She couldn't stand here with all these sad, maudlin thoughts cartwheeling through her head.

The sky was gray, ominous, rising out of half-melted graying snowbanks, the whole earth appearing dull, without color. Edna shivered, tried to shake off the rising sense of omen. Why these melancholy forebodings now?

Too much emotion, she supposed. Too much of everything, trying to fix an unfixable family, allowing herself false hope, when a good dose of reality was like a smack in the face.

Dave and Emma Chupp and eight offspring would likely return to their former way of life the minute she drove out of view. She could wield all this power while she was here, but inevitably, they'd return to who they were, and perhaps live a happier life than she would ever have.

So for the remainder of her stay, she did what she did best, which was to nurture, clean, do laundry, bake and cook and iron. She bossed those boys around, who crossed their eyes, stuck their thumbs in their ears and wiggled their fingers behind her back, called her "elephant" instead of Edna, and mimicked her gait when she wasn't looking.

She had one solid victory, however.

Every week, Dave Chupp drove his horse on Saturday afternoon, tied him to the hitching rack at the Dollar General, and bought a large cardboard box containing the cheap brand of disposable diapers. And Emma had scrub rags and dust cloths for years to come, plus the bonus of rags to tie around her children's necks when they came down with the flu.

CHAPTER 5

THERE WAS A MESSAGE ON HER PARENTS' VOICE MAIL WHEN SHE returned.

A group of single girls planned a trip to Florida, on the bus. Would she like to go? Delia Miller's number was the return.

Edna let it go. It was too dark, too cold on a Saturday night, so she scuttled back in the house, shivered, held her hands to the stove's warmth.

Her father sat in the oversized recliner; his fingers dovetailed like a good drawer, his eyes closed, and his round eyeglasses slid down his nose. He opened one eye, then closed it again.

Her mother was shelling walnuts, cracking them with the old nutcracker, her arthritic hands gnarled like an old tree root. Then she'd use the silver pick that always reminded Edna of a dentist tool to carefully remove the meat from the nutshell.

She slid into a chair opposite her mother, ate a few walnut halves, then spoke of Dave Chupp and his wife, the way things went at that house.

Her mother shook her head from side to side, clucked like a hen.

"Ach well, Edna. You know she'll have more babies. Sometimes a tired mother like her raises some amazing children. It seems as if they run wild to you, but they have a healthy amount of space to grow, to develop their own attitudes. Plus, you have to bear in mind, that kind of child is no worse off than the ones who have to walk the line with controlling, abusive parents. Just let it go, now."

"I do, Mam. I really do let it go. It's not my life."

Her mother. "No, it's not."

The wisdom of the elderly, Edna thought.

"Should I go to Florida?" she asked.

"Who's going?"

"A bunch of girls."

"Well, I guess that's up to you."

"Delia Miller, Annie, Robert's Annie, you know who I mean."

Her mother nodded, popped a walnut into her mouth.

"But I never thought I'd go. I don't really approve of it. That's all you hear in church. I don't think I should spend my money just for my own pleasure."

Her mother raised her eyebrows.

"You shouldn't look down on others. Or judge."

"I know. I wasn't."

But Edna had done both and knew it. Of course, she wanted to go. Who wouldn't? But no, she wouldn't go, not with that bunch of girls, anyway. They fit the description of an airhead so perfectly. Each one pretending they loved the single life when their eyes were like magnifying glasses looking for an available man.

Edna leaned back in her chair, crossed her arms and watched her mother pick walnuts, her gaze shifting from her mother to her father, large and asleep in his oversized chair. No, it would not be right for her to run off and leave her parents in the dead of winter. She must say no.

"Well, that's enough for tonight."

Her mother drew herself up, extracted the indispensable straight pin, opened her mouth to pick her teeth, wet nutmeats all over her tongue.

Edna swallowed, grimaced, but didn't have the heart to say anything. Her father coughed in his sleep, opened both eyes, and reached for the handle at the side of his chair to lower the footrest. He leaned forward, heaved his great bulk out of the chair and shuffled across the kitchen.

Edna sighed, jerked her head in the chair's direction.

"Seriously, Mam, look at that. Two empty coffee cups, a Pepsi can, cookie crumbs. What is he doing, drinking that stuff?"

"Oh well, one won't hurt him."

"Of course it will, and you know it. His legs and feet are often numb now. Who's going to care for him once he sprouts a bunch of open sores on those legs? No more Pepsi, Mam."

"Tell him, not me. You know if I don't let him have it he'll go down to the corner."

"He can drink diet."

"He won't drink diet soda."

Her father lumbered back into the kitchen, belched, patted his expanse of shirtfront, said he was hungry.

"It's bedtime, Dat," Edna said curtly.

"I need my peanut butter crackers before I go to bed. Can't have my sugar too low in the morning."

"Dat, you need to stop eating those packets of Ritz crackers with peanut butter. You're getting barely any peanut butter and too much sugar. Carbohydrates that turn to sugar. Spread a slice of celery with it, if you have to have peanut butter."

His eyes narrowed, and he began to chuckle.

"You know what I heard about celery? The only thing it's good for is to convey dip to your mouth."

Edna didn't laugh. Her mother lifted an arm and scratched where it itched. Her father brought a packet of crackers to the table, went back to the refrigerator, lifted a can of Pepsi, looked at Edna's sour face, and then put it back. He poured a large plastic tumbler of milk, drank half while he stood at the counter, brought the remainder to the table. The kitchen chair groaned in protest as he lowered his bulk into it.

"Dat, you need to lose weight. I'm worried about your sugar."

"Nothing insulin won't fix."

He waved a hand in dismissal. Insulin was his bridge to procuring and relishing good food. Diabetes was easy for him. Shoot that stuff in his body every day, and everything was normal, including Pepsi and doughnuts down at the corner.

The Quick-Mart down where Route 101 met 62 was her father's idea of a good time. Sit at the counter with a cup of coffee, greet all your neighbors and friends, then sit all morning and talk about things that aren't important. He would order toast and jam, carbohydrates and sugar. After that, it would be a few eggs, over easy, on a pancake, doused in syrup, and not the sugar-free kind, either.

Then he'd come home, tell Mam he can't have any of her pie, or cookies, whatever she made, eat a light lunch of vegetable soup, a plate of cheese. And she believed him when he said he was doing real good with his sugar.

The only reason Edna knew all this was because of his brother Ray, who was often with the truck that delivered hay to many of the homes where Edna was a *maud*. He'd laugh about his brother's antics, relate in full detail what a *schliffa* he was.

It was a growing despair that sprouted in her chest like a mushroom, crowding out any humor or sense of leniency as far as her father was concerned. It simply wasn't funny.

She would be the one to look after them both. Everyone else had a life. She had no husband or children, no permanent address away from home.

She was unattached, a built-in nurse that came with the property.

"How was the two weeks this time?" he asked, scratching

his stomach, his fingernails like small rasps as he worked them across the fabric of his shirt.

"Oh well, you know, it was Dave Chupp's."

"They had another one, that's right. How many does this make for them?"

"Eight."

"Really? Why, that's a right nice family. Everything went well, I suppose."

"Yes."

What else could she say? Her parents were elderly, so they could only fathom the good in every person, didn't need to hear the hard parts, the tough times. Sometimes Edna imagined having a husband to whom she could relate every aspect of her day. Even her thoughts.

Well, she had Dora, her best friend and confidante, but she had her own life, her days filled to the brim with family, work, activities in the community.

She'd have to call her one of these days. Maybe tomorrow.

It was off to church the next morning, under lowering skies that bulged with snow, the wind easterly, damp and cold. She'd tried to persuade her parents to stay home, but they would have none of it, her father becoming quite noisy, and stating that he needed a healthy dose of spiritual food.

Edna thought he did, too, the way he could never pick up the cross of self-denial, sitting down there at that Quick-Mart eating pancakes and toast with jam on it, rolling around in his earthly pleasures like a pig in slop.

"Now, Dat, if it snows this forenoon during services, you are staying kaput. In the house, till I ask someone else to get the horse ready. You hear?"

"I don't hear you, no. I have a perfectly good pair of boots with a rubber tread, and feel quite capable, thank you."

"Mam, help me out here."

But her mother shrugged, chirped something about him being alright, which made Edna want to snort in frustration. How many years young did they think they were?

"Well then, if the snow starts coming down, we're not staying for lunch."

"Oh, I think we will. You know I enjoy church *essa* very much. All those pies, cheese, and ham. Yum."

So was it any wonder she entered the house of worship as disgruntled as a wet hen in cold weather? Her parents just tried her good humor to the limit.

Of course, the minister hit the sore spot, speaking at length about respect for the elderly, the true honor that was becoming lost, parents a burden for the children, the children likewise a burden on them.

Where was the voice of authority? Respect?

And Edna bowed her head in shame, knowing full well how far off her designated rung of the family ladder she was, yapping at her parents like an agitated terrier from the back seat. She had to do better.

Had to.

Alright, if her parents wanted to stay and were not afraid of the fine bits of snow that were beginning to fly past the window, then she would respect their wishes. Indeed. She set her mouth into a pious shape, her eyes becoming limpid pools of martyrdom. Ah, how good it felt to peel off the layers of dross, the impurities of her nature, leaving a shining vessel of polished gold for Jesus.

She clasped her hands, turned her face toward the minister, felt the blessings clothe her like an expensive fur. Yes, life was not worth living if you couldn't practice a bit of self-denial.

The snow was driven in by a stiff wind now. Edna could hear the clattering of a loose piece of the soffit and feel the draft at her feet. Her eyes repeatedly went to the window, where the snow appeared to be whirling even faster. She swallowed her anxiety, set her face to the minister.

She sang heartily during the closing song, then watched to see if her father would get his hat from the hook and venture outside.

Her breath caught. She bit her lower lip.

Yep. There he went, his black felt hat smashed down to his eyes.

Oh dear.

Harley Troyer stepped over, stopped him by putting a hand on his arm, spoke to her father, nodded, and smiled. Harley then left to get his own hat and accompanied her father out the door and down the steps.

Thank goodness. *Thank you, God.*

In the buggy, she huddled beneath plaid woolen blankets like a child, closed her eyes, and vowed to let her parents drive, respect their ability to stay on the right side of the road, spot oncoming traffic, and be able to see in the increasingly white world outside.

"Alright, here we go. Whoah there, Dob. Careful. You'll fall. Roads are downright slippy."

A long wait. The hissing sound of tires on snow, the whoosh of air as they passed.

"You see anything, Mam?"

"No. go ahead, Dat. The coast is clear. But close your window as soon as you can."

"Come on, Dob. Git up!"

The smack of reins across his fat back.

Edna wanted to yell, "turn signals!" She did not hear the blinking clicks that should have been in use to avoid a crash.

"Hurry, Dob. Car coming."

She felt the turning, the rocking of the buggy as it rolled across the road. She almost bit her tongue in half, her teeth clacking in panic when the sound of a horn sounded loud and long, followed by the outraged yell of a motorist who barely escaped an accident.

"What? What was that?" her father asked, his head swiveling from side to side.

"I didn't see anything." Her mother said mildly. "Close the window, now, Dat."

Edna sat straight up, every well-meaning bit of spiritual advice flung away with the woolen blankets.

"The turn signals!" she shouted. "You forgot again, Dat!"

"Edna, now you simmer down," her mother said evenly.

"No use getting riled up. We made it," her father added.

Why? Why was she stuck with her elderly parents? Nothing would ever change. She felt waves of irritation coupled with self-pity, then the sense of martyrdom she'd felt in church. *Yes, Lord. This is my lot. Give me patience and an understanding heart.*

Edna stayed cocooned in her room the remainder of the day, napping, writing letters, thinking about Florida, and wondering when her next job would be on the message line. She was ready to go.

It wasn't until the middle of February that the call came through. Allan and Laura Mast, a young couple who lived twelve miles away, clear on the other side of Topeka, had a baby boy. She could wait to come till Monday morning, since the mother was spending the weekend.

Before leaving, Edna helped her mother bind a quilt and make a pot of vegetable soup. She sewed a new dress in olive green, a different color for her, but one that would bring out the olive tones in her brown complexion. She packed her duffel bag with the usual assortment of colorful dresses and white aprons, made sure she had her L.L. Bean moccasins and plenty of ankle socks, flannel pajamas, and a heavy robe. Some houses she stayed in were positively freezing, especially the upstairs of old farmhouses.

She had never been a *maud* for Allan and Laura and had no idea where they lived. She looked forward to meeting a new family. This baby was not their first, but she had never been told how many they had.

On Monday morning, her father told her gravely that Orva Schlabach's wife, Sarah, had taken a turn for the worse. They gave her only weeks to live.

"The poor girl. I can't imagine Orva's despair. And those children. Emery said the oldest boy is thirteen."

Her mother shook her head. "What a tender age. So hard under normal circumstances. No longer a child, but not grown up yet. Ach my."

Edna was drawing the zipper around the top of her black duffel bag. She heard only part of her parents' conversation but stopped to ask how they expected to keep house without a mother. Usually, members of the family would help out, taking their turn.

"I don't know. I guess they aren't talking about that yet, hoping for a miracle at the last hour," her mother said gravely.

Edna felt bad for the young mother, the husband, and children, but had only met them at Dave Chupp's, so she had no close emotional ties to the family. Occupied with her preparations, she pushed it to the back of her mind and let it go.

The Allan Mast residence was located only a few hundred feet off the well-traveled route 891. It was a new two-story house covered in gray siding with a long, wide porch out front, the walls covered in decorative stone that matched the siding perfectly, concrete urns placed on either side of the welcoming red front door.

A barn/shop combination accompanied the house, in a darker shade of gray metal, with the same stone beneath a smaller porch. Shrubs of different varieties were placed at attractive angles, with bird feeders and birdbaths below young trees, which only added to the pleasant setting. The lawn spread to the road and beyond, covered in the melting snow, but Edna could tell everything was groomed and polished.

She was met at the door by a woman who looked young

enough to be the mother, dressed in a neat purple dress, her covering and hair flawless.

She extended a hand, a bright smile of welcome on her face.

"Hello. You must be Edna Miller." She said quietly.

Edna heard the patter of little feet, and a dark-haired, dark-eyed child clasped her arms around the purple skirt, peering up with an inquisitive gaze.

"I am Edna. Do I have the right place?"

"Yes, you do. How did you find it?"

"Oh you know. All you need is the address and those square wonders called GPS devices get you there."

"Oh, absolutely. Well, come on in. We're glad to see you. Although I'm not ready to leave yet. This baby boy is a darling."

She set her duffel bag on the rug; her eyes took in the beige and white palette of the house, the tasteful furnishings, the large rugs placed on high-quality wood flooring.

From the reclining position on the large, gray, overstuffed couch, a soft voice greeted her.

"Good morning. You must be Edna Miller. How are you?

"I'm fine, thank you. And how about you?"

"Well, considering I just had a baby boy, I'm O.K."

She sat up, put the fleece blanket to an adjoining chair, smoothed her blond hair and adjusted the black *dichly* that covered the back of her head.

She was very pretty, with her blue eyes and a porcelain complexion, only a shadow of weariness beneath her eyes. Slim, with her robe cinched around a small waist, the young mother looked to be still a teenager.

Edna looked from the dark-haired child to the blond, blue-eyed mother, a question in her eyes.

A tinkling laugh, with perfect white teeth.

"Oh, I know. Alicia is all mine. Ours. She's the spitting image of Allan. As dark as he is. Now go look at little Adrian."

The mother beckoned her to a small bassinet, covered in white.

Edna bent to lift the blue crocheted blanket away from the pale little face, the bald head complete with only a dusting of fine whitish hair. He was a beautiful boy; he just lacked hair and the dark coloring of his sister.

"Isn't that something?" Edna whispered.

The mother chuckled. "I hope he will keep his blue eyes. But you know how they say the brown eyes usually dominate."

Edna nodded.

She was led to the kitchen table, which was seemingly in the same room as the living area, the open floor plan creating a large, airy atmosphere. It was a sunny home filled with light and happiness. A steaming mug of coffee was placed in front of her, along with a plate containing a warm cinnamon roll.

"Laura, you want your tea?"

"Sure. I'll be out. Come, Allie, you want some tea?"

So she was Allie. With all the children Edna had encountered at her job as a *maud*, this one was almost too cute for an accurate description.

She didn't look real. A doll, really, and by all appearances, as sweet-natured as she was pretty.

She climbed up on a chair, her knees bent, her little elbows propped beneath her chin, turned her dark eyes to Edna and said in perfect Dutch, "*Das bisht glay, gel?*" It meant, "You are little, right?"

Edna laughed, wanted to reach out and grab her for a good, long hug, but drank her coffee and said, "Yes, you're right. I'm not very tall."

Laura smiled and told Edna she couldn't take responsibility for everything that came out of Allie's mouth.

"That's alright. I have heard a lot worse from children."

"I'm sure. Do you enjoy your work as a *maud*? You know, you should be called something nicer, like caregiver, or nurse, or something," Laura said, turning to look at her mother, who nodded in agreement.

The whole morning spent at the kitchen table was focused on her, both Laura and her mother curious, eager to hear about her life.

They told her she could probably write a book, and how interesting that would be to read of all her different experiences.

"Oh, I couldn't do that. I'm no writer, and I could hardly be truthful. People would see themselves, so no."

She shook her head, a shadow of remembering Dave and Emma Chupp crossing her face.

"I can well imagine," Laura said kindly.

Edna was surprised to feel the sting of tears behind her eyelids.

She prided herself in being unscathed, untouched by the homes that were less than enjoyable, tried to keep the negative thoughts at bay. But when kindness came unexpectedly, she let her walls down a bit and she felt the bitterness of defeat, whether she admitted to it or not. But to relate past experiences, to go from one house to the next spreading gossip, well, it simply wasn't done.

No matter how tempted she was, it wasn't right to speak ill of anyone. Each family had a history, an upbringing, and were placed on earth in different circumstances. We all have nature and genes created by God, whose knowledge and wisdom were mysterious, so who was she to judge?

She dug into the warm cinnamon roll, drank coffee, and felt as if she had known these two women her whole life.

She did laundry, baked pies and cookies in the bright kitchen, complete with the best bowls, a mixer, and every staple in the pantry she could imagine. Tupperware containers were set in orderly rows and labeled, holding oatmeal and brown sugar, 10x sugar, instant pudding of every variety, baking cocoa, and chocolate chips.

The sunlight, with little Allie talking in her lisping voice, the kindness that radiated from Laura, all of it was a dream come true. After what felt like the insurmountable challenges she had faced at the Chupps', this home seemed almost unfairly wonderful.

When Allan Mast came home from work, tall, dark, and handsome with the conventional good looks of a movie star, his kindness and appreciation like Laura's, it seemed as if she should pay them to enjoy her time with Allie, basking in the praise as Allan bit into his first forkful of her apple pie.

One day blended into the next as she performed her duties, often resting on the couch with Laura, as they talked and laughed, cuddled the baby, and read stories to Allie.

One afternoon Laura asked Edna if she'd ever thought about the names of her husband and children. Allan, Alicia (Allie), and Adrian. And she was plain old Laura.

"Our names spell 'Laaa.' Like a stuck La-la."

They laughed together, happy to be in each other's company. Edna knew she had found a true friend, one she would aspire to imitate the rest of her life.

But she found herself watching the clock as the hands moved slowly from the two to the three, every afternoon. There was only a small amount of work, a house that seemingly never became dusty or dirty. Cleaning was a breeze, with a battery-powered Hoover that sucked up the dirt every bit as efficiently as an electric vacuum cleaner.

After day six, she finally admitted to herself that she was bored. Just dreadfully bored with the perfection of it all. There was no challenge, no using of her abilities to set everything right, no satisfaction of making a difference to some overworked, underappreciated mother. She felt as if she was being smothered in Cool Whip, all light and frothy and delicious.

On Sunday morning she made a pot of her famous sausage gravy with homemade biscuits she mixed from scratch. The praise was warm and genuine, even from Allie, who broke bits of biscuit into her gravy and scooped it into her mouth. The orange juice was perfect, the coffee piping hot, just the way Allan liked it. The pancakes were absolutely the best thing they'd ever tasted, and the syrup warmed just the way they loved it.

She was the best thing that ever happened to them.

Baby Adrian hardly ever cried, and when he did, it was only a few hoarse little whimpers that were immediately remedied. The Huggies diapers were soiled at regular intervals, disposed of into the Diaper Genie that left no odors whatsoever.

Allie played with her assortment of dolls and toys, and had been perfectly potty trained months before the baby arrived. She went all by herself, awash in her mother's praise.

So why wasn't Edna immediately soaring to the heights this kind family instilled in her? She was loved and appreciated beyond anything she had ever experienced, and should've been, well . . . happy. But the truth was, she could hardly wait till the two weeks were over. Edna thought about this strange occurrence, wondered if perhaps she was turning into a sour old maid who was so used to wallowing in misery that anything this close to perfection only served to send her scuttling sideways, crablike, under the rock of her own dark expectations.

But Edna decided she couldn't help being bored. She liked a challenge, hard work, and tumbling into bed at night so bone-weary she fell asleep as soon as her head hit the pillow.

When the second Monday morning of her stay finally arrived, she left the house well stocked with homemade bread, granola cereal, casseroles in the freezer, and a layered chocolate cake with caramel frosting under its glass dome on the Pfaltzgraff cake stand.

She left with her usual wages plus a hundred-dollar tip, swimming in effusive praise, warm hugs, pictures Allie had drawn and colored, and a gift card for Target in an undisclosed amount.

Allan and Laura Mast were an exceptional young couple. They were what every young couple aspired to be on the day they were married.

And for this, Edna could thank God and give Him the honor and praise.

But she knew she needed more.

CHAPTER 6

Spring showed a few flirtatious colors, yellow and purple crocuses peeping up among soggy brown leaves and layers of melting snow that still lay on the north side of the buildings and in low places. Water dripped from eaves, lay in puddles in gravel driveways, and dropped onto snowbanks and left indentations in a straight row.

Edna thought she could smell the change in the air as she hung out laundry, appreciating the color of soft earth that promised new growth. Her fingers were freezing, however, with the cold breeze turning them red and aching. Nothing she wasn't used to, so she lowered her hands and shook them well to restore circulation.

She was washing her parents' bedding, every blanket and quilt she could find, the afghans her mother crocheted in brilliant colors, and covers off the pillows on the couch. Edna even washed all the many little throw rugs that were drawn across the floor, like patches of ice perfect for causing her parents to slip and fall.

These throw rugs were a necessary part of her mother's well-being, evidently, so whatever, but they were being washed. And they would likely be washed many times in the future since her parents had paid seven hundred dollars for a Yorkshire terrier. A tiny brown and black dust mop that peed on the rug by the door whenever her parents failed to hear his whines, which was more often than Edna had any idea.

She couldn't believe it when she came home from her stay at the Masts and this small dog came clicking across the linoleum like a dust mop come to life. She gazed down into two sparkling brown eyes that looked up at her with all the wisdom of small dogs, sizing her up and deciding she was worth some excitement, whereupon the terrier let loose a very small amount of yellow urine.

"Oh, now, Trixie. She does that," her mother trilled, scurrying to grab a wad of paper towels.

"Mam! A dog. Why a dog?" Edna wailed.

"Oh now, Edna. She's so cute. Dat and I need some entertainment. She's downright the cutest thing we ever saw. You should see her with Dat."

Grinning broadly from his perch on the oversized chair, with all the pride of a new father, he shook his head in wonder, said she stood in front of his chair and yipped the most adorable little barks until he reached down to lift her up to his lap.

"Just like a child," he chortled.

Edna bit her tongue, literally. Her eyebrows lowered, her nostrils flared, but all the protests stayed buried beneath a layer of parental respect.

She did not like dogs. Especially small dogs. Especially Yorkies, those yipping little ankle biters. Now how was she going to live in the same house with a brown dog the size of a good *shoe lumpa* that seemed to leak from his bladder whenever anyone talked to him. As if her aging parents weren't enough to send her clutching at the edge of her sanity.

She banged the door to the laundry room after the last load was on the line, those denim trousers that seemed as wide as a blanket, really. She bet her father's waist was at least a forty-eight.

She rinsed the tubs, swept the floor, then filled the blue

plastic bucket with hot water, added a squirt of Palmolive dish detergent, got a rag from the shelf beside the wringer washer, and set to work cleaning the brown and gray linoleum.

She hummed, whistled below her breath, her right arm making swiping motions as she cleaned. She heard the distinctive clicking of tiny dog toenails on the floor, sat back and waited, thinking. *Huh-uh. Oh no, you don't. Not on my clean floor.*

On she came, in her rocking little gait, her brown eyes eager to greet this person who resembled her own species, down on her hands and knees like that.

"Hey! Git!"

Edna made shooing motions with her hands. Trixie regarded her with bright questioning eyes, her stubby little tail whirring. She decided Edna wanted to play and bounced on over, her mouth open, her tongue lolling.

"No! Git! Get away from this wet floor."

She placed a hand beneath the tiny dog and lifted her, giving her a good head start to the kitchen. Trixie didn't want to go to the kitchen, she wanted to play with Edna, so she turned around and started back.

"Mam!" Edna wailed. "Come get your dog!"

Her father lumbered to the door of the laundry room, bent over and snapped his fingers.

"*Komm*, Trixie honey. *Komm.*"

Oh, so now it was "honey." She glared at her father, who smiled back at her and shook his head.

"You'll get used to her. She's a real companion. A joy to have around."

"I bet," Edna said bitterly. She pictured herself washing urine-soaked rugs and pillow covers wet with dog saliva, eating soup with dog hair in it.

Her mother cooked her usual breakfast of fried eggs and cornmeal mush, tomato gravy and thick slices of toast made from homemade bread in the broiler section of the oven. There was a small crockery pot of butter, a glass container of strawberry jam, water, and coffee. Her parents did not like the taste of orange juice, too sour they claimed, and so they swallowed Vitamin C pills and called it good enough.

The kitchen was sunny and pleasant, her parents both pleased to have her there, with conversation flowing easily. Her mother was looking forward to having Sadie come for coffee this morning, which Edna was pleased to hear. Her husband, Harley, had gone to Canada with his coworkers at the welding shop where he spent most of his days, so Sadie said she deserved a treat and would spend the afternoon shopping.

"Harley loves to fish, and this is the opportunity of a lifetime," her father commented, spreading an enormous amount of butter on the thickest slice of toast Edna had ever seen.

She opened her mouth and closed it again. If he wanted to sit there eating half a loaf of bread, then she guessed he'd just have to.

The remainder of the morning passed quickly, with dishes washed, kitchen swept, a fresh pot of coffee put on the stove, and a variety of cookies and bars arranged on a plate in anticipation of Sadie's arrival.

Her father clapped his straw hat on his head and hurried out to meet her when the horse and buggy came into view, with Sadie making an appearance shortly after he left.

"Mam. Edna. My, it's good to see you." Sadie hugged her mother, then Edna, a warm, cushioned hug from her sizable younger sister. She smelled faintly of horse, leather reins, and fresh, damp air, and the lingering odor of a slightly wet and well-worn black jacket.

"Why, Sadie, no children?"

Sadie shook her head. "Nope, not this time. Julie and Lucy are at Vernon's for the day, well, all night, actually. The boys are spending the day with their cousins, Chip's boys. You know how Fannie is, the more children she can accumulate, the better."

"So, you're going shopping all by yourself?" her mother asked.

"Oh no. I was hoping you'd go with me."

"Well, we'll see."

The excited Trixie appeared, bouncing on all four feet, running in circles, yipping her high-pitched sounds, and sure enough, leaving a small yellow puddle on the linoleum.

"What is this?" Sadie laughed, bending over to scoop up the wriggling dog. "Isn't she the cutest thing? Mam, you should get a few litters of puppies out of her, you know that? She's adorable."

Edna felt a stab of anxiety, pictured the kitchen floor come to life with ten more Trixies, dotting the linoleum with tiny yellow puddles, yapping and bouncing. Grimly, she reached for the paper towels below the sink and swiped at the puddle, her face red, her eyes snapping with distaste.

"Dat brought her off Henry Garber, that Mennonite who raises Yorkies. We just enjoy her so much. She's a bit of entertainment for both of us."

"What about you, Edna?"

Sadie watched her sister with knowing eyes.

"Not my choice," Edna said, in clipped tones.

Sadie laughed good-naturedly, her round eyes flattening as her full cheeks pushed them up, her teeth white and prominent.

"You know, Edna, you better be careful, or you'll turn into a sour old maid."

"You think so? Not everyone likes dogs, married or unmarried."

"That's true."

They sat at the kitchen table, poured coffee, brought out the plate of cookies, and caught up on all the latest news from Sadie's perspective, which was talked about in full detail. She elaborated on school problems, incompetent teachers, and a school board unwilling to work with them.

Edna snorted inwardly. Everyone knew Harley and Sadie's

children were slow learners, so inevitably, the teachers received the blame. The very reason Edna refused to teach school. Children were pliable; it was the parents you couldn't change. No way, much easier to do laundry, cook, and clean house.

"Well, we should get going here. My first stop is the dry goods store. I'll need a new black suit the way I hear it's going with that poor Orva Schlabach's wife. I can't imagine how she must suffer, in pain from her cancer, knowing she must leave her poor children and husband. They said last week she has a few weeks, or that's what the doctor gave her.

"The worst part, the one I can barely fathom, they say that the oldest boy is simply in denial. He's very troubled, hard to handle, to begin with. The only one who was ever able to do anything with him was Lizzie."

Her mother's eyes filled with tears, her mouth turning soft with emotion.

"Oh, you'd just like to spare him everything he'll have to go through at such a tender age, dealing with his grief. He'll have a hard road ahead."

Edna rinsed the coffee cups, put the remaining cookies in a plastic container, wiped her hands on a towel and went back to her room for a sweater.

Everywhere she went, Orva Schlabach's plight was thrown in front of her, like an efficient roadblock. She did feel pity, yes, but it happened many times. God evidently designed it that a mother was taken away, so what was there to be done? She wished everyone would stop talking about it.

She'd be glad when everything was over. He'd find himself a suitable wife soon enough, and everyone would likely survive. Perhaps she was turning into a lemony old maid, but was that so wrong?

People needed to be strong; it was that simple. She'd found that out soon enough. You took whatever was placed in your life and made the best of it.

The day turned out to be the most fun she had had in a long time, sitting in the back of Sadie's clean buggy, with her mother in the front seat with Sadie, conversation flowing fast and easy, the way mothers and daughters were.

Free to speak of whatever was on their mind, the sun shining, breezes that spoke of the promise of spring, Edna forgot about the new dog, the reality of the next job that loomed before her, or any troubling thought that entered her mind when she was alone.

Their first stop was Yoder's Dry Goods and Notions, a long low building with a brick front, the porch lined with all sorts of useful tools like garden rakes, hoes, cultivators, and the PVC rings with attached clothespins.

Four vehicles faced the front of the building, with two horses tied to the long hitching rack. An elderly man was scooping piles of horse manure onto a wide metal shovel.

"Good morning, ladies," he called out, straightening his bent back, his white beard framing his friendly face.

"Hi!" Sadie answered, turning her back for a moment as she stepped down from the buggy.

"Stay there, Mam, till I tie Maxie, O.K.?"

"You need help?" the elderly man asked.

"No, thanks. I got it."

He nodded, then turned to resume his shoveling.

Edna waited till Sadie tied the horse, then helped her mother from the buggy, before climbing over the front seat and down on the paved parking lot. She adjusted the strap of her purse on one shoulder and led the way through the swinging glass doors. She breathed deeply, the smell of candles, herbs, and new fabric—a pleasant odor, one that held the promise of discovering new things.

She bought fabric for two new dresses, a dark teal and a lime green that was too bright, but she thought, oh well, spring is just around the corner, and I am, after all, still a young girl. She would feel pretty in it, lighthearted.

She picked up a package of steel hairpins, and a new hair-net to keep the roll of hair secure on the back of her head. She bought thread to match both dresses, then walked over to the housewares section, and browsed through stacks of plastic containers, dishes, and kitchen gadgets. As always, she wondered how young brides felt, establishing their own domain in the kitchen. Edna found herself wistfully eyeing the brand-new display of stainless-steel cookware, the two-burner griddle, and the twelve-quart kettle she would use to cook plump red tomatoes from her garden, turning them into spaghetti sauce. There were also fresh new kitchen sponges, dishcloths, and tea towels.

She turned away, a sense of loss like a mist that obscured her view. Well, it was what it was. Other girls could have all that, but God had chosen a different path for her.

She wandered to the back of the store to survey the decorative items. An exceptional picture of the silhouette of a tree, in stark black, against a gray background grabbed her attention. It would look great above the love seat in her room. It was only then that she noticed the printed words in darker gray.

The Serenity Prayer.

"God grant me the serenity to accept the things I cannot change, to change the things I can, and the wisdom to know the difference."

Very meaningful. And quite unexpectedly profound. Tears pricked her eyelashes as chills covered her, the words spoken directly to her heart.

O.K., Lord. I know this is a direct message from You. I'll take it and do my best to practice it throughout my life.

She bought the picture, with no trace of the usual guilt, the indecision that normally upset her choices.

Her sister met her in the aisle, raised her eyebrows while nodding toward the large purchase.

"Wow, sis, you're in the splurging mood, huh?"

"Yup. Sure am," Edna answered, with a saucy toss of her head.

She didn't need to know how the picture had touched her heart. Best to hide the longing for her own home or husband from the eyes of her sisters or her parents. Let them be comfortable with their version of Edna's single position in life.

"She's too independent."

"Doesn't even think about a man."

"She's happy and carefree. Why bring up the subject?"

Sadie had about half a grocery cart full of useful items, her cheeks red and eyes bright as she searched the shelves for more necessities to begin her spring housecleaning.

She stood in front of the new wall mops, undecided, a finger to her full lips. "I need one of these so badly," she muttered.

"Get one," Edna told her briskly.

Sadie turned to her. "Do you have any idea how many dollars' worth is in this cart? I had to get a new drip coffee maker. Oh, Edna."

She reached out to slap her forearm.

"I forgot to tell you and Mam. Harley turned on the coffeepot, the feed man came, and he rushed out of the house. I returned from taking Robert to the dentist to find the house full of smoke and the coffeepot ruined. Positively blackened beyond redemption."

"Wow."

"It was more than wow. It was more like Arrrggghh. I was upset."

"I bet."

Well, she didn't have a husband, so she didn't have to put up with that. Harley was kind of a loser that way, forgetting things, always had that questioning look in his eyes as if he wasn't sure if he was coming or going. But you couldn't tell Sadie that. She worshipped the man.

Always had.

Back in the buggy, they decided to eat lunch at the local diner, just a quick sandwich.

More horse tying, helping Mam from the buggy, and through more swinging doors. They said hello to more of their Amish friends, settled themselves into a booth and ordered coffee.

The waitress was Amish, too, a young girl who took their order with the bored expression of the unchallenged.

"Isn't she one of Ben Miller's girls?" Sadie asked, in a voice barely above a whisper.

"Ask her." Edna said.

"Well, I don't want to appear nosy. She's too fancy, anyway. If that covering was any smaller . . . Whooo."

"Now, Sadie, your girls aren't grown yet. You have to be careful." Her mother said, a smile making the admonition seem like a gentle reminder.

The girl returned, stood on one leg, a hip to the side, and asked what she could get for them, cracking her gum, her gaze going out the window instead of looking at them.

"I'll have the special," her mother said quietly.

There was no acknowledgment of her mother's order, simply a left-handed jotting on her tablet, coupled with more gum cracking.

"A bowl of chili and the cheeseburger with onion and pickle, please."

Sadie's voice sounded like a first-grade child asking to use the restroom. Edna rubbed her hands together in anticipation. She'd get her attention.

"What is on the chicken wrap?"

"Chicken."

"I know there's chicken. I mean, is it chopped, with cheese, like a cheesesteak, or is it a slab of chicken breast, plain, or is it marinated, cut-up chicken breast, or breaded chicken pieces?"

Edna's face was a mask of innocence, as the girl struggled to follow. She quit popping her chewing gum, her dark eyes going to Edna's, followed by a bewildered expression.

"Could you repeat that?"

Edna rambled swiftly through the same question.

The girl shrugged. "I have no idea."

"Why are you working here, then?" Edna asked stonily.

Sadie kicked her shin under the table, her mother looked straight ahead, blinking furiously with embarrassment.

The girl's face colored, and she said breathlessly, "Let me go ask."

"Good idea."

As soon as she disappeared, Sadie hissed, "Ed-NA!"

"What? She was rude."

When she reappeared, her full attention was given to Edna, her manner helpful and courteous.

"The wrap is marinated, cut-up chicken breast. The chicken cheesesteak is the one that's chopped."

"Then I'll have that."

Bewildered, the waitress arched an eyebrow.

"Which one?"

"The chopped. But no onions. Put extra tomatoes on it. And light sauce. They spread sauce on the wrap, right?"

"Yes."

Edna could easily tell that she had no idea whether they did or not, but let it go.

"Are the waffle fries crispy?"

"I think so."

"What about the onion rings? Do you make them to order, or are they laying under a warming light? Because if they are, I don't want them."

"Right."

The harried girl scribbled furiously, wet her finger with the tip of her tongue, flipped the page, and resumed writing.

"If the waffle fries are made to order, I'll take them. First. If not, give me the onion rings, but only if they're fresh. What are your soups today?"

"Chili, chicken corn, and beef macaroni."

"What's in the beef macaroni?"

Meeting Edna's eyes now, the girl did her best to list the ingredients, saying it was really very good. Edna waved her hand, "No, I don't want any."

"Alright. Can I get you anything else, ladies?"

"Coffee. We need a refill," Edna barked.

She returned immediately with fresh coffee, more creamer, and a handful of straws for their water glasses.

"I'd like to order an unsweetened tea, please," Edna said.

After the tea was placed in front of them, Edna riffled through packets of sugar, artificial sweetener, till she found Splenda, then tore open three packets and added them to her tea, her mouth expressionless as Sadie told her in quiet, menacing tones that she would never, ever come into this place with her again.

"She needed to be straightened out, Sadie. It's only a matter of time before she'll lose her job with that attitude."

"But she's Amish," Sadie protested.

"I don't care if she's Amish or English, Chinese or whatever. She shouldn't be a waitress if she can't be courteous."

Her mother sipped her coffee.

"Edna's right, Sadie," she said, still smiling, her eyes with the constant light of kindness.

"Well, I'm embarrassed. I'm going to leave her a large tip."

Edna merely lifted her chin and sniffed.

The food was delicious, the atmosphere homey and inviting. Henry Garber stopped at their table to say hello, and to ask about the new dog.

"Oh, we're so glad we have her," her mother chortled, wiping her mouth with a napkin. "Dat just loves that wee little thing, doesn't he, Edna?"

Edna nodded, swallowed, smiled up at hairy old Henry Garber and his willowy wife with what she hoped was a genuine smile and not a toothy grimace of pure falsehood.

"Oh, he does," she squeaked, pushing the words out with considerable effort.

The bulk food store, "Countryside Foods," was a constant whirl of motion, smells, and sights. It was a huge store, almost a supermarket, and was a popular and well-managed market.

Her mother and Sadie were soon busily navigating the aisles bent over their lists, so Edna had time to browse. She picked up cookbooks and idly flipped through them, lifted oranges and sniffed them, then wandered the spice aisles, turning labels, before moving to the front of the store to check on her mother.

She stopped, half turned, and lifted a hand when she recognized the man everyone was talking about—the one whose wife was dying.

He was of medium height, a trimmed brown beard, with short brown hair beneath a narrow-brimmed gray hat. Edna squeezed a bag of cornmeal then let it go, before throwing a quick sidelong glance in his direction.

He was talking to an older man, his shoulders slumped with weariness, his hands in his pockets. His face was ashen, gray with care, his eyes wells of colored wretchedness. He bent his head, nodded, as the older man placed a hand on his shoulders.

He turned away, came toward her, stumbling blindly, his eyes half-closed with the force of emotion that brought the thick tears that rained down his cheeks, and his lower lip caught in his teeth as he struggled to contain the ravaging grief that tore him apart.

He never saw her.

She remained rooted to the floor, unable to move out of his way.

Never had she witnessed such agony.

She called out just before he walked into her, the toe of his heavy work boots hitting the side of her Skechers. She put up a hand to balance herself, found a coated arm and hung on.

"Oh. Oh. I'm sorry."

His hand found her waist, held her upright. She found herself very close to the face of pure and total sorrow, the tears making small wet lines down the drawn cheeks, the trembling, masculine mouth.

"Are you alright?" he stammered.

Edna looked up, into the light-colored eyes, that held bewilderment, apology, and untold grief. It was as if he had seen the tip of the iceberg that he knew would eventually try and sink him, the reality of it all too harsh to bear.

She experienced a total loss of speech. Wave after wave of raw pity swept through her. She had to do something for this broken man.

"I'm fine. I should have moved. If . . . if you need me, I'm Edna Miller, I work as a *maud*. Here is my number."

"Thank you. I appreciate it." She watched him walk away.

CHAPTER 7

THE FIRST MORNING OF HER TWO-WEEK STAY AT JAMES DETWEILER'S was cold, gray, and threatening rain. The flat Indiana landscape was dotted with snowbanks that were mottled with dirt and reluctant to melt into the muddy surface of the earth. The warm breezes had been herded out by a bone-chilling, wet wind that sank its teeth into coats, hats, and scarves.

Edna paid her driver, lifted her duffel bag, then faced the front porch and took a deep breath. Front porches had a way of disclosing plenty about the family that resided within the walls of a house, so by this one's appearance, she could tell it was one of the homes that required all of her energy and drew on her reserve of goodwill until there was nothing left.

It was a farm, which highlighted rule number one. Plenty of work. A washhouse or laundry room that inevitably reeked of cow manure, clumps of it clinging to Muck Boots and Tingley overshoes. No matter how much she mopped or scrubbed, there were always fresh stains on sneakers, with hay and straw scattered on rugs and lying in corners. The front porch held a faded deacon's bench piled with brightly colored bags of dog food, hockey skates, hockey sticks, and leftover coats. White plastic buckets stood on either side of the limp screen door, like sentries, guarding the entrance in all their cheap glory. A half dozen skinny barn cats lay in various positions, a few grooming themselves, others lifting their heads to acknowledge her arrival. Broken wind chimes tinkled haphazardly from a hook and hung beside two plastic hummingbird feeders, whose red color had weathered to a dull pink.

Edna wondered how many hummingbirds they'd fed this winter.

She exhaled a long sigh, then bent to pick up her backpack and made her way to the door. Before she reached it, the screen door was pushed open from the inside by an arm the size of a log, followed by a booming voice.

"Katsa! Shoo! Off the porch."

The cats lifted themselves, stretched, and sat down, the six pairs of yellow eyes heralding her approach.

"Hello. Oh, hello, how wonderful to see you coming to our door! You are the most welcome sight ever."

Edna could only describe the woman as massive. There was no end to her. Three hundred pounds was a kind estimate.

Oh my goodness.

"How are you? I'm Edna Miller."

She put out an unsteady hand to shake hers, but was ignored, then swept into a bone-crushing hug and a deep rumble from within the excess poundage.

"Welcome. Welcome. Children, come meet our new *maud*."

Instantly, the kitchen was filled with little ones of various sizes and colors, some blond, others with muddy brown hair, all dark-eyed and cherubic, their faces alight with interest.

"Now, Diana, this is Edna Miller. She's going to live here for a few weeks. Edna, this is Diana. She's five."

The woman stood aside, beaming, her eyes bright with pride as the little girl stepped forward to place her hand in Edna's.

"How do you do?" she asked politely.

Edna was completely taken aback. The children were clean; their hair combed flawlessly, their dresses made in the latest style, the hems almost touching the floor, and their small black coverings neat and straight.

In turn, there was Annalise, then Kent and Brendon, winsome little chaps who shook her hand gravely, each one presented with the same air of pride from the oversized mother.

"Now, you must come see the new one. Oh, she's that adorable. She's number nine."

She moved across the kitchen the way many large women did. She seemed to sail, moving quite swiftly, like a large tugboat. She led Edna to a white bassinet pushed into a corner beside a huge recliner and bent to lift a bundle wrapped in a cream-colored blanket of expensive crocheted fabric. She held her out to Edna, saying, "She only weighed a little over six pounds. Came early. Isn't she cute?"

Edna had to admit she'd hardly ever seen a more perfect little girl. Her face was round, her eyes like crescents, little half-moons fringed with wispy lashes that promised a heavy growth.

"She is absolutely picture perfect, isn't she?" Edna said, sincerely.

"Oh, I know. Ours are all that cute, though. We named her Audrey. Audrey Rae. Isn't that cute?"

She waited expectedly for Edna's agreement, her eyes eager on her face.

"I'm Susie, so you know who to yell for if you need help."

She laughed, then took the baby and sank into the recliner, reached down to pull the lever at the side and stretched her legs comfortably as the footrest moved into positions.

"Sit down, sit down. We want to get to know each other. The work will be waiting when we get to it, O.K.? Relax. Do you drink coffee? I just made a fresh pot."

"I do. I'll get it, if you tell me where the mugs are," Edna offered.

"To the right above the stove. Now, Edna, we don't always live like this. The baby came, and everything went kaflooey in short order. The girls did well over the weekend. So did James, bless his kind heart. You know I have the best husband in central Indiana, you wait till you meet him. He's a gem, an absolute keeper."

Her bright eyes rested on Edna's face, expecting agreement, as she carried two mugs of coffee to the recliner.

"Oh sorry. I need my creamer. Diana honey, would you please bring my creamer and spoon?"

Instant obedience, carried out quietly.

"Thank you, sweetie pie."

"You're welcome, Mam."

"So, Edna, there are four more children in school, all girls. We have seven girls now, and two boys. I was hoping for a boy, but girls are always welcome."

She bent her head, crooning, "Aren't you, widdle Audrey. "

"We have Karen in eighth grade, which, of course, I'll be so glad to have her out of school to help, but I can't tell her that. I told her to enjoy her last year of school and remain carefree; she's still so young. Then we have Katrina in sixth grade, Sharon in fourth, and Shannon in second.

"All of them such a big help, so sweet and responsible. You know, Edna, I have no idea how the Lord ever blessed me so abundantly. I'm just swimming in happiness right now, and I do nothing to deserve it. My Mam and sisters close by, all so helpful with casseroles and desserts. Fern brought three, mind you, three baked lasagnas for the freezer, and her lasagnas are the best. Absolutely."

She lifted the baby to her shoulder.

"Now tell me all about yourself, Edna. You know we live so far at the north end of the Amish community. I don't believe I know your parents, or any of your relatives for that matter."

"Well, there's not much to say. I'm single, obviously, and twenty-nine years old. I live with my parents who are in their seventies, so that has a whole list of craziness."

Susie choked on her coffee as she burst into laughter, the

deep belly laugh of one who "gets it," then shook her head from side to side.

"I can well imagine. I know my mam had her hands full with her parents, in their nineties, they were. Both of them."

She paused, her head tilted at an angle.

"I may as well be honest, though. I cannot imagine why you are single. You're like a chickadee. So small and round and dark. You're just the cutest thing. You'd think the guys would be falling over each other for you."

Edna gave a short laugh. "Not exactly. I have never been asked out. Not once."

"Well, then God must have a special role for you, somewhere, somehow. There is just no rhyme or reason to your being single. Actually, I was prepared to meet this tall, skinny, sour old thing, you know. People have their idea what an, excuse me, old maid looks like. And you don't fit that description at all.

"Look at me. Happily married, a whale of a woman. No seriously, I have a water retention condition and must go off my Lasix when I'm pregnant, I swell up like a balloon. This is probably my last baby, which makes me very sad, but it's too dangerous now, with my blood pressure and all that goes with it. They had to take Audrey five weeks early, so I have a feeling I'll have orders from my doctor.

"So now I'll naturally keep decreasing all summer. My normal weight is a bit over two hundred, which is quite enough. But I'm elephantine, now. The fat lady at the circus."

She laughed at her own description, then sat back and closed her eyes.

"My head is swimming, sorry, Edna. When these pills start to work, I tire easily and get light-headed. Listen, you just go ahead with laundry and cleaning up the way you're used to it. I have a washer that runs on air, use it like an automatic. James has the tank full."

Another pleasant surprise.

The laundry room was large, with plenty of windows dressed in fancy shades, the washer in a closet behind folding doors, shelves lined with Tide and Downy, Clorox and all kinds of stain removers and colorfast bleaches. Edna lifted the lid of the white, automatic washer, checked out the knobs and thought, *Hmm. Well, my word.*

She sensed a presence behind her and turned to find Diana, her hands clasped in front of her.

"If you want, I can show you where the hampers are, upstairs."

"Sure. That would be a great help."

"O.K. Follow me."

Laundry was almost unfair. The clean clothes were spun so well they seemed dry, the clothes basket light in her hands. She washed dishes and windows, then mopped the laundry room floor between loads until lunchtime when she was introduced to the amiable James. He was tall and built like a linebacker, with the bushiest blond hair she'd ever seen, and a wispy beard that seemed like an unsuccessful attempt at completing his manliness.

He grinned widely, extended a huge paw (she couldn't think of hands that size) and shook until her teeth rattled.

"We're glad to have you. I told Susie more girls should make a career out of being a *maud*. You travel all over, don't you? It's a wonderful thing."

"Thank you. I mostly enjoy my job. Of course, some places are better than others, but I seem to thrive on hard work. Plus, I enjoy housekeeping."

"That's good. A wonderful calling. Susie asleep?"

He looked toward the empty recliner. He bent to receive both boys, who came running at the sound of their father's voice. He pulled them on his lap, giving them his full attention, as Diana and Annalise stood at his elbows, waiting their turn. Edna was fully and efficiently dismissed as he listened to the chatter of the little ones.

"Kent wet his bed," Brendon said gravely.

"Well, he can't help it. Too much chocolate milk last night, right, buddy? We love our chokko milk." He rumpled Kent's hair, and the boy nodded solemnly.

Edna heated Campbell's tomato soup, made grilled cheese sandwiches, opened a jar of pickles, and then apologized for the quick lunch.

"I hadn't taken a farmer's lunch into consideration."

"Don't apologize. It looks delicious. Just what I was hungry for. Nothing beats a good grilled cheese sandwich and tomato soup on a cold, dreary day like this."

Oh, but you wait, Edna thought. *Wait till I bake apple pies and cinnamon rolls with caramel icing and fried chicken or pot roast with Lipton's onion soup mix.* She looked forward to cooking for him, as genuine as he was, and as rewarding as it was bound to be.

She had to admit, this once, that the front porch had been deceiving. The farm was truly well kept, the old house remodeled, not with the latest or most expensive materials, but with common sense. New drywall where it was needed, kitchen cupboards replaced with good-quality custom-made cabinets, new flooring, with painted trim that looked as if the old, routered wood had been used wherever possible. The house contained some clutter, of course, but underneath, it was reasonably clean. The laundry room had only a faint odor of cow, or "bovine cologne," as Edna dubbed it.

So she entered seamlessly into the life of James and Susie Detweiler, went right ahead with the work the way Susie wanted it done, which was basically whatever she saw necessary. By the end of the first week, the house had taken on a new shine, windows gleaming, linoleum wiped clean with Pine-Sol, every small piece of furniture moved and dusted, bedding washed, dried, and put back on the beds.

She discovered the basement that first Monday after the

lowering skies dropped fat raindrops that increased all forenoon, until it could easily be called a deluge.

She carried the wet laundry to the basement, found a large,
warm area open to the east with low windows and French
doors, There was linoleum on the floor and paneling on the
walls, wooden clothes racks and plenty of clotheslines suspended
from the ceiling, and a coal stove giving out radiant heat.

There was a Ping-Pong table, a shuffleboard table, air hockey,
an extra refrigerator, and a set of inexpensive cabinets complete
with a sink and stove.

The school-aged girls were grown versions of the four youngest. Blond, brown, all dark-eyed, their dresses made to fit well, as
neat as pins, their white coverings clean and well-shaped. But most
of all, there were the impeccable manners on display again. They
emptied their lunch boxes themselves, washed the Tupperware
containers, dried them, and put them back. They went to the
basement only after Edna told them they didn't have to help with
supper, and after they sat at length with their mother who listened carefully as they told her about their day. They did have a
quiet, desperate struggle after one of them thought the other held
Baby Audrey too long, but that was only to be expected, for sure.

She made a meatloaf that first evening, covered thickly
with ketchup and brown sugar, a bit of mustard. Baked potato
wedges were covered in olive oil, garlic, and Parmesan cheese,
with a salad made of iceberg lettuce, tomatoes, and broccoli
florets, which, she was horrified to find, barely reached to fill
everyone's plate. James had an enormous appetite, with Susie
being no slacker in the food consumption department, either.

She shrugged inwardly but did not apologize. This was how
she learned. She should have known by the size of them, but
then, you could never tell. That fuzzy, peach-colored beard
threw her off, she figured.

After supper, the two oldest girls covered their hair with ban-
danas, shrugged into old gray sweatshirts, and went to help their

father with the milking and calf feeding. Sharon and Shannon were expected to help clean the table, to do dishes, and sweep, which Edna found to be a great help.

The family had a routine, a well-managed order to their days, but Edna could never quite figure out how it was all accomplished under an atmosphere of relaxation. Things didn't run smoothly all the time, so if something did not get accomplished, it was alright, tomorrow was another day.

The front porch got a thorough cleaning, though. Edna dumped the cat food, which she had mistaken for dog food, into the plastic buckets and carried them to the laundry room closet. She found lids and a permanent marker, and wrote "CAT FOOD" in capital letters. She found a home for hockey skates and sticks, all the unused coats, then swept and scrubbed the cement porch floor, replaced the welcome mat with a slap, set the broom on its handle to dry and that was that—no more misleading porches in her domain.

She fell in love with Katrina and Karen, the two oldest. She never met girls with so much liveliness and happiness, complete with an outsized sense of humor. Well, look at the parents, she thought. Same genes.

On the third day, Wednesday, she had finally been able to bake bread, resulting in warm, fragrant loaves, the tops glistening with butter and resting on the counter under a tablecloth to keep them from drying out.

The girls, always hungry, sniffed appreciatively, rolled their eyes, and asked Edna where it was.

"What? Where what is?" Edna asked, feigning innocence.

"Bread! It smells like fresh homemade bread." Katrina said.

"Oh come on, I didn't bake bread."

"Liar, liar, pants on fire," from Karen.

Taken completely by surprise, Edna's mouth fell open.

"What? My mother would never have allowed such language in the house."

"Whoopsie. Neither does mine," Karen hissed, rolling her eyes in the direction of the recliner, where Susie lay with her eyes closed.

"I'm sorry my mam takes on the form of a walrus when she has a baby." Again, Edna's mouth formed an O of astonishment.

They laughed lightly, quietly, in the beginning, but the laughter kept bubbling up over and over until they were sprawled on kitchen chairs, their arms hanging helplessly at their sides, wiping their eyes to rid them of unexpected tears.

"Be nice!" Edna hissed.

"We are nice. We tease her about it. She just laughs. It's a condition."

"I know. She told me. She says this is probably the last one."

"Oh, I hope not. I love the babies."

"Oh bread, where art thou? Thou art forever fair in mine eyes," Karen sang out.

"I canst sniff thee, yet thou eludest me," Katrina mimicked.

There was just so much to love in this unexpectedly well-adjusted family, that Edna often found herself thinking back to her arrival, the inward shifting of gears as the porch came into view.

You just never know, and that was the truth.

Midweek, James Detweiler came home with armloads of groceries, bearing the grave news that some Schlabach woman had died, leaving a husband and three motherless children. He didn't know them, but that was the talk around town.

Edna stood still, absorbed the news without any outward sign that she had heard, but immediately thought of the man at the dry goods store.

Orva, they called him. Orva Schlabach.

So it had happened then. Her cancer-riddled body was free from pain, or rather, her spirit left the body here below to be properly taken care of, to be viewed and mourned.

Edna felt nothing. A dull acceptance, until she remembered the look in his eyes as he had stumbled away. She should not have been there, seeing that. It was as if she had viewed the private photographs of a man that did not want her to see them. Edna felt a tugging lack of energy, a lassitude she couldn't understand. She folded clothes and put them away, made a pot of chili, dragging herself from one job to the next, wishing she could lie down and rest.

When she finally found herself in the shower, the spray of scalding hot water released an unstoppable flow of tears that lasted far into the night as sleep eluded her. If someone would have asked her why she was crying, she would not have had an answer.

She awoke the following morning to the high, insistent pinging of her travel alarm, felt the immeasurable sadness, stumbled into the bathroom, peered at her swollen eyes, and knew she had to perk up.

Ridiculous, this moping around.

Edna threw herself into the work, then tumbled bone-weary, already dripping with sleep before her head hit the soft, feather pillow at night. She put Orva Schlabach and his three children out of her mind and continued her life.

She had coffee with Susie every morning after the children left for school. She would have it no other way. Three was a whole day for her to finish cleaning or baking or whatever.

This morning Susie produced a package of Oreos, ripped open the top and took out five or six, dipping them rapidly into her heavily creamed and sugared coffee.

"You know, Edna, I feel as if I've known you my whole life. I will miss you so much when you leave. The girls just love you. You'll have to stay in touch. Write or call sometimes. Or, even better, come for a visit."

She stretched, yawned and rubbed her eyes.

"Not much sleep last night. Whew! But James is so good

with a crying baby. He always takes a turn, especially if he knows I'm exhausted. I mean it, Edna, I have the best husband in the world. I didn't do one thing to deserve it. And look at the size of me. It's awful."

"I don't think size has anything to do with it."

"For some men it does. Look at David Erma. She diets all the time to stay trim for that man."

"Oh, well."

They sat in a comfortable silence.

"You think you'll ever get married?"

Surprised, Edna looked up, straight into the discerning dark eyes.

"Why would I? I can't believe anyone would want me anymore."

"What do you mean by anymore? As if you've reached the golden age of seventy."

She clucked at her own joke.

"No, I mean you know as well as I do that an Amish girl's best prospects are gone once she reaches the age of twenty-four or five."

"You think?"

"I think so."

"Not for everyone. Look at JoAnna Mast. She was in her thirties when she married Elvin Weaver."

"A widower, right?"

"No. A single guy. And not unattractive, either."

"Well, you know. Whatever."

Susie pushed away the package of Oreos.

"I have to stop eating them. They give me heartburn."

Edna laughed with the natural humor that wavered between sisters, or a mother. She had never met anyone quite like Susie. She was like an artesian well, with kindness and goodwill flowing from her oversized heart, coupled with a deep interest in others' opinions, always finding the best in those around her, yet she had no idea how downright good she was. She carried her husband and children's love like a banner that floated above her, gave them all the credit, neverendingly thankful. She was what God intended women to be.

A deep shudder ran through her, a sickening jolt of the knowledge of her own pettiness, the selfishness that ran through her veins like an unhealthy disease. She couldn't even be accepting of a tiny little dog with an overactive bladder.

"What's wrong with you?" Susie asked.

"Nothing."

"Something crossed your mind. Your face."

"I thought . . . well, it's true that we deserve what we get, right?"

Puzzled, Susie wrinkled her brow.

"You mean . . .?"

"Well, I'm just saying. You know, outwardly, I'm a good person, the way everyone is, mostly. But I am not nearly as unselfish as you."

"Why would you be like me? I had nine children. Let me tell you something, Edna. After nine babies, if you still have selfishness, you're just bound to be the most miserable person on earth. You know that verse in the Bible where God told Adam he had to work by the sweat of his brow and Eve would bear children with pain? Women are finicky creatures, prone to think of themselves, picky as all get-out. So the whole of God's design is, indeed, a wondrous thing. We are saved from ourselves through bearing children, which may sound harsh, but it really isn't. Babies teach us what God wants us to be."

"What about single girls? I'm just on the slippery slope into a cauldron of misery?"

Edna could not quite keep the bitterness from her voice.

"What's a cauldron?" Susie asked, followed by her infectious laugh.

Edna glared at her.

"Oh, come on. I'm not wording this well at all. Of course, we all have the very same opportunity to accept the gift of salvation through Jesus Christ, Edna. It's just that I understand what God has in mind, and am eternally grateful. Motherhood is a wondrous thing, and I hope you'll get to experience it."

She looked puzzled for a moment.

"But surely, in your work, you feel attached to the little ones, feel a sense of ownership, of love."

"Why would I? They're not mine."

"Of course not. And here I go rambling on about the virtues of having babies, feeling superior. I don't mean it that way, Edna."

Edna nodded, a small smile hiding the lump in her throat.

"You didn't say anything wrong. It's just that . . . ever having someone, you know, getting married, the whole bit, seems like an ever-growing impossibility, the older I become. I just have to accept it. My sister Sadie says I'm already turning into a sour old maid. Lemony."

Susie's voice rose.

"No, you are not. You are the most delightful *maud*. I hear you in the kitchen with the girls, and they love you. Absolutely adore you, Edna. You are blessed to have this gift of being an outstanding *maud*."

And like a long-dry sponge, Edna soaked up the water of Susie's encouragement, and sang as she sorted laundry in the laundry room.

CHAPTER 8

THE TWO WEEKS WITH JAMES AND SUSIE DETWEILER WAS SHORTENED by the alarming message that her father had been taken to the hospital in Topeka.

By ambulance, which meant her mother had called the emergency number, no doubt making her way to the telephone in too much of a hurry, which could have been disastrous as well.

Guilt left her feeling robbed of good humor as she arrived, the towering brown building looming over her sense of duty, taunting her with its air of English professionalism.

She disliked hospitals, doctors, efficient caregivers that never failed to instill a sense of stupidity, of incompetence. She should have been at home, catching on to her father's deep cough, the escalating fever. No doubt her mother had used an entire jar of Vicks, resorted to Unker's and Vitamin C in diarrhea-inducing dosages, along with enough Tylenol to tranquilize an ox.

Upon arrival, she turned to the driver, a smiling gentleman who reminded her of Susie, his face lined with horizontal wrinkles that all turned upward, like the corners of his mouth.

"There you are, young lady," he said, his old, watery eyes assessing her worried face.

"Yes. How much do I owe you?" Edna asked, pulling her purse on to her lap, reaching for her wallet.

"Not a thing, honey."

He placed a gnarled, swollen hand on her arm, and rubbed gently.

"This is free. Your poor old father is sick, so why would I take your money?"

"Well, thank you. But please let me know if there is anything I can do for you sometime."

"I most certainly will. Now you take care of your old man, O.K.?" Edna nodded, opened the door, and stepped out. She took a deep breath as if to cleanse her arm from that old hand. She could almost guarantee she wasn't normal, the way irritation flared the minute he touched her arm, called her honey. She was not his honey, not even remotely.

She stalked across the parking lot, bristling, with the sense of being thrust into a situation that was entirely against her will.

She didn't even know her father's room number.

The giant lobby was filled with people whose faces registered varying degrees of concern. She turned away from any friendly overtures, marched up to a long, low desk without returning the man's greeting, brusquely inquiring about David Miller.

"Room 504," he answered, after a lengthy tapping on computer keys.

"Thanks."

Fifth floor. Great. How was she supposed to find the elevators?

She stopped, found signs with arrows pointing to them, and kept going, finding a small group waiting in front of the heavy, automatic doors. Edna entered with them and stood in the farthest corner, her arms crossed defensively across her waist.

The elevator rose, then stopped, with most of them exiting the enclosure, so she did, too, without checking the numbered panel with buttons to push for the floor she needed. She stepped out, stood hesitantly, turned left, to find directions for rooms to 301.

Right. 304. This was not so hard.

She walked with a purposeful step to Room 304, finding the door ajar, so without knocking, slowly pushed it open, expecting to find her father and siblings. Instead, a thin, graying woman looked up from the reclining bed, a question in her half open eyes.

"Oh, excuse me. I have the wrong room number."

She backed out before the woman in the bed could answer, retraced her steps, boarded the elevator, punched the button below the five, and hoped for the best.

504, he'd said.

She found the room, tapped lightly, then let herself in, easing slowly in as if she might not see anyone she recognized.

Her mother rose immediately.

"Oh, Edna. I am so grateful you're here. Fannie and Sadie won't be in till this evening, or the boys. The time gets awful long, just sitting here.

"They are taking him somewhere else in a few minutes, to do tests. Something about the infection in his bronco tubes."

Edna groaned. "Mam, did the doctor say bronchial?"

"I don't know what he said," her mother said softly, and then began to cry, soft little hiccups with tears splashing on cheeks as papery and thin as Kleenex.

"Ach, Mam, I'm sorry I wasn't here. I just . . ."

"Edna."

A hoarse whisper from the bed. "I'm glad you're here."

He extended a hand, the fingers beckoning.

Edna went to him, placed a hand on his shoulder. "How are you?"

"I'm alright. I am. They'll fix me right up in here," he gasped, then began a fit of coughing, like sandpaper across a rough surface.

"They will," she assured him.

Under the fluorescent ceiling lights, her father appeared bloated, his hair parted in greasy yellow strands. Dry flakes of old skin clung to his feverish forehead, his nose crisscrossed with blue veins, moles, and pockmarks. The teal green hospital gown was pulled to one side, exposing his thick neck crosshatched with skin tags, unsightly polyps of overgrown skin cells.

She had never seen her father without a shirt collar that rode up on his neck. He seemed vulnerable, an aging oversized baby, dependent on other's judgment. An odor escaped from under the thin sheet, an unwashed body, made up of lumps of flesh, old yellowed fingernails.

Edna took a deep breath, steadied herself and looked to her mother, who was pocketing an old crocheted handkerchief, her eyes tired and rheumy.

"I should have been at home," she stated matter-of-factly. "You are both fast approaching the age where you will need someone close all the time. Which will have to be me, right?"

Her father had fallen asleep in his weakened condition, but her mother repeatedly shook her head, no, no.

"You have to provide for yourself, Edna."

Two white-coated men came into the room, greeted them vaguely, then proceeded to unhook wires, the bed lowering electronically, and without further words, they wheeled him out the door and turned left.

Dear God, keep him safe, Edna whispered.

It was viral pneumonia. Her father spent over a week in the hospital.

The boys and their wives visited frequently, as did the sisters and husbands, with Edna traveling to and from the hospital every day. Her mother insisted on spending the night with him, obstinately refusing to budge when her children tried to persuade her otherwise.

"They won't hear him when he calls," she told them.

"Mam, listen, it's the nurse's duty to check on him all night long. You know how it is at a hospital at night, you get very little rest, O.K.?" Edna pleaded.

"Edna, now you be quiet. This is my husband, not yours," she said firmly.

She only lasted two nights, and then became so exhausted she fainted in the bathroom, which gave Edna a horrible fright. After that, she realized the time had come to treat them like children, and make them obey.

Of course, Edna's mother folded like an accordion, without a whimper, accompanying Edna home and sleeping without a sound all night long.

Much to Edna's relief, Trixie was whisked off in her small plastic carrier, with Sadie's children eagerly awaiting the dog's arrival.

Edna scrubbed every inch of the linoleum, washed every rug in very hot water and a drop of Clorox, then clapped her hands to rejoice all on her own.

And so began her month's stay with her parents.

The letter arrived that second week when she thought she must surely lose her mind from sheer boredom and the endless repetition of caring for her father, whose spirits wavered between irritation and self-pity, her mother jogging back and forth, waiting on him hand and foot.

And of course, Trixie returned, completely spoiled, having forgotten every attempt at being housebroken.

She found the letter between a subscription renewal notice for *Birds and Blooms* and a propane gas bill. It came in a plain white envelope addressed to her in a cramped writing style that was definitely masculine.

Her heart leaped, dropped, then began a slow, methodical thudding. *What in the world*, she thought, and took the letter back to her room, opening it with fingers that shook so badly she tore the envelope and a good portion of the letter written on plain, lined notebook paper.

Dear Friend,

(Her first thought was, I'm not your friend. What's wrong with Edna?)

After much prayer and consideration, I have decided to ask you if you would be willing to begin a friendship with me? I would like to pay a call on the evening of the twenty-first.

I remain anxious to hear from you.

Yonie Hashbya

Her first reaction was to assure him that he'd remain in an anxious state for quite some time. Yonie. Oh, help. Wasn't that just like him? Wasn't this simply a continuation of her whole life? Dealt a hand of cards she would never be able to comprehend?

She didn't want Yonie, plain and simple.

Her whole life, he'd gone to the same church, attended every sale, every volleyball game, every event she had ever attended. He was a good five years her senior, short, curly-haired, wearing those wire-rimmed glasses that made his eyes look as small as raisins. Or chocolate chips.

He had a pronounced limp from a fall off a tractor when he was a boy, she remembered that. He was severely pigeon-toed, and everyone agreed he was a bit slow, although certainly kindhearted. He'd do anything for anyone, always the first at any fund-raiser.

He was also wealthy, having inherited his father's welding shop, producing all sorts of hayracks, feeding troughs, snow removal blades, everything anyone asked of him.

But could she come to love him, in time?

If she ever wanted a husband, here was the door of opportunity.

The letter slid out of her nerveless fingers, fluttered to the floor and lay there.

Well, prayer was most definitely necessary, but she had to

deal with the thoughts that marched like an unstoppable loco-motive through her head. She rubbed both of her temples with her fingers, squeezed her eyes shut to clear the chaos, then threw herself back against the cushions of her sofa and exhaled.

There were her parents. Her job. What would people do without her? She could not leave her parents alone. What would her sisters say? Who would give her the best advice?

Edna could not rein in her scattered, wing-borne thoughts. For one, she could never again tell anyone she had never been asked to go on a date with an eligible young man. She had been asked now. Written to.

How often had she imagined this letter in a handful of mail? Now it had happened, but not from the one she had always thought might write to her someday. Never from him.

His name was Emery. Emery Hoschtetler.

He was exactly nine months older than her, thirty years old now, and still unmarried, which made it harder for Edna to keep pushing away the "perhaps," the hope she knew was empty, but found herself hanging on to anyway. Even to herself, she didn't admit the power of his attraction.

Why was life like this for some, and for others everything went according to plan? Her plan for marriage and living hap-pily ever after always included Emery, from the first moment she had spied him, straddling a bench as he greeted his friends at the Sunday evening hymn singing.

There was nothing outstanding about him, no golden-haired movie-star perfection, nothing that set him apart from a dozen other young men. It was simply the way he walked, the way he held his shoulders, the wide grin that flashed on and off. He had straight brown hair, nondescript eyes behind heavy glasses, but his nose was sharp, his skin darkened from the sun.

She had fallen hard. Heart-thumpingly hard. The image of him filled her days, the fantasy of if and when he would ask her to be his girlfriend.

Emery and Edna. Given their names started with the same letter, she told herself constantly that it was meant to be, destiny. God's will, her own will, her parents' will.

Thirteen years and nothing had ever happened.

Well, sometimes things had happened. He smiled at her, or talked to her, but always with a group, as a friend, and nothing more. She knew now she had been pathetic, single-minded, desperately drowning in the pool of her longing, kept afloat with one smile, one "Hey, Edna."

Her girlfriends knew. They sat together giggling, talking, talking, sharing feelings, discussing boys, planning outings to spaghetti suppers and horse sales, fairs and festivals. But one by one, her girlfriends were chosen, became wives and then mothers, growing away from her by the sunlight of their lives, leaving her in the shade of being older and single.

Oh, there was a time when she would not have thought there was anything wrong with that title. Her shoulders squared, her face took on the practiced look of happiness and self-sufficiency, of being a career woman. Albeit an Amish one, so minus the high heels and attaché cases. Her wardrobe and luggage consisted of sensible Skechers, white aprons, and a roomy duffel bag.

Pride was a constant pillar of support. She never allowed the people in her world to see below the mask of happiness, the energy, and constant work tackled with an almost manic vigor.

She was alright. Always. She had everything under control. As the years went by, Emery remained an active figure in her imagination, but in the mist of nostalgia. He moved to another county, opened his own leatherworking shop, so Edna let go, more or less.

Now here she was, still alone, and Yonie bobbed to the surface of her life. *Oh my. Now what?*

How did one go about loving someone you had no attraction to? Was it possible? Was it required?

She needed her sisters, so she slung a sweater over her shoulders and sat in her father's tiny office to use the phone.

She got Fannie's voice mail.

"Fannie, this is Edna. There's an emergency coffee tomorrow morning. It has nothing to do with our parents, so don't panic. Bring your cream-filled coffee cake. See you."

Sadie's voice mail. Same sales pitch from Edna.

Her parents had no idea her world had been rocked., They went about their day reading get-well cards, counting out pills, peeling blinds, and turning the thermostat up or down, taking Trixie out or wiping up after her. Her mother cooked the evening meal, a delicious but simple bean soup and fried sausage patty sandwiches with bread-and-butter pickles, slices of Swiss cheese, and tomatoes.

Edna wasn't hungry, she said, which sent her mother into a tailspin, asking what she'd eaten for lunch, did she think maybe something had gone bad? Was she coming down with the flu?

She retired early, dressed in her nylon pajamas after a hot shower where her tears ran freely with the steady stream from the showerhead.

She cried for the loss of Emery, who she finally had to set free, with the proposal on paper from none other than Yonie Hershberger.

So that was the new level in which she should view herself. She knew there shouldn't be such a difference. Wasn't one human viewed with the same measure as another? In the eyes of God, anyway.

Till late in the evening, she wrestled with her options. The later it became, the more this whole thing irked her. She brushed her wet hair, heavy and dark, viewed her face with all fairness.

Average. She was not hideous. Her face was small, round, like the rest of her. It was not a beautiful face, with outstanding features. It was a plain, nondescript face with ordinary features.

Like Emery.

She could no more help that intrusion of thought than she could help breathing. He lived in her subconscious, all the images of the past years like a child's View-Master. Click. You pulled the lever down, and there was a brilliant photograph of him, riding his black horse at the sale. Click. There he was again dressed in his Sunday best, his hair perfect, his smile making her knees go weak. Another click, and there he was, loading his plate at the oyster dinner.

She had to rid herself of these images, had told herself that over the years, but now, tonight, she meant it. If a false hope would keep her from loving Yonie, then it was time.

She slept a few hours before her alarm rang at six, shuffled to the bathroom and glared at her reflection.

The letter. All of the previous evening's doubts and fears presented themselves again. But it was a new day, with Sadie and Fannie coming to help her untangle from the web in which she found herself.

Her father appeared perky, color in his cheeks again, as he sat up at the kitchen table, looking sadly at the lone fried egg and shaking his head.

"You know, life is cruel. Those doctors have no idea how small and worthless one fried egg is without mush."

Edna shook with laughter.

"Funny, funny, Dat. But if you want to stick around for a while yet, you're going to have to change your eating habits. It's oatmeal for you."

"Rolled oats. Not that quick stuff."

"Whatever. No more mush for a while. Your cholesterol was off the charts."

Her father cut sadly into the fried egg with the side of his fork, laid the cut piece on a corner of his toast that contained not a smidgeon of butter.

He bit off a section, chewed, then said with a wistful

dignity, "You know, isn't there a selection of artificial butters at Walmart? Some of them are made from olive oil, I believe."

"Of course, Dat. We'll look for something you like on our next trip to town."

"I'd appreciate it."

His bowl of oatmeal was met with the same humble obedience, punctuated by fits of coughing and a tired sigh before he scraped his chair away from the table.

"Think I'll drink my coffee on the recliner," he mumbled. "*Komm*, Trixie."

The small dog's ears perked up, and she followed him obediently, then was picked up and placed in the big man's lap.

"You're only allowed a fourth of a cup of dog food, and I can only have one egg. Fellows in misery."

Trixie raised her face, opened her mouth, and yawned, with the super-long tongue dangling. Edna watched her balefully, thinking how rat-like she was, while Trixie eyed Edna with humor in her brown eyes, as if to tell her she was the fortunate one, sitting up here while Edna did the dishes.

Can I help it if I'm not a dog lover, you little sprinkling can? Edna thought, then rose to begin clearing the table. She finished the dishes, then told her mother about her sisters' visit, complete with a coffee cake.

"Alright, what is the emergency?" They asked in unison, as they washed their hands in the laundry room sink, dried them on a towel, and headed for the kitchen.

"My hands still smell like horse," Sadie said, holding them to her nose. She retraced her steps, soaped and washed again, sniffed her hands before she dried them.

"I can't stand the smell of horse sweat on leather reins."

"Try Trixie's messes," Edna said sourly.

Fannie rubbed Edna's back.

"Oh, come on, darling sister. The poor hapless creature. She's so cute."

Her mother nodded. "She is. I feel bad that Edna has to clean up after her, but we can hardly get her broken."

"Well, it's cold yet. Wait till the weather moderates, then she won't mind going out."

"Emergency? Remember? What is the emergency?" Sadie asked.

Edna was pouring coffee, so she kept her face hidden. Unexpectedly, her heart slammed against her chest, and she felt the color drain from her face, accompanied by the absolute certainty that she was going to cry.

Bewildered, their mother's eyes questioned.

Edna faced them in spite of her spiraling emotions, blurted out the news of the letter.

"Yonie? Wha-at?"

"Yonie Hashbya? Simply unbelievable."

And from her mother, "Why Edna, you've been asked."

As if her whole life had been a journey to this point. Mam could leave the earth and go to her heavenly reward now; her youngest daughter had been asked, with marriage the end result. Her motherly mission had been accomplished.

"So, the emergency amounts to?" Fannie asked.

"What should I do?"

"Tricky, tricky," Sadie said flatly.

"He'd make you a wonderful husband, and you know it," from Fannie.

"Aye. Aye." Sadie interjected.

Edna slurped coffee, burned her tongue, grimaced. "Would you marry him?" she snapped, looking from one inconclusive face to the next.

"No."

"Probably not."

A long, uncomfortable silence, rife with words that should be spoken but polite kindness refused to let out.

"Alright, here goes," said Sadie. "You know you were never

asked for a date because of your obsession with that Emery Hoschtetler. It was as if you wore a thick layer of armor that was a repellant. Like insect repellant."

Edna snapped to attention.

"Nobody knew it. Not one single person. Well, a few of my girlfriends. But not you or Mam."

"Too bad if you think so. It was written all over you."

"Now, don't be mean, Sadie," her mother chided gently.

Edna felt the strength drain from her arms. She sagged against the back of her chair, looked from one sister to another.

"O.K. It was. Too bad. It's all in the past. So what? Now if I want a husband, it's going to have to be Yonie. Is it alright to marry someone for the sake of being married? Does love come later, if you give yourself up? Or should I be happy in my single life? You know if I marry, you guys are going to have to step up to the plate and do your share with Mam and Dat."

"You're not going to marry him," Fannie said bluntly.

Sadie slid her eyes sideways with a warning look.

"You could try one date."

"I think you should," Mam said firmly. "How will you know if you like him or not unless you spend an evening with him?"

"But, Mam!" Edna wailed.

From the recliner, her father's weak voice wobbled across the room.

"Yonie Hashbya? By all means, you'll take him, Edna. Here's your chance for quite a ketch. That man is the salt of the earth. You better take him."

Short of breath, he halted, laid back against the headrest of the recliner. Touched by her father's weakness, Edna told him soberly that she would. She would allow him to come see her on the evening of the twenty-first. Fannie cut another slice of coffee cake.

"Well, alright. Emergency taken care of. Right, Sadie?"

"I would say so."

"You'll write to him?" her mother asked, anxiously.

"Yes. I will. I'll try that first date if that's what you think I should do."

Her father smiled, her mother looked pleased, but Sadie and Fannie walked like puppets when they left. As if they were being forced into something they could barely carry out.

The buggy fairly bulged with their outraged conversation the whole way home. Their parents were too old-fashioned to try and make Edna enjoy a date she never wanted in the first place. They couldn't stick them together like Legos, there was no way that strong-willed Edna was going to date poor Yonie. It was the worst match in the history of romance.

Edna was not the type to let love happen by giving herself up. She knew her mind immediately, and her whole mind was taken up with that waspish Emery Hostetler.

"You know, she acted shocked that we were let in on her little secret."

"What she sees in him, I'll never know. He's skinny, walks around like a banty rooster. It's just how Edna is. Contrary. If I can't have him, I don't want anyone."

"It's just too deep."

The horse slowed to a walk, the road turning slightly uphill.

"Hey, get this thing moving. I have laundry to do. Chip finally fixed my washer."

Sadie opened the window, slapped the horse with the reins, and said, "Mark my words, that date is going to be a disaster."

CHAPTER 9

Edna, of course, never heard her sisters' dire premonition, which was a good thing, the way she battled for weeks, staunchly determined to meet this thing head-on.

When the day finally arrived, she ignored the sinking of all her resolve, showered, dressed carefully in the new rose-colored dress she had sewed in the latest fabric, a light black sweater for the evening that was bound to be carrying hints of early spring. She combed her hair with a bit more care than usual, sprayed it liberally with hairspray, before adjusting her white covering. She felt pretty, even if the result was not what she'd hoped. The dress was too vivid, too rose-colored. She'd tried too hard.

Her parents nodded their approval, a spark in her father's old, tired eyes. His health had improved, but the pneumonia had taken away more of his already waning strength. Her mother told her she looked very pretty in that new dress, and she hoped she would enjoy her evening.

"Thank you, Mam. I think I will."

She was ready at 6:00. The house was cleaned up, the dishes put away, Trixie on her father's chair. Enda scanned the floor and the rugs for telltale dark spots and was relieved to find none.

When a horse-drawn buggy finally appeared, Edna was taken aback at the beauty of the horse. Black, high-stepping, the buggy gleaming.

Well.

She went to the barn, in the traditional way, to help him unhitch. It was a lovely evening, the sun already setting the sky on fire with the beautiful colors of orange, blue, and yellow, the breezes carrying a hint of flowers, new earth, and developing plants.

He was about her height. They were both short. He was very short for a man. He stood on tiptoe to run the reins through the ring mounted on the harness.

"Good evening, Edna."

He turned, and his face was an open book, pleasure written in joyous paragraphs. She took his proffered hand, shook it, and returned his greeting.

"Hello, Jonathan." She couldn't say Yonie.

He waved away the formality. "Oh, just call me Yonie."

She smiled, met his eyes. Hidden behind the heavy lenses, surrounded by sturdy black plastic, they were only small indentations in his round face. His nose was quite prominent, his mouth round, like his eyes. He was clean-shaven, his hair cut well, so that was something.

"So, did you want to go somewhere?" he asked, turning to lead the horse through the door and into an empty stall.

She waited till he reappeared.

"You hadn't indicated anything when you wrote, so I thought we'd stay here, if that's alright."

"Certainly. Of course."

He walked over to the buggy, reached behind the seat and produced a wrapped box, complete with the most beautiful arrangement of ribbons and bows she had ever seen. She lifted her hands in delight. He gestured for her to follow him to the porch where he held out the box to her.

"My goodness!" she breathed.

"For you, Edna," he said, handing it over with so much pride, he was fairly bursting. Edna found this strangely endearing, and took the package with genuine feeling.

"Thank you. You shouldn't have done this. It's too much."

He giggled. Edna didn't know men could make such a feminine sound.

The box tilted. *Oh, there's something alive in here,* she thought. Then she noticed the breathing holes.

The box whimpered.

No, no. Please don't let this be a dog. Oh please.

But that's exactly what it was. A Yorkshire terrier. A teacup Yorkshire terrier. Brown and black.

All of Edna's upbringing could not save this moment. She opened the door, unsure what else to do.

"Um, my, um, here's Trixie!" she said brightly, as the small dog's keen sense of smell found her own kind, bouncing and yipping and leaving small puddles of excitement on the floor.

The ill-concealed outrage turned her face a darker shade as she swooped to pick up the dog and carry her to the door, to set her outside less than gently.

She saved the ribbons and bows, folded the beautiful wrapping paper, looked at the trembling dog, a portrayal of twice the work, twice the annoyance.

She reached out to hold the puppy, forced herself to say, "He? She?"

"You don't like him?"

Yonie's face was the picture of damaged pride.

"I do. He's really cute."

The evening was endless, Edna keeping up her end of the conversation, a seesaw with her being the heaviest. It was hard work. The presence of the dog colored every word she said, as she wondered with wild desperation how she would ever manage.

Yonie was kind, hopeful, entertaining. He was actually a good conversationalist, but knowing this was going nowhere and never would, she could not concentrate on their talk. What was she supposed to do with the dog?

He offered to take him back, which almost changed every-thing, the despair replaced by a rush of gratitude that almost felt like love.

He didn't ask for another date, only looked at her from the whitish-blue glare of the headlamps, thanked her for a good evening, climbed into the buggy and left. Edna turned, sighed deeply, and walked slowly back to the house.

Then, with the night scented with budding tulips and daf-fodils, the new grass and overturned earth, Edna felt a deeper sense of longing, a longing for something in her life that she knew she wanted.

To be loved by a man, the way Chip loved Fannie.

Harley and Sadie. Her three brothers and their wives, all joined together by God the day they said, "I do." Till death do us part.

She supposed she'd wasted the best years of her life, waiting on Emery, but was that so wrong? Would she ever give up that hope? He was still single, so why should she?

But she knew the futility of her thoughts. Edna pictured the evening without Emery lurking in the perimeter of her being. Yonie might have appeared different, maybe completely desir-able. Oh, she had no idea.

This business of dating and romance was too hard, like being tangled in fishing net underwater.

She'd go on to her next job, throw herself into the work, care for her aging parents, and forget about it.

Her message line contained two messages, the first one left by a man, saying they'd asked a niece to help out, that with milk prices what they were it was too much to pay wages to a *maud*, but they'd keep her in mind.

Edna felt a sense of loss, she enjoyed the Miller family over on Route 618, their bright house and homey atmosphere.

The second message was from, well, she wasn't sure exactly who it was. A sister to Orva Schlabach. Would she consider housekeeping through the month of April? Something about produce and greenhouses, her brother Ben and his landscaping business, something about hardscaping.

What in the world was hardscaping? Her message was one of those that began with "How are you? We're having a beautiful spring day, and isn't this weather lovely?" All those idiotic questions when she knew full well there was no way on earth she could answer them. The rambling message could have been condensed to a few quick sentences and one important question. Would she be willing to keep house for Orva and his three children, ages fourteen, nine, and six?

She would. With marriage to Yonie erased by the first date, her father's health improved, she would be able. So she left a message back, asking for directions, an address, and when she would be expected.

Short, brisk, and to the point.

The whole thing of leaving messages with telephones housed in outdoor buildings was maddening. She thought of organizing a protest, maybe a march, like people do.

That wasn't the Amish way, though. It was all about submission, respecting those in authority. First God, then the ministers, bishops and deacons, husbands, parents, the list went on and on. You were raised this way, being Amish, so minor irritations like doing without telephone service in the house were like cold sores. Eventually, they went away until the next one popped up.

Rebellion came and went, like waves of the ocean. If a major rebellion came and stayed, members of the church would generally leave, buy a car, use electricity, search for a church that made more sense with their way of looking at things. The horse and buggy were too harsh, the *ordnung* too strict. Inevitably, there was confrontation, parents pleading tearfully to the *ungehorsam*, their pride seriously wounded.

The remainder of their lives, they would carry the blame, the shame of unfit parenting. How nice to have every child grow up with the same views and values as their parents, walking obediently in their footsteps.

A great blessing.

Members of the Amish church, however unfortunate as it may be, were all endowed with human nature, which meant each individual thought for themselves, and did not always adhere to the *ordnung*. At council meetings some would sit with a bowed head and ears red with the burning of his or her conscience.

And some saw no wrong in the pocketed cell phone, the occasional bottle of beer. They felt no conviction from God, but they'd never tell the minister their ways.

Was it possible to love your parents and cause them grief? Well, at any rate, Edna always figured you got into complicated territory once you allowed a rebellion to take over your life. To listen to messages on an outdoor phone was a small price to pay for continued peace and unity with the family, the ministers. To give in to each other was a gift, and one that brought lasting peace. God was the final judge, so Edna didn't need to worry her head about it.

Edna believed folks in all walks of life were saved, would hear the trumpet of the Lord with gladness, the deciding of it best left alone.

But she did think it was silly to have to go outside to use the phone. And what if her parents had an emergency and needed to call for help when she wasn't home?

"Dat, we need to get you a phone in the house," she announced the minute she reached the kitchen.

Her father looked up from *The Connection* and grinned, shifted the toothpick in his mouth, asked, "Now where did that come from?"

"If you or Mam would have a heart attack or a stroke, you'd have to go out the sidewalks, through the office door, just to dial the emergency number."

"Then I guess we'd do that."

"You need a cell phone."

She walked across the kitchen to the magazine rack, ruffled through it until she found a copy of *Reminisce*.

"Here, look at this. A cell phone with big numbers. No internet. Nothing. Just a handy gadget in case of emergency. I'd feel so much safer after I leave."

"Now where are you off to this time?" her mother asked, leaning forward over the sink to pinch off brown geranium leaves from the cluttery display of flowers.

"I guess to that man whose wife died a while back."

"Where's his family?" her mother growled, pushing her glasses up with a forefinger, before peering more closely at wilted geraniums.

"I think I have mealybugs," she muttered.

"His sister left a message. It's spring, so they have business, I guess. Landscaping, greenhouses, I don't know."

"Well, my word. Don't think it's right, now, Edna. Family should be caring for him and his three children. See, more and more, we're drifting to the ways of the world. This poor man should not have to hire a *maud*."

Her mother's words were delivered over the sink, with her head tilted back to see through her bifocals, muttering about her mealybugs.

Her father got up to shuffle to the kitchen table, sitting heavily and gazing with a child's wistful expression at the refrigerator.

"Mam, I guess the cottage cheese and sliced peaches are all, right?"

"Did you look? If I have these mealybugs again. . ." she answered.

Edna went to her room. She didn't have the energy to argue with her parents about the phone. With her father on medication for both cholesterol and high blood pressure, her mother fairly capable, they should be alright for a month. She'd make sure the girls checked on them.

She heard the click of small toenails, then watched balefully as Trixie walked into the room, making her way steadily to Edna, where she stood, lifted her head, and stared at Edna's face with sad, accusing eyes.

"You pee on my rug, Trixie, and you're dead," she muttered.

Trixie put her head to the side, searching for a welcoming sign, trying yet again to be invited up on the overstuffed love seat.

Edna glared a warning.

Trixie turned, her head down, and walked slowly across the expanse of the luxurious beige rug, came to the edge, sniffed, and hunkered down to relieve her bladder mightily.

"Trixie! No! No! Bad dog!"

Trixie took off running, her feet pounding the hallway in swift bunches of her legs, her toenails like mini castanets, clicking on the linoleum.

"Mam! You get your leaking little fleabag! She peed all over my rug!" Edna yelled, hysterical with frustration.

"*Komm*, Trixie. *Na, na. Komm.*"

"Ach, Edna, we're going to have to do something different."

"You're right, Mam. It's me or the dog."

And both parents were glad it would be Edna.

As she folded clothes in proper stacks, she found herself still smarting from the bruised dignity of that first date. Here she was, packing the same old piece of luggage with the same old work clothes, going to yet another home where she would enter without a clue, thrust through a stranger's doors, and expected to carry on the management of a household. A great weariness settled about her shoulders, leaked into her arms, and left a stone in her chest.

Was this her own reaping, having rebelled against marriage to someone of her kind, like Yonie? Lofty ideals that flowered into unreachable fantasies, with Emery on a sky-high pillar of dreams, year after year going by without seeing herself for what she was.

She folded one white apron on top of another, her thoughts colliding, banging around in her head until she stopped, sat on her bed, and lowered her face in her hands. She had to do better than this.

Where was her usual sense of ambition? Of meeting challenges head-on, looking forward to each new home, new people? She should never have agreed to that date with Yonie, the way it had deepened her sense of failure, the development of this painful soul-searching.

This time, she walked up to another porch, her feet dragging, doubt following her like a cloud of black gnats.

This house of sorrow.

It was a white vinyl-sided house with a wide front porch, a row of three low windows, black porch rockers, and a black porch swing at one end.

The lawn would soon need mowing, chickweed strewn across the too thin mulch in the flower beds. The welcome mat was askew, with boot tracks leading to a pair of lace-up camouflage boots.

Before she could lift her hand to knock, the door was opened from the inside; a tall woman of medium build in a purple dress was greeting Edna with a smile on her face.

"Come right on in, you must be Edna Miller."

Edna set her duffel bag on the floor, turned to shake her hand.

"Yes. I am. How are you?"

"I'm fine. Well, as good as I can be, with everything. I'm Orva's sister, LydiaAnn." Edna was surprised to see quick tears sprout from her blue eyes.

After a month?

Uncomfortable with the unexpected emotion, Edna cleared her throat, felt helpless as she searched for proper words.

"Well, of course. You'll want to know where to put your . . ." LydiaAnn pointed her chin in the direction of her duffel bag.

The whole morning was awkward, with LydiaAnn struggling to keep her composure, showing her to her room upstairs, a large well-lit area complete with a comfortable-looking queen-sized bed. There were also two large dressers, a writing desk, chair, and a tasteful comforter and matching curtains.

She would have to share the bathroom with the children, but Edna assured her she was quite used to that in other homes.

"Orva is at work. He has his own siding business. Construction. He's putting in long days since Sarah died. We're really worried about him. It's just . . ."

Her voice trailed off. She turned to look squarely into Edna's eyes.

"It's a mess. The oldest boy just turned fourteen years old. Neil. He's a handful. His mother was very special to him. I don't know how he'll be with a stranger in the house. Orva has not faced reality yet, we're afraid, so he's detached himself from responsibility as far as Neil is concerned. There is just one hurdle after another, with both of them.

"Marie is nine, and Emmylou is six. The girls are manageable, both in school, of course. It's just Orva and Neil."

She shook her head, a hand going to her mouth.

For a fleeting moment, the thought entered Edna's mind that she should just leave. Go upstairs, pick up her bag, tell LydiaAnn she wasn't about to let herself into a situation like this, call her driver, and go home.

It was so unlike anything she had ever experienced, these cloying doubts, this monumental task before her.

It had to stop.

So she mentally dusted her hands, squared her shoulders, took a steadying breath, and said she'd be fine.

They shared the remainder of the apple cake with a cup of coffee as LydiaAnn went over the basics of laundry, what the children ate in their lunchboxes, the Yeti thermoses in the men's lunches, which day Neil went with his Dat and which days he helped his grandfather on the dairy farm two miles away.

"Emmylou is frightfully spoiled, which is understandable, having had a sick mother for so long. You just deal with the children as you see fit.

"Orva seems to be in another world, as you'll notice."

Immediately, Edna thought of the day at the bulk food store, the raw, unvarnished grief in his eyes. She sipped coffee to hide her thoughts, toyed with the fork, her eyes averted.

Too soon, LydiaAnn was on her way home.

Edna rinsed the coffee cups, noticed the sticky countertop, the smudged stove, the dust on the gas heater in the corner. The house was laid out sensibly, a large, bright kitchen with custom-made cabinets, an oval kitchen table with matching chairs, a wide doorway to a large living room that ran along the front of the house. The three low windows presented a view of the driveway, a grove of trees, the sweeping front lawn.

The room contained grommet drapes on each side of the windows, an overstuffed sofa and chairs, a multicolor braided rug, a low coffee table, and houseplants in ceramic pots that all appeared dry, neglected.

Well, the house was definitely cheery, open and inviting, so that was something. The laundry was already flapping on the long wheel line in the back yard, thanks to LydiaAnn, so she'd check the pantry and refrigerator for the food situation before she began cleaning.

She'd be alone till late afternoon, when the girls came home from school, then Orva and Neil between five and six.

She opened the door of the refrigerator to find it stuffed to overflowing with plastic containers, leaking bags of hot dogs, and lunch meat stuffed into torn wrappers. There was cheese in sandwich bags left open, rotting grapes, oranges covered in green mold, ketchup containers stuck to shelves, and spilled dressing, with the cooling fins in the back surrounded by thick layers of white frost.

Nothing to do but get right down to work. Edna was used to these gas refrigerators, so she turned the knob on the bottom to "Minimum," opened both doors and began unloading the containers. She found garbage bags in a drawer and started pitching all the moldy food, the Cool Whip containers of dubious edibles, the limp celery, and sagging carrots.

As usual, work was her therapy. Adrenaline ran through her veins as she unhooked shelves, washed them in hot, soapy water, set a cake pan beneath the frost-encrusted cooling fins, then tackled the pantry.

It was a lovely pantry, with a small window set high with wide shelves along three sides, a bin for potatoes and onions, a rack along the door for mops and brooms, a hook for the dustpan and brush. Everything else was a fiasco. Too many meals had been brought in, with no one taking charge of empty containers, which seemed to take up most of the shelf space.

Opened bags of potato chips and pretzels were tossed into corners, along with torn boxes of Tastykakes, peanut butter crackers, and granola bars.

A trail of grape Jello powder was already drawing small red ants. A hunk of black bananas on the floor scared her so badly she let out a high squeak. Didn't these children eat anything healthy, ever? Evidently not, by the looks of all these spoiled fruits and vegetables. Well, she'd change that, for sure.

She bent to the job at hand, scoured and scrubbed and organized. Every dish that belonged to someone else was placed on a table in the laundry room, filed according to initials. Thank goodness for Amish housewives and their perpetual marking of precious Tupperware, Princess House, and Pampered Chef, those versatile but pricey kitchen items they needed to keep in their possession.

Edna found the telephone in the nearby garage, felt like an

intruder in Orva's personal space, but went on to open a door and find his office. His desk was long, low, and made of metal, like a schoolteacher's, the top littered with every imaginable contractor's item strewn haphazardly. Calendars, deer antlers, fishing rods, old license plates, glass bottles on a high shelf, a map of Indiana.

Edna found the telephone and left a community message in a brisk voice. She chose to remain anonymous, saying only that the items left at Orva Schlabach's should be picked up at any time.

That done, she returned to her organizing. There were too many empty black-lidded Modular Mates from Tupperware. She washed and dried them all, dumped the opened bags of snacks into them, stacked them in order, and proceeded to the next shelf. When she began to feel light-headed, she looked at the clock, amazed to find it was well past the noon hour, so she quickly folded a few slices of ham into a roll, added sliced tomato and mayonnaise, grabbed the potato chip container, and sat down, suddenly ravenous. She polished that all off, and then went in search of the chocolate chip cupcakes she'd discovered, ate two, and belched loudly.

She grinned to herself.

Nothing like good old-fashioned hard work to set your whole world right. All those crazy doubts and fears, the building pressure of clutching anxiety was gone like a balloon on a string released from a child's hand. This was all very doable, the same as all the jobs she'd tackled before.

Three children at those ages couldn't be all that bad.

Orva would gather himself together and step up to the plate, take on the duties he needed to again. Neil would be O.K. Everything would turn out to be fine, she knew.

She went back to work with a song whistled low under her breath, finished defrosting the refrigerator, arranging everything back on the shelves, before getting down on her hands and knees and wiping the whole kitchen floor with a new, orange cloth. The sun shone, the smell of wet earth came through the window she'd opened a few inches, filling the house with clean scent.

She went to the back patio to bring in the laundry and was surprised to find another wide expanse of lawn sloping down to a rock garden built among layers of stone, surrounded by a grove of evergreens, and one huge, old maple tree. Daffodils had already bloomed, their shriveled heads falling off the green plants, a variety of colored tulips everywhere, with pink and lavender creeping phlox still a carpet of beauty dangling over the enormous racks.

She stood, clothes basket in hand, taking deep breaths as she surveyed this garden, as wave after wave of delight washed over her.

Who had done this? Had Orva put all the labor into this lush garden for his beloved wife, only to lose her?

CHAPTER 10

SHE HAD PLANNED TO HAVE ALL THE LAUNDRY FOLDED AND PUT away before the girls came home, but she had miscalculated, evidently, not being able to find the correct drawers. Edna heard the front door open and close, the sound of children talking, before she turned and made her way down the stairs, the clothes basket in hand.

"Hi! I'm Edna Miller, your new *maud*. Welcome home."

She was greeted by two pairs of green eyes that gazed at her from a fringe of dark lashes, two grim mouths that did not smile, or open to utter a word.

The oldest, Marie, shrugged her shoulders, and the youngest one, Emmylou, simply turned away and went to the living room, sat on the couch and began to peel off her socks.

Edna put the clothes basket away, returned, and asked brightly whether they were hungry. Another shrug came from Marie, with the return of a barefoot Emmylou, clutching her black socks and glaring.

"You're not my mom," she said. "And I'm going barefoot. It's warm outside."

Edna smiled. "Alright."

Astonished, the child's mouth fell open in disbelief.

"We aren't allowed to go barefoot unless we see a bumblebee," she said. Her voice was high-pitched, with a lisp so pronounced it was like a burr.

"Who said?" Marie asked from the pantry.

"My mam."

"Your mam is dead," Marie said forcefully.

"No, she's not dead. She died. She's an angel now. Dat said."

"Whatever."

Incredulous, Edna turned from one girl to the next.

"So can I go barefoot?"

Edna was at a loss. Of course, she remembered her mother's words, or she would not have spoken of it. To say no would only bring the expected reminder that she, Edna, was not her mother, ending in disobedience. A yes would give her the advantage of her disobedience to her deceased mother's words.

So Edna shrugged and told her to do whatever she felt best.

The girl stood, deep in thought, and watched Edna get down the recipe box and flip through it before sighing.

"Guess I'll put my socks back on. No bumblebees yet."

She returned to the couch and began the meticulous process of putting on the long, black socks.

"Who put our snacks away?" Marie asked, unhappily.

"I did."

"We don't like our snacks in containers. Mam never did."

"You'll learn to like it."

Edna kept her eyes on the recipe cards, felt the scorching look from the nine-year-old Marie.

"You're not our mother."

"No, I'm not. But I'll be here for a month, so it's my kitchen for the next thirty days."

She spoke firmly, busily flipping through the recipe box.

"Neil won't like it."

"Who's Neil?"

"My big brother."

Edna found the recipe she was looking for, or one close to

her version of lasagna, so she didn't bother answering, a shot of irritation stopping her kind answer.

She knew Marie was lacing up her boots for combat, using her big brother as a scare tactic, and they'd barely been in the house for ten minutes.

Little upstarts. Motherless or not, this attitude was ridiculous. Edna wanted to slap them both. Seriously, who did they think they were? Well, too bad, girlies, I can put on my own combat boots.

"See, if you throw snacks on shelves without reclosing the bag or securing it, they go stale in a hurry."

"The same thing happens when you leave the lid off," Marie retorted.

"No kidding," Edna said, indulging in much-needed sarcasm.

Marie sniffed, loaded potato chips into a cupped hand, and headed for the couch. Edna's first reaction was to stop her, but she thought better of it. Power struggles could sneak up on you, and before you knew it, you were on your knees. Let Marie have this small victory. Potato chip crumbs were not the end of the world.

She busied herself cooking tomato sauce and ground beef, shredding cheese, boiling lasagna noodles, whistling low, only slightly aware of the girls' whereabouts, until she felt a small figure at her elbow.

"What are you making?" Emmylou asked.

Edna bent to look at her, found the green eyes wistful, genuine.

"I'm making lasagna."

"Mm."

"You like it?"

"I do. My mam made it sometimes. My dat likes it."

"Good. Then we'll have a good supper on our first evening."

"Mm-hm."

Emmylou was silent, hovered at her elbow, a small sprite

of uncertainty. But it was something. A redemption from the disastrous beginning.

The table was set, the lasagna bubbling in the oven, filling the house with its cheese and tomato goodness. Edna was tossing the salad, tentatively hoping no one would notice the browned edges on the iceberg lettuce, the wrinkled grape tomatoes she'd tried to revive in cold water, the peeled but salvageable carrot.

Old crusts of homemade bread were turned into garlic toast, with the heels of sharp cheddar shredded on top.

She grasped her lower lip in her teeth and willed the thick thrumming of her heart to slow when the white pickup truck with ladders attached to a silver ladder rack and a giant toolbox straddling the back bounced in the drive and pulled to a stop.

She wiped the countertops for the fifth or sixth time, opened the oven door just as often. She heard the door of the laundry room open and close, and the rustling of clothes and shoes before turning to greet Neil, and was met with so much open hostility it took her breath away.

She opened her mouth, closed it.

"Hello, Edna."

The quiet voice of Orva Schlabach was like a benediction. A blessing.

"How are you?" she asked, still reeling from Neil's measured hatred.

"O.K. I'm managing. And you?"

"Good. I'm well, thank you. I . . . well, just made myself at home after LydiaAnn left. She was very helpful, though, getting me started."

"Good. She's a wonder, that woman. Seven children at home and she's spent more time here than anyone else, since . . ."

His voice trailed off, unable to say what they both knew. He looked at Edna, then really looked at her in a straightforward manner, which left her exposed to wells of so much suffering, she would not have thought it possible.

"Yes. Well, it's . . . supper's ready," she said briskly, and turned away.

Neil's place remained empty. Orva went to the stairwell, called his name three times, then turned away.

"He's not hungry."

Edna kept her eyes lowered, bowed her head when Orva did. She thought, here we go, chalk one up for Neil.

Edna had placed Orva at one end of the table, herself at the opposite end, opting to stay away from the wifely position to the left of the husband.

She watched him from under her lowered lids as she ate.

He was not tall, but of medium height, and wider in the chest and shoulders than she'd thought. With his blue denim shirtsleeves rolled up to his elbows, his arms were thick, heavily muscled, covered thickly in brown hair. His hair was brown, a bit wavy, cut short for a married man. His face was lean, tanned, not picture perfectly handsome, but honest, likable. A faithful face.

She found herself drawn to his well-maintained composure, the grace and forbearance of his grief.

He helped himself to an outrageously large chunk of the lasagna. Edna had to keep her mouth from falling open. A third of the whole pan.

"This is so good," he said, quietly.

How could a man say something that fell so neatly into her expectations of almost perfect? He praised her cooking in simple language, without garnishing with flowery outbursts that were not true.

That was all he said, before falling into his usual state of reverie, the first of many that Edna would observe. The girls ate well, chattered on about their school day in spite of preoccupied grunts from their father.

"So, you're staying for a month?" he asked before she served dessert.

"That's what they asked me to do," she answered.

"That's alright. Although I don't know what we'll do after the month is up."

"We'll see," Edna assured him.

His eyes found hers, questioned.

"You have other jobs and aging parents, is that right?"

"Yes."

Without another word, he pushed back his chair and went out to his office, the dessert she brought out forgotten. Edna felt as if he'd slapped her.

Marie ate half her cake before pushing back her chair, with Emmylou copying her moves. Edna stopped them both with an instruction.

"O.K., girlies. When I'm here, let's practice our clean up routine. You're responsible for cleaning the table, while I wash."

Marie eyed her coldly.

"We never did dishes for Mam."

"That's alright. You will for me."

"I'm going to tell Neil."

"Will he mind?"

"Sure."

"Then go. See what he says."

They clomped happily up the stairs, opened a door. Edna heard murmuring voices, running footsteps and more downstairs clomping.

"He said we don't have to. He said you're not our boss."

Triumphantly, with wide grins, clearly the winners.

Edna gauged the power-o-meter immediately. She had no chance, not with that vicious glance that meant Neil had the upper hand, not her. Well, round number one was lost. Without parental backup, she had no chance, so she let it go. Subdued, she cleared the table, scraped the dishes, then washed, polished the stove, and saved the remaining lasagna for Neil before drying the dishes and putting them away.

She walked down to the rock garden and stood in the early evening glow of the sun sliding behind the horizon. Edna felt a sense of awe.

Someone had spent hours designing this. She felt sad to see the amount of weeds from up close, then thought, *Why not?* If he didn't like her weeding this beautiful spot, then he'd just have to come down here and tell her.

She plucked a few tall dandelions, the yellow heads already gone to seed. She dug out chickweed and a few tall, spindly thistles, and dug into the soil with her fingertips. She found patches of vinca loaded with white blossoms that would bloom profusely in blue in a few weeks. There was ivy planted in crevasses, daylilies in lower, oblong patches, and echinacea that had barely pushed through the soil. She straightened, rubbed her back. Her eye caught a movement in the window upstairs.

Neil.

Well, let him go eat cold lasagna. If he didn't eat with the family, he could eat whatever was left. She'd talk to Orva about this when she found him alone.

More than a week passed before he walked down to the rock garden where she was still weeding, a job she tackled every evening after supper. She'd pruned the forsythia, hoed up the available mulch, and was separating the daffodil bulbs when he walked up.

"How's it going, Edna?"

"Well, O.K., I guess. I need mulch, and feel bad asking for it."

She laughed and hid her face as she bent to retrieve forsythia cuttings.

"You've done a lot of work down here."

"I guess I have. It's not work, though."

"Order mulch. You want me to do it?"

"I'd appreciate it."

"Why don't you sit here a while?"

Orva pointed to the bench made of cement that was placed among the daffodils, the huge incline of stone, plants, and pathways before them.

"O.K. My dress and hands are filthy."

"It's alright. I just appreciate what you're doing. This was Sarah's personal oasis after she found out she had cancer. I had a landscaper come in and do it. My brother-in-law. The hill was already there, they just brought in the stone. Designed it and everything. He's a genius."

This was the longest speech she had ever heard from him.

She felt his nearness, and wished she was not covered in dirt.

It was now or never, so she plunged into the subject of the children's lack of manners, Neil at the helm.

She sensed her loss before she had finished.

"They've lost their mother. We have to go easy on them."

"But . . . You're not helping these children, Orva. Neil frightens me with that look in his eyes."

"What look?" Orva asked, turning to stare at her in alarm.

"He is so full of resentment. Of hatred. He hasn't begun accepting or giving up what God has put in his life. Why do you allow him to stay away from the supper table? The only meal you're all together."

"Sarah could make him listen. I never could."

"Never?"

"Well, of course when he was younger. But not after she got sick. It was as if he wrapped himself in a shell and stayed there."

Edna was quiet for some time, then told him about Marie refusing to clear the table. Again, she felt him slipping away. She was losing him before she had finished talking.

"Edna. I appreciate your concern. But these children have lost their mother. We want to do what we can to make their lives happy. Provide a quiet and restful atmosphere in the house so they can find peace."

Edna drew a sharp breath. She wanted to shake him, pound

her fists on that solid chest. Children did not thrive on total lack of discipline, to be allowed to cater to their own whims, obedient parents jogging after them, and willing to hand over whatever it was that made them happy.

He was wrong.

But it was not up to the *maud* to correct him. She was on her own. If she wanted to change anything she'd have to work on it by her wily little self.

Without another word, she rose and walked slowly up to the house to find Neil in the kitchen, his head in the refrigerator. He'd already eaten two cold burgers.

Edna was still hopping mad, and she had no intentions of letting these two men get away with this.

"Neil."

No answer, not even a backing out of the refrigerator.

"I'd appreciate it if you ate with the rest of us. Is there a reason you can give me? Surely you're hungry when you get home from work."

He turned and straightened. Tall. He was as tall as his father. His eyes burned into hers.

"You think you can come here and boss us around, you can guess again. My mam is the only person I listen to, and she's dead. So go home and leave us alone."

Edna bowed low, her one foot extended.

"Touché, Neil. You got your point across. May you enjoy many cold burgers and countless bowls of cereal."

She smiled.

Neil's eyebrows came down, only slightly, a dead giveaway to his ill-concealed bewilderment. He snorted, an exhalation of impatience.

"Funny."

"I'm not funny. You're the one who's different. Eating all that cold junk."

Almost, he smiled, then caught himself.

"I'm happy."

"Good. You just stay that way. Oh, and would you come down to the rock garden a few times when the mulch is delivered? I'll pay you ten bucks an hour but for no more than an hour. Can't afford more."

"Ten bucks? For what?"

"For hauling and spreading mulch."

"Nah."

"You sure? Ten dollars? You could work five evenings. That's fifty dollars."

"You can't afford it."

"I know I can't. I'm just trying to get you to like me."

This time, he turned away and went upstairs to his room. Edna had caught the beginning of a smile and knew he was determined to keep his armor of anger secure.

She got the girls ready for their bath and curled up with them on the couch for a few chapters of the book they were reading together.

She finished, then asked if they'd brushed their teeth, which resulted in a vigorous denial, heads swiveling from side to side.

"No way. I hate brushing my teeth."

"Go, Marie. Please brush your teeth. O.K.?"

"I told you. I don't like to brush my teeth. The toothpaste is sour. It hurts my gums. It's gross."

Emmylou sighed and slipped an arm beneath Edna's. "I'm too sleepy."

"I'll go with you," Edna said, removing Emmylou's arm, hitching herself forward to get off the couch.

The girls did not protest as she led the way upstairs. Edna watched as they brushed and rinsed well, then followed them to their bedroom.

They had twin beds with homemade pink and white quilts, dolls and books. Bits and pieces of beads and paper, stamping supplies, and other art supplies were scattered across the white desk.

"Alright, hop into your beds."

They slid under the covers, lay stiffly on their backs, and stared at her.

"We forgot something," Edna said quietly.

"Prayers," Marie whispered.

"That's right. Prayers. I'll let you do that on your own, O.K.? Good night, sleep tight."

"Mam helped us when we were little. Before she got sick. But she couldn't come up the steps anymore."

"Stop it, Marie. I'm going to start crying. You can't talk about Mam. See that box of tissues? I cry in one every night. A little bit."

The lisping voice touched Edna, so she bent, took the child into her arms, and held her close, rocking her softly.

"You'll be fine, girlies. I promise. I'll be here to care for you for more than two weeks, maybe even longer."

Marie sat up straight, blinking in the light of the battery lamp.

"You are definitely bossier than our mam was. But if we can get used to your bossy ways, it's much better having you here to pack lunches and make out supper."

She rolled her eyes, with emphasis on the "definitely." Her tone was so serious, that Edna's shoulders heaved as laughter shook her.

Dear child. Finding her own way up the steep slippery steps of living without her mother, at the age of nine.

And so she took Marie in her arms as well, surprised to find how hard and how long the child clung to her before she pulled away and sat back.

She sighed a long sigh, then shook her head.

"You know, if you did that every night, I could much easier do without my mam."

Edna searched her face for signs of sincerity, then reached out and touched her cheek. "Then I will."

"Good."

With that, Marie scooted herself over, stretched out and put her arms behind her head, stared at the ceiling and asked, "You think my mam has wings now? I mean, I know she's healthy again, but every person in Heaven is an angel, right?"

"I think you're right. She must be very happy."

Marie nodded. Emmylou sniffed loudly and told her to stop that, her mother did not have wings. Her mother looked the same way she always had.

Edna said of course she did, then tucked them in, kissed them both and said good night. She hesitated when she saw Neil's closed door, but tapped lightly, put her mouth close to the door and said, "Good night, Neil."

She received no answer, and didn't expect one.

Orva was on the recliner in the living room, the daily newspaper held up, the battery lamp above his head creating an oval of white light.

Edna made her way quietly to the kitchen, rinsed the few cups and plates, wiped the tabletop where Neil had spilled his chocolate milk, then got the broom from the pantry to sweep up crumbs.

She glanced at the area of light. Her heart leaped when the paper was lowered, the crackling sound almost frightening in the quiet house.

"Edna?"

"Yes?"

"You're planning on staying till the end of the month, right?"

"Yes."

"I think maybe you'd better make plans to stay longer, if it's possible. I thought maybe you could go home for the weekend, to stay with your parents. They need you, too."

"Alright. It sounds like a plan. Yes. I think it will work. I have two jobs coming up in May, though. So perhaps you could find someone else through that month."

"You can't say no to them?"

"I . . . don't know. I guess I could."

"The children seem to do so well with you here. I . . . we need you, Edna. I feel as if a huge burden has been lifted right off my shoulders. I heard your conversation with Neil. That in itself is amazing. You have a gift, Edna. It seems you know what he needs. He's such a serious boy, the same as his mother. Your kidding around seems to draw him out."

"Oh, well . . ."

Edna was at a loss for further words. Finally, she told him that Neil certainly didn't like her, though.

Orva got off the recliner, folded the paper and put it in the basket. He looked at Edna with an expression she could not begin to understand. Then he walked out the front door without another word, closed the door firmly behind him, leaving her alone. She made her way up the stairs, wondering what she had said to cause the abrupt departure.

The long, hot shower felt wonderful, erasing the brutal aching between her shoulder blades. That rock garden seemed unconquerable at times. She'd no more than finished weeding the whole thing when a fresh growth of broken dandelion and thistly roots sprouted all over again. But it was so beautiful. Edna imagined a stone patio, an outdoor oven, comfortable chairs, a table with an umbrella, urns, and pots of flowers.

The possibilities were endless.

She had to realize this was not her home, her lawn, or her garden. She was the *maud*. That was it. She couldn't help it if she encroached on motherly territory with those two girls. How quickly they had turned from angry little ones to normal children, who were left to grapple with life's fears and failures on their own. She could come to love them, in time.

Would she say no to other *maud* duties?

She knew she wanted to stay here. Even with Neil's bewildering anger, with Orva's grieving, his face a maze of feelings, she wanted to stay.

The house was hers, comfortable, clean, and organized.

But that was the trouble with a man. He brought all kinds of unrest into your life. It was like crossing a stream, hopping from one rock to another, you never knew which foothold would prove to be stable, and which one would tilt, throwing you into the water of turmoil and doubt.

Take this conversation.

Suddenly, he'd cut it off, went out to the porch to brood, likely. Men thought only of themselves. Didn't he think about her feelings at all?

Well, she had no business worrying about what he thought of her. She was the established *maud*, nothing else. He was enveloped in sorrow, reeling from the death of his wife, so naturally, he was entitled to his time alone on the porch if he didn't like where the conversation was going.

The road to her future was plain as day. A road dotted with multiple homes, containing Amish people of every variety, a vegetable soup of personalities and habits acquired from their own lineage, their various upbringings.

She was free to come and go, without being cast into the complexities of family life. If people didn't get along, lived together in wrecked harmony, it was nothing to her. She'd seen plenty of that. Children in pain, selfish parents occupied with a less than compromising union.

Here, though, after only a few weeks, she had unknowingly shouldered the responsibility of the children's well-being, which she found unsettling.

She cared about Neil, wanted to dig out the root of his anger, the place he occupied too often. What caused it?

The girls and their box of tissues, used ones crumpled in the small pink waste can, affected her deeply. They were so brave, and yet, at night, their mother's death brought the harsh reality of their sorrow.

Edna imagined a vast, dark sea, with glowing little lights

bobbing on the surface, motherless children who sought comfort when no one else but their own mother could supply it. In a sense, these children had lost a valuable commodity, the depth and richness of a mother's love, with their father awash in his own cocoon of grief.

That night Edna found herself sobbing into her pillow.

CHAPTER 11

SHE WAS SENT HOME FOR THE WEEKEND, ORVA BEING THOUGHTFUL that way. Her own home did nothing to dispel her sour mood. She felt displaced, with a restlessness she could not explain.

She cleaned the bathroom late Saturday evening, a DeWalt battery lamp hung from a hook in the ceiling, using a bucket of steaming hot Spic and Span water with a clean rag, Windex and paper towels, Clorox tub cleaner, and a container of heavy blue gel in a black bottle of bowl cleaner. The physical exertion helped alleviate her mood, helped to lower the lid on her rising steam of frustration.

Her parents smelled. The whole house smelled of old lard in cast-iron frying pans, bubbling cornmeal, oil of camphor, rugs soaked with Trixie's constant watering. And Edna had discovered the source of an unpleasant odor in the region of the blue Rubbermaid trash can. Trixie was not notifying either one of them when nature called, so her mother rolled the dog doo in a Kleenex, stuffed it in a plastic bag, and threw it in the trash, without telling anyone.

Edna had a strong suspicion the shower was not used as often as it should be, the way her mother's dress and apron front appeared dotted with grease and dried on drops of food. Her father's hair hung in matted clumps, the surface of his face fuzzy with white bristles.

She gave them a pep talk in the kindest way possible, which was met with a slow response of mixed language, part justification, part rebellion, and partly blaming each other.

Like children.

She scoured and scrubbed, threw the faded rugs into the rinse tubs in the washhouse, tore off the fuzzy toilet seat cover, sniffed it, and pursed her lips.

"Mam, you can't use a lid cover. I told you too many times. It's not sanitary for old people like you," she yelled.

"Ach now, Edna. Just wash it on Monday. I don't like a toilet without a lid cover."

"I know you don't. But . . ." she whispered behind her father's chair, rolling her eyes in his direction.

Her mother threw her hands in the air, before grabbing it out of Edna's hands.

"Don't throw this out," she said sternly.

"Then it needs to be washed more often," Edna told her.

Her mother sniffed before returning to the kitchen to check on her cornmeal bubbling in "blups" on the stove. She lifted the lid and bent over it with a wooden spoon, muttering about the time.

Weary and just a bit miffed at her parents' relaxed lifestyle, Edna told them good night and retreated to her calming bedroom. She closed the door and flopped on the recliner, lifted a forearm across her forehead, and stared at the ceiling.

She had to dig deeper, do better, stop this criticism.

She was not their boss. They were her parents. Sometimes she just wanted out. Out of Indiana, out of the area jammed with Amish who knew everyone else and his brother, sister, uncle, cousin. Away from eyes who watched her moving from house to house, always ambitious, happy, oozing energy and goodwill while caring for aging parents.

So unselfish. So dedicated, they said.

A blessing in the community.

They had no idea the things she struggled with. None. They

were lumped into a crowd, stacked on stadium seats to get a better view.

She thought of Orva too often. She couldn't deny the magnetism of his lonely life, the bewilderment of his aching sorrow. She felt ashamed of the intense physical urge to put her arms around those sloped shoulders, to assure him everything would be alright.

She was confident "they" were already marrying them off. Poor children needed a mother. Who would be better?

She imagined herself on her wedding day, the sad-faced Orva elevated to heights of love for her, surrounded by smiling children who approved of this union, understood and accepted her as their new mother.

The wind came up, springing out of nowhere and riffling the downspout, moaning around the corner of the house. Edna lowered the footrest of the recliner and hurried to close the window as large splats of rain hit the glass.

Oh good, she thought, a spring rainstorm, so pleasant to hear at night. But then she thought of the rock garden, the vines and ivy, the shrubs that needed moisture, and the half-finished mulching she'd done. She wondered if the girls would remember to close the upstairs windows.

Poor Emmylou. She'd cried when Edna left. She should have stayed there. She pictured herself side by side with Orva on the black porch swing.

Edna knew dear Sarah occupied his mind and heart. Barely two months had passed since her burial, and here she was, like a common teenager, thinking selfish thoughts.

She paged through the stack of mail on her lap. Credit card offers, sale folders from J.C. Penney and Marshalls, a stiff yellow card with her name printed neatly in the lower right-hand portion of the envelope.

She ripped it open by inserting a thumbnail under the flap, viewed the card that said, "Thinking of You," in plain gray letters on a white surface. She figured it was from one of her girlfriends. Then she saw something.

What?

She went cold, then hot all over. The knuckles on her hands turned white as she gripped the card, then she began shaking, trembling visibly.

Dear Edna,
Greetings in Jesus' Name.
How are you? I have been thinking of you lately, and feel as if the time is here to ask you out. Would you consider going with me to the Dutch Village on Saturday evening? The 24th?
I would like to become better acquainted with you.
A friend,

Emery Hochstetler

A friend. After all these years. My word. A friend.

Well, there had never been a question. Emery had occupied her thoughts much of the time during her years of *rumschpringa*, and had become an obsession, and here she was at the ripe old age of thirty, and all her dreams were coming true.

Emery Hochstetler.

She let her arms hang limply off the side of the recliner, the card on her lap. She stared at the ceiling, her thoughts railing from one remembered picture to another. Here was Emery, standing by his buggy, one foot crossed over the other, propped on the toe of his shoe, an elbow slung across the buggy wheel, laughing with that easy grace, that unaffected sound that came so naturally. Emery standing in line with the boys of his youth group, filling his plate, piling it high, talking and kidding around with anyone or everyone. Girls gravitated toward the sound of his laugh, as did children and old men.

To be in love was a cruel place to be.

She had always loved him, with a one-sided love that had never been received. Most girls would have taken offense, tossed their heads and said, "Sorry, bud, there are more fish in the sea." But not her.

Oh no, not her. She'd kept her eyes on the goal, slavishly, limpidly, she'd carried that love like a precious gem, always knowing where it was, in the deepest chambers of her heart. Every once in a while it was taken out and polished by the soft white cloth of absolute devotion.

She didn't display her feelings outwardly. Edna had done her job well, and this, this unbelievable card, was her reward. He had come to love her, in the end.

She lifted the card and reread it, slowly, savoring every word. Emery had not written about seeking God's will, or said a word about prayer. But she felt sure he had done all of that in secret.

So she wrote back on plain white stationery, in what she hoped was impressive handwriting. She also hoped the words were properly restrained, so that he had no idea how her heart raced to think of being in his presence.

She told her parents, of course, who reacted with a display of astonishment, then properly congratulated her with kind words.

"When it rains, it pours," her father commented wisely, his pleasant face lined with pleased wrinkles.

"It seems everyone is writing to you," her mother said, mincing her words into a hash of false humility. But Edna knew her pride was overflowing.

Her sisters shrieked and raised their hands in the air, brought them down on their laps and shrieked again. They drank so much coffee and ate so many day-old doughnuts from Shop-Rite that they were overflowing with energy and washed all her mother's windows and scrubbed the porch.

Edna went back to Orva Schlabach's house, fell into the usual routine, managing housework, laundry, cooking, and baking with accustomed ease.

All her extra time was spent on the lawn and garden until her already dark complexion turned the color of a smooth cappuccino. Her anticipation of the coming Saturday evening added a sparkle to her dark eyes, color to her cheeks, and a brilliant smile that flashed on and off all week.

Orva took notice.

They sat down in the glow of the evening sun, the table set with tall glasses of sweet tea, burgers she had made on the grill, a large dish of baked macaroni and cheese thick with toasted, buttered breadcrumbs, and a salad that contained every new vegetable from the garden—spinach, spring onion and radishes, tiny slivers of red beet—and was drizzled with a homemade dressing.

Emmylou sat beside Edna, her small face scrunched up at the salad. She leaned over and patted her knee, softly, but insistently.

"What, Emmylou?"

Edna leaned over to catch the little girl's hesitant whispers.

"What?"

Edna leaned even lower, concentrated on understanding. She sat up, tried hard to keep from laughing, but gave up and let it happen.

"What?" Orva asked, smiling. "What did you say, Emmylou?"

She shook her head.

Orva looked to Edna, a question in his eyes.

Edna shook her head. She'd tell him later when Emmylou wasn't around.

She noticed Neil took second helpings of everything, then reached for the macaroni the third time, but kept his eyes averted.

After the dishes were washed, she set off across the lawn to begin mulching, taking up where she'd left off the previous

week. After she'd dumped the garden cart a few times, spread
it around new growth, bending the brown tulip pants to layer
it on top, her eyes caught a movement at the upstairs window.

Yes, there he was, again.

He knew her offer, so it was up to him to join her. Marie did,
spreading mulch with her soft child hands, prattling on about
everything and anything.

Orva came across the back yard, his brow furrowed.

"Where's Neil?" he asked brusquely.

Edna had never heard that tone of impatience from him
before, so she straightened, then shrugged.

"He could be helping here. That boy does nothing if he can
get away with it."

He made his way to the house.

Edna cringed, but as always, she let it go. What went on in
a family was nothing to her, so she practiced the usual indif-
ference, bent her back, and kept working. It was fine for her to
encourage husbands to do good, or to lightly correct children,
but when it came to family disputes, she stayed out of it. At one
point she thought she heard loud voices, but then decided she'd
likely imagined it.

Evidently, she hadn't.

Orva marched Neil down to the mulch pile, gave him a pitch-
fork and the wheelbarrow, along with clipped instructions. Neil
never as much as glanced in his father's direction, just lowered
his head and forked mulch.

He brought load after load, but refused to speak or make eye
contact with her, and pushed his little sisters aside when they
tried to engage him in any conversation or activity.

So much bitterness, Edna thought sadly. So much anger contained in one at a precarious stage of adolescence.

Glad to have the evening come to a close, Edna returned to
the house to find Orva on the porch swing, drinking the last of
the tea.

"Come out here, Edna," he called.

She washed her hands, took a quick swipe at her hair and went to join him. The porch swing seemed too intimate, so she sat on the rocker facing him, her hands placed primly in her lap.

"Tell me why you're so happy this week, Edna. Did something special occur over the weekend?" he asked.

Edna took a deep breath, set the rocker in motion.

"Actually it did. I had a letter from an old friend, asking me out."

A few seconds went by before Orva spoke.

"That is good news, of course. I assume you're accepting?"

"I am."

"Who is the fortunate man?"

"Emery Hoschtetler. His Dat is one of Dans Jake's boys."

Orva's brow wrinkled, but he shook his head.

"No one I know. But, hey, I'm sure this is exciting for you, right?"

"Oh my yes. I'm known him for years."

"Your age?"

"Yes."

"Never married?"

"No."

"How old are you, Edna?"

"I just turned thirty."

"Really? You aren't so much younger than Sarah was."

Then, as if the mention of her name brought back the pain of her passing, his face turned dark and brooding. Here in the waning light of evening, she could study his features like an open book. She had thought him quite ordinary looking when she met him, but his face had taken on a familiarity; the snubbed, wide nose, the mouth that could appear thin and strained, but softened easily to a broad smile, and eyes that were light in color, but were neither green nor blue, certainly not brown. His eyes were not large, but seemed larger with the glimmer of color, like a jewel.

She could tell when he was sad, when he was missing Sarah, and when he tried to be happy for the children's sake, which seemed to be the hardest of all.

"Sarah was one of the best people I've ever been privileged to meet."

That was the beginning, the opening of the verbal faucet. Edna leaned back in her rocking chair, felt smaller and smaller as the words continued.

"She was my life, my love. I fight bitter feelings against God for taking her. She was never very strong, which was why I did so much for her. She could never work in the sun on a hot day. Her head hurt immediately.

"Having babies took its toll as well. That's why we have only three. Neil was almost nine pounds, and I feel as if carrying him was too much for her."

When he paused, Edna searched his face but found it inscrutable.

Was this, then, his whole problem with Neil? He never bonded as a father and son should, perhaps still placing blame on an innocent child for his wife's health. It wasn't a new concept. She'd seen it before.

Orva had no idea of the root of unforgiveness in his heart toward Neil, and if she were to tell him, he'd be furious. Shocked. In denial.

Many fathers and sons, especially oldest sons, simply lacked the ingredient necessary to cement a relationship. Edna had seen this same scenario played out in many Amish homes, the problem often magnified by an overprotective mother, who tried to replace the lost father-love by her own ministrations of care for her son, which the father saw as a misdirected love that should rightly have been his. And so jealousy rode in on this ill wind, creating a crevice in the solid family structure.

"She babied that boy," he broke out, his voice cracking.

"She served him hand and foot, now look at him. He's so spoiled no one knows what to do with him. He thinks I'm nothing. Nothing, mind you. I can't do much about it. If he's like this at fifteen, who knows what will happen at sixteen? He's not going to do what I want him to."

He paused.

"I've always felt as if I was on the outside, with him and Sarah in a glass bubble. I could never reach him."

Before she could stop herself, she asked quietly. "Have you tried?" She could feel those light eyes penetrating the darkness.

"What do you mean, have I tried? Of course I have. What father wouldn't try?"

"But how did you try?"

Orva was obviously at a loss for a decent explanation, so the seconds ticked by before he cleared his throat.

"I mean, I noticed you have everything any woman or child could want, except the usual boy things, like ponies, dogs, skateboards, you know, rip sticks and other stuff boys would normally have around."

"I hate dogs."

"But maybe he doesn't."

"Dogs are nothing but trouble."

"Maybe not for him."

"You sound like Sarah."

"Orva, listen. I'm well aware that this is none of my business, O.K.? I like to think that I am a bit of an expert on human relations, having worked in so many homes. Neil is hurting. His anger and swagger will serve as armor for now, but the sad part is that it won't stay in place forever. And it will drive him to make bad choices later in life."

The porch swing was flung back, the chains buckling as Orva got up, his temper driving his speech as he talked into the darkness.

"Shut up!" he yelled. "You have no idea! Go back to your home and date old Henry or Emmett or whatever you said his name was."

His shouting became thinner and thinner as his steps hit the blacktopped drive. Edna heard the rasp of the barn door handle followed by a solid slam before silence grew around her. Too shocked to do anything, Edna stayed in her rocker, shrank even farther against the back, unable to think.

Finally, she wondered if Marie and Emmylou had finished their bath, so she rose from her chair and walked across the porch.

The usual bedtime preparations helped assuage her troubled state of mind. She set the four lunch boxes in a row on the counter, filled ziplock bags with potato chips, included small containers of ranch dressing, and put cupcakes in Tupperware sandwich keepers.

Pattering footsteps on the stairs produced two little girls in pink and blue plaid pajamas, their hair like tangled wet mops over their heads. Sheepishly, Marie produced a hairbrush.

"Our hair is really messy," she said.

"I see. It looks as if you had a long bath."

"Shower!" Emmylou corrected her.

She brushed out the wet tangles, put their hair in ponytails, fixed them each a glass of chocolate milk, and climbed the stairs with them.

"Edna, we heard Dat yelling," Marie confided as she turned down her quilt and fluffed her pillow. Emmylou turned to watch Edna's reaction, her thumb in her mouth.

"Oh, it's alright. He was upset at something I said about Neil."

"Mam and Dat used to fight about him," Marie said quietly. "Well, not fight. But Mam cried sometimes."

Edna nodded, thinking, out of the mouth of babes. Nothing was ever perfect. After death, folks remembered the good. They held the wheat to wind, watched the chaff blow away, sorted the good memories and felt guilty to so much as admit to themselves that, yes, there had been bad times, and yes, it was who we were.

Death was final. It was real, and reality was like a slap in the face for many people, and left them reeling in grief and disappointment, regret and denial.

But he had loved her. This Edna believed.

Neil had been like a festering boil between them. Only God knew whether they had spoken of this before her death.

She spoke the littler German prayer of her childhood with the two sweet-smelling little girls, kissed them, tucked them in, and couldn't resist a tickle below Emmylou's chin.

"Hey!"

Emmylou turned away from her, grabbing covers, giggling helplessly.

"Good night. Sleep tight."

"Good night."

"You should marry our Dat."

"Oh, he wouldn't want me." Edna said quietly.

"Maybe he would. I'll ask, O.K.?"

"Night."

Edna made her way to Neil's door, tapped softly and said, "Good night." She didn't expect an answer and, of course, there was none.

She was wiping countertops when Orva came in, his eyes swollen, his heavy shoulders drooping even more. He walked straight to her, and said in a voice gravelly with weariness, "I'm sorry."

He stood too close. If he'd move back a little way, she would look up at him, measure the intensity of his sorrow, sift through the lights that changed with his emotion. All she wanted to do was just put her hands on those heavy forearms, clench slightly, then slide them up to his shoulders, those solid weary shoulders stooped with too much care, too much living with circumstances he couldn't control.

He was only one man. He could do only so much. Men got all tangled up in a deepening love for a woman, often hating anything or anyone that got in the way of this slavish devotion, creating a toxic soup of jealousy and hurt. A tenderness, so true she hadn't know she was capable of, began somewhere in the region of her chest, but mostly spread to her hands, leaving them terribly alone. She had never known hands could feel alone, but hers did.

She did. She placed them on his forearms. She clenched very softly. She looked into his tear-streaked face, found the lights in his swollen eyes, watched as they turned from amber to green, then to the deepest black of agonizing grief.

"It's O.K.," she whispered.

With a sound like a groan, or a sob, she couldn't be sure, his arms came around her small plump body and held her close. He shook with the force of his weeping. She felt his tears on her hair.

She had never been held by a man and had often wondered how it would feel; if it would ever occur in her lifetime, who it would be, and whether she would love this man.

This was not love. Only tenderness, the need to comfort, to reach out and hold a child, a suffering person, old or young.

She did, however, feel initiated, baptized by this grieving widower's sorrow. No, it wasn't romantic love; it was far more than her highest expectations. This love was almost spiritual, a profound understanding and kindness, from her to him.

"It's alright, Orva, really."

He released her, drew out a rumpled navy blue patterned handkerchief and blew his nose, mopping his face before facing her again.

"It's just so hard, losing Sarah, and having already lost Neil."

He was an honest man, this Edna knew. Not many men

would admit to that or shoulder any of the blame. Strong women had crumpled under the pressure of misplaced blame.

"You haven't lost him."

"Yes, Edna. I have."

The wind picked up outside, dashing an old brown leaf against the window screen. Edna jumped. They both laughed. She went to turn the small handle, closing the window. They watched as a streak of lightning shot down from the north, a jagged white line of fierce power.

"Windows closed upstairs?" he asked.

"Yes. It's a bit chilly to have them open at night."

He paused, watching her as she hung the dishcloth on the small peg by the sink. She turned to face him. There was nothing between them, she told herself, was there? She felt comfortable, at ease, unselfconscious.

"When you say I haven't lost Neil, what do you mean?"

"Are you going to fly off the handle again?"

He smiled, then laughed outright. "No."

"Get him a dog. Or better yet, offer to take him to pick out a puppy at a kennel. Or the animal shelter."

"I don't like them."

"Neither do I. It's not what you like. This isn't about you. It's about Neil. You parents all think you don't have to give in sometimes. Hello? You do."

Orva shook his head, but his eyes followed her as she left the kitchen and made her way to the stairway.

CHAPTER 12

IT WAS HARD TO LEAVE THE SCHLABACH RESIDENCE ON SATURDAY after lunch, with Marie and Emmylou close to tears, begging her to stay. The lawn was freshly mowed, the mulching completed, the house clean, and the laundry finished.

Edna was in high spirits as she entered her parents' home, threw her bag on the table and said the Saturday night of her dreams was here.

Nothing took away her mood of high anticipation, not even Trixie, who sauntered into the kitchen, yapping dizzily before turning around to deposit a few squirts on the rug. Edna was so beyond caring about life's little annoyances, she didn't complain about dead flies and crumpled brown geranium leaves. Spring was turning into summer, so the windows were often open, allowing a clean breeze to carry out most of the scent of Vicks and camphor and Hall's eucalyptus cough drops.

Her father was not at home, which alarmed Edna but took away only a portion of her goodwill.

"Where is he, Mam? Is he sitting down at that hole-in-the-wall Quik Mart?"

"Yes, he is, Edna."

"You know he drinks way too much coffee and eats those doughnuts nonstop."

"Not nonstop. Two or three."

"He's not supposed to have any."

"It's not going to kill him. And besides, he's so miserably unhappy when he gets bored and wants to visit with his friends. I see no harm in it, Edna."

Edna shrugged and threw up her hands. "Whatever."

"You're not the one who has to live with him. I am. So if he chooses to go down there, I'm not going to hold him back."

"Alright, Mam."

It seemed as if she had waited all her life for this moment. This Saturday afternoon of choosing the dress, the shoes, showering and combing, using her best cologne, taking down one dress, only to change her mind and replace it. Many girls would have had a colorful jumble of discarded articles of clothing and shoes, but Edna was far too meticulous, too organized. Everything went back on its hanger; shoes set back where she'd gotten them in the first place. She finally settled on a rich royal blue dress in a pebbly woven pattern, with black shoes that were not too stylish for a Saturday evening. She decided on no sweater, after which she changed her mind and grabbed a very light one with three-quarter-length sleeves.

She was just so plump. She looked like a turtledove. Walked like one, too. He'd never ask her out again, she just knew it, then berated herself on her lack of faith. She was, she told herself, thirty, not sixteen.

He hadn't told her which way he'd be traveling, by car or buggy. No big deal, she guessed, as warm as the evenings had been.

She was ready when a neat one-seated buggy pulled up to the barn. The horse was not outstanding, simply a brown Standardbred without much style. The harness looked new, made of shiny biothane with lots of silver attachments.

"Wish me luck, Mam, Dat," she called, as she hurried breathlessly out the door.

"Good luck, dear. Enjoy yourself."

"Bring him in. I want to meet him," her father called after her.

Emery stood by the buggy, tall, sinewy, with that easy, cat-like grace she so admired. His shirt was some kind of beige, that was all she could remember later. His face appeared older, more mature, with laugh lines around his mouth, his nose sharp like a beak.

Had he always had that kind of nose? My, it was something. Like a bald eagle's beak. Really bent and hooked. Oh, but it was alright. Everything about him was pure Emery. The small brown eyes. The mouth that widened into the likable grin.

"Hey there, lady!" he yodeled.

Taken aback, Edna smiled, although her smile felt chopped by that less than traditional greeting.

"Hello yourself," she answered.

"Good to see you, old buddy. Terribly long time no see."

Edna stopped a few feet away from him, allowing space to size each other up, to digest changes in appearance, to connect real life with memories of bygone years.

"You look the same, Edna. Haven't aged at all."

"Neither have you," she answered with full sincerity.

And he hadn't. Every move he made, the way he turned, the way he talked and laughed and patted his horse, was the stuff of dreams.

Seated beside him in the buggy, the heady scent of evening mist and climbing roses added to her sense of being lifted to a realm that was not of this world. The chirping of robins in the woods across the road added the beauty of background music. She had never experienced this sense of total and absolute happiness.

She was jarred out of her sweet reverie by a hand clapping down on her knee and giving it a squeeze. She had barely been able to keep from screaming in fear, before a hand snaked across her back, clamped on to her shoulder and pulled, followed by a kiss on her cheek.

It was a wet kiss that left a trail of saliva. Without thinking, Edna reached up to wipe it off.

"Ah yes, my little buddy Edna. I think we're going to have ourselves a nice evening together."

Little buddy? Clamping a hand to her knee?

Edna brushed the thought away, waiting till the euphoria settled over her again.

"So, tell me about yourself, you still *maud schoffing*?"

"Yes, of course. What else would I do? Careers aren't exactly waiting for uneducated Amish girls."

"Of course there are. Look at the money some of these girls at the RV factories are pulling in. Thousands of dollars."

"You call that a career?" she asked dryly.

"That kind of money? It's a career."

"You don't measure a job by the money you make," Edna countered.

Emery disagreed. It was all about the money. You could learn to like anything, as long as you made enough money. He was a supervisor at the factory.

He'd made so much money he'd bought a farm so that he could invest.

The next step was a wife.

The clammy hand of confusion took a firm grip on Edna's shoulders. The smile on her face remained bright, but the evening had turned a few shades darker as she realized Emery was over thirty now. How could she expect him to stay unchanged? His personality was a bit . . . how could she say this? Over the top, ebullient? But she knew it was their first date; they were both nervous. She figured that eventually, he would calm down. She could not expect perfection at her age.

When they pulled up to the hitching shed in the back of the Dutch Village restaurant, there were three more teams tied up at the hitching rack, leaving barely enough room to squeeze in beside them.

Immediately, Emery opened the window on his side and began slapping the horse loosely with one rein.

"Come on, you old hag. Get over here."

Chirping and contorting his face into every grimace she could imagine, he kept calling out directions to his bewildered horse. Edna wished he'd step out of the carriage and lead the horse where he needed to go, but this didn't happen.

"Hey! Git! Git up there!"

Edna literally bit her tongue to keep from correcting his inept driving.

"Stupid old nag. He's about the dumbest horse I've ever seen. I'm getting rid of him."

With that, he leaped out of the buggy.

Edna thought about the dumbest driver she'd ever seen. So many horses were blamed for their confusion when the driver was the one who needed to be sold.

She sat calmly, her hands clenched in her lap, as he led the horse to the cast-iron railing, tied him securely, then made his way back to her, holding out his hand to help her down, that infectious grin lighting up the evening, pushing away every doubt or turned-off thought she may have had.

The Dutch Village was a well-known tourist spot, so as usual, folks from every walk of life were filling the restaurant to capacity. People spilled out the doors, sat on benches holding cards that would be called when a table became available.

"No reservations?" she asked Emery, looking up into his face.

"What? Oh, no. Didn't even think about it. You mind?"

"No. This is fine. It's a nice evening to wait out here."

A harried person walked among the crowd, handing out cards, saying the wait should be no longer than twenty minutes. Emery struck up a conversation with a couple who were from Connecticut. This was their first trip to Amish country, and they were completely thrilled, asking improper questions without reserve. Emery answered with questions of his own, erupting in a splatter of hawkish, knee-slapping hilarity at their confusion.

Edna stayed quiet, the heat creeping up into her face.

She smiled brightly, kept her shoulders square, her posture straight, and hoped they would never encounter them again. Thank goodness names weren't exchanged.

Their table was perfect, set in a small alcove, with only one other couple. The lighting was dim, and the water glasses held plenty of ice, just the way Edna liked it. Emery had good manners, holding her chair for her, which made her feel like a princess.

The food was as delicious as they had both anticipated, and the conversation flowed freely. Edna relaxed, laughed and talked, studied the planes of his face, and decided, yes, this was the Emery of her dreams.

He was a delightful conversationalist, easy to understand and knowledgeable in many subjects. They talked of the past, the uncertainty of youth, and the difference in attitudes and expectations at their age, now.

The waitress appeared, asked whether they were interested in dessert. Emery ran his hands over his stomach, grinned, and shook his head.

"Not for me, thanks. But it's up to the little lady."

He watched her face.

Edna ordered a slice of pie. Coconut cream, her favorite.

After the waitress left, Emery's eyes twinkled.

"You sure you need that?"

A stab of irritation shot through her, but she corrected it with a bright smile.

"I probably don't need it, no. But I love their coconut cream pie," she said evenly.

"Had it a few times, have you?" he asked.

Edna felt like Trixie when her father gave her one of his dog treats.

Should she be glad to receive Emery's approval? Should she be bouncing up and down, yapping and exulting that she was allowed to have a slice of pie?

"Yes," Edna answered tightly.

At evening's end, Emery kissed her. Edna was unprepared for the sudden swoop of his arms, and the sensation of wet lips pressed to her own. She had dreamed of this moment, waited for it all her life, in fact, and felt nothing.

Nothing but the need to extricate herself from the impression that left an airless panic, as if a garbage bag had been pulled over her head.

Emery released her, smacked his lips, and said he was ready for the next date whenever she was. She was concentrating on keeping her hands at her sides when she desperately wanted a Kleenex from her purse to wipe off the moisture.

"Yes. Well. How about two weeks?" Edna said brightly.

"Why not next weekend? I really enjoyed this tonight, Edna. You're a lot different than you used to be. I'm glad to see you've really grown up, and I enjoy your company. Besides . . ."

Here he broke off and laughed like a hyena.

"You're so soft and squooshy."

Edna laughed with him, to be polite, telling herself it was simply his offbeat sense of humor. He was like a dog that veered off unexpectedly, following whatever scent he fancied, delighting in things that only he could know.

Spontaneous. That was the word for it. Free-spirited.

"Alright. Next weekend. But I have church," she said.

"I do, too. I could stay for the night, take you to church."

Edna hesitated.

Her parents would have to drive alone. Well, they'd be capable, likely.

"My parents need supervision sometimes, but perhaps we can drive behind them."

"Sure. We can do that."

She helped him with his horse, watched the small blinking lights as he drove out the lane, turned right, and disappeared. Slowly, she turned, her head lowered, and walked back to the house. She paused on the porch, taking in the scent of the climbing rose, the dew that was settling on the newly mown grass. The daylilies had opened, pure lemon yellow and so beautiful, but were closed for the night, their wings folded like resting angels.

A cricket set up its night music. Out on the highway, a truck changed gears, with the flow of traffic a soft buzz in the night.

Ah well.

Like the old climbing rose, you couldn't have the sweetness without a few thorns. Sunshine and rain, days when things settled drearily around your shoulders and days when life was all beauty and light. First dates were probably all awkward, every one. She could tell Emery was the nervous type, so perhaps his off-the-wall humor would settle down. She'd have to give this time.

The following day was the in-between Sunday, when there were no church services. Amish tradition had services every other week, leaving a day of rest for visiting friends and family. So today Edna was grateful for the chance to sleep in, to luxuriate in having nothing that needed to be done all day.

She reached over for her alarm clock, tilted the face to check the hands' placement, then rolled over and went back to sleep.

Her bedroom was illuminated with golden sunlight when she woke up again. She waited for the joy, the remembered gladness of having enjoyed her first long-awaited date with Emery, but lay staring blindly at the ceiling, her fresh morning thoughts stirred into a vague pudding of nothingness.

Her emotions had peaked to heights of euphoria, then plunged into the depths of doubt, finally buoyed by the assurance that nothing was perfect.

Did first dates always turn out this way? Was it normal?

She could choose to feel disappointed or choose to be thrilled, realizing he was smart, entertaining, funny, and good looking.

But that kiss.

She rolled over, stuck her face in the pillow and groaned.

Kisses were overrated. Not just kisses, but all romance and touching and hugging and carrying on. Honest only to herself, Edna knew she had felt the same way she had as a child when she was kissed by some warty old aunt.

Yuck.

It would get better. She'd get used to it. Or he'd improve. Dear man, he was so nervous he was fairly walking on pins and needles, all evening.

When she really thought about it, she found it hugely endearing. To think she had made Emery Hochstetler nervous. Imagine. Yes, it had all happened too fast, and she simply didn't have the time to absorb all of it yet.

Her parents' faces were an open book of curiosity, and Edna did not leave them wondering about her evening. She gave them a shining account.

Her father grinned widely, his round cheeks like polished apples.

"Oh, that Emery. Good for you. Glad you enjoyed it. I suppose he'll be coming around again?"

"Next weekend," Edna chortled.

Her mother raised her eyebrows, batted her eyelashes coyly.

"My, the man knows what he wants, doesn't he?" she said in a girlish tone of voice.

"I guess."

Edna enjoyed her bacon and homemade waffles and the cut-up strawberries and whipped cream. Her mother's old waffle iron never failed to produce the plumpest, most golden waffles she'd ever eaten.

"Oh Mam, you know how much I love your waffles," she groaned, reaching for yet another half.

"I love to make them, Edna. You know that."

But Edna knew it was a celebration, like a birthday cake for her date with Emery. Her parents took so much pleasure in her happiness that it brought a rush of love to their wrinkled, aging faces. It made no sense to assault them with tales of his little quirks, the inability to understand some of his ways. She'd simply keep those things to herself.

The little girls were delighted to see her early on Monday morning. They tumbled down the stairs in their eagerness, their hair all *schtrubbly*, smiles crinkling their faces.

"Edna, we are so glad to see you. We're hungry, and . . ."

Emmylou eyed her, then beckoned. "Come here."

Laughing, Edna went and bent over till Emmylou could whisper in her ear, "You have to wash. I don't have any clean underwear!"

Horrified, Edna straightened, sucking in her breath in a mock gasp.

"Really? What did you do with all of them?"

Marie said solemnly, "She had diarrhea."

Emmylou nodded. "I missed my mother a lot. Marie helped me."

"I'm sorry to hear it. I should have been here."

"You shouldn't leave on the weekends," Marie said, eyeing her with a mournful expression.

Edna wanted to reassure the girls that she would stay, but knew her dates with Emery would require her to leave. She decided the best approach would be to tell the girls the honest truth, introducing them to the fact that she had another life, one that did not include them.

They took the news with brave faces, nodding like little women.

"O.K.," Emmylou sighed.

"You should not be dating this other man," Marie said bluntly.

Edna watched their faces, guilt creeping up over her own.

"Why not?"

"I hoped . . ." Marie lifted her shoulders and let them fall. "I hoped that you could live here with us until we all die. You wouldn't have to marry Dat; you'd just live here."

Edna smiled. "Oh, I don't know how that would work."

"It could."

So much confidence, hopes so high. Edna couldn't bring herself to deny Marie this little plan she had dreamed up, so she said, "I suppose it could."

She hung all the laundry on the line in the bright morning light and watched a pair of bluebirds at the house in the backyard, their brilliant coats shining in the dappled shade beneath the maple tree. She noticed the green show of weeds between the rows of carrots and turnips, saw the wilting tops of the red beets and knew it was time to do them up into pickled beets.

The yard needed to be mowed and trimmed.

This was her domain. This was where she thrived, and happiness came easily. Adrenaline was already coursing through her veins, as she planned ahead. After laundry, she'd clean up the children's rooms, make the beds and dust the furniture. She'd hoe the weeds, then pull the red beets, wash them, and get them started cooking before she put a cake in the oven.

There was not one baked item left, the monster cookies and chocolate pie were all gone. Well, it was O.K.; with no one to cook for them they'd naturally eat whatever they could find.

She whistled and sang, scurried from room to room, smiled

and laughed and talked nonsense with Emmylou and Marie, who trotted after her and dropped bits of information.

"Dat was grouchy yesterday."

"Neil stayed at Ervin Chupp's the whole time. Dat was mad."

Edna processed these bits of information, but nothing upset her tranquility. Emery was settled into her life, the impossible had actually happened, and as long as she could erase the low points of the evening (that knee clutching), she was, indeed, blessed beyond measure. Dreams did come true.

Over and over, she told herself she could not expect perfection at her age. A thirty-year-old single girl could not be picky with the men in her life, or she'd stay alone.

For one honest moment, being alone seemed like a smooth, untroubled alternative, a road less traveled, perhaps, but a peaceful one.

She fluffed the pillows on Neil's bed, pulled up the sheet and tucked it in, then the navy blue comforter. The breeze coming through the window was already promising the heat of early summer. Soon the green beans would be ready to pick and freeze, then the cucumbers. She'd make her mother's seven-day sweet pickles, and serve them with grilled cheese and tomato sandwiches. She wondered if Orva liked sweet pickles, or if he was the sour dill type.

She drew back the curtain to watch the bluebirds again and knocked something off the windowsill. She was shocked to find a red and white package of Marlboro cigarettes. The ashtray was stuck on the ledge between the windowsill and the screen, a brown lighter beside it.

She replaced the cigarettes slowly, her mind churning.

He was fifteen years old. Not with the youth his age, or *rumschpringa*. But a bad beginning, acquiring an addiction so soon. Edna felt heartsick, then let it go. Neil was none of her concern, especially now that she was dating Emery.

All this was hidden from the little girls, who were sitting on the floor flipping through a copy of *Outdoor Life*.

She tried putting the incident from her mind, and clattered down the stairs and out the door. Once she reached the garden shed, she retrieved a hoe and began cleaning up the carrots and turnips, assuring herself over and over that to tell Orva would solve nothing, but that was not sufficient to erase the guilt of knowing.

Neil was not a typical adolescent. He was hurting, the timing of his mother's death something that never failed to bring sorrow to Edna.

Why did God take Sarah, knowing Neil needed the comfort and stability of his mother's presence? All the anger, the hatred, and disrespect channeled into the first act of rebellion that would hardly be the last.

Wasted youth. Edna knew the path well, having watched more than one young man approach his sixteenth year without the armor they would need to withstand peers who would eventually lead them onto the wrong road. The road of instant gratification, that Band-Aid slapped onto painful rebellion that only served as a breeding ground for infection of every kind.

She lifted the heavy cucumber vines, already supporting tiny green cucumbers and yellow blooms. Fat bumblebees buzzed from one flower to another, busily pollinating, keeping the garden in heavy production by the intricate design of God.

Surely, if He cared for all these little creatures, He would watch over Neil, keep him in the palm of His hand. She found herself praying in bits and pieces, but mostly offering up one young boy's life to the Lord's care.

She mixed a chocolate cake, her arms whirring with the power of a good stainless-steel whisk, and popped it in the preheated oven as the girls announced the beets were finished. She praised their work, set two large kettles filled with red beets and water on the stovetop, then went back to more garden work.

All day, this was her frantic pace, but at the end of the day there were twenty-six quarts of pickled beets lined up on the counter, laundry folded into drawers, or hung in closets, the garden tilled and hoed until not one weed was visible anywhere, but only vegetables in straight rows with fresh, dark soil between them. Orva walked along the rows, a toothpick protruding from his mouth, his head bent. Edna would have paid a lot, much more than a penny, to know his thoughts.

Neil had come home from work and threw his lunchbox and thermos on the table before taking the stairs two at a time and staying holed up in his room the remainder of the evening. Sometime during the night, he crept downstairs and ate a large portion of the chocolate cake, and all the leftover meatballs in barbecue sauce.

Edna packed his lunch the following morning and thought if she was his mother, he'd go one day without a lunch, then two, until he obeyed and sat down to his supper, the way a young man should.

Chapter 13

Through that summer and into fall, Edna was whirled into a courtship that left her head reeling with euphoria one moment, insecurities the next moment, and finally a time when she admitted to herself that she was utterly exhausted.

There were weekends of hiking, biking, picnicking, staying at cabins with other couples, hymn singings, potluck suppers, ball games and volleyball, croquet and outdoor barbeques, horse sales and benefit auctions.

There were neighboring church services to attend with Emery, where she recognized hardly a soul. Edna felt left out and alone, but would never have had the courage to say anything to Emery.

He was a constant bubble of energy, laughing, moving, talking, his mood infectious, igniting the same high-powered wattage in Edna. She glowed with happiness, spoke more than anyone had ever expected, and became quite the social butterfly among her peers. They all expected the engagement that fall, then a Christmas wedding, but when nothing was announced, folks lost interest, and Edna's surmised nuptials were forgotten.

It was a few weeks before Christmas when she sank into her reclining sofa at home in her room, sighed a deep, cleansing sigh, and knew she had reached her limit. Slow, hot tears trembled on her heavy lashes, broke away and slid down her cheeks as her chest heaved with exhaustion.

Things were just a mess at Orva Schlabach's. She was so close to telling him to look for another *maud*, her heart had pounded in her chest, and she'd felt the color drain from her face.

But she couldn't bring herself to do it.

Neil was worse than ever, on the verge of leaving home. A juvenile delinquent in the making. Marie was having trouble in school, Emmylou came home with a black eye, having gotten into a fight with a second-grade boy, which was incomprehensible to Edna.

A girl! She'd never heard of it.

And told Orva so.

They were seated at the kitchen table, late at night, after the girls had been put to bed, and the tapping and goodnight call at Neil's door completed. She'd found Orva seated at the table with a slice of apple pie on a plate and a glass of milk.

Since dating Emery, she didn't really see Orva anymore. He was never around much, and if he was, it was in the presence of the children.

She didn't notice Orva, his moods, his sorrow, his smiles. The incident of seeing the heavy shoulders, the desire to comfort him, had been lost in the shuffle of long weekends with Emery. She was never quite sure what kept her there at Orva's, except for the little girls who needed her every day.

She'd basically given up on Neil, who didn't give her the time of day, ever. She may as well have been a fly on the wall for all he cared, so she figured two could play this game and ignored him. He was lucky she fed him, and that was the truth. But every night, she'd pause, tap her knuckles on his bedroom door, and say goodnight. He never replied.

"Orva, you know Emmylou has a black eye from getting into a fight at school."

Edna blurted this out while her back was turned, folding the dishcloth after wiping the countertops.

"I wondered what happened to her, but she wouldn't tell me."

Edna turned, with her hands on her hips.

"The girls need attention. You haven't visited their school, you show no interest in their grades. I know you're busy, but wouldn't it be a good thing to check up on them occasionally?"

"Probably."

And that was the end of his input. The clock ticked loudly on the wall, the spigot dripped a few times, then stopped. Edna could hear him swallowing his milk and the side of his fork hit the plate.

"Well, I'm off to bed," she said quietly.

"No. Sit down."

She glanced at him in surprise, then stood behind a kitchen chair, her fingers gripping it tightly.

"Sit down, Edna. I need to talk."

Silently, she pulled out the chair and slid into it.

"I need help with the Christmas shopping. I don't know what to buy for the children. Sometimes I feel so detached from them since Sarah left us. It's almost as if the children are growing up without me. As if I'm watching from a distance. I don't know. I can't explain it. A mother is sort of like the glue that keeps the family together, I guess. Would you consider spending a day shopping with me? Or should I just hand over my wallet?"

Unexpectedly, he looked straight at Edna and grinned, a tired, boyish lopsided grin that made him appear much younger.

She laughed. "The wallet. Just hand over the wallet."

He laughed with her. She wasn't sure if she'd ever heard him laugh before but liked the rumbling sound.

"No, seriously. Would you be embarrassed to be seen with me at the local stores? We could go to Elkhart, to the big stores."

Taken aback, Edna raised her eyebrows.

"Why would I be ashamed to be seen with you?"

"You're dating that Emery."

"Yes. But this would not be a date or anything. I'm working for you."

"No, it wouldn't be that."

She lifted puzzled eyes to his. She found his amber eyes with a light that was not humor or teasing or . . . or anything. But there was so much in his steady, unwavering gaze. Edna was thrown into this golden light, the light that erased the kitchen and the tabletop, the hissing of the propane lamp, the rectangle of night in the window. Her heart beat rapidly, with a dull banging in her chest, but still the moment lasted and lasted.

"Uh, no. It . . . uh . . . wouldn't be a date. So, sure. Whenever is a good day."

"Tomorrow?"

Her baking day. "Whatever. Yes. Yes, I guess so."

"Edna, this may be too offensive, too personal, but I often find myself wondering if you're happy. Is this Emery the one you want to spend the rest of your life with?"

Edna's gaze fell. She scratched the surface of the tabletop with her fingernail, softly. She tried hard to find the proper words, but there were none. She decided to test the winds of honesty, take a chance and bare her soul to this quiet, lost widower.

"I don't know."

"You don't know."

Their gazes locked, held. Edna was bathed in the glow of his amber eyes that now turned dark, as if storm clouds had rolled in.

"Not really. I am in love, though. I love him. He's fun to be around, you see, he's the man of my dreams. He's the reason I never dated. I held out all those years. And now, well, I guess you could say, my dreams have come true. He's what I always imagined. It's just . . ."

Orva waited.

"I'm tired. I'm completely exhausted. You've heard the term, whirlwind courtship?"

Orva nodded.

"I'm whirled straight off my feet. I'm tired. And dizzy."

He smiled.

"But you'll marry him when he asks you?"

"Yes. Oh yes."

Orva said nothing.

Should she ask him? Why him? She wanted to ask the question that ruffled all her thoughts of late, that left her lying awake at night, mulling over the awful chasm that stretched before her, yawning at her feet now.

"Um . . . I . . . hope you don't think this is inappropriate, Orva. But there is one serious doubt in my mind about marriage to Emery. He . . ."

She waved a hand in dismissal. Orva urged her on, gently.

"Well, this is so childish. But . . . Do you need physical attraction to marry someone? I can hardly stand some of his . . ."

She could not bring herself to say kisses.

She wanted to fade into the back of her chair, to slide under the table. Why had she even thought of asking a personal question? Her sisters had already warned her about her lack of response to Emery's clumsy overtures. Can him, they'd said. Get rid of him. He's not for you.

Your head is filled with fantasies of Emery Hochstetler.

The first time she'd mentioned some of his inept attempts at romance, they'd shrieked with laughter, real knee-slapping belly laughs that brought a lump to Edna's throat and rebellion against their mockery.

"Just marry Yonie Hershberger," Fannie gasped.

"At least you'd have a house dog," Sadie yelled.

It still hurt, the insincerity, the situation that seemed so humorous to them was very real to Edna. She'd often wanted to confide in a true friend, but had never worked up enough nerve. And here she was, bumbling along like a frightened schoolgirl.

The silence stretched away into the night, with Orva's gaze situated somewhere over her left shoulder, his face like stone. "Forget it." Edna whispered. "Don't worry about it."

He roused, as if his thoughts had been far away.

"I was a married man, Edna, and I loved my wife completely. She was my friend, my helpmeet. I am a man, of course, but I would imagine that physical touch is important. You do love him, but have no desire to be touched by him?"

Edna's face flamed miserably.

"You can tell me," Orva urged, softly. And she did. They talked far into the night, openly, honestly. She was amazed to learn of Orva's personal sorrow long before he knew his wife was sick. So much hidden rejection, so many nights when he doubted himself.

She explained everything to him, in the end. He encouraged her, smiled, then laughed openly at some of her descriptions.

"He wants to go to Florida. He wants to take me to Florida for two weeks. In February. I've never been there. He'll want to go to the beach. I'm just not ready to . . ."

She lifted her hands to her face, then shook her head back and forth.

"I have dreamed of this. Played it over and over in my mind. Here I am, and all I have is exhaustion. I'm just so tired.

"Thank you. Thank you for this talk, this time. I can't tell you how much I appreciate your concern."

"It's more than that, Edna."

When she hurried across the kitchen, she knew she was taking flight like a scatterbrained little bird, but there was no preventing it. She had to get away from this man with whom she had a shared her deepest fears and insecurities.

The evening had rolled along like a freight train, seemingly unstoppable, with time meaning nothing until they both realized it was after midnight, and yet they talked.

Something had fallen away as the night wore on.

Pride. Dishonesty. The armor of hidden insecurities.

Edna had never mentioned Neil. Well, it was best left alone, that subject.

The dog had never materialized, with Neil's vehement denial of ever wanting one. Orva's hurt, sheepish grin after Neil's fiery onslaught had finally died away. Yes, the place was full of drama and unhappiness with Sarah gone, but she always wanted to come back to Orva's home, every Monday morning without fail, blindly following her deepest instincts, the need to protect, to help.

She lay awake, her eyes open wide, pondering Orva's words. One day at a time.

Her hands shook as she ran the fine-toothed comb through her hair the following morning. Her eyes smarted with lack of sleep; her brain felt as if someone had taken a potato masher through it.

But Edna sent Neil on his way to work with a packed lunch of a bacon, egg, and cheese sandwich wrapped in aluminum foil. The girls went off to school with a handwritten note from Edna.

Dressed in a somber navy blue, she belted her black pea coat and grabbed her purse when Orva called up the stairs when the driver arrived. He was standing beside the SUV, watching her approach, his hat pulled low over his forehead. He smiled, then opened the door for her, waited till she was settled, and closed it gently.

Unbelievable. Edna blinked. She blinked again. No one had ever helped her into a car. And it seemed like the most natural thing on earth, as if she was as precious as, well, something that had to be taken care of.

Not something, but someone.

She was someone.

Enough now, Edna. Just take the day as it comes and stop all this philosophy.

She watched the scenery flashing past the window, the farms, pastures with Holstein cows cropping the brown grass, hoping to find the last green shoot beneath the fading vegetation. Horses frolicked behind acres of white fences; bicycles, buggies, cars, and trucks in a constant flow.

Orva listened as the driver kept up a steady conversation, mostly one-sided, which seemed to work well. Occasionally, Orva would offer a viewpoint, which only served as a launching pad for another volley of words.

They slid to a stop at a red light.

"Where's your first stop?" the driver asked, turning to look at Edna.

"I didn't think about it yet. Orva, do you have any suggestions?"

"Why don't we start at Walmart, for the girls' gifts?"

"That's fine."

They spilled through the doors with the throng of holiday shoppers, were approached by an effusive greeter and handed a cart. Orva stepped back and spread his hands to offer the cart to her.

"I'm no shopper," he said wryly.

She smiled and pushed the cart to the children's toys, then to the aisle that contained only dolls and accessories.

"Emmylou would be thrilled to have one of these," Edna said, picking up a large pink box containing a beautiful baby doll with a shower of thick blond hair, blue eyes that opened and closed, a pacifier, barrettes, and a comb and brush set.

Orva agreed immediately, and Edna set it in the cart.

"Clothes for the doll?" she asked.

"Whatever you think is fine with me."

They chose Lego bricks the girls could use, to build homes with families and cars, swimming pools, and swing sets. Edna told Orva that Marie would spend hours constructing villages, designing houses. She was a quiet child who could immerse herself in the intricacies of erecting things out of Neil's old set of Legos.

Orva frowned, then told her if she talked like that, it made him certain he was lost in his own world of selfish thoughts, since Sarah's passing.

"You know my girls better than I do."

"No, no. It's only that I've been there all day nearly every day every day for over nine months."

"Has it been that long?"

"Yes, it has."

They purchased board games and books for the girls, then spent hours at Target and the biggest sporting goods store Edna had ever seen. Here Orva bought hockey equipment for Neil; the best, most expensive items, then bought him a gift card to purchase more items of his choice.

"Hungry yet?" he asked her quietly, as they stood in line to pay for their purchases.

"Starved."

"You pick."

"Steakhouse? Italian? Chinese?

"Your choice. This is for you."

"I know you'll like the steakhouse."

"But will you?"

"Of course."

Their table was private, set in a small dimly lit alcove, the booth with backs so high it was impossible to see the other diners except for the one table across the aisle, which was empty. Edna felt shy quite suddenly, unable to think of one endearing thing to say.

This did not seem to bother Orva at all, leaning back against the back of the seat, his arms crossed, looking around at the paintings on the walls, the western antiques grouped on the opposite wall.

They ordered tea and read menus, discussing the variety of appetizers and entrées.

The food was perfect, but Edna had a hard time enjoying it. How did one stop comparing Emery to Orva? Why was life so terribly complicated? All these years of being alone, turning into a lemony singleton with no prospects, and here she was, almost engaged to the man of her dreams, and wondering why she felt this way with Orva.

It's more than that, he'd said.

What did that mean, then?

It was all about last evening. They never should have had that conversation. Edna felt so wobbly and unsure of anything now. Orva was a man who had suffered, came through bad times, continued feeling at a loss with Neil, and was crowned with a humble spirit.

Emery was exhausting. He dragged Edna from one event to the other, her smile bright and reassuring, carrying her love like a pink banner for everyone to see. Then one evening, pouring her heart out to this man, this quiet, hurting man . . .

She caught her breath.

"Edna?"

He reached across the table and found her hand. He laced his fingers into hers, slowly, gently.

"I want you to know that you are a beautiful woman. One who needs to think hard before you agree to marriage. Will you do that?"

The blood drained from her face, her breath in ragged gasps.

She could not form words, so she nodded.

"You see, Edna, it will soon be a year since Sarah passed, and I would never step into another man's territory. I have Neil to think about. No woman in her right mind would deserve to live with him."

Edna could only stare into his eyes, shocked to hear him say that.

"But . . . but I have lived with him."

"You have. That's true. But you would never agree to be his stepmother."

Edna bit her lip to keep from blurting out the truth.

She would. Oh, she would.

Her eyes filled with tears. She bit down hard on her lower lip, but the tears came regardless.

"Edna," he said gently. "I didn't mean to hurt your feelings."

She shook her head, reached blindly for a Kleenex in her purse. Her chest heaved with emotion, but she could only shake her head repeatedly.

Orva released her hand.

"I just . . ." she choked, coughed, took a sip of her tea. She pushed a lettuce leaf around her plate with the edge of her fork.

"I pity Neil. That anger is his only weapon to stave off the world, so they don't see the little boy crying inside of him. He blames you that his life has gone crazy."

"He hates me."

Edna shook her head. "He hates himself."

Orva did not speak. His face was lined with grief, mirroring the exhaustion in Edna's face, underlying bewilderment creating a vulnerability, a mixture of suffering and insecurity. Their eyes met, and spoke volumes.

He reached for her hand, his thumb caressed her palm, gently, so lightly, every move an act of caring.

"You understand him better than I ever will."

"He's hurting, is all."

They allowed their eyes to linger, to speak the language of newfound friendship. It couldn't be love, Edna reasoned. It was not possible to be in love with Emery and get carried away like this.

There had to be a name for what she felt for Orva.

The thought of what it would be like to kiss him entered her mind.

Then she would know. Was one man so different from another?

What if Orva did kiss her and it was as perfect as she always imagined Emery to be?

When she slid out of the booth, he stood up, took her coat and helped her into it, the way English men with good manners did.

Her knees were weak with an emotion she could not name.

She buttoned her coat. His hand stayed on her back, lightly.

"Promise me, Edna."

"What?"

"Promise me you'll take your time to consider Emery's proposal when it comes, O.K.?"

She looked up at him (he was not so tall) and nodded.

"I promise," she said soberly, and felt the prick of honest tears, again. He drew her slightly closer by the pressure of his hand then stepped back, put his coat across his shoulders and shrugged into it.

He waited for her to lead the way, and she felt like a princess, wearing the tiara of this man's trust.

"Now for your gift, Edna. You tell the driver where to go."

"Oh, I don't need anything. My room is stuffed full at home. Seriously."

"Surely you want something. I'm not good at choosing gifts for women, so you think about it, O.K.? Maybe a gift card or something?"

She smiled, nodded.

The weekend with Emery went well after Edna determined to set her priorities straight. She was ungrateful and spoiled, critical of Emery, was all it was. Orva was lonely, at a loss with Neil, and all she felt for him was pity.

They went to see a Christmas pageant at the local Baptist church, then to Olive Garden with two other couples, both younger, but good friends of Emery.

He was attentive, polite, rubbing her shoulders with long,

thin fingers, laughing uproariously at his own jokes, ordering wine as if he was accustomed to this every day. It was pure Emery, and Edna became relaxed and happy again, putting Orva and Neil out of her mind efficiently. Yes, this was indeed the man of her dreams at last.

They lingered at the kitchen table, planning the trip to Florida. They'd stay in his grandfather's house, ride the bus down and back. Edna drank cup after cup of black coffee, listened to his well-laid plans, and nodded repeatedly.

"Sounds exciting," she said, with far more enthusiasm than she felt.

"Oh, you wait till we get down there, girl. We'll paint the town red!"

She felt her toes curl under the table and pursed her lips to stop the grimace. Would she ever get used to his expressions?

Girl? She hated when he called her that. It was so conceited, or something.

Christmas came and went in a whirl of activities, wet snowflakes, gifts, food, and more events and dinners and hymn singings. Emery gave her a set of white china with a plain gold ring around the outside, a beautiful plate, with cups and saucers, and serving dishes and stemware to match.

It was very expensive and very beautiful. Edna kissed him in gratitude and was rewarded with his declaration of undying, true love.

And she was happy, happier than she'd ever been.

She spent Christmas Day with her parents, a quiet time filled with love and simple homemade gifts, with roasted chicken and mashed potatoes for dinner. She read the Christmas story of Christ's birth alone in her room, eating a bowl of popcorn and pondering her fate.

But she knew the most precious time was spent with Orva and the girls. Neil arrived with his friends, who dropped him off to open his gifts, which he did with more grace and enthusiasm than Edna could have hoped.

"Thanks, Dad."

The look on Orva's face wrung Edna's heart and left it clunking painfully in her chest. The poor man.

"You're welcome, Neil."

"It's really good equipment. Kevin says I'll make the team."

The remainder of Christmas was cast in the rosy glow of Neil's approval. Orva was happier than Edna had ever seen him, and for this, she was grateful. But she kept herself in the role of *maud*, allowed no intimate glances, and simply did her duties with a bowed head and only an occasional smile.

She had accepted Emery and would see it to the finish. It was who she had always wanted.

Edna lay wide awake upstairs in her cold bedroom, listening to the sound of Orva walking, pacing from the kitchen to the living room and back again.

CHAPTER 14

Aᴛꜰᴇʀ ᴛʜᴇ ʜᴏʟɪᴅᴀʏꜱ, ᴛʜᴇ ʟᴏɴɢ ᴡɪɴᴛᴇʀ ᴇᴠᴇɴɪɴɢꜱ ʟᴇꜰᴛ ᴇᴅɴᴀ restless, the days long, the workload barely enough to keep her occupied. She complained to her mother, who informed the sisters, who decided it was time she put in a quilt frame, there at Orva's, with the impending engagement and all.

Edna fumed and fussed, saying she already had three quilts that would be stored in cedar chests and never used. Why would she want a fourth?

"Oh when you houseclean in spring, you switch the quilts on the guest beds, wash them, and fold them away," Fannie informed her. "Nothing smells better than a fresh quilt that has been stored in a cedar chest."

"Look, I have no idea where my home will be. What if I live in a small house? A double-wide trailer? Then I won't have room for a cedar chest, and certainly not a guest room."

"And, you might live in a huge two-story farmhouse," Sadie said.

So the following week, her mother and sisters arrived at Orva's, the quilt frame on the back of the pickup truck, children in tow.

They had never been to Orva's, so the day was immensely interesting to them as they checked out every room, every closet, the pantry, exclaiming and admiring while the children ran wild, the way they always did whenever Sadie and Fannie were together.

Edna had gotten out of bed to make cinnamon rolls, at the unaccustomed hour of four. Eager to see her mother and sisters, it was not that hard to roll over, shut off the alarm, and dress hurriedly before tiptoeing down the stairs and into the kitchen. She used the battery lamp by the sink and tried to make a minimum amount of noise.

She heated milk, set the yeast to rise, got out the eggbeater to whip the eggs, which must have woken Orva, who began pulling drawers open in the bedroom.

She put coffee on immediately.

When he appeared in the shadowy kitchen, his hair tousled, his eyes bleary with sleep, carrying a pair of socks, Edna grinned sheepishly.

"Sorry. I'm making cinnamon rolls."

"No need to apologize for that."

"I did tell you my mother and sisters are coming, right?"

He nodded. "Good. That's great. You said something about putting in a quilt frame."

"They insist. I already have three."

"Well, the fourth one may be necessary at some point."

"Huh."

She mixed the flour and leftover mashed potatoes until she had a smooth, elastic dough.

"Do I get any of them?" Orva sked.

"Probably not till this evening. They won't be ready till at least eight."

He helped himself to a cup of coffee, sipped, then caught Edna's eye and smiled.

She lowered her head and did not return his smile. He was too close. The cozy atmosphere in the kitchen was too intimate, the smell of fresh coffee and rising yeast dough and his clean white socks, his tousled hair and sleepy eyes, his old denim shirt stretched across his shoulders.

She caught her lower lip in her teeth and bit down, her senses scattered now. With all her strength, she tried to hide the overwhelming need to be close to him, to belong to something, someone.

But she did. She did belong to Emery, who loved her the way she knew was right.

Her heart thudded dully in her chest when she felt his approach.

She busied herself at the sink, rattling bowls and spoons as if the sound would frighten him away.

He did not touch her or speak to her. He merely warmed up his coffee from the pot on the stove, then went to his office to do bookwork.

She saw the yellow light from his office windows, saw him moving around, turning up the gas heat. The snow appeared gray and cold but glistened in the light from the windows.

Edna shivered, then took a deep breath to steady herself. She got out his lunchbox and Neil's and began to throw food blindly into them.

There was something seriously wrong with her. It was so deeply shameful, this attraction to Orva. She had no right to feel this way, happily dating Emery, in love with the man of her dreams.

The thought of feeling this . . . whatever it was, for Emery would be so perfect, so easy and wonderful, to long to feel his arms around her, to expect the nearness of him to be what it was with . . .

Yes.

With him. With Orva Schlabach, the widower with three children. To finally realize this, to admit it to herself, was like being hit by a sledgehammer, draining her energy, the joy, and anticipation of her mother and sister's arrival. There was no way on earth she would ever speak to them about this; it was too personal, too deeply embarrassing. Edna knew they thought she always had her act together, forging her way through life with confidence and that famous brisk energy, working, managing households, tackling one menial task after another.

Here came love, and she dissolved like wet cotton candy, turned into a blubbering, insecure disaster.

Edna swallowed, bit back her tears, filled thermoses and punched the dough with more strength than was absolutely necessary. She made egg and cheese sandwiches for everyone, was snappish with Emmylou when she complained about having her hair pulled too hard, answered Orva in monosyllables when he spoke directly to her, and sighed with relief when they all went out the door.

Her sisters' arrival lifted some of the heaviness. As she knew they would, they eyed her too closely, raised their eyebrows when she set down cups of coffee and asked what was up with the dark circles under her eyes.

Her mother praised the cinnamon rolls, loved the house, said "My, Edna. This is a beautiful home." Her dear wrinkled mother with the wide hips and the hunched back, the merry way of meeting life head-on, unwrapping everything that seemed complicated with a shrug of her rounded shoulders and an, "Oh well, the Lord has a reason."

Almost, in the light of her mother's love and rock-solid faith, she became undone and poured out her troubles for them to examine, sift through, and come up with a sound solution.

Her pride took the driver's seat, though, and she pasted an imaginary smile on her face and listened to her sisters' lively banter, held the little ones, ate too many of the cinnamon rolls with pecans, and drank cup after cup of coffee until her head buzzed with caffeine.

The quilt frame was a rollaway kind, as Edna called it. It had a T-shaped, wooden support on each end, two long round pieces of wood with heavy fabric attached, an inch of space at the bottom to pin the quilt, roll it up, and put the batting on top, after which came the beautifully pieced top, the actual quilt.

"I don't know about the purple, Fannie," Edna mused.

"Why? What's wrong with it? You know it's pretty with that olive green and golden yellow. It's all the style."

"Well, since you pieced it, and you say so, I'll take your word for it. It's O.K."

They sat down to quilt, with thimbles, small needles, and miniature scissors to snip off the ends of the thread. It was as easy as breathing, pushing the needle up and down with the end of the thimble, over and over, a mindless skill that brought instant contentment to all of them.

It was a ritual, a tradition among them. Their mothers had all quilted, and their mothers before them and on back to precolonial times, even before the forefathers had made the perilous journey across the Atlantic in waterlogged, creaking sailboats a tenth of the size of modern-day carriers that plied the waves.

"So which is best, to quilt on the seams, or to stay away an eighth of an inch?" Sadie asked, leaning back to rub her temples.

"I have to make an appointment, get my eyes examined," she said, grimacing.

An indignant howl came from the toddler.

"Hey! Here," Fannie rose swiftly, her folding chair toppling to the floor.

"Neva, let him have that. Come on, give it to him."

Neva held the spinning top to her chest, pouting, her little stomach pushed out, her feet planted firmly, toes pointed out. Sadie entered the fray, trying to get little Evan to give it up.

"That's hers, Evan. She had it first."

Her mother smiled at Edna.

"Here we go again," her eyebrows said.

Edna laughed.

It was family. There was just nothing quite like being in

the company of sisters and sisters-in-law, mothers, nieces, and nephews. No one else understood each other quite the same way or created an atmosphere that allowed you to be more yourself.

Which Edna certainly was, spinning in her own vortex of doubt, humiliation, and fear, dumped into the certainty of her pride, which resulted in an unusual silence as she quilted steadily.

Fannie leaned back, thrust her feet out and lifted her hands above her head. "My neck!"

She twisted her head first one way then another, her eyes closed. She turned to look at Edna.

"What is up with you, Edna? You don't have a thing to say."

"She's in shock, thinking about going to Florida with Emery," Sadie said, her voice rising into a singsong on the word Emery.

Edna merely smiled.

"Aren't you?"

Bewildered, Sadie leaned in to gauge her sister's mood.

"Yes, of course I am. Just mind your own business."

"Ooo. Touchy, are we?"

"Well, what a dumb question. Everyone or anyone would be looking forward to a Florida vacation with their boyfriend."

More eyebrow raising and eye rolling behind her back, her mother shaking her wisdom-filled head, her mouth drawn in a thin line.

Fannie announced, "Someone's here."

Edna looked up, and saw the black truck. The siding crew. Orva was home before lunch. Something must have happened.

The laundry room door opened, he made his appearance in the kitchen, an old rag held to his forehead. Traces of blood were on his cheeks, in his eyebrows, but he said hello, in a normal friendly tone of voice.

Edna was on her feet; the color drained from her face, the dark circles under her eyes like purple bruises.

"Orva! What happened?"

"It's not much. I should have been careful. It's too windy to be putting siding on today."

He disappeared into the bathroom, returned with the small plastic basket containing adhesive tape, Band-Aids, and gauze.

"Here. Here. Sit over here."

Edna was fluttering around him, guiding him to a chair, lifting the rag away, gasping.

"It's pretty nasty. Why don't you just go to the Urgent Care?"

"You think I should?"

"Mam, Fannie, come over here. What do you think?"

Dutifully, they inspected the injured forehead, shook their heads and told him to go, the wound would definitely require stitches. Edna hovered, brought a clean cloth, paper towels, and a bottle of peroxide.

"Oh, I forgot to introduce you. Orva, my mother and sisters, Sadie and Fannie. Mam, this is Orva Schlabach."

They acknowledged each other, smiled, then watched Edna become even more flustered, bringing him a clean shirt, her face flushed. Fannie jabbed an elbow into Sadie's side, they caught each other's eye and winked.

That Edna. Things were not the way they should be, but no one spoke of it or hardly dared to think about it.

February arrived, with its unpredictable bouts of stormy weather and balmy days. Crocus and hyacinth bulbs pushed small green shoots up through the mulch but then got the tips frozen by a low temperature with a sparkling frost. Piles of gray snow melted into gravel-ridden slush, until the next storm blew in, covering everything with a new and pristine cover of fresh snow.

Edna's nerves were shot. She hovered on the edge of anticipation and doubt as if she were winding her way up a steep mountain, on a very narrow trail, the unknown yawning to her left, a steep precipice on her right.

Orva had hired Minerva Yoder to be his *maud* for the three weeks Edna and Emery would be gone.

On hearing this news, Edna's heart had plummeted until she felt physically ill. Why Minerva? She was in Edna's group of single girls, blond and willowy, soft-spoken, vivacious. The last person on earth that should be with Orva for three weeks. The thought had made her cheeks burn, until she lifted both hands to her face as if to ward it, and certainly the accompanying jealousy, off.

She knew Minerva was the opposite of her. She was smart, witty, outgoing, confident. The hardest part was the fact that she cared, knew she shouldn't. So if she was in love with Emery, why did this burning jealousy raise its head like a fiery dragon?

A few days til Saturday now, and Edna's face turned pale with fatigue and lack of sleep, her eyes dark pools of misery and uncertainty. She threw herself into the work, making casseroles, lasagna, baking so many bars and cookies it seemed as if the freezer was full of them. She cleaned with a vengeance, made sure every piece of laundry was done then sat down late that Friday evening, convinced she had done everything she could to make it easier for Minerva.

She knew Orva was in his office. She watched the rectangle of yellow light, willed it to turn dark, wanted him to walk into the kitchen to talk to her on this last evening, but when the light glowed steadily, she forced herself to walk slowly upstairs, to the shower and to bed.

She heard him come in. She heard every footstep, everything he did, until the bed creaked and the house settled into the nighttime quiet.

And still she did not sleep. Her thoughts were rampant, darting down avenues of confusion, then guilt, then despair. She prayed fervently, finally, when it seemed as if she would surely lose her mind.

How did one receive an answer from God? How did you know when He answered? If only He would stand beside her bed and say in one simple sentence what He wanted her to do. Was she only a spoiled youngest child, who wanted and wanted, longed for and desired Emery Hochstetler, and once he was hers, she wanted someone else?

If she went to Florida, a thousand miles away from Orva, with Emery, would everything fall into place, love blooming in the beauty of the sea and the sand and the palm trees? She had to retrieve that old feeling when she thought of Emery, the intense longing to be his girl, the way her life had always been.

Far into the night, she agonized between faith and her own will, trying to decipher one from the other. Perhaps Orva was only a test from God, trying her true love for Emery. Who knew?

She was up very early the following morning, making coffee, moving quietly in the dim light of the propane gas lamp.

She had slept very little, so coffee was a necessary ingredient to think of facing her day. She jumped when the laundry room door opened, could hardly believe it would be Orva. She'd thought he was still in bed.

Her mouth went dry, her heart pounded.

"You scared me," she said shakily.

"Didn't mean to."

"Coffee's ready."

"Good."

She poured him a cup, and one for herself.

An awkward silence stretched between them.

Orva sighed.

"So tell me, Edna. Are you looking forward to your Florida vacation?"

She toyed with her coffee cup, kept her eyes lowered.

"Yes. Yes, of course I am."

"I'll miss you. The children, too, of course. They'll probably treat Minerva the way they treated you in the beginning. Remember?"

Oh, so now it was Minerva. Not Minerva Yoder.

Edna punished him with no reply. Another awkward silence followed.

"What's wrong, Edna?" he asked, with so much tenderness she felt an immediate sob rising in her throat.

"Nothing. That's a dumb question."

"But . . ."

He paused. "You're so pale, with dark circles under your eyes, as if you are exhausted. We're working you too hard, aren't we?"

She took a deep breath for courage, then told him she was exhausted, but not because she worked too hard. It was, well, other stuff.

"Stuff?" Orva sked, then grinned a slow lopsided grin.

"You wouldn't understand."

"Maybe I would."

She got up to refill her coffee cup, but stood at the sink gazing out into the early morning darkness.

"Look at the quarter moon. Isn't that the most beautiful thing? It's so clean this morning you can see the imprint of the rest of the moon, but only a slice is bright enough to notice."

She felt him behind her. He didn't speak. She reveled in his nearness, knew it was all that was missing in her life. She was not surprised when his hands cupped her shoulders and gently turned her to him.

She went into his arms with a natural gladness that made everything right, dispelled the agony of making the wrong choice. She knew there was a place in her heart that only Orva could fill.

She looked up, found his eyes and knew the golden light that turned steadily darker was for her.

"I'm sorry, Edna. I wasn't going to . . . I told myself I would let you go without telling you . . . anything. You belong to Emery. I have no right to do this."

Edna sighed. There were no words to fill the space that needed to tell him the truth.

Slowly, so slowly, he bent his head. He hesitated, drew back. "Edna, I . . ."

She could not bear to step away, to do the right thing.

She lifted her face, then hesitated, and turned her head to lay it on the comfort of his solid chest.

"Oh Edna. What are we going to do?" he whispered.

She stepped away, and stood alone, so alone, her arms hanging empty at her sides. Orva kept his eyes on hers. With a small cry, she was back in his arms, and when he kissed her it was both of them at the same time, a perfect longing fulfilled, orchestrated by the maestro of denied love, of attraction long subdued, of proper tradition obeyed and respected.

She didn't think, only knew this man's kiss was everything she had ever longed for, imagined, and far beyond. He was perfect, his nearness a necessary ingredient, like air and oxygen, water and fire, an elemental coming together.

There was no time. No beginning and no end. The kitchen slowly came back into focus, and they stepped away hurriedly, hearing Neil's feet hit the floor, then his door opening, water running in the bathroom.

"I apologize, Edna."

She shook her head, tears already trembling on her lashes. He reached out to wipe them away with the tip of his finger, then took her face in both of his hands.

"I have no right to put you through this. I will never do anything again to make you feel confused."

She could only shake her head.

"Tell me you don't despise me, please, Edna." He whispered.

"Never," she whispered.

They heard Neil clattering down the stairs, and both quickly turned away, Edna to the sink, busying herself rinsing coffee cups, and Orva to turn the propane lamp up.

"Morning, Neil," he said.

Neil never answered any morning greeting, so Edna never offered one, merely kept her back turned as he hurried through the kitchen. Orva shrugged, and said, "There. Right there is why I have no right. If you know what's good for you, you'll enjoy your vacation, continue to see Emery."

And then Edna spoke. She poured out her heart. She told him exactly why she was in agony, afraid she was a spoiled child, wanting what she could not have, until she acquired it, and found the longed-for person like sour grapes.

"You do understand, Orva, right? It's so hard to have enough confidence to say, oh, I don't like Emery after all. He's nothing like I always thought he would be. I mean, surely God led him to ask for me, after all these years. What if I am not thankful, just take him for granted?"

"But do you love him, Edna? Do you want to be with him every hour, want to touch him?"

With a small cry, Edna fled to the safety of the kitchen sink. When she turned, her face was so pale, her eyes so agonized, that Orva knew he was treading on dangerous territory.

"I'm sorry," he said, yet again.

"No," she burst out. "No. I don't want to be with him. I can't stand his kisses. I feel nothing. And that is the reason for my unhappiness. How does a person know?"

"A person places his trust in God's leading. Which we will both do, with broken spirits, so that He can show us the way. What we experienced this morning is very real, but let's give it time. Only through our faith and willingness to obey with humble hearts can we find the right path."

His words were like a healing ointment to a gaping wound. Yes, here was a man who had been through the fire, been burned and polished beneath the Master's hand until he glowed. A respect that seemed almost like reverence brought a sense of peace as she allowed herself to trust his words, the truth that brought understanding.

"Although, here I am telling you all this, when in reality, I am the one who needs to be told. I waver often, doubting God after He took Sarah."

Edna took a deep, steadying breath.

"So then I'll go to Florida." She gave a small laugh. "It's ironic, really, the judgment I've passed on these folks who go to Florida every year."

"We never know what life will bring, do we?"

"For sure. I always thought it seemed so senseless, wasting all that time and money. Now I'll see if it is a waste, or if it will be a major event that I'll look forward to each year. I'll turn into a Florida snowbird."

They parted that afternoon with a gazing into each other's eyes, trying to convey all they felt, hoping to trust the three weeks would bring no change. Maria wrapped her arms around Edna's waist, and told her she probably wouldn't be alright for three weeks without her. Emmylou pouted and told her to come back as fast as the bus could bring her.

"Minerva Yoder will take good care of you," Edna assured them, then kissed them both goodbye, and with one last look at Orva, she carried her luggage to the car, got in beside the driver and left, answering his attempts at conversation in quiet monosyllables.

At home, she retreated to the safety of her room, packed her belongings in a large rollaway piece of luggage, tried to summon a sense of anticipation. She was looking forward to a vacation, new sights and a whole other world she had heard about so often from her friends, but felt the stab of reality too harshly, thinking of Emery.

He was so sure, so eager for this time together, and she the proverbial shrinking violet.

Well, it couldn't be helped. By some twist of fate she'd met Orva and if Emery wanted to wait thirteen years while she turned into an old maid then it simply was what it was.

She enjoyed the evening meal with her parents, didn't allow Trixie or all the senseless clutter to dispel her good spirits, simply let her troubles fall away and put on an aura of happiness for her ageing parents' sake. Her father teased her, saying Sadie and Fannie were going to have to plan a wedding as soon as she returned, now wouldn't they?

Her mother smiled and nodded, but knew in her own wise way that still water ran deep, and Edna was as deceptive as a forest pool.

She ached to erase the tension from her face, to calm her stumbling heart, to tell her love wasn't perfect and to marry a widower with three children wasn't easy, that was certain.

CHAPTER 15

THEY STEPPED OFF THE BUS INTO A BURST OF WARM SUNSHINE AND blue unclouded skies in a charming town called Pinecraft. There were hordes of bicycles, three-wheeled tricycles, cars, trucks, pedestrians, but mostly a vast array of Amish folks of every *ordnung* imaginable.

There were lawns so green it almost hurt her eyes, and flowers of every color and shape, blooming bushes and small trees, but the most beautiful of all were the palm trees, so foreign to anything she'd ever seen. To see a photograph of the tree did not do it justice, she decided, but kept this bit of observation to herself, seeing how Emery was taken up with reading addresses, muttering to himself as he figured out how to get to their destination.

"I didn't tell you we'll be staying with my brother and his wife, also my grandfather. They said they'd meet us here, but I don't see anything, yet."

"Oh."

Edna was surprised, then relieved. She had not wanted to be prudish by questioning the fact that they were staying together, unmarried, but in the back of her mind, she had wondered what the arrangement would be.

"Taxi! Taxi!"

Emery dashed into the slow-moving line of traffic, almost

colliding with a startled old gentleman on a three-wheeled bike. Edna held her breath, felt the perspiration break out on her forehead standing in the heat of the day, which was lovely at first. But she was accustomed to her winter climate and became decidedly uncomfortable.

She was relieved when he was able to stop a white and black vehicle with the letters "Taxi" emblazoned on the front. Their luggage stowed in the back, she fell in beside Emery, suddenly grateful for the air-conditioned vehicle and its swarthy, talkative driver.

Emery gave him the address, then fell into a lively exchange of words, while Edna gazed out the window, unable to keep her attention on anything but the darling little houses, painted white or blue or lime green or coral. They had front porches or screened-in porches or patios, and were decorated with outdoor furnishings, potted plants, and items from the sea.

What a charming town, she thought. She could hardly wait to rent her bike and explore the many streets, visit shops and stores.

She grinned to herself. Here she was, right smack in the middle of the folks she had always looked on as frivolous, money squandering, self-seeking individuals without a bit of conscience about those less fortunate.

What a difference it made, then, to be here, to enjoy God's wonders with an open heart, to feel a love and kinship with other Amish folk who came to Florida as a getaway, a moment's reprieve from their dutiful, work-filled days at home.

Well, she had some attitude adjustments, at any rate. They found the house on a street that looked much the same as all the others, except for a cul-de-sac and a low-lying marsh that stretched out from there. They were greeted enthusiastically by a thin, bent, aging man with a heavy white beard and a sunburned, balding head, his quick actions reminding Edna so much of her energetic fiancé.

"Hello! Hello! So glad you made it. So this is Edna?"

He held her hand, shook it repeatedly, his dark eyes alert, quick to notice his surroundings, to gauge the mood between them. Edna thought of Moses, an ancient prophet with the gift of leadership, conversation, and the wisdom of communing with God.

"Hello. Yes, I am Edna. It's good to meet you."

"I'm Harvey. Harvey Miller."

So he was Emery's grandfather.

"Eli and MaryAnn are at the beach, but they'll be back in time for supper."

Emery was carrying luggage, sending the taxi on its way.

Before Edna could take stock of her surroundings, he had pushed past her looking for bedrooms to store the suitcases.

"Only one extra bedroom?" he called out from the end of the small hallway.

"Afraid so. You'll have to sleep on the couch," the old man called back, grinning and winking at Edna.

"Are you serious?"

Emery came out to the living room, surveyed his surroundings with distaste.

"I have a bad back. I don't know about this arrangement at all."

Immediately, Edna spoke up, always the fixer, the helper, the one who made life easier for everyone.

"I can sleep there. No problem."

The old man shook his head. "No, no. That won't be necessary."

"Why not? She offered," Emery said, looking hopefully at Edna.

"Sure. I can sleep out here."

She unpacked her bags, stowing her clothes in drawers and on hangers in the closet. The room was small but comfortable, with a full-sized bed, a low dresser with a mirror, a chest of drawers, and a wicker chair in the corner. The walls were painted white, with a serviceable quilt in shades of green; the pictures appeared to have been plucked from a thrift shop without thought. A faded pink candle leaned to the right on a green plate, beside an old wooden cedar chest with a flaking woodland scene shellacked to the top.

Edna longed to go shopping, to decorate this room with items that made sense, here in this tropical climate so close to the ocean.

Emery clattered into the room, all effusive words and manic energy, stuffed his clothes in the chest of drawers, threw his luggage on the wicker chair, then came over to give her a quick hug. He lifted her off the floor in a grip so compressed her covering slid back, followed by one of his wet kisses.

"My sweet Edna. Are you happy we're here?"

"Oh yes! Of course. This is lovely. We'll have so much fun."

"Good, good. I'm glad you like it. You want to go rent our bikes now?"

"Why don't we just relax a while? I need a drink, maybe something to eat. A snack? We didn't have lunch."

"Sure. We can do that. Sure. Come on. Doddy can rustle up something."

They sat at the kitchen table with glasses of ginger ale mixed with pineapple juice, saltines, and cheddar cheese.

The old man proved to be what Edna had imagined. Full of wisdom, with an energy about him that made him seem like a much younger man.

"Yes. I bought this house in '85. Mam and I enjoyed many vacations here with the children. Back then, it was allowed to bring the school-aged ones. Nowadays, no children can be taken out of school, which is a good thing. We're very fortunate having our own schools, so we need to obey the rules of those who look out for us."

"Huh. The government? Buncha crooks. That's what they are."

Harvey Miller's eyes fastened on his grandson's face, but he kept his peace. He found Edna's eyes on his, and something passed between them, a flicker of shared understanding, of both being in disagreement with the fractured attitude Emery displayed.

She bent her head, busied herself cutting cheese slices.

The kitchen was adorable, small, compact, with white kitchen cupboards and blue walls, a black and white patterned linoleum that appeared to have been the recipient of many activities, worn where the traffic was heaviest, punctured and torn in other places. An old gingham curtain hung in the window above the sink, a tin container on the windowsill, and a white refrigerator decorated with dozens of souvenir magnets, recipes, bills, and Bible verses.

Edna would hang a Roman shade in a white basket weave, paint the walls white, and replace the worn linoleum. She'd put glass bottles on top of the cabinets.

She'd get rid of the awful magnets.

But she reminded herself again, this was not her house, merely a place to stay for a three-week vacation.

Eli and MaryAnn returned, sunburned, laughing, delighted at their arrival, welcoming them warmly. Edna had, of course, met them before. They were a childless couple in their early forties who took every opportunity to go sightseeing to various locations at any given time, spending most of the winter months in Florida with his widowed father.

MaryAnn was tall, with long arms and legs, resembling her husband who was like a twin to Emery. They were all willowy, athletic, energized to the point of mania, and Edna only hoped to be able to keep up.

"How was your trip down?" Eli asked, helping himself to a handful of saltines.

"Great. We had a good trip. Good seats, comfortable, lots of fellow travelers to chat with. Time went fast, really."

Emery leaned back in his chair; his dark eyes lit with enthusiasm.

Edna groaned inwardly. She had no idea he felt that way.

The trip was long, boring, and seemingly endless. The seats were beyond miserable, and the bathroom facilities horrendous. And yes, his constant talking had grated on her nerves. She was hungry, thirsty, tired without being able to sleep, constantly trying to avoid the clinging of his arms, or hands, or . . . well, his brain-sapping conversation and cloying words. She finally gave up trying to decipher her inward shrinking and irritation, chalking it up to the underlying exhaustion that was so much a part of her life. She thought she'd feel better after a week of sun and rest.

She made a wholehearted effort after hearing Emery's rosy account of the arduous bus trip, and berated herself for turning into a person she didn't know; a bitter, battle-weary old maid who wavered from being determined to love Emery and make an honest effort this time, to admitting there was something better out there.

Her first evening Emery sat with her on the couch, asked kindly if she was sure she'd be alright, then went into a long account of his back injury when he was bucked off a horse at eighteen years of age.

Edna listened, nodded, smiled, her eyelids drooping, her back aching from hours of sitting.

"See, Edna, if we were married, you could sleep with me," he said quietly, then wiggled his eyebrows comically, his face mere inches from hers.

His breath smelled like fish.

The flounder MaryAnn made was absolutely the best fish Edna had ever eaten. She stuffed it with a mixture of crabmeat, breadcrumbs, spices, lemon juice, and mayonnaise, then broiled it to perfection. Served with baked potatoes and shredded cabbage, carrots, onion, and toasted almonds, plus ramen with a vinaigrette dressing, it was so good that Edna tried to eat delicately, but had been hungry for so many hours that she found herself filling her plate twice.

All these tall, thin people. She felt like a dumpling.

She smiled at Emery and said yes, but they weren't married, so she'd be fine on the couch. Of course he needed to take care of his back.

The following morning Edna was the first one awake, so she rose quietly, turned on the coffee maker, dressed, and poured a fresh, hot cup. She let herself out the back door to the small patio enclosed by magnolia trees, and what appeared to be a climbing vine with small yellow flowers scattered all over it. The large waxy leaves of the magnolia looked artificial, so Edna extended a hand to stroke the glossy growth.

"Checking to see if they're real?" a voice asked softly.

Edna turned, embarrassed, but relaxed to find MaryAnn in her summer housecoat, her hair in a ponytail, her eyes swollen with sleep.

Edna laughed.

"Don't feel bad, I did the same thing when I came here the first time. They're beautiful."

"They sure are."

"Did you sleep well?"

"I was exhausted after my bus trip, so yes. I slept like a log."

"Good."

MaryAnn frowned, a pucker appeared between her eyebrows.

"What is up with you sleeping on the couch, though? Why doesn't Emery let you have the bed?"

"He has a bad back. He explained it to me last evening before he went to bed. A horse unseated him when he was a teenager."

"Really?"

"Yes."

Edna nodded soberly.

"Well." MaryAnn took a deep breath, exhaled slowly, and sipped her coffee thoughtfully. Edna relaxed and watched a mockingbird glide in for a landing on the highest branches of the magnolia tree before opening its mouth, and imitating the cry of a seagull to perfection.

They laughed together.

"You know, this patio always brings back memories of when Eli's mother was alive. She was like you in many ways. Short, a bit chubby . . ."

"You surely mean fluffy, don't you?" Edna asked, her eyes twinkling.

"Whatever. She had dark hair and yes, so sweet, just like you."

"I'm not always sweet. Hardly ever, to be correct."

"Oh, you are sweet. You're perfect for Emery. He needs someone just like you. I'm so happy for you. You make a great couple. Think he'll ask you to marry him on some romantic spot on the beach?"

A wave of despair came as unexpected as lightning, leaving her speechless. She could only concentrate on her breathing, gulping enough oxygen to stay afloat, without succumbing to the tsunami of exhaustion that left her glued to her chair. She had to grip the handle of her coffee mug to keep from dropping it.

"I don't know. He might," Edna said breathlessly, then smiled quickly to mask the unexplained onslaught.

She was subject to a searching look, a narrowing of dark eyes.

"Is everything alright?"

"Yes. Of course. We're . . . I'm fine."

"O.K. If you say so."

"Certainly. I don't know why you would think otherwise. We're very happy. Being in love is so unbelievable. Just a whole new world of getting to know each other, growing together."

Edna realized she was babbling now, so she got up to

disguise her confusion, poured out her cooling coffee, and let herself into the kitchen, quietly, to refill her cup. On her return, she'd regained her sense of balance. She looked into MaryAnn's eyes and smiled.

"Tell me about your life, Edna. Is it really true that you've always waited on Emery?"

"Oh yes. He was the only one for me."

MaryAnn clasped her hands delightedly, raised her eyes to the blue skies, and sighed. "So terribly romantic, isn't it?"

"It is. A dream come alive!" Edna gushed.

She was acting a part so well she knew she could have been a Nazi spy, a shark in a loan company, the best imitation . . . well, anything or anybody. A certain sense of power made itself known as if she held the ability to control her own destiny.

If she had said everything was fantastic, that love was everything she made herself believe it was, well then, it was.

The door swung open, and Emery appeared in clean denims and a white T-shirt, barefoot, and his hair uncombed. He was holding a mug of coffee.

He sat on Edna's lap, the ever-present skinny arm snaking across her shoulders. A line of dried spittle ran from his mouth to his chin, with a strong whiff of last night's flounder and crabmeat.

"How's my best girl this morning?"

Without waiting for a reply he launched into a vivid account of his perfect night's rest, ending with, "Man, did I sleep!"

Edna wanted to smack him. Her thigh was aching badly, the backs of her knees smashed into the woven resin chair. She shifted uncomfortably, spilled some coffee, and the color rose in her cheeks.

MaryAnn watched.

"So now, I am ready," Emery shouted. "All I need is a half dozen eggs over easy, about ten slices of bacon and a stack of pancakes.

"What say, Edna baby?"

"Sounds good. If you'll get off my lap, that's what I'll do. Make you a big breakfast."

She smiled without looking at him.

MaryAnn watched over the rim of her coffee cup.

Breakfast was a happy affair, sitting around the oval kitchen table with eggs and bacon, large cups of coffee, fresh tree-ripened oranges and grapefruit, before the warmed casserole dish was set on the table, along with the maple syrup and homemade blueberry syrup.

"Pancakes! Wonderful! " Emery yelled, lifting the lid of the dish and burning the tops of his fingers, then letting the lid clatter onto the tabletop.

"Ow! Man, that's hot! Shoulda told me, Edna."

Edna's mouth was set in a thin line without comment.

But the sun shone, the air was balmy, laden with the scent of the ocean, the magnolia, and bougainvillea, the yellow jasmine, all dispelling any negative reaction to a less than perfect boyfriend.

Florida was magical, the days filled with anticipation of experiencing new sights and sounds, getting to know other Amish people, many of them already acquaintances.

She found herself on a rented bike, cycling everywhere, waving to friendly folks in cars, on foot, or on three-wheeled battery-operated bikes that droned past like bumblebees.

They ate seafood in restaurants, and they cooked it at home. She learned to like steamed oysters and clams in hot sauce, ate prodigious amounts of shrimp dipped in cocktail sauce and red snapper broiled and drowned in lime juice and cilantro with roasted cherry tomatoes.

MaryAnn became a dear friend and confidante. Every morning they were up early, drinking coffee and sharing their lives. Edna learned of the deep heartache and disappointment of a couple unable to have children, the dashed hopes, the desperation, until finally, they accepted "Thy will be done."

Edna's nose burned, her eyes filled with quick tears of sympathy as she listened to MaryAnn. She spoke honestly, sparing no details, a forthright account of inner turmoil, and a marriage that was seriously strained. They cried together, laughed together, took long walks, sat in restaurants and people watched, drank tea, and ate French fries.

Eli and Emery spent their days fishing or joining Edna and MaryAnn on the beach. Edna loved the sea, the endless expanse of blue water that met the sky on the horizon and melded into the same brilliant hue.

She loved the white sand, the tropical breeze, and all the seabirds. She waited on Emery's proposal without thinking of the outcome.

And not once did she mention Orva Schlabach, Neil, Marie, or Emmylou. She only allowed herself to think of him, to ponder on what had occurred in the kitchen on the nights when she lay awake, her lower back bothering her. She adjusted pillows, took Advil, and lay flat on her back on the rug by the couch as she heard Emery's deep, rattling snores.

The sleeping arrangement could not be helped. Wasn't it her duty to call him "Lord?" To wait on him, to see to his comfort?

The good wife. In the years she had been a *maud*, she'd seen plenty, and instinctively knew when the wife truly loved her hardworking husband, cared for him without self, Edna's own highest aspiration.

And so she would practice to be that woman before marriage, to practice goodwill and submission.

She lay awake and tried not to listen to the rattling snores from the bedroom, while mulling over and over the feeling for Orva, the almost spiritual connection to the essence of him. He was everything Emery was not.

But why? Emery was a good man, an uncomplicated,

overactive, loud, painstakingly honest man. She assured herself of this.

Until that fateful day.

For the first time, she'd allowed MaryAnn to glimpse her own hidden turmoil, to take stock of her soul-searching. It started by MaryAnn asking her where she had been working and who was taking her place.

"I was with the widower, Orva Schlabach. He hired Minerva Yoder, a good friend of mine, until I return."

MaryAnn watched Edna's face, saw the misery creeping across her features like darkness enveloping a twilit evening. She watched Edna bite down on her lower lip, watched the eyelids cover her eyes, the windows to everyone's deepest emotions. Edna got to her feet abruptly and tossed her coffee across the railing, then returned to sit on a hassock, all agitation and suppressed emotion.

MaryAnn said quietly. "So that's not good."

"Oh, it's O.K. Why wouldn't it be? Nothing wrong with that," Edna replied, but wouldn't meet her eyes.

MaryAnn gave a short laugh.

"Obviously, there is."

"What do you mean?"

Startled, Edna's eyes flew open, found MaryAnn's, and was caught off guard.

"It seems to rattle you, either the fact that Minerva is there, or just the fact that you had to leave Orva."

"Oh, stop it. It's nothing like that. I just pity the little girls. And Neil is a problem. He's fifteen, bending all the rules. Orva can't do anything with him since his mother passed away. I just . . . well, it's complicated."

MaryAnn believed her but knew this morning was only a glimpse, only a small part of Edna's inner churning.

And she felt a great sympathy.

Edna walked to the little café named "Just Coffee," slid into a booth, and ordered a bagel. They made their own here, huge, chewy, and crusty, with flavored cream cheese so good she always asked for extra.

An iced coffee would rev her up, prepare her for the long bike ride to the bookstore with Emery.

"Hi! How are you, Emery?"

The waitress stopped at the booth next to hers, the high back dividing the diners well, giving them the maximum amount of privacy.

"Great. Doing great."

"Still having a good time?"

"Oh, you bet."

"So how's your girlfriend holding up?" the waitress asked, laughing.

"Oh, you know. Whatever. I told you she's got some age on her, and she's on the fluffy side, you know."

The waitress giggled.

"Tell you what. You want a good time? I'll ask my Dad to take us out for shark. He's got a forty-footer. Speedboat."

"Really? That would be absolutely the greatest. Sure I'll go."

"The girlfriend?"

"Nah. She's got a sunburn. Gets motion sickness. We can't have her puking all over the boat."

Edna's face felt as if it would go up in flames. She reached over, grabbed her purse, and slunk out the door, her mind completely blank save for the fact that she had to get away, the more distance she put between herself and that café, the better.

Some age on her? Sunburned? Puking? And the improperly familiar way she'd spoken to him, calling him by his first name. Surely this wasn't their first overly friendly encounter.

Edna walked. She balled her fists and stalked on leaden feet. She ran, jogged, her skirt flapping, her purse banging against her knees, with her mind still blank and her heart like a stone in her chest. Her back was soaked with perspiration, and her chest was heaving, so she found a park bench by a pavilion, hidden from view by the magnificent growth of magnolia. She wiped her face with the hem of her skirt and allowed herself to calm down first, hoping for rational thoughts and the dignity to think this over in a mature, Christian way.

What would Jesus do? That wise, old question.

If a man sins against you seventy times seven, thou shalt forgive him. Slowly, the admittance came. She could forgive him and would do just that. But she could never marry him. He had not one ounce of respect for her. Couldn't have, talking like that to a waitress.

Some age on her. Really. She may as well be a swaybacked old mare, where he pulled down her mouth to pronounce her long in the teeth.

She was hurt, furious.

Slowly, then, the fog lifted. The mist that had always created a sense of uncertainty, an obscuring of a clear pathway. No, she could not marry Emery.

And perhaps would never marry Orva, either. Was that so terrible? She would not decide her own destiny, or grasp desperately for what she wanted or didn't want.

She would merely live, appreciate the sunshine in Florida, the magical days of vacation, soak up the sea and the sand and the palm trees and wait on God's wonderful love and leading.

She would bare her soul to MaryAnn, who was a dear and kindhearted woman who knew suffering in her own life. And she would understand.

Edna would now understand herself. She would be completely truthful with herself and others. She had never loved Emery. Not since the first date.

And with a blinding pain of reality, she knew she loved Orva with all her heart, her whole being. He was her soul mate, but these things were all in God's Hands, and not her own.

CHAPTER 16

THE RIDE TO THE BOOKSTORE DID NOT HAPPEN, EDNA SAYING SHE had a headache (how handy that old malady came in), her sunburn bothered her a lot, so if it were alright, she'd stay here.

He was concerned. Kind.

Edna could not meet his eyes. She turned her face away.

"What's wrong, sweetheart?"

"I told you, I have a headache."

With that, he left, leaving Edna alone in the house. Harvey had gone to the park to play shuffleboard, Eli and MaryAnn off somewhere, who knew, the way those two found a new and different adventure every day. Edna lay on the couch with a glass of ice water beside her, a gigantic sour mood descending like a blanket that threatened to smother her. Self-pity disguised itself as martyrdom, the "why me?" After all the years of service and hard work, why couldn't God be more merciful to her? Here she was, a thousand miles away from her parents and Sadie and Fannie, this awkward situation flung in her face, and she did not deserve it. She'd always tried to do what was right, prayed to be forgiven for her judgmental attitude, knew her faults, and tried to overcome them.

She thought of Eli and MaryAnn, then. They did not pity themselves, or question the fact that they were childless. They just went ahead with their lives and made the best of what God handed them.

Life was mysterious. God was, for sure.

You just couldn't figure everything out on your own. If Orva developed feelings for Minerva, then that was her signal to be just like Eli and MaryAnn, to be an inspiration to others by accepting her single status.

And what was wrong with that, being single?

This solid thought came crashing down when she thought of Orva, his sad eyes, his, oh, just everything. The way he talked, the way he poured a cup of coffee, the way he sat on a kitchen chair, leaning back and crossing one foot over the other, with his wide shoulders and heavy arms, the way his face lit up at the sight of Emmylou.

Somehow, she'd have to shed all that like a winter coat, and simply divest herself of the warmth and beauty of her feelings for him.

Her head was pounding now, so she rolled over, sat up, put her head in her hands and groaned. She was reaching down for her glass of ice water when the door opened, and Harvey stepped in. His face was red from the heat, his breathing quick and fast as if he'd been hurrying.

"Edna, I'm supposed to deliver this message to you. You worked for this Schlabach fellow? A widower?"

"Yes?"

"There has been an accident. A young boy is in critical condition, and this Schlabach wants you to know."

"A boy? His boy? Neil?"

"I don't know."

Edna felt the color drain from her face and felt the agony of being so far away when Orva needed her.

"Thank you for telling me. I'll call. If he needs me, I'll return."

"Alright. You're O.K. then?"

"Yes. I'll be fine."

Edna called his office number, received his business voice

mail, as she knew she would, and left a brief message saying she'd return if he needed her. She left the telephone number of the house where she was staying.

Then she sat by the phone, wringing her hands, chewing her fingernails, pacing, returning to sit by the table and stare out the window, waiting for a ring. Just one ring, to let her knew what really happened.

She walked out to the back of the house, paced the yard, told herself everything would be alright, which was followed by the anxious thought of how Orva would deal with the death of his son, less than a year after Sarah.

She stopped, listened. Was that a ring?

She hurried to the back door, but it was nothing. She told herself Orva was at the hospital. He wouldn't call any time soon.

Where were the little girls? Was Minerva good to them? Did they have to go to school as if nothing had happened? Edna felt a moment's panic, wanting to be there, but she couldn't without a phone call from Orva.

Emery did not get in till the sun had already slid behind the horizon. He was sunburned, exhausted, and went straight to the shower. He would have disappeared into his bedroom if Edna had not waylaid him in the hallway.

"We need to talk."

"We do?" The mockery plain as day.

She felt an utter calm. She spoke quietly, unhurriedly.

She was going home. She was breaking up, ending the relationship. She said nothing about his conversation with the coffee shop waitress, to spare him the embarrassment. If she forgave him, then why rub it into his face? They needed to part on peaceful terms. Childish accusations just weren't a part of this.

Emery seemed to become angry at first, then relieved.

"But I did love you. I do. I still do."

Edna bristled but kept back the harsh words.

"We had a good thing for a while, Emery, but there's no sense committing our lives to each other without the real thing, which I think we both know is sadly lacking."

She told him then about the accident, and that she was needed at home. His eyes narrowed, and suspicion crossed his face.

"So it's Orva?"

To admit her longing would only serve to infuriate him, to deny it would be a lie, so she merely shook her head.

"He needs me. The girls need me. Neil is like my own son. He's a troubled boy who was deeply affected by the loss of his mother. I have to see him, if he lives that long."

Emery nodded. His eyes softened. Edna could almost have loved him.

"Alright, Edna. I have to let you go. I'll get over it."

You already are, Edna thought. You always were.

There was nothing left to say.

They sat in silence, both staring at the floor, both aware of the fact that more should be said, such as discussions of past feelings, gratitude, or the possibility of a reconciliation. But there was nothing either one could bring to the surface.

Edna got up, went out to the kitchen and opened the refrigerator door, anything to get away. Emery sighed, got up, and let himself out the front door. Edna listened, then went to the window to watch him walk away, his hands in his pockets, his head bent.

Edna felt nothing, then turned away.

She did not leave the house, still waited on the phone call that did not come. She spent the evening with Eli, MaryAnn, and Harvey on the back patio, the warm fragrance of the evening bringing on a sense of melancholy.

Edna felt sad, leaving Florida. The warmth of the tropical climate, the beauty of the sunsets, the clear water of the ocean, the white sand and profusion of flowering bushes and trees, the stately palms, would always hold a place in her heart. She would now understand the longing to spend the winter months in a location so different from her home state, the freedom of being away from work and responsibility, a time of rejuvenation.

Never again would she stand in church and look down her nose, sniffing those "better than thou" sniffs.

"You're not really here, Edna," MaryAnn said quietly.

Edna looked at MaryAnn without seeing her.

"Hello?" MaryAnn said, laughing.

Edna smiled.

"You know I'm leaving on the six o'clock bus. If a certain phone call arrives."

MaryAnn nodded.

Eli and Harvey retired early, leaving MaryAnn and Edna in deep conversation. They talked, they cried and laughed and sympathized.

A bond grew between them that would last a lifetime.

When the phone jangled to life, Edna leaped to her feet, her heart racing as her eyes raked the caller ID.

Yes, it was him.

"Hello?" Quietly, out of breath.

"Edna?"

"Yes."

"It's Orva."

"Yes."

Couldn't she say anything but yes?

"Sorry I'm late. I just got back."

"How is he?"

There was a long pause.

"Orva?"

His voice was choked, garbled. "It doesn't look good. He's on life support."

Her heart plummeted. The room spun.

"But he's expected to live?"

"They won't say."

What was left to say? How did one go about comforting a person who recently lost his wife, and was confronted with another tragedy so soon?

"Orva, I'm sorry. Do you want me to come home? To the girls?"

"They are asking for you."

"I'll come. I'm scheduled to leave on the six o'clock bus."

There was another pause. Then, "I don't know what Minerva will say. She's . . . kind of taken over."

So here it was. The rest would follow. He'd fallen for her. Tall, willowy, blond Minerva.

"So you'd rather not have me? I don't want to create a problem."

"You won't. I'll tell her, Edna, believe me, it isn't a problem. Just come home."

His voice broke, then.

"Come home, Edna. I need you."

No words could express the music in her heart. She bit her lip to keep from saying words she would regret later. She merely said, "Alright."

"When will you be here?"

"Sometime on Thursday forenoon, I imagine."

"Should I meet you at the bus station?"

"My parents or sisters can. I mean, if you need to be at the hospital."

"I'll be there. In Topeka, right?

"Yes."

"I'll see you then. Have a safe trip."

"I will."

Her heart sang. She replaced the receiver, let it drop slowly, softly. She turned to go to the back patio, then took a deep cleansing breath, let out all the pent-up stress of the past twenty-four hours, before clasping her hands in a euphoria that was, of course, weighted with worry for Neil.

She let herself fall into a lawn chair, her arms and legs dangling, her head propped on the back, her face lifted to the night sky.

"I'm going home."

"That was him?"

"It was."

"And?"

"He wants me to come home. He needs me. He said he'll talk to Minerva. She's taken over."

"Glory be."

And still, they talked. Edna knew she would not sleep if she did not lay on that couch. That creaky couch with the lumpy cushions that slid out from under her every time she changed positions. And Emery with his bad back enjoying a good night's sleep, evidently, by the eruptions of expelled breathing that came from his room.

And so she left Florida, riding on a comfortable bus with more Amish and Mennonites, all sorts of plain people who were returning to their homes after a few weeks or months in Florida. She dozed, but mostly she gazed out the window and watched the scenery, or read the book she had picked up at a little bookstore, and tried to stay calm, without the hard work of an imagination that ran wild.

"Mind if I sit here?"

Edna looked up into a ruddy, tanned face surrounded by graying hair and a pair of the bluest eyes she had ever seen. Tropical waters.

"Sure. Here, let me put my bag on the floor."

He lowered himself into the adjoining seat, extending a hand. Tentatively, she reached across and took it.

"Elmer Stoltzfus."

"Lancaster?"

"Yes. How did you know?"

"Stoltzfus is not a western name."

"No, it isn't."

There was not an awkward moment after that. He, too, was a widower, but it had been nine years since his wife passed away. Nine long years of being alone, the children all married with families of their own.

He'd often considered marrying again, but felt unfaithful to the memory of his Ruth, and said she was as perfect as Ruth of the Old Testament story, their love blessed beyond comparison. He talked constantly of his deceased wife, the union was a gift from God, and to be honest, he was a bit leery of second marriages as they often didn't go well.

"Too many men marry when they're still grieving, heartsick, and lonely. Any woman looks good to a man who lives by himself after a while, let me tell you."

He gave a short laugh.

Edna looked at him, horrified.

"What?" she asked, without thinking.

"It's true. Don't look so scared. I'm serious. Second marriages are a downright catastrophe, or can be. You know, it gets messy. Children involved. And if those children are not your own flesh and blood, it can be hard to . . . well, I've seen it."

Edna sat up straight, her nostrils flaring with indignation, but instead of giving him a piece of her mind, she kept her mouth closed.

"So, what's your status?" he asked.

Status? As if she was expected to fill out a questionnaire. Put an X in the box. Married. Single. Whatever.

She bristled, wouldn't speak.

"I mean, I noticed you're by yourself. Going home?"

"Yes." Stiffly.

"To . . .?"

"Indiana."

"I thought so, by the bowl-shaped covering. You're single? Or did your husband opt to stay home and milk cows?"

"Yes. In fact, he did. He's at home, milking cows. I went to Florida for my health."

She patted her chest, cleared her throat.

"Bronchitis. Florida climate does wonders."

"I see. Well, I'll move on here. I need to talk to my cousin who's seated in the back of the bus. Have a good read."

"Wait."

He sat back down.

"I lied."

"You what?"

"I don't have a husband, I just said that to . . . actually, I don't know why I said that."

He put back his head and laughed, a full, deep, pleasant sound that made her laugh as well.

"Funny girl, aren't you? That's what I like about you westerners. You have this great sense of humor. That was your way of getting rid of me, right? Look, I'm not in the market for a wife. I just thought you looked alone, kind of scared, maybe, as if you weren't too sure what was going on in your life, so I wanted to see what you had to say. You looked interesting to me."

Edna laughed.

"I've been called a lot of things, but never interesting."

"You seem like someone who is very intelligent. Has seen a lot in life, but is confronted with something that makes her nervous."

Edna smiled wryly.

"I'd say you have supernatural powers, or else you're an excellent judge of character. All except the very intelligent."

And so they traded life stories, decided they'd both been tossed about by life's high seas, but he was easily old enough to be her father, at fifty-seven years of age. Time passed swiftly, and when the bus pulled into an Arby's, they ate together, then passed the remainder of the trip in each other's company.

Elmer Stoltzfus restored her faith in men. He had come across as abrasive and nosy, but Edna learned he was only honest, curious in a good way.

His life lessons were many, a string of events in which he had acquired a keen insight, especially in diving unprepared into the shark-infested waters of holy matrimony. Edna smiled when he said marriage was not for the faint of heart, except for his Ruth. An angel. An absolute saint on earth. But he had seen so much.

His own daughter and son-in-law had an awful time of it. They'd been for counseling, counseled till they were blue in the face, but it hadn't made a whole lot of difference.

His honesty was refreshing, his optimism catching. He spoke freely of an all-powerful God who directed lives, whether people were aware of it or not. A faith that seemingly moved mountains.

She pondered his words, thought how he thrived on golden memories and a devotion to God alone, a curiosity about his fellow men and women, and a spirit that longed to help folks to a higher ground when he knew they were stuck in their own defeat.

His advice to Edna about Orva was to go slowly. There was plenty of time. Orva was at the crucial stage, when his loneliness was his driving force, especially if he had had a solid marriage before.

Edna took his words into her heart. He was right, she knew.

So when the bus pulled into Topeka, she kept herself from the anxiety of peering out the window, watching for Orva, hoping he'd stay true to his word. The cold wind was like a slap in the face, but she'd dressed for the wind's knife edge, knowing what the beginning of March could be in Indiana.

And there he was.

Solid, dressed in a heavy gray coat. A neat black hat. So handsome, so right, so Orva.

The light in his face was like a beacon, guiding her on.

"Edna."

It was a statement, a reassurance.

Surrounded by a sea of Amish folks coming from the bus, there were only the expected formalities. They waited for luggage, kept their eyes on safe objects like the bus or people they both knew, and called out greetings.

Again, he opened the car door for her and she gathered her skirt, placed her feet delicately, feeling every inch a princess.

But Edna remembered Elmer Stoltzfus's words.

With the girls in school, they found Minerva Yoder alone in the house, busying herself at the stove, cooking dinner, the table set for three.

So he'd told her.

"Welcome back, Edna."

She extended both hands and Edna took them gratefully.

"How are you, Minerva?"

"Good. I'm good. Moving on, now that you're here."

"Are you glad to be doing that?" Edna asked.

A slight pause, then a cheery "Oh yes. Back to the bakery literally. I miss it. And my Mam will be happy to have me back."

She placed a casserole on the table, and a plate of sliced cheese.

"How was Florida?"

"Great. Actually, I love it there. All I want to do is return as fast as I can."

"No wonder, you have a special memory now. And a bright future with Emery, right? Or didn't he pop the question the way everyone says he will?" Minerva asked, laughing, glancing at Orva.

He sat at the head of the table as if carved from stone. Expressionless.

Edna shook her head.

"Actually, he didn't. Our trip was cut short by Neil's accident."

"He came back with you, though. Right?"

"No. He stayed."

"I see."

It was obvious that Minerva did not see, that she was more than a bit irritated by the disclosure of no engagement, no bubbling bride to be, and no promise of having Edna removed. But there was nothing to do about this except sit down at the usual place, arrange her utensils and bow her head with her hands folded in her lap when it was time, without disclosing any of the inner rough and tumble of her thoughts.

When the prayer was finished, they all helped themselves to the casserole, which needed salt, but was pronounced delicious by Edna in a breathy self-conscious tone of voice that bewildered Orva. It went unnoticed by Minerva.

"So, is Emery returning in the coming week, or . . . ?"

Minerva faced Edna with a calm expression, friendly, curious.

"I'm not sure. We . . . he's staying at his grandfather's house, with his married brother Eli."

"You stayed there, too?"

"Yes, I did."

"Ooo. Close quarters to think you are only dating."

Absolutely nothing to say to this, Edna thought, so she didn't.

Minerva turned to Orva.

"So, I'm here with the girls tonight, right? Edna is going with you?" Orva glanced at Edna, then looked away.

"She wants to see Neil, I believe."

Edna nodded.

There followed an awkward silence, forks sliding sideways across plates, the breaking of waxy cheese and polite chewing, with mouths closed. The wind sent a porch rocker tapping against a window frame, a tree branch scraping on the porch roof.

Edna found her room filled with Minerva's belongings, the bathroom piled with an array of liquid soaps, shampoo, conditioner, toothpaste, flossing string, hairbrushes and combs, hairspray, hairpins, bands and bobby pins.

There were lavender bath salts, eucalyptus oil, bubble bath, and French Country bar soap, a loofah sponge, a long-handled bath brush and a ball of nylon netting on a rope.

She managed a shower surrounded by bottles and objects she never used, dressed quickly and hurried down the stairs, knowing they'd be leaving at one o'clock. Orva emerged from the bedroom fastening his shirt buttons, but avoiding her completely as he entered the bathroom and closed the door behind him.

Minerva had finished the dishes and was sweeping the floor in long, swift strokes with the soft kitchen broom. She looked up when Edna entered the kitchen, smiled and asked if she just got rid of all her junk, or if she showered around it.

"Oh, it's fine. You must enjoy your bath time."

Minerva stopped sweeping, set her broom against the cabinet, and sighed. A faraway look came into her eyes, and she smiled a rueful grin.

"Oh, you know, Edna. From one single girl to another. If we want to be pampered we have to look out for ourselves, because no one else is ever going to do it. You know how fortunate you are with Emery?"

Edna nodded.

There was no sense in telling her. Word got around soon enough, among the plain people who lived their lives woven together like a fine basket.

No, she did not have Emery, and there were no regrets, not now, not ever. The mystery had been solved the second she saw Orva standing in the bus station in Topeka.

His maturity, his quiet strength, those sad eyes.

It was as if God had handed her a sign, written plain as day. The future was constructed of the hope of his love, but if it was not to be, then she would come to accept it, in time.

But never would she mourn the friendship with Emery.

CHAPTER 17

Edna's distaste for hospitals stayed hidden away in Orva's presence. The quiet, dimly lit room with its confusing network of wires, tubes, screens with numbers and jagged lines, the monitors and wheezing and clicking, and the smell of antiseptic and cleaning fluids were stark reminders that this was the ICU.

These things surrounded the bed, yet Edna could see only Neil, his head almost covered in white gauze bandages, his face swollen to an alarming size, his eyes closed in two curved dark lines. He was attached to so many devices that Edna stopped halfway across the room, afraid she would upset or disturb the rhythm of one or all of them.

Orva went ahead, bent over and touched his chest.

"Neil. We're here. I brought Edna. Remember Edna, our *maud*? We'll sit with you for a while."

He turned to Edna.

"We're supposed to keep talking to him, they told us."

Edna approached the bed hesitantly.

"Hello, Neil. It's me, Edna."

She reached out to touch his cheek. It felt waxen, like a statue, but it was warm. She watched his chest rise and fall, over and over, and wondered if the machine was the only reason he was breathing at all. She turned to Orva, tears in her eyes.

"Is there . . . ?" She gestured with her hand.

Orva stepped closer, bent his head so she could speak very softly.

"Brain activity?"

"Yes. He is not considered brain dead."

"So there's hope."

Orva nodded, bit his lip.

They sat side by side. Orva explained in detail what had occurred the night of the accident. Neil was in a car with his friend Owen, and both had been drinking, with dangerous levels of alcohol in their blood. They ran a stoplight and went up over a curb and into the side of a brick building in downtown Topeka.

Neil had head injuries, a ruptured spleen, broken ribs, a dislocated shoulder, and an arm broken in many different places, the bones shattered.

"Neil was in bad shape after Christmas. It seemed as if the hockey equipment only served to remind him of what he should be. He wanted to meet high expectations, so he set goals for himself, but failed them all."

Edna shook her head, then turned to meet Orva's eyes.

"But why? He was doing so well. I had high hopes that if he actually joined the hockey team, it would build his self-worth."

"It proved to be the opposite."

They sat together in shared disappointment, in dashed hopes. They roused when there was a tap on the door, followed by a slight girl who appeared much too young to be an RN.

"Hi," she said quietly.

"How are you?" Orva sked, with a genuine concern, getting to his feet.

"I'm fine. How's Neil today? I'm just coming on to the three o'clock shift, so I'll be in and out. My name is Kerry."

"I'm Orva, Neil's father."

He turned to Edna. "This is Edna, my housekeeper."

Edna smiled, said hello in a subdued voice. Housekeeper? Was that what she was to him? Why not friend?

But this was no time to think of herself. It was all about Neil and Orva, the pain of enduring his wrong choices, of bravely going ahead to face the unknown with his son lying so near death at such a tender age.

She watched the girl tap a keyboard, watch a screen, take Neil's temperature and blood pressure, before adjusting the light blanket that lay across his chest.

"Is he still running a temperature?" Orva sked.

"Yes, he is."

There was no more information offered, and nothing for either of them to do but let her go. Questions would have to wait till his doctors came in, which would not be till morning.

Edna was content to stay here with Orva in this room with Neil.

She wanted the world to go away, and leave them cocooned in this quiet sanctuary where everything seemed possible. Everything. When he did not speak, she remained quiet, comfortably aware of his presence, the nearness of him.

"Are your parents allowed in?" she asked.

"They'll be in later. Sarah's parents, too."

Edna nodded. She watched Orva get up, lay the back of his hand on Neil's cheek, then step away, before turning to go back.

"Neil. It's Dat. I just want you to know I love you. I haven't told you since you were a little boy, but I do. I want you to wake up and get better. I need you, Neil."

He waited, watching his son's face with so much heartbreaking concentration as if Neil would blink or lift the corners of his mouth in response. When nothing happened, Orva sighed deeply and walked back to his chair, sinking into it like an old man.

Edna couldn't help it; she placed a hand on his arm.

"It's O.K., Orva. He'll be alright."

"If only I could feel that way. I'm so afraid I'll never get another chance to tell him I love him. I've been too hard on him. Too jealous of Sarah's tender care and concern. No one knows how I resented it. In my mind, she babied him terribly."

"It's alright. Not unusual at all. I've seen it plenty of times." Orva nodded.

"You want coffee?" he asked suddenly.

Blissful thought. A numbing sleepiness had crept up as she relaxed, and she realized how weary she really was after her long bus ride.

"I would love a cup of coffee."

She walked to the door with him and was rewarded by Orva reaching out to open it, then stepping back to allow her to go first.

"Which way?"

She looked up at him and found his eyes, a light of tenderness in them that brought a wave of newfound confidence in her.

The cafeteria was down two floors, to the right, then left, a confusing array of doors and lights and hallways filled with a variety of nurses and doctors and visitors dressed in winter coats carrying bags of gifts or clothing, or clutching vases of flowers, their faces a mixture of smiles or frowns, frightened expressions or bored ones. Some of them acknowledged Edna and Orva's presence with nods or tentative lifts of the corners of their mouths, but mostly they stared straight ahead as if they were invisible.

They walked through a door with the lighted cafeteria sign, found a table, and sat across from each other. Edna thought wryly how she would never enter a restaurant again without sizing up the height of the divider between booths, a painful memory that seared her confidence, even now.

But she said nothing to Orva.

Some things were best hidden away, especially the ones that made you feel like a loser, a real bona fide victim.

Orva found her eyes on his, and asked quickly.

"Tell me, are you still O.K. with Emery? In spite of not being engaged?"

Edna shook her head.

A waitress appeared. She was short, round as a barrel, her curly hair like a metal sponge, and her tablet propped on her protruding stomach.

"Something to drink?"

"Coffee for both."

Orva turned back to Edna.

"Tell me. What happened?"

Edna sighed. "It's a long story."

"Tell me." More urgent now.

"I don't know if I want to."

"Edna, I have to know."

"Why?"

His eyes on hers, intently now.

"You know why."

The waitress arrived with two cups of coffee, heavy white mugs that smelled wonderful. Without further conversation, she set down a white dish containing small plastic containers of half-and-half, then left without asking if they'd like to order food.

Edna took a deep breath, then launched into a vivid account of her stay in Florida, the unraveling of all her dreams. Orva watched her face intently, his eyes going from soft to angry, then back to soft as he absorbed her words of indecision, of self-blame and the Herculean attempt at love by determination, followed by the bitter scene in the coffee shop.

Their coffee cups long empty, they remained seated as words poured from Edna's mouth. She finished up with the Lancaster companion on the bus home, his words of warning about second marriages, confusion clouding the emotion in her eyes.

Orva shook his head.

"That is a long story, Edna. And one worth repeating. Thank you for sharing all of it with me. You have absolutely been on quite the journey. So, do you feel God has led you so far, only to leave you?"

"You know, Orva. I have no idea. I only know that I have perfect peace by not wanting anything right now. If God wants me to remain single for the rest of my life, then I'll be happy in that situation."

"Will you?"

"Yes. I reached that conclusion in Florida, complete with fireworks and a marching band."

Orva laughed. "I love your mind. Your way of talking." Edna smiled at him, lifted one eyebrow, and asked if that was all.

"Your apple pie isn't bad."

He sobered, then told her quietly that he appreciated her, for so much more, but he wouldn't rush anything. Neil was the one they would think about now, and his recovery, if there was one. The heaviness on his mind lowered his thick shoulders, followed by a long sigh, his eyes gazing off to the right as if he could find an answer in the noisy, crowded cafeteria.

Back in Neil's room, there was no change, his swollen face in exactly the same position as it had been.

Toward evening, when birds dipped and swooped in the lavender skyline dotted with the jagged outline of buildings, his parents arrived, with Sarah's parents following a few minutes later.

Introductions were made, with tears and hugs and well wishes. Edna felt an immediate connection to these loving people, who seemed accustomed to comforting their son and did it easily, genuinely.

Nurses came and went, voices were quieted, then resumed. As twilight came, they all agreed, it was time to go, and Orva and Edna could return with them. More tears, the bending over Neil, touching his face, speaking kind words of love and encouragement.

When it was Edna's turn she said, "Good night, Neil. I don't have a door to tap on the way I normally do, but good night anyway. I love you."

At home, the girls threw themselves at Edna, clung to her with all their strength, told her there would be no more Florida vacations for her, ever. Laughing, Edna folded them in her arms and held them, rocking them back and forth, but found herself fighting tears.

What a difference since that first time, she thought, when they were all belligerence and rebellion.

Minerva left in a huff of indignation and a train of suitcases, thanking Orva coldly for her check and telling the girls goodbye with no sentiment.

Emmylou shook her head wisely.

"She won't have much hair left by the time she's old with all the stuff in the bathroom."

Marie corrected her, saying half of those bottles were full of stuff to make your hair healthy, then she turned to Edna and wanted to hear about Florida.

They made grilled cheese sandwiches and opened a bag of potato chips, mixed a pitcher of grape juice, and sat around the kitchen table till Edna said she had to call a driver and go home to her parents.

The girls protested, but Orva hushed them, saying her parents were old and lived alone, and they needed her.

He followed her to the laundry room as the headlights moved up the driveway, swept her into an embrace so tender, yet so firm and sure. It was the assurance she needed, the perfect wordless way of saying, "We are more than friends and you are so much more than a *maud*, and I will be here for you, today and tomorrow."

She laid her head on his wide, comfortable chest, wrapped her arms around his waist, and closed her eyes for only a moment. She marveled at the difference in Orva's embrace. It was so perfect, like finding the missing piece of a jigsaw puzzle. His arms around her were a completion of something left undone.

She found the house dark, her parents having gone to bed. She let herself in quietly, then sniffed, grimaced, and groaned inwardly. What was that smell?

Well, nothing to do about it this late at night. She was numb with exhaustion. She found the battery lamp, made her way across the kitchen before she heard, "Edna, is that you?"

"Yes, Mam. I'm home."

"Wait. I want to see you before you go to bed."

"It will have to wait, O.K.? I'm exhausted."

"Alright. You don't have to get up early."

"I won't."

Enda took a quick hot shower, then fell into bed and to sleep so quickly she barely remembered covering herself with the quilt. She woke to morning light, a soft, gray fog that blanketed the brilliance of the sun, the white of the light cover of snow, even on the branches of the maple trees closest to the house.

She heard the banging of pans, the coffeepot, doors opening and closing, her parents, usual morning routine. She stretched, rolled over, and went back to sleep.

When she did get up, it was close to nine o'clock, and she was ravenous. She could hardly scramble eggs fast enough, or butter toast with enough speed. She found herself nibbling on the crust of a loaf of bread, her mouth watering as she worked.

Between bites, she told her parents about Florida, her breakup with Emery, and her decision to be happy being single if that was what God wanted. She told them about Neil, in soft, quiet tones.

Her parents were attentive, kind, cheerfully accepting her decision, and glad to think of having her with them as they aged. Edna nodded, and kept the secret of Orva all to herself, reveling in holding something so precious and so intimate. Her eyes glowed with an inner light; her cheeks bloomed with rosy color, her tanned face became golden, her dark hair streaked with highlights from the sun.

She whistled as she cleaned. She found everything in lamentable shape, the sink in the bathroom dotted with toothpaste, the mirror splattered with unnamable dots of debris. The commode was disgusting, but she gamely swabbed and scrubbed, and wiped away until everything shone with cleanliness and smelled of Clorox and bathroom cleaner.

As she backed out of the bathroom, on her hands and knees, Trixie bounced up, cocked her head sideways, and yapped a few short bursts of sound.

Edna turned her head and eyed Trixie levelly.

"Git!" she muttered.

A few more yaps that sounded like "Rack, rack."

"Come here, Trixie."

Her father clapped his hands.

Edna got to her feet, grabbed the bucket of soapy water and turned to find Trixie walking calmly into the bathroom, across her wet floor.

"Hey!" Edna yelled. "Come here, Trixie. Come. Get over here, you little fleabag."

Her father laid his head back, his eyes squeezed shut, and his large frame shook with the force of his mirth. He leaned forward, wiped his eyes and said, "Uh, ho."

"I mean it, Dat. I don't like her, and you think it's funny."

It was good to be home, good to hear her father's laugh, to know they had been well taken care of while she was away. She knew Sadie and Fannie would do their share in the future, as well. Her thoughts rambled as she cleaned, dusted, washed windows and washed the porch floor with a broom and a bucket of soapy water.

The fog dotted everything with cold moisture. Drops formed on the edge of the spouting and hung like gray teardrops. Tree branches cut through the gloom like a ghostly web, as cars moved slowly on the highway. Starlings were lined up like so many small crows, their raucous cries from the barely visible lines strung between heavy poles. Sparrows twittered in the forsythia bushes along the fence.

She finished cleaning the porch, then went to check the many birdfeeders that hung from low branches.

Edna thought they needed refilling, so she took them all down and washed them in soapy water, then dried them.

"Ach, Edna," her mother lamented. "You'd wash the porch roof if we let you. Now why did you clean the bird feeders?"

"They needed it. Don't you know it should be done occasionally? Birds can get diseases from caked-on moldy birdseed."

"You think? Look at this, Edna. My begonias will be blooming in a few weeks."

She pointed to a large plastic pot containing a bedraggled plant that appeared to be resurrected on one side, the other side waxy and almost leafless.

"Wow, Mom. Isn't that something? You were always so good at overwintering plants. Good for you."

Her mother's face shone with her daughter's praise.

Now where did that come from? Edna thought. She had meant to tell her mother she should turn her large plants, so they would grow more evenly, but had said what came from the goodness she felt within.

Was it the acceptance of her lot in life? Or was it being freed from the hard work of trying to love Emery, keeping that artificial smile on her face until she thought she would be permanently disfigured? Or was it the quiet promise of being Orva's wife, a mother to his children?

He'd go slow, he said. Which was a promise, wasn't it?

Elmer Stoltzfus's words cut through her dreams, separating

the wishes from reality. He had warned of second marriages with children.

But did anyone feel about the person they married the way she felt about Orva? Nothing could be too hard, and nothing could tear her away from him, or separate them. If love was wanting to be with him every single minute of her life, to search the light in his eyes, to pour him a cup of coffee and wait for that smile, then she had been blessed by God indeed.

She had already won over the girls, and could easily live in the same house as Neil, even if he often chose to ignore her.

Well, always, actually. He disliked her, if she was truthful. But then, he disliked everyone, so she could accept that. It didn't matter, so long as he was ok. She just wanted him back to his healthy self.

She hitched up old Dob after the fog thinned and a slow rain began to fall. He stood as quietly as he always did, then backed faithfully between the shafts when she said, "Back, Dob," while she lifted them high, then lowered them to insert the points into the leather loops on the harness.

She attached the traces and the britchment to the shafts, unfolded the reins, and climbed into the buggy before slapping his sizable rump with one rein, saying "Gittup, Dob."

The horse moved off in his easy pace, his head straight out, held comfortably without being reined up, as the strap that was attached to the bridle and clipped to the shoulder pad of the harness kept it up.

Her father thought them too cruel and never used one.

She kept to the shoulder of the road to allow cars to pass comfortably, always sensitive to irate motorists who thought horses and buggies an unnecessary nuisance.

She reached down to check if she had her shopping list in her purse, found it, and then kept her attention on the road.

Old Dob was certainly not what you would call a handful, she thought wryly. This horse had to be twenty-five years old.

She pulled gently on the right rein to turn him to Yoder's Bulk Foods, pulled up to the hitching rack, climbed out, reached under the seat for the neck rope, and tied Dob to the rail. She was the only team, which was unusual, but the foggy morning likely kept people off the road.

She said good morning to everyone she met, then pulled a grocery cart from the long line and got out her list.

Cornmeal. Brown sugar.

She headed for the items in the baking aisle, selected a five-pound bag of each, before moving on to the refrigerated cases for a bucket of lard.

Her mother fried all the cornmeal mush in lard, no matter who tried to change her. Olive oil, canola oil, Crisco, all of it was dismissed by a downward wave of her hand and soft snort.

Whoever heard of frying mush in olive oil? Who said it was better for you? They didn't know. Not until they ended up with cholesterol levels completely off the charts, Edna thought, shaking her head as she set the white, plastic bucket in the cart.

But some things could not be changed, and lard was one of them.

"Hello!"

A hearty voice boomed behind her. She turned to find Emery's brother Marvin, the oldest in the family, a tall, overweight man with a booming voice.

"Oh. Marvin. Good morning."

"So how's it going, Edna? I'm surprised to see you back already."

"Emery is still in Florida."

"Really?"

"Yes, I came back to be with Orva Schlabach's children. His oldest boy was in a car accident."

"Yes. I heard about that. Poor man. Seems as if he just lost his wife, and now this."

Edna felt the heat rising her face.

"So, you getting married?" He laughed good-naturedly. "I thought to myself that if Emery proposes, he'll do it right. Take his girlfriend to the sunny South, right?"

Edna smiled, nodded, but said no, he hadn't proposed.

"What? You're kidding."

"No."

"What's he waiting on? A blue moon?"

Should she tell him? Quickly, she decided against it, not wanting to deal with any drama that might crop up. At the age of thirty, there was a certain stigma attached to single Amish men and women. A label that reminded those around you that you were overripe, like a brown banana, or a tin can that had set on a grocery shelf too long. Marriage between two thirty-year-olds was cause for celebration.

She just smiled and shook her head.

"You're looking good, with that tan."

"Thank you."

"I'll have to call him. Remind him that it's time."

He winked and moved on.

Edna shuddered. She imagined a hand clamped on her knee, the ease and flamboyance of all Emery's overtures. How close she had come to subjecting herself to a lifetime of submission.

She bought mini tea bags, a container of Folger's coffee. She knew her father was told to drink decaf, but he'd have none of it, filling his oversized stoneware mug to the brim repeatedly. Only, of course, if he wasn't sitting down at the corner Quik Mart quaffing coffee and eating doughnuts.

She smiled to herself, imagined she may be doing just that at his age, so she better be careful. She did love a good doughnut.

So filled with benevolence toward her aging parents, she bought a dozen shoofly whoopie pies, a bag of Hershey's Kisses, and one of miniature Reese's cups. She smiled at the fumbling girl at the cash register, said that was alright that she'd rung up the wrong amount.

She knew a few months ago she would have frowned, thought grocery stores should not hire incompetent girls like her, snorted to herself.

Where did all this goodwill come from?

She decided firmly and without a doubt that she was in love.

CHAPTER 18

GOING BACK ON MONDAY MORNING WAS A JOY. SHE PACKED HER bags, twirling in her bedroom from dresser to bed, her skirts flying in a cloud as she turned. Humming softly, her face alight, she barely recognized herself in the mirror, this vibrant person who was tanned, healthy, eager for life.

Love was a wonderful feeling, one she did not deserve, but she grabbed every bit greedily, wrapping herself in the softness and comfort, like a sheer veil of silk.

The wheels of the vehicle did not turn fast enough, so she found herself bracing her feet against the floor as if pressing down on them would speed things up. The driver, a wrinkled man with bristly white sideburns and a greasy cap pulled low on his forehead, kept up a continuous monologue of boring subjects which did not interest her at all, so she made occasional noises of acknowledgment which seemed to be sufficient.

Finally, they turned in the drive, and she was transported on feet with wings attached, running lightly up to the porch and into the living room. She took a deep breath, closed her eyes.

She was here, in this house. Her house. This house would be her home, to live with the man she loved, to help him raise his children, to have and to hold, all of them. She felt a sense of belonging, a homecoming, as if she had been wandering without a compass and had finally found a clear direction.

Upstairs, she unloaded her luggage, then gathered all the laundry in the bathroom and the girls' room. She checked Neil's room but found nothing, so Minerva had done all his. She stood, thinking of Neil's battered body, Orva's pain of having failed him, and said a prayer, asking God to heal them both.

She sang as she hung laundry in the frigid air, hummed as she cleaned the laundry room and swept the kitchen. She washed leftover dishes, emptied trash cans, then got down one of her cookbooks and began a batch of chocolate chip cookies, Orva's favorite.

Her dreams knew no boundaries that day, her exuberance a gift from God.

When the girls got home they threw their lunchboxes on the table, then ran to receive the hug they craved, the human touch that was not that of their mother but a haven of safety nevertheless.

"How was school?"

"Good. Every day is basically the same," Marie said airily.

Edna raised an eyebrow.

"Really? Nothing new ever?"

"Not really."

"Uh-huh!" from Emmylou. "Jeremy spilled his chocolate milk all over his desk and had to wipe it up, and he was crying. You know why he had to wipe it up? Because. Every day he slides around on his seat, leans way back, puts his feet in the aisle, just acts like a monkey when he eats his lunch. Every day he does that. So Teacher Janie made him clean it up and not just paper towels, either. He had to get a bucket of water, with soap in it, that yellow stuff in a bottle that we use to mop the floor, and a rag. He was crying, but it made no difference to the teacher. She didn't pity him a bit."

She shook her head and lowered her eyebrows.

"She can be mean. All us little girls think so. She makes us do over our arithmetic."

She paused, then eyed Edna like a parakeet, tilting her head to one side before she began again.

"Did you know the English kids in public schools? You know, the ones who ride the big yellow bus? Did you know they say math for arithmetic? It comes from the word mathematics. It's the same thing as arithmetic."

"And, I'll tell you another thing. Megan Yoder likes Nathan Yoder, but they can never get married because both of their last names are Yoder."

Marie rolled her eyes.

Emmylou disappeared into the pantry and returned with a box of Ritz crackers, then pulled a chair to the counter and scrambled up on it, opening doors.

"Here, Emmylou. I'll get your peanut butter," Edna offered.

"I got it. Where's the marshmallow cream?"

"Dat ate it all," Marie offered, pulling on the paper of a Ritz cracker stack.

Emmylou scrambled down, returned the chair, and yanked a drawer for a knife, then sat down and concentrated on spreading peanut butter perfectly, without breaking the cracker.

"Hey! And you know what? Lisa Miller had a hundred percent in spelling all year. I had only one wrong so far. You know how to spell 'little,' Edna?"

Amid all this happy one-sided chatter, Edna noticed how very different the two girls really were. Marie was quiet, bordering on introverted, never showing much emotion, skimming across the top of life's complexities, unruffled.

Her school days were all described as "Fine" or "Good." Many occurrences passed over with a shoulder shrug and a "whatever," whereas Emmylou was a veritable walking newspaper. She'd make a great journalist, if she wasn't Amish, Edna thought.

She formed meatballs with the ground beef she'd thawed,

mixed a tomato sauce to pour over them before popping them into the oven, and set the chocolate chip cookie dough into the refrigerator to chill before she baked them. She then peeled potatoes while the girls went to feed the bunnies and barn cats.

She checked her appearance in the bathroom mirror, tucked in a few stray hairs, adjusted her covering and smoothed her skirts.

He'd be here soon.

Would she still find his face welcoming? Would he want to draw her close to him but wouldn't with the girls in the kitchen?

Oh please don't let him come home with that closed expression, she thought. She set the potatoes to boil, opened a package of frozen broccoli, her breathing faster now, as she watched for the truck that would appear after five.

She took so many deep breaths she thought she might hyperventilate before the truck appeared, and Orva stepped down, carrying his lunchbox and water jug, his coat streaked with dirt, his hat pulled low over his eyes.

How could she describe his face, even to herself? There was no gladness, no light in his eyes, only a closed coldness, as if he held her away from him with a push of his hand, sending her reeling into the opposite wall.

Deeply hurt, she turned away, lifted the lid of the potatoes and poked a fork into them before turning off their burner and draining the water.

He disappeared into the bedroom, emerged with clean clothes over his arm, and closed the bathroom door firmly behind him, the click of the lock a firm reminder that he was not her husband and she was not his wife, and he had every right to assert his independence and troubled mood whenever he wanted.

She mashed the potatoes with a hand masher, bit her lip to keep her emotions in check, steamed the broccoli, and made a cheese sauce.

She set the table, poured water, and waited for the sound of the shower to stop before dishing up the food.

"Go ahead and eat. I'm not hungry. I'm going to the hospital." Edna was desperate for eye contact, anything to reassure her that he was fine, that he was alright with her being there in his kitchen.

"Is he worse?" she asked, her voice rattling.

"No. I don't know."

He left and did not return that night. He had not asked her to accompany him, hadn't touched his supper, which left Edna facing the long cold evening alone, the ghosts of all her inadequacies seeping through doorways, taunting her.

He doesn't want you, they crooned. *He never did.*

Forced into the presence of the Heavenly Father by the spectre of her fear and self-loathing, she found a measure of peace before drifting into a troubled sleep. But Edna woke abruptly to find all her fears increased.

She had told herself she would be happy without Orva. Happiness should not be based on another person, but on the acceptance of God's will.

But the battle to lose the self, to shed the longings of human flesh, and human will, was monumental as the night wore on.

Where was he?

Would he spend all night in the hospital, alone?

She imagined another car wreck, the police at the door, Orva's mangled body. Neil's death, too much for Orva. One macabre incident led to another in her fatigued imagination, her spirit broken by the rebuttal.

And yes she prayed, and fought bravely with the sword of her faith.

She got the girls off to school without giving away any of the night's struggles, swept the kitchen, and then turned the oven knob to 350 degrees.

She'd bake the chocolate chip cookies, then go through the girls' dresses to repair ripped seams, torn pockets, lengthen skirts, and throw out the ones that were too small, stained, and worn out.

To keep busy was an elixir, the best medicine for a weary soul. And she prepared herself for the words that were sure to come.

She did not realize he was home till he came through the laundry room and into the kitchen. She was using a turner, lifting hot cookies from the cookie sheet, a hotpad folded over it.

She looked up, a question in her eyes.

He had aged during the night, his face lined with fatigue, but there was a light in his eyes that smoldered, and turned them darker as he approached.

She put down the cookie sheet, unfolded the potholder, laid down the turner as he came closer.

"Edna," he choked, his voice a hoarse whisper.

She was swept into an embrace that was anything but gentle. He crushed her against him, and his lips searched until they found hers. Too shocked to fully comprehend, Edna rose from despair into a dizzying wave of hope and gladness that took her breath away.

He released her, stepped back, his arms at his sides.

"I'm sorry, Edna. Again. But . . ."

She would never forget the shift in his beautiful eyes. A man's eyes should not be described as beautiful, but his were just that.

"I want you. I want to marry you. Now. I can't spend my nights and days at the hospital without you. I love you. I love you so much I can't function anymore. I want to wait, to go slow, to win your heart, but . . ."

He let his shoulders fall, his big hands hanging loosely as if there was nothing else to do with them.

"I don't blame you if you're disgusted. Neil lying in the hospital, nothing is certain, and here I am, asking you to . . . I know it's risky. I am a widower with three children."

He stopped, shook his head.

"Edna, listen. I can't eat. I can't sleep. It's bad. Just . . . just say something. I'll take no for an answer. It will be better than not knowing."

Edna could not find one word to answer him. The song in her heart rose to a crescendo that drowned out the power of her speech. Thick and full and rich, the joy of knowing that he loved her, wanted her, and had asked her to be his wife propelled her softly, gently into his arms, her own going up to his shoulders and around his neck, her lips lifted to his with all the joy of a found heart. A heart that had never known true love till this moment. Time was obsolete, the world and its sorrows vanished, replaced by the perfect design of two people in love.

Her eyes shone into his, the light in one igniting the other.

"I love you as much as you love me. I will marry you. Yes."

"Oh my precious love," was all she heard, before she was swept back into his arms.

They were brought back to reality by the distinct odor of burning chocolate chip cookies. Edna rushed to the stove, but laughed as she lifted a smoking tray of blackened cookies, shaking her head, embarrassed suddenly.

"It's O.K., Orva," she laughed.

She made a pot of coffee, finished baking cookies while they talked, planned, rejoiced in their newfound love brought to light. Secrets of the heart were shaped into reality, too much joy to comprehend except in small pieces.

No one could know. Neil came first. Orva needed her with him until his recovery. The doctors spoke well of his ability to recover, but it would be months.

In the spring, maybe. In May? It seemed a long way off.

The girls stayed with their grandparents for the night, their pink Dora the Explorer backpacks bulging with pajamas and bedroom slippers, the Uno and Skip-Bo games, homemade valentines, and fresh chocolate chip cookies.

Edna dressed in a mint green dress, sprayed cologne liberally, remembered she was engaged and applied even more.

Oh, how she loved him.

The hospital room could not contain their joy. They sat side by side, spoke in quiet tones, unfolded their lives for the other to examine.

Edna dozed with her head on his shoulder, then walked over to Neil's bed and knocked softly on the railing.

"Good night, Neil."

Edna stepped back when he lifted his right hand, then let it fall, before turning his head from side to side.

"Orva!" she gasped.

Everything turned into controlled chaos after that. The nurses were soon followed by a doctor, then another. Lights were turned on, screens monitored, beeps turned into hums, and voices rose above other voices.

Tears rained down their faces as his swollen eyes opened, blinked, then closed, only to open again. Orva would not leave his bedside until the doctor who was authorized to take him off the life support machine arrived.

Then he stood with Edna, her hand clutched in his.

And so began the healing.

Neil remained in the hospital for another three weeks, long days and nights for an impatient youth. His friends came to visit, greeted Orva and Edna cordially, which lifted their morale considerably. Car accident or not, they were wayward Amish youth who deserved a second chance.

On the day he was brought home, the tulips down by the rock garden bloomed for the first time, gently opened by the warm spring sunshine. Thin, pale, and exhausted, he flopped into the hospital bed by the living room windows and fell into a deep, restful sleep.

Edna cooked nutritious meals, plied him with multivitamins.

His dark hair was long and unkempt, but there wasn't much to be done about that. Orva stayed at home the first week so he could help him to and from the bathroom, which was a trial in itself, being in the same house, the same room without revealing their secret.

They managed to revert to the man of the house and *maud*, with neither of them suspecting the knowing in Neil's eyes or the ensuing confusion.

One afternoon, Edna sat by Neil's bed, one leg tucked up beneath her, rocking gently on the recliner, reading a magazine. She was shocked when he turned his head, the hair falling over one eye.

"Hey," he said.

He never called her Edna.

"What?" On guard, prepared for arrows of hurt that would pierce her skin.

"You know how it was when you woke me?"

"I woke you?"

"Yeah. You know, when I was on life support."

"Oh. Yes?"

"You know how you always tapped on my door and said good night?"

"Mm-hm."

"Well, that's what woke me."

Edna blinked back quick tears. "Seriously?"

"Yeah."

"So . . . you used to hear that?"

"Every time."

"You probably thought I was crazy. You know, a little off."

"No." He laughed, which came out as an unusual rattling sound.

"I don't hate you, you know," he said.

"You don't?"

"No. I hate it that my mam is dead."

"I know. That has to be awfully hard."

"It was. Not so much anymore. But I miss her a lot."

There was a silence fraught with unspoken words. Edna went back to her magazine. The recliner rocked, squeaking softly.

Then, "You and Dat? You got something going on?"

Frightened, Edna swallowed, tried to speak, but stammered, unable to find the right words, the words that would not offend him.

"Well . . . it's just . . ."

"Do you or don't you?" he asked quietly.

"We do."

"You gonna marry him?"

"After you're healed and back on your feet."

For a long time, he said nothing, and then he turned his head away. Edna went back to her magazine, but the sentences ran into each other like traffic accidents so that she couldn't comprehend anything.

What was going through his head? He would hate her for replacing his mother, of this she was sure.

She heard the whisper of his hair on the pillowcase as he turned his head. In profile, he looked so much like his father, except thinner and younger.

He sighed.

"Before the accident, Dat marrying you would have made me so mad. But I heard a lot of his words. You know. He's . . . well, cool. So I'm down with it."

"You're down?" Edna asked, not understanding.

He laughed. "I'm O.K. with it."

"Thank you."

He nodded, "It's cool."

She told Orva, who received the news with no small amount of incredulity. Prayers were answered, he said. He hadn't prayed for perfection, only the healing of the hurt in Neil's heart from his mother's death.

He hadn't asked for a complete and total conversion from bad to good. Only the healing that would bring this about, in God's time.

"He's so young. We'll likely still have our times, but the seed has been sown, and he'll find his way back. Praise God."

By the middle of April Neil had the casts removed and was upright, walking with the aid of a walker on wheels.

He still wore a neck brace, but it, too, would be removed in the coming weeks. Orva and Edna hunched over the kitchen table with a calendar, planning the date of their wedding, where to hold the services, who would host the reception, and the guest list.

"Fannie and Sadie, my two sisters, will be beside themselves with only a month to prepare. We had better plan this for the last week in May."

"Whatever you think, Edna. But that is like a year away."

"No. Six weeks."

"Too long."

The little girls were told, with shrieks of approval and lots of acrobatic maneuvers across the kitchen and into the living room.

"I knew it! I just knew it!" Marie shrieked.

"You'll be my mom, I'll have a mom," Emmylou cried, extending her arms and racing around in circles, like an unbalanced bird.

Orva put his arm around Edna's waist and drew her close. They smiled into each other's eyes and thanked God in the hidden recesses of their hearts.

Her family was fit to be tied, literally.

If only she'd thrown hints, given them a clue, it wouldn't be half as bad, Sadie and Fannie shrieked. The sisters-in-law took the news with less fanfare, but then, they weren't the ones who had to do a wedding at their house.

Sadie lifted both hands to her flaming cheeks.

"Why didn't you give us a warning, at least?"

"Because of Emery." Edna stated flatly.

"What's he got to do with it?"

"Well, we did break up only recently. This whole thing is a scandal."

"Oh, pooh! You and Emery were broken up before you started. He was like a mirage to you. You know, you crawling across the desert dying of thirst and he was always there, like a mirage. He was never real. He likes English girls too much."

Edna's head shot up, her eyes widening.

"What?"

"Well, he does. Everyone knows it. We just never had the heart to tell you."

Edna contemplated this bit of information, before deciding to stay quiet about the coffee shop episode. If it was true, the gossip her sisters were implying, then perhaps the overheard conversation was a blessing in disguise, but there was no point in destroying his reputation even more. She knew there was truth in Sadie's outspoken observance.

"You broke up before you started." Broken down into gentler phrases, it simply was not meant to be, a common saying but very meaningful now.

Sadie searched Edna's face keenly.

"That's what happened, right?

"Well, not really. I mean . . . oh, forget it, Sadie."

"Tell us, Edna."

And so she did. They laughed and cried together, listened wide-eyed, burst out in righteous indignation at her description of the sleeping arrangement.

"Oh, he'd definitely be a winner," Fannie said, her mouth so full of butterscotch pie that it sounded like "witter."

"Swallow your pie!" Sadie shouted.

Edna laughed without restraint, cut another slice of pie, and decided you could search the world for something closer and better than sisterly bonds and you would never find it. Love and romance was another category, a God-given love that was high on the list, but sisters were priceless. They understood everything about you, no matter how hard you tried to hide it. They loved you even when they disapproved of you, and always forgave you for every crazy thing you ever did.

"I can't get ready for a wedding in a month," Fannie said, repeating herself for the third time.

"Orva is alright with the end of May."

"What's the difference, Fannie? Six weeks or a month?" Sadie broke in.

"Two weeks, that's what the difference is. Two whole weeks of painting and cleaning up. We have to move most of the shop stuff, you know."

"I'll tell you what. We'll just get married in town. One witness, you or Fannie, which one will it be?" Edna asked.

And so began the busiest six weeks of Edna's life. Keeping Orva's home running smoothly, weeding the gigantic rock garden, spending as much time as she could helping her sisters, sewing the wedding dress, choosing and sending invitations, finding fine china and silverware, matching tablecloths and placemats; it was all a bit too much.

She made lists, crossed them off, made more lists.

Every evening she fell into bed, so exhausted sleep was dreamless, a blink in time and she was awake at the sound of the alarm.

Her take-charge attitude was thrown off kilter by a sense of unreality. Sometimes she wanted to pinch herself to make sure everything was real.

At night, when they had a moment alone, they knew it was the best time of their lives. Or at least for Edna.

"There is only a young love once," Orva told her quietly. "Only when you're young is when you're free-spirited, diving into love and marriage without have experienced it. It is a love like no other," he said, his face saddened by memories.

Only for a short time, Edna felt slighted, before he folded her tenderly in his strong arms. He told her she was the best thing that God had ever given him, to give him hope and a new life with a beautiful girl he certainly did not deserve. Words that built her confidence in him, in spite of being a second wife.

She knew she was not beautiful, but kept this to herself. If beauty was in the eye of the beholder, then that was alright.

She had no reason to doubt his love, his attraction to her. He told her repeatedly how strong she was, and so capable of running a household smoothly.

"Well, Orva, when you say that, it's much more believable than when you tell me I'm pretty."

"I never told you you're pretty. The word is beautiful. And you are."

He smoothed her hair away from her face, sighed, and said sometimes he could hardly stand the love that flooded his chest.

"It's like congestive heart failure. I'm *fa-schticking* on all this love." And she smiled softly.

CHAPTER 19

By THE TWENTY-SIXTH OF MAY, THE WARM BREEZES AND BRILLIANT sunshine had effectively blown the gray days of winter to wherever they went till another season of cold rolled around. Trees were decked out in their green dresses, every flower bed and patio displaying new color as women everywhere filled pots and planters, edged shrubbery and perennials with hot pink petunias, buttery marigolds, and flamboyant geraniums in a variety of daring reds.

Lawnmowers buzzed across new grass, leaving neat stretches of turf like the finest carpet. Gardens were filling up with straight rows of peas and beans, red beets and carrots, clumps of cucumber vines peeking through the tilled soil.

Sadie had done her best. Her husband, Harley, had worked along with his energetic wife, listened to her insistent voice, mostly, but sometimes veering off course and doing things his way. The long white shop with the two garage doors was turned into a wedding chapel in due time, scrubbed and painted, carpet laid, benches set.

About a half mile away, Chip and Fannie had their shop decked out for the reception, or the dinner, as was the Amish label for the wedding meal.

Rows of tables were set with white dishes, glass tumblers, and silverware, dinner rolls, butter and strawberry jam, apple

butter, and honey. In the background, many friends and relatives were working to see that the wedding dinner went seamlessly, frying chicken, boiling potatoes, making gravy. It was all
a sort of controlled chaos, with women chattering like colorful
birds, each one a competent cook who had prepared a wedding
meal many times.

They were the cooks, an honored position.

Edna was dressed in navy blue, with a white cape and apron, a
new covering on her head, new shoes on her feet, and a glow on
her face that everyone said made her appear prettier than they'd
ever seen her.

Wasn't it something, they asked each other. So perfect for
Orva. But they'd seen it before, the widower marrying his *maud*.
It was not unusual.

The wedding sermons were preached by two uncles, the
short first sermon by a spirited young minister who spoke of
Sarah's passing, which produced quite a few handkerchiefs held
to streaming eyes, especially for the family who had endured all
the pain and questioning of the years of her cancer-ridden world.

Yes, they nodded. God had taken away, so there was peace
in acceptance. You didn't question his ways when he took a dear
sister, daughter, mother of hurting children.

They were glad to welcome Edna to the family, relieved to
hand over the duties of helping Orva and the children. Now they
would have a mother to pack their lunches, keep their clothes
clean, cook and sew and bake. But even more important was
the fact that Orva would not be alone, but have someone by his
side, a helpmeet, someone to love.

Neil sat on the bench, still thin, but the color in his cheeks
was returning, the pallor of his face turning into a healthy tan.

As he listened to the sermon, watched his father stand before
the bishop with Edna by his side, pronouncing the quiet "ya,"
and the congregation rising in prayer after they were pronounced

man and wife. Many people cast covert glances in his direction, wondering what he was thinking, his face set like stone, his mouth in a grim, inscrutable line.

Was a stepmother ever truly welcome to a teenager?

Or did they all harbor a form of resentment against this woman who was thrust into their life by the father's choosing?

What about Mam? She was gone, forgotten so soon, while the father went chasing after anyone who seemed readily available. Evidently, everyone thought it was O.K., the way they set up this wedding, dressed up, and sat here with shining approval. But it was too soon. Much too soon for the grown son to take in this finality, this forgetting of his beloved mother who was dead, buried in the Amish graveyard with a too-small, too-unadorned gravestone stuck into the earth above her wooden coffin that lay rotting beneath it.

And so amid the happiness, the gaiety and celebrating, there was only the smallest sprout of the bewilderment and uncharted navigation of the coming years.

Orva and Edna were now man and wife, married, joined in holy matrimony by the bishop, bound together as one in the eyes of God and man.

Edna had never felt such joy, so much love, and acceptance by his people, and Sarah's. They were so generous in their praise, giving her no reason to feel she had entered into this union too soon or with too much confidence in her own ability.

Humble. Edna Miller was humble, so sweet, they said. She'll win over those children, even Neil. And they so obviously loved each other.

The entire congregation was awash in high hopes and goodwill, kinfolk and friends who were inspired to see what God had wrought in his great love for the suffering Orva and the lonely Edna.

They piled their wedding gifts on the back of Rick Anderson's pickup truck, helped both sisters restore their shops back into

working condition, and began their life in the house Edna loved
so much.

Marie and Emmylou went on with life, swaddled in the secu-
rity of having a mother. They went to school with good food
in their lunches, the memory of Edna's hug across their lonely
shoulders, and faced life head-on with newfound confidence.

Her parents brought her furniture from the large bedroom
down the hallway, her father presiding over the hardworking
men as if he was the foreman of a moving company. Her mother
hovered, laughing, throwing little knick-knacks in the packed
boxes. Saying she'd want these when she became homesick.

"Here, Edna. Take Trixie," her father said, handing the
bewildered little dog to her. "I know you'll miss her."

And laughed uproariously at his own joke.

"Goodbye, Edna," her mother said, reaching for her. Edna
was gathered into a warm embrace, and felt the patting of her
hands as if to assure her that all would be well with them.

"But, Mam, will you be alright?"

"Why of course we will. You girls will check up on us. Dat
is much better than he was for a long time on that medication.
We'll be fine."

"I'll be back every Thursday to clean."

"Now, if something comes up don't get all stressed about
our cleaning. I can clean, too, you know."

Edna smiled at her mother, thought of the bathroom and
Trixie, the dead flies and dropped geranium leaves. Her parents
stood together, waving, Trixie draped across her father's arm,
her head to one side. Edna told Orva that dog had never been
happier than she was to see her leave.

By the first week in June, her new life as Mrs. Orva Schlabach
began in earnest, the house rearranged to her liking, her furniture in various positions, mixed with the things that had been
Sarah's.

The first wind of unrest blew in when she took down a few pictures and replaced them with her own. She was innocent about this change until Marie asked what she'd done with her mother's pictures.

"I stored them in the attic, Marie. Why?"

Marie put a finger to her chin, tilted her head sideways, and said it got too hot in the attic for her mother's pictures, and she wanted them in her room. Eyes glaring, accusing.

Surprised, Edna took in the baleful look, the defiant stance. "Oh, alright, Marie. I didn't know the attic got so hot."

"It does."

She turned away, and Edna felt properly scolded. It was far more than the pictures. It was Marie holding on to her real mother, the memory of her, resenting the thought of her new mother replacing the one she still missed. Edna went to the attic, brought down the pictures, asked Marie where she wanted them hung.

Marie surveyed her room, then asked to have them put above the bed, where she could see them before she went to sleep.

Edna did as she was told, then searched Marie's face for signs of approval, but there was none, only the attitude of having been slighted in the first place.

She tried to put the incident out of her head, told herself repeatedly that it was nothing, a normal wish for a child who had lost her mother. But the whole thing stuck in her mind like a painful bruise until she approached Orva with the unsettling disclosure.

He listened patiently, of course, he always did, which soothed Edna's ruffled self-confidence. He put an arm tenderly across her shoulders, pulled her close, and said he was sure this was nothing out of the ordinary. Marie simply felt displaced without the usual things on the wall.

"Of course," Edna said softly. "I understand."

A few weeks later it seemed that the pictures on the wall

laid the groundwork for a string of incidents that were like interlocked pieces of a jigsaw puzzle that eventually formed the border of an entire image; a scene that pushed its way into Edna's joy, took away her serenity as efficiently as a thief in the night. She knew the danger of this thief lurking in the shadows, knew she had to stop thinking of herself, stop being childish, but one incident became so significant she came to Orva again.

"Orva, can I talk to you about Neil?"

Orva laid down his magazine, pulled the lever on the recliner, moved over to make room for her, patting the seat beside him, that look in his eyes that always melted her heart. He wanted her, desired her in the way every a husband wants his wife, and this was all Edna needed to overcome the adversity she faced with the children.

She loved him with all her heart, a consuming love that only multiplied as the weeks wore on. He was all she had ever imagined and more. She could put up with the children's periodic lack of acceptance.

She settled beside him, leaned into his solid chest, felt secure and cherished as he drew her close. He kissed her and told her he loved her, which brought quick tears.

"I'm sorry to keep bringing up these childish things," she began.

"It's O.K., Edna. We were bound to have some problems somewhere along the line. It's O.K."

"No, it's not O.K." Edna corrected him

"How is it not?" he asked.

"I'm just being too sensitive. I often feel as if I'm not welcome here. I mean, not really like that, but . . . I don't know how to say it. It's as if I was still the *maud* and the children resent everything that goes outside of that."

Orva took a deep breath. She felt his chest heave, and felt guilty for putting him through this.

"It's probably perfectly normal."

And so she didn't tell him about Neil slamming his lunch on the counter, eyeing her with a look that could only be described as distaste, and telling her never to put tuna salad on a roll again. That it got soggy and gross, before adding the fact that his Mam never did, she put it in a container.

"I'm sorry," Edna stammered, hating herself for not thinking that perhaps the tuna salad would make the bread soggy, but was in a hurry that morning and let it go.

Neil didn't acknowledge her apology, he simply turned on his heel and clomped upstairs with as much noise as he could make, slamming things in his room.

To let me know how much he hates me, Edna thought.

She'd been so sure, after the accident, so confident that Neil would be different. He'd said he was "down" with it. He wanted her to marry his father. So why was everything so wrong?

That evening, she turned her back to Orva for the first time, saying she had a severe headache, which was true. After she heard his deep breathing, she pulled the sheet over her head and let the tears come till she found a measure of peace.

Well, hadn't the minister spoken of sunshine and rain, the way every minister described marriage? But rain, gentle rain that nourished the earth and created dark days, was nothing compared to this onslaught of ill will, an unexpected hurricane to the heart. Orva remained kind and understanding, but how could he know the depth of the hurt?

They were, after all, his children.

So each morning, Edna awoke with fresh resolve to overcome these times when the children's resentment paved a road of difficulty for her.

She put chicken and tuna salad in a Tupperware container, made sure the rolls were fresh and soft, put plenty of ice in the gallon water jug. She scoured the white lid of the Coleman coolers with Comet, till it appeared new, proud of the fact that her men went to work with clean lunches, packed thoughtfully.

The heat of summer arrived in a cloud of humidity and blazing sunlight that left Edna gasping for air at nine o'clock in the morning.

The laundry hung stiff and straight in the hot morning sun, the cucumber vines already wilted in the garden, and the geranium leaves curling from lack of moisture.

She sat at the kitchen table, drinking her lukewarm coffee, listening to the stirring upstairs as the little girls woke to a new day.

She always looked forward to their appearance on the stairway, and this morning was no different. With school over for the summer, they were a constant source of entertainment with their chatter.

She stretched and yawned, then got up to start a batch of bread. It was too hot to bake, but Orva loved her homemade bread and rolls, so she tried hard to have it fresh out of the oven at least once a week when he came home from work. Neil did not like the homemade rolls for his sandwich, so she always kept the store bought on hand for him.

She was learning.

In the short time that she lived here as Orva's wife, she had one textbook after another set in front of her, forced to accept, remain optimistic, and yes, learn. When she became disheartened with Neil's attitude, or the girls' lack of respect, she tried to rise above it and remain cheerful and smiling in spite of the sinking feeling in her heart.

She measured yeast in lukewarm water, stirred it absent-mindedly as her thoughts went from one incident to another. Marie was on a mission, it seemed, to make sure Edna stayed in her place, ever since the pictures were hung in her room. The hugs of bedtime were gone, with the excuse that she was too old to be tucked in like a baby, turning her back, tilting her head to look at the pictures on the wall that had been her mother's.

It was a small form of rejection, but one that drove a cloud above Edna's head for days, especially when Emmylou followed suit, saying she was not a baby who needed a hug before she fell asleep. The kick delivered when she was down was the day Neil refused to eat even one item in his lunch, saying the banana on the bottom was overripe and had ruined everything.

"Don't you know to wrap bananas in plastic wrap? Mam always did," he said with a look of so much disdain it took her breath away.

He must really hate me, she thought, for the hundredth time. She turned her back to him, refused to answer.

This boy needed discipline. He needed a sharp rebuke from his father and needed to know that speaking to his stepmother with all that adolescent condescension was unacceptable. But it would never happen, Orva living in constant fear of provoking his son.

And so the tiny seed of bitterness was planted, with Edna bouncing from times of hope that the situation would improve, to moments of wondering if no one had an eye for any wrong-doing, while she remained the sounding board for everyone's grievances.

It was too hot in the house to eat supper, and certainly too uncomfortable to eat in the kitchen, so Edna fired up the grill, prepared burgers and sausages, made a bowl of potato salad, and cut a large watermelon in chunks, placing it all outside on the patio table that had been a wedding gift from her single friends.

It was not an inexpensive table and chairs, but one that would withstand all kinds of weather, lots of company, and abuse in general.

The chairs were heavy, with pivoting seats that tilted forward or backward, and there were bars between the table legs to rest feet so that after a meal, chairs could be tipped back to relax with a glass of iced tea.

Edna was so proud of this patio set, a dream come true for her. How often had she walked among the summery displays at

Snavely's, daydreaming of owning one of these, but without a patio or a home of her own, and certainly no husband, it wasn't possible, none of it.

Neil had taken to eating with the family after the accident, so tonight, he collapsed into a chair, raked a hand through his hair, and sighed.

"My leg gave me a lot of trouble today."

Tanned, with his shoulders widening like his father's, Neil was turning into a handsome young man, if he could ease the tension in his mouth, learn to smile and relax, accept life's twists and turns without the peevish pout.

Orva looked at him.

"I told you not to go up on that roof."

"Someone had to do it."

Orva didn't bother answering, simply went ahead squirting mustard all over the burger on his plate. Edna looked at Neil, then looked away hurriedly, seeing the black light of irritation that flared far too often.

To ease the tension, Edna spoke out of turn, saying perhaps another worker could have gone up.

"You weren't there. You have no clue what we're talking about."

The snarl on his top lip was as plain as day, his eyes boring into hers with just the right amount of contempt to make Edna feel the usual wave of despair, the jolt of unacceptance.

She busied herself cutting watermelon, her lips drawn back in a tense smile and her eyes blinking with humiliation. She looked to Orva for support, but he was already occupied with Emmylou's sausage, cutting rapidly with his knife.

Determined to rise above this mundane exchange of unpleasantness, Edna took a bite of watermelon, chewed, and smiled brightly.

"Mm-mm. This is the best one yet."

Orva raised his eyebrows. "Really?"

Edna nodded. "I'm learning to leave them on the vine a bit

longer. I think that thing that attaches it to the vine, whatever it's called, needs to be withered more than I thought. The watermelon becomes sweeter."

Orva shook his head.

"You're a wonder in the garden, Edna."

"Why thank you, Orva. You know I love gardening. There's something about the challenge of growing melons, though, that's especially rewarding."

She met Orva's eyes, allowed her love to show, a warmth spreading across her face.

Neil pushed back his chair with enough strength to knock it on its back, grabbed his plate, and slammed through the door. Edna thought she heard him mutter something about "Kissy kissy," but she couldn't be sure.

Orva looked up, shrugged, and went on eating his burger that was dripping with ketchup and mustard.

"What brought that on?" Edna asked. She was only answered with another shrug, another bite of burger.

Edna's uneasiness prevailed as she washed dishes. Orva's shrug was the most inefficient, uncaring thing she'd seen yet. Why couldn't he show sympathy or understanding where Neil was concerned? She could not ask for a kinder, more considerate husband, but with Neil, there was always this competition, this need to show superiority. He could have been nice about Neil's leg pain instead of telling him that he did wrong by going up on the roof. Neil had meant well and was doing his job. Immediately after delivering that put-down, Orva praised her melon-raising ability.

Why couldn't Orva see it? He was blind and deaf when it came to dealing with his oldest son, again, even if things had been so different when Neil had been in a coma. Nothing had changed, now that he was back to his usual self. But approaching Orva and telling him of this major fault hadn't worked the first time, and very likely never would. She wished she had enough wisdom to work on a miracle between these two by some brilliant act of psychology. But she knew that, too, was a plan without a possibility.

She simply had to maneuver her way through this labyrinth of emotions as taut as a guitar string, and hope to hit the right chord.

Her tears fell in the dishwater, plunking off her face like a child's. She sent a plea Heavenward, for wisdom, for support, and thought again how she needed the serenity prayer more than ever.

"God grant me the serenity to change the things I can, to accept the things I cannot change, and to be able to tell the difference."

Or something like that. Telling the difference, that was the sticker. How did one go about knowing when to speak, when to take action, and when to shut up and accept a situation that was clearly out of one's control?

Neil had always confided in his mother, an act of confidence driving the wedge between him and his father. Clearly, Orva had harbored childish jealousy of Neil and his relationship with his mother. Was that because he felt she loved Neil more than she loved him? The need to have a serious talk with Orva overtook her. She had to talk to him, now, this evening. To stay quiet would only allow this festering wound to become even more toxic. Her way had always been to face a situation head-on, take the blows as they were hurled, and live with the consequences. This situation was the first one that left her crying weak tears in her dishwater, cowering in indecision.

Enough. She was Edna Miller, well, Schlabach now.

She washed her hair, showered, cuddled up to Orva on the sofa in the living room after the children were in bed, laying her head on his shoulder, stroking his chest and telling him that she loved him. He sighed and drew her close, answering her love with words of his own.

He buried his face in her wet hair, drew in a deep breath and said she smelled so good.

"Edna, you know you are the best thing that ever happened to me, and I love you more every day. You fulfill me in ways I didn't know were possible. You are my whole life."

Edna was quiet, allowing the words to rotate and shine, as if she was sifting through diamonds with her fingers, catching all the brilliant lights she possibly could. Everything seemed possible when she heard his declaration of love this way.

And so she launched her concern, immediately.

She felt him tense up, draw away from her. She stopped speaking, held her breath, before plowing through her fear.

"Surely you can see, Orva, like tonight on the patio. Neil needed to hear that he did something right by going up on the roof, not something wrong. He was only doing his job. He isn't one hundred percent healed, you know. Then, on top of that, perhaps you'd better not praise me when he's within hearing distance. He doesn't like me, you know, and to hear your enemy being praised is hard for all of us, especially a struggling teenager."

"You're not his enemy."

"Of course I am. He doesn't like me."

"There's a difference."

There was a moment of silence fraught with exploding emotion.

"No, Orva, you're wrong. Neil can't stand me and does anything he can to let me know. You're not aware, because I don't tell you half the stuff he says to me."

"Why don't you tell me? I'd straighten him out."

"No, you wouldn't. You're scared to death of him."

Truth, especially when spoken in an accusing tone, can have the impact of a sledgehammer, and this was exactly what Edna's words brought out in her husband.

With a sharp intake of breath, he drew away from her,

pushing her aside. He leaped to his feet, breathing hard, his hands balled into fists, his chest heaving.

"Don't, Edna, don't. Don't you ever tell me I am afraid of my own son. You know there is not an ounce of truth in that sentence. I did not marry you to come into my family and make all this trouble. We got along just fine the way we were, and I plan on keeping it that way."

With that, he stalked out of the house, into the still, hot night, leaving Edna sideways on the couch, with an impending sense of threat.

CHAPTER 20

Edna was shucking corn in the back yard, sitting on a stacking lawn chair, a wheelbarrow on one side, the garden cart on the other, a huge stainless-steel bowl at her right, and a pile of light green corn husks at her feet.

She took up another ear of corn, pried the ends loose and ripped the husks downward, then broke off the end and picked up the small vegetable brush to rid the corn of its silk.

Another broiling August day, she thought wryly, but it wasn't too bad sitting here in the shade. She eyed the wheelbarrow stacked high with deep green ears of corn, imagined it would take all day before it was cooked, cooled, creamed and cut, put in ziplock freezer bags and put in the gas chest freezer in the basement.

Now where were the girls? She'd asked them to help at least ten minutes ago, and so far, she'd not seen anything but the house and surrounding lawn and flowerbeds. Which was enough.

She'd never tire of this beautiful home. She'd always view her home as an undeserved blessing, an old maid with no prospects finding herself the wife of a desirable man, the co-owner of a house that was far beyond anything she had ever imagined. It was a joy to mow grass, plant flowers, shrubs, and order mulch to distribute among the many perennials and ornamentals, before standing back and soaking up the pleasure of her hard work. Everything, including the everyday tasks of doing laundry, sweeping and dusting, scouring bathrooms, washing windows, were labors of love.

Not that the house and its duties came with no strings attached, she reminded herself, as the craziness of the previous evening horned in on her thoughts. It had been the worst of their bad times, as always with Neil in the center.

But Orva was afraid of his son, and Neil knew it. That was the number one reason Neil spoke to her with no respect for her feelings.

He could lord it over his passive father, so she was lumped in the same category, an annoying parent who knew nothing about anything, who bumbled through life having the unlicensed right to put an unwrapped, overripe banana in his lunch, and he had every right to tell her so.

Searing anger shot through her. She should stand up to Neil, bark and yell like a trooper, deliciously telling him everything he needed to know. She daydreamed about the words she would say, then resigned herself to the fact that it would never make a difference, the way she'd botched everything last night.

Oh, Orva was mad. Was still angry with her, as far as she could tell. They'd kept each side of the bed warm, with a sizable area in the middle that neither one had touched. She'd considered apologizing, then scrapped that idea, justifying her confrontation with the thought of having merely told him the truth, and if it was hard to digest, well, then he'd have to get over it.

She had not cried one tear. She was too angry at both of them, acting like spoiled children. She shucked corn harder and faster than necessary, wondered if all married couples had times like this.

She knew Chip and Fannie did, but that was no mystery, for sure. Fannie loved to boss Chip around, always thinking she knew best in every situation, and Chip was not the kind to let his wife walk all over him. So they had frequent bouts of arguing, sinking into their specific silences, until they made up and got along wonderfully until the next round.

Harley and Sadie were more level, but that, no doubt, was on account of Sadie being meek and quiet, an almost perfect helpmeet.

Yes, Edna had seen plenty in her years as a *maud*, her mood receptor honed to a fine instrument. But did those couples ever become as upset as Orva had been last evening?

Well, she'd have corn on the cob for supper, steak on the grill. Butter him up a little, see what happened. If it weren't so hot, she'd make butterscotch pie, but it was too uncomfortably humid to think of eating that sweet dessert.

No watermelon; knowing these men, they'd start up the endless round of praise and put-downs again.

Now where were those girls?

"Marie! Emmylou?" she yelled.

No answer.

Annoyed, she got up, shook the corn silk from her skirt and hurried into the house, sliding the screened patio door harder than she should have. She sniffed. Something was burning. Bacon or ham.

The kitchen was blue with smoke, a blackened pan set on the countertop, greasy, rumpled paper towels thrown across the table, empty plates with the residue of blackened bacon and crusts of toast.

She pressed her lips together in a thin line, calling out grimly, "Marie!"

A thin reply wafted down the stairs.

"Get down here. Now!"

Two frightened faces appeared on the oak stair railing.

"What were you doing in the kitchen?

"Making breakfast."

"But there's lots of smoke, Marie. You burned the bacon.

You are not allowed to make bacon without me, O.K.? Now get down here and clean up. You can wash your dishes."

With that, Edna stamped back to the kitchen, lifted the pan to find a black ring on the granite countertop, just as she'd feared.

Orva had told her about the high-quality countertop, and it was not meant to hold very hot pans.

Oh my. Now what? In the mood he was in already, this would certainly cement his displeasure.

"Look what you did."

She showed the darkened circle accusingly, watching their faces intently.

Marie's eyes opened wide. Emmylou peered over the countertop and gasped.

"What happened?" she asked.

"You set the hot pan on the granite countertop. You can't do that. You could have had a bowl of cereal if I was busy with corn."

Marie stepped back. For an instant, Edna thought her face would crumple, and she'd cry. Instead, her eyes fell to half-mast, her lip curled, and she spat out the words, "You can't boss me around. You're not my mother."

Her face turned red, and her voice rose until she shrieked the word "mother." Emmylou began to cry, quietly.

Edna grasped Marie's forearm in her hand, shook her gently and said, "I am your stepmother, Marie, and I expect you to listen to me. You know better than to fry bacon without my help. Now you clean up this mess, and we'll have to show the ruined countertop to your father."

"He won't care."

"We'll see. After you're finished, come help me with the corn, the way you were supposed to in the first place."

"I hate doing corn."

Edna wanted to slap her, standing in this smoky kitchen that already felt as if it was approaching ninety degrees. Her shoulders ached from the corn picking, her foul mood enhanced by the atrocity of the previous evening. Would anything ever be right again?

Was this union with Orva destined to be riddled with ill feelings and wrong moves?

God grant me the serenity . . .

To accept the things I cannot change . . .

Well, she wasn't about to accept Marie's cheekiness. That little girl thought entirely too much of herself, same as Neil, and if she didn't nip this in the bud now, she would never accomplish any form of discipline.

Emmylou was different, too young to know her sister was being too bold.

Grosfeelich. Marie's attitude was plain *grosfeelich.* She'd had the upper hand with those pictures, and here she was a gain, expecting Edna to accept everything she wanted to do. She thought of the sympathy she'd felt for the poor motherless girls, the love she felt sure would come easily, the showers of blessings that would follow.

So what was going wrong so soon? Was this a pattern that would be drawn up month after month, year after year, until it pried her and Orva apart? The thought was despicable, sickening. She couldn't let this happen. She had to control the children in a loving way, but she'd need Orva's support, wouldn't she? Wasn't that the way decent, loving families operated, like a smooth, well-oiled machine that was maintained on a regular basis?

The temperature climbed steadily until late in the afternoon when the thermometer on the north side of the house registered only a shade below 100 degrees. Edna's thin dress stuck to her back and armpits, and the outdoor cooker boiled and steamed as she cooked the yellow ears of corn, then plunged them in the cold water. The Rubbermaid totes were filled and running over, with the garden hose draped over them with a steady stream of water coming from the nozzle. Marie and Emmylou were soaking wet, generously allowing the ice-cold water to spray wherever they wanted, laughing uproariously, the morning's incident forgotten, eating corn and talking to Edna about little girls' thoughts and events.

By the time Orva and Neil came home, Edna had everything cleaned up. The last quart bag had been taken down the steps to the freezer, and she was turning on the grill to prepare steak, while the corn bubbled away on the stovetop.

She felt her heart racing. Would he still be angry?

She occupied herself, busily scraping residue from the grill racks with a wire brush, her back turned. She straightened, stood to face him and welcome him home, but stopped, her mouth open in disbelief when he let himself into the house without acknowledging her presence.

So it was worse than she thought.

Heartsick, her hands trembling now, she finished cleaning the racks, the strength draining from her arms. She vowed never, ever, to confront Orva about Neil again, and bit her lips to stop the tears from pricking her eyelids.

She jumped when she felt Orva behind her.

"Edna, I'm sorry."

Gently he turned her, and gently he took her in his strong arms. She shook with the force of her sobs. He stroked her back, murmured endearments, told her it was all his fault, not hers. She clung to him and said she was the one who should have kept her mouth closed.

Marie found them in a close embrace, laughing, with Edna wiping her streaming eyes and her face red with the heat and the force of her crying. Marie stepped away, around the corner of the house to run on bare feet to her rabbit hutches, opened the door, took out a bunny, and held it in her lap.

The steaks were tender on the inside, crispy on the outside, just the way Orva and Neil liked them. The sliced tomatoes were perfect, laying on a bed of mayonnaise atop fresh home-made bread, the corn steaming with a river of melted butter glistening like liquid gold.

Edna and Orva chatted about everything, their gazes holding and locking, their smiles wide and frequent. Neil said his knee buckled under him on the job, and Orva took on a look of concern, asking him if he wouldn't need to have a doctor look at that leg.

Neil nodded, said gruffly, "Maybe I should."

Orva asked Edna if she'd mind calling his orthopedic surgeon, seeing if she could get him in as soon as possible, and Edna was lifted to the heights of euphoria, thinking how clearly the Lord had heard her pleas for help.

To change the things I can't accept . . .

That was the evening that Neil carried his own plate through the screen door, into the kitchen, and lingered at the sink for a self-conscious moment before saying gruffly, "The steak was really good, Edna."

She turned to face him, but he was walking away, so she said, "Thanks, Neil." He didn't answer. He'd called her Edna, not Mam, but that was O.K. Perfectly alright. He had spoken to her all by himself, given her a compliment.

Was there no ceiling for joy and gratitude?

Orva found the blackened countertop later that evening, lifted questioning eyes to Edna. Without missing a beat, Edna explained about Marie and the bacon, saying she should not have been as frantic about getting the corn done all in one day.

Orva frowned, ran his fingertips across the ruined surface.

"I'll have Marlin Yoder come look at it. He's the one who installed the cabinets. Marie shouldn't have been frying bacon. I'll talk to her."

"I did. But it would be best if you talked to her as well. Sometimes I just upset her more."

"Why don't we both talk to her?"

Edna was doubtful but accompanied him to the rabbit hutches, where Emmylou was holding two white rabbits while Marie cleaned the hutch with a short-handled hoe, taking out the wisps of hay and droppings.

Emmylou handed over two bunnies, her eyes shining. Marie stopped scraping, straightened, her eyes clouded with suspicion.

"Hey. Marie. Good job." Orva said, smiling at her.

"I do it often, you know."

"Good. That's good. Marie, I saw the ruined countertop, O.K.?"

She nodded, all defiance and little-girl bluster.

"I don't want you frying bacon again, without Mam's help, O.K.?"

"My mam is dead."

Orva recoiled, his eyes wide.

"Marie! You should not say that to Edna."

"She's not my mam."

This was Orva's first encounter with Marie's hardened attitude, and Edna could tell he was reeling in the face of it.

"Marie, she is your mam because I married her."

"She's not going to boss me around, though."

Orva nodded toward the house, gave Edna a small shove, and said softly, "Take Emmylou."

Edna walked along the flagstone sidewalk, with Emmylou skipping behind her. When Edna sank into a patio chair, Emmylou climbed up on her lap, laid her head on her shoulder, and said it wasn't her that didn't want a hug at night, it was Marie, who was being a brat.

Edna held her close and said Marie was simply having a hard time accepting her as a new mother. It was a long time before Emmylou answered, but when she did it was the most memorable little speech Edna had ever heard.

"Well, my mam is in Heaven, you know. She was awful

skinny and it hurt everywhere in her body. Now she's an angel, and she sings up there with Jesus every day. It's better now. I miss her, but you're here, and you help us a lot."

She sighed. "Plus, Dat likes you, I think."

Oh, he does, he does. Edna's heart sang as she sat on the patio and felt the cool of the evening creep across her feet and legs.

Summer gave way to the cooling breezes of October. The leaves on the maple tree turned to a blinding shade of gold, the smaller maple at the edge of the lawn to an orangey red so brilliant it appeared to be fiery.

Edna was cleaning house. *House-butza.* The twice-yearly deep cleaning that most women who were raised in Amish homes adhered to, the tradition handed down for generations, the roots in Switzerland where the forefathers lived their scrupulous lives on well-kept farms, working from dawn to dusk.

Although it was rare for the modern *hausfrau* to lug buckets of hot, soapy water up the attic stairs to get down on her hands and knees to scrub the wide planks of the attic floor. Some of the old cleaning practices were no longer viewed as necessary and were replaced by common sense.

She did start in the attic, however, and planned on working her way down. She had garbage bags, broom, brush and dustpan, Windex and paper towels for the windows.

She shivered as she mounted the attic steps. She should have started this job on a warm day but thought once she got going, the exercise would keep her warm enough. She had only been in her attic a few times, so she never took the time to assess the boxes and broken pieces of furniture.

She groaned when she saw the accumulation of dead flies and upturned stinkbugs, the silvery flash of silverfish that were very much alive—despicable little things. If you saw one of those little critters, there were hundreds, probably thousands more in every available hiding place. She may as well give in immediately and write "foggers" on her store list.

She stood on top of the attic steps and surveyed the jumble with eyebrows drawn, mouth taut. By all appearances, no one had ever organized seriously, the way cardboard boxes, broken chairs, and plastic bags were scattered about. She decided she'd start at the far corner and work her way over. This would take up most of her day, so there would be no bread baking and likely vegetable soup for supper.

What a mess.

It didn't take long to realize there was enough old furniture here to fill another house. She opened and closed dresser drawers, dusted, wiped, then pushed, pulled, and yanked until she had a semblance of order.

She was beginning to enjoy this, as she viewed the clean, orderly corner she'd already accomplished. But she couldn't help wondering why Sarah never cleaned her attic. This dusty jumble was more than a few years of neglect.

No one had been up here for a very long time, likely as long as the house was here. Well, who knew? It was certainly none of her business, so she wouldn't ponder too much.

The top of the cedar chest was warped, and the varnish was peeling as if the heat in the attic had damaged the smooth finish. It was not an old cedar chest, but one a local Amish furniture builder had designed.

That was strange. Why wasn't this beautiful chest in the guest room, the way all cedar chests were, containing lovely hand-stitched quilts or hooked rugs, all items handed to young brides from her family?

She tried lifting the lid but found it to be impossible.

Locked.

Hmm. Curious now, Edna ran her hands over the entire surface of the chest. Nothing. She stood looking down at it, contemplating her options. She should walk away, let it be. *Don't waste time on this*, she thought. But still.

She got down on her hands and knees, reached up under it with her fingers, searching for a bump, a key taped to the underside. People hid keys all the time, and often in an area close to the locked door.

A bump in the far right corner.

Aha.

A piece of tape, with, yes, the smooth head of a key.

Should she open this?

She was married to Orva, and this was her house, his belongings were her belongings. Wither thou goest and all that. Even their God was the same, so yes, she had every right to open the chest.

It wasn't hard to pick the end of the tape loose or to extract the key, a plain silver one that fit in the slot like magic. Edna turned it to the right, felt the welcome click of the lock, and easily lifted the lid.

She held the battery light over the contents, her brow lined with perplexity. Baby things.

She reached down to stroke a small blue quilt. So soft. She lifted the corner, to find more soft baby shawls, receiving blankets, and a small box filled with sleepers and onesies, all in shades of blue or white.

Baby boy items.

Edna wondered why the chest contained these items that had obviously been Neil's, with nothing pertaining to the girls. She dug deeper, searching for anything pink, little dresses or nighties, but there was nothing.

On the opposite side of the chest, there was another box, a decorative box with navy blue and white artwork with a gold clasp. Gingerly, Edna lifted it, slowly opened the lid to find hundreds of photographs.

Obviously Neil, but who was the English girl holding him?

She peered closely, then picked up another one.

Her again. With Neil.

Edna thought it must have been his babysitter, or perhaps an aunt who had left the Amish faith. She shuffled through more pictures.

Neil as an infant. Neil being held. Always by this same girl. She was so young. She couldn't have been more than seventeen or eighteen at the most, perhaps even sixteen.

Puzzled now, she riffled faster, picking up and laying down picture after picture. She finally concluded the photographs stopped after the baby—was it even Neil for sure?—was three or four.

Walking. Riding a trike.

Slowly, she closed the lid on the box, laid it back on top of the other baby items. She picked up a pair of tiny white sneakers, little overalls, and striped T-shirts—a little English boy's clothes.

She had only met Sarah twice, then at the last stages of her cancer, the disease that left the body shrunken to near weightlessness.

Surely this pretty girl without a trace of plain clothing could not be Sarah. She couldn't think that.

Determined to find out what exactly had occurred here, she set out a few items, dug to the bottom of the chest, searching for answers.

At the far left corner, standing upright, a packet of letters tied with a blue ribbon, which Edna thought must be the baby cards she had received.

Tentatively, she lifted them out, noticed immediately they were not cards, but plain white envelopes addressed to Sarah Miller.

Edna gasped. Haverstock, Maine.

Oh, my goodness.

She glanced over her shoulder, guilty now, as if Orva had come home from work early and found her digging around in his first wife's past. Or Neil. Neil would never speak to her again.

Should she read the contents of the letters? It would solve everything. She surely couldn't turn back now, having come this far. She found her hands were shaking now, and she felt hot, then chilled.

Slowly, she pulled the top white envelope from the stack, unfolded the lined tablet paper, and began to read.

"Dearest Sarah,

"Greetings of Christian love in the name of Jesus. Every day, you are in my heart and mind. Every day. I want to write a letter to you, let you know we will never rest till you come home with your dear little boy."

So it was her, Sarah. The thought stuck her with force. Orva was not Neil's father. Sarah had Neil with someone else, left the Amish faith because of her shame. Or was it shame? Had she followed Neil's father to Maine, only to be rejected by him?

Children being born out of wedlock was uncommon among the Amish, but it did happen, and when it did, the couple or the single girl were accepted with love and sympathy. There was support carried in Christian love that rode on the winds of forgiveness. Although the stigma of shame and humility was attached as well, a mark that sent the girl from an innocent young maiden into the circle of the married woman, no matter her age.

Had the Amish way been too much for the shy Sarah to bear? And who was Neil's father? There was not one photograph of any young man.

Edna read on.

"We miss you every day and pray on. You know what is right, Sarah dear, so we will pound on the gates of mercy till you return.

"I'm so afraid you are suffering financially since Shawn left."

Edna drew in a deep breath.

Shawn. An English youth. Or man.

But why wasn't his picture taken with Sarah and Neil?

Edna steadied herself with a deep breath. She sat back on her heels, then sat down, stretched her legs out and leaned back against the chest, her thoughts rampant. She was definitely intruding, sticking her nose into a situation from the past, one that was buried, forgiven, laid to rest.

But the fruit of Sarah's disobedience lived on.

Neil. Ach my, Neil.

And there awoke in Edna a fierce love for this handsome, hurting, troubled adolescent. God had put Neil on this earth for a reason, and what other reason but to be accepted and loved the same as everyone else, no matter the circumstances of his birth? He could not help being born.

Did he know Orva wasn't his father? But he resembled him somewhat. She had noticed the width of his shoulders, the build so like Orva's, but was that only a coincidence?

Now what?

Should she tell Orva? Approach Neil?

She knew immediately the latter would be much the same as stumbling on a land mine, with an instantaneous eruption. But Orva would be different.

He would be willing to share this information of the past, surely.

CHAPTER 21

DAYS WENT BY WITH EDNA IN TURMOIL. ORVA CAME HOME FROM work, happy, talking about his day, teasing the girls as if his whole world was centered, stabilized, and he was the recipient of one glorious day after another.

Neil was his usual sullen self but had actually progressed to the mature decision to sit at the supper table and eat with the family. In spite of separating himself by his silences, Edna took it as a small step toward acceptance.

So why blow everything by mentioning the cedar chest in the attic?

It was in the past, forgiven, forgotten. But thoughts swirled.

Did Neil know? How much had Sarah told him?

She found herself watching Neil's face for signs of . . . of what?

She wasn't sure. A clue, perhaps.

The first cold, windy day in October, when Edna watched the bare limbs of the maple trees slashing the sullen, scudding clouds, she wondered to herself how they could be putting siding on any building. As all wives of builders do, she worried that someone would get hurt, or take risks, causing an accident.

Marie and Emmylou slammed the door in the laundry room, shucked their coats and scarves, kicked off their shoes, and came into the kitchen, where Edna was coating chicken pieces with a mixture of cornmeal, flour, and spices, her own special coating for fried chicken.

Breathing in and out with exaggeration, their cheeks red from the wind, they threw their lunchboxes and book bags on the counter.

"It is cold!" Emmylou breathed.

"It is going to snow!" Marie shouted.

Edna smiled. "Oh, come on. It's not Thanksgiving yet. It won't snow yet."

Marie gave her that special look that meant she was in error. "But you don't know."

Edna laughed. "No, I don't. You're right."

"You don't know a lot of things."

The sadness weighed heavily, then, like a wet blanket. With Marie, there was always the disrespect, the pushing of boundaries, testing Edna to see how far she could go before being scolded or reminded of her disrespect.

To find the proper level of love and discipline was like balancing on a beam. Too far to the left, and you lost everything. Too far to the right, and ditto, the same result.

What had changed?

They had wanted her, begged her to be their mother. Evidently, being a *maud* and mother were polar opposites, which left Edna trying to decipher every motive, every lack of respect or hidden slur. If these girls were her own, she would administer some good old-fashioned discipline in short order, and wasn't sure it would not come to that, yet. Children needed boundaries. They needed rules, which was a sort of safety net for their well-being. Oh, she'd seen plenty in her days as a *maud*. Timid mothers who tried to please their children to earn their respect merely allowed them to have the upper hand, with the result a total lack of honor. Or caring.

The same with passive fathers, who turned a blind eye while the children followed their own way.

Edna sighed.

It was all uncharted, or was it?

Hadn't she learned by experience? Nothing had ever taken away so much of her self-confidence as being a stepmother to children who made no secret of their disapproval of her.

If only she could approach Orva with all her fears and insecurities where the children were concerned. He was a kind and loving husband in every aspect, but could not seem to understand Edna's struggle with the children.

His children were doing O.K. What was she complaining about?

And so Edna went to him less and less, knowing what the outcome would be.

A shot of irritation.

She turned to Marie.

"You know, Marie, I know a lot of things. I know a little girl who needs to stop being unkind to her mother."

"You're not my mother."

"I am your mother. Your own mother is in Heaven, and I am here. Your father married me, we all live together in the same house, so I expect you to listen to me and stop being so mouthy. Go hang up your coat and put your shoes on the rug. After that, you need to feed your bunnies. I saw their water dish was empty this morning."

Marie's eyes narrowed. She opened her mouth, then closed it again. Turning on her heel, she motioned to Emmylou, who sat at the table with a pile of mini pretzels and ranch dip, methodically swirling them through the dip one at a time before popping them into her mouth.

"Wait," she said.

"Hurry up."

Edna said nothing, merely watched as Emmylou popped the last pretzel into her mouth before following Marie into the laundry room.

Edna peeled potatoes and watched the tree branches lash back and forth, like her own restless thoughts. Brown leaves swirled across the lawn and skidded across the macadam drive-way into the corner of the shop, where a good-sized pile had already accumulated. The trees bent and swayed, the wind toss-ing the top branches into a wild dance. Birds dipped and soared, with their wings held out to catch the main current or beating frantically to gain momentum.

She heard an unsettling crash on the front porch, hurried to find one of the wooden porch rockers blown end over end. The wind tore at the storm door, lashed her skirt to her legs, tugged at her covering strings as she bent to set the rocker upright.

Glad to be back in the cozy kitchen, she wondered if the men would not be home early on a day like this. Surely it wasn't safe to work outside. As if in reassurance, the black pickup truck slowed, turned, drove up to the shop, and disgorged Orva and Neil before making its way back to the road.

Orva disappeared into his office, but Neil hurried through the wind, into the kitchen, slammed his lunch and thermos on the counter before saying to no one in particular, "I hate him!"

Shocked, Edna turned, her eyes wide.

"Don't look at me like that. He's crazy. No way should we have been on the job. But you can't tell him."

"But, Neil, he's your father. He knows best."

"He thinks he does."

Then he burst out, "And he's not my father."

The blood drained from Edna's face. She gripped the edge of the kitchen table for support. She could not meet Neil's fiery gaze.

"He's not, you know. Obviously. I don't *have* a father."

With that, he turned and left the kitchen, stomped up the stairs, clopped down the hallway, and slammed the door, hard.

Edna didn't take time to think. She took the steps lightly, tapped on his door without expecting an answer, and said,

"Neil, you do have a father. God is your father. He spared your life, so be thankful."

"Yes, right."

The sarcastic answer was a blow to Edna's confidence, but she let it go at that. No sense in pushing unwanted words on an unwilling recipient, so she padded away, moved softly down the stairs. She opened a package of frozen corn, placed it in a saucepan, and added butter and salt before setting it on a back burner. She had harvested, shucked, cut, and frozen this corn, so it was immensely satisfying to cook this pot of her hard-earned bounty. She wondered if the sweet dill pickles were good. Or the mixed pickle. She headed to the basement for a jar of each.

All the everyday, ordinary tasks helped to keep her thoughts centered, to keep her calm in the face of all she had experienced throughout the day. She didn't allow herself to dwell on any of it as she greeted Orva when he came into the kitchen, putting her arms around his solid waist as he bent to kiss her.

He smelled of cold air and aluminum, of lumber and electric tools and the faint smell of mud.

"How was your day?" he asked, stepping back to search her eyes.

"Good."

Bright and cheery. An expert at hiding her true feelings. But it was time to say something, to test the waters. She took a breath and gathered her courage.

"So, a few days ago I was in the attic. Housecleaning."

He stepped back, his face registering surprise.

"You were in the attic?"

"Yes. Is there something wrong with that?"

He shook his head as if to clear it. "No, no. It's alright, of course. I'm sure it was quite a job. Sarah didn't clean the attic, said it was not her responsibility, something I never understood. I thought perhaps in her home the men actually did keep the attic clean and organized, so I never bothered myself about it."

He sniffed. "Something smells really good."

Edna smiled. "Fried chicken."

She mashed the potatoes and made gravy from the pan drippings, while he washed and scanned the daily paper, shook his head at the latest goings-on in Syria, holding the paper on his lap like a blanket as he spoke of his outrage to Edna.

She smiled. She was a married woman. A wife. A confidante. Someone needed her, asked for her opinion, and wanted her. She was a helpmeet to Orva. She stood beside him, walked beside him, was enveloped and cocooned in his love. She was so secure in her belonging. All her years of being single could never compare to this love between them, in spite of its flaws. At times like this, his inability to deal with the children in the way she thought was proper paled in comparison to the burning light of her love, carried like the Olympic torch.

She called Neil to supper, but there was no response.

She questioned Orva, who shrugged his shoulders, said let him go. He'd been a bear all day.

Edna bit back the anxious words, poured the water into the water glasses, and sat down, waiting on Orva to bow his head, the signal for hands to be folded beneath the table and heads bowed in silent prayer.

Emmylou spoke immediately when the prayer was finished.

"Marie was not looking at her plate."

"I was, too," Maria said sharply, glaring at her.

"Huh-uh!"

Orva didn't seem to hear this exchange; he merely helped himself to an enormous portion of mashed potatoes, reached for the platter of chicken.

"Dat. Marie wasn't putting patties down," Emmylou said.

"I was!" Marie insisted.

"Putting patties down" was the children's version of praying before a meal, a common expression among Amish all over the United States. It was just that, putting children's hands below the table, bowing heads. One-year-olds in high chairs learned to put patties down, often asserting themselves by raising dimpled little fingers on to their tray before their father raised his, resulting in a sideways glance and a light tap from the mother.

"What? What's wrong?" Orva sked.

"Marie wasn't putting patties down right. She was looking out the window. I saw her."

"How do you know, Emmylou? You weren't bowing your head, either?" Orva asked, a twinkle in his light eyes.

A smirk from Marie, a knowing nod of righteousness.

"Emmylou, you need gravy?" Edna asked, watching her face with kindness.

She was always the one everyone else seemed to take advantage of, the smallest, the one who was easy to boss around. Marie had a streak of unkindness where Emmylou was concerned, and the situation was not getting better.

Emmylou nodded, dipped the back of her spoon to make a hole in her mashed potatoes.

"There you go, Emmylou."

Edna smiled kindly into the questioning eyes.

She had seen plenty of children with bad table manners, the parents far too preoccupied to notice the licking of table knives, the lunges across other plates to reach bowls of food instead of asking, leaving vegetables and potatoes uneaten and helping themselves to dessert.

But she had never seen a teenaged boy sequestered in his room whenever something didn't suit him. It still bothered Edna, the way it always had.

"So what happened at work? Neil was pretty upset when he came home."

"That's only normal. He's always mad at work."

"But isn't there something you could do?"

"I can't stop the wind."

"No, I didn't mean it that way. I mean, can't you talk to Neil, sort of talk him out of his bad mood?"

"We don't talk at work."

Edna sighed. How hopeless. It seemed only days since Orva had stood crying beside Neil's bed, and her hopes had been elevated, sure things would change, and here they were, worse than ever. To fix a sour relationship between a father and a son was apparently in the same category as hundreds of other impossibilities. You just had to keep your opinion to yourself, stay quiet, and accept it for what it was.

Especially now, since the discovery in the attic.

"Wasn't the work dangerous today, though?" she asked.

"We were actually finishing up a job. Mostly trim, so it wasn't too bad. Neil had the hardest job. He was up on a ladder."

"Are you sure that was a good idea with his leg?"

"Doesn't hurt him. Makes a man out of him."

Edna struggled through the days of autumn. She loved Orva the husband but did not understand Orva the father. He was absent so often, and at home he was stuck in his office, doing bookwork, and running his lucrative siding business. Always, there was plenty of money. Money to buy groceries, to purchase shoes and clothes, necessities for the house, and to pay drivers she hired to take her to see her parents. If she saw a new piece of artwork, an area rug, a large houseplant for the living room, or anything she would have walked away from before she was married to Orva, she bought now, without hesitation. He always approved of her purchases, put money into her account, told her she deserved it.

So she figured her blessings outweighed the times of trouble, nothing on earth was perfect, and took it for what it was. A mixture.

Whenever she was alone with Orva, she wanted to bring up the subject of the cedar chest, of Neil and Sarah, but could not find the courage to begin. Neil knew Orva was not his father, so what else was there to say?

She asked her parents if they had heard anything about Neil's first wife when she was young, told them about the cedar chest in the attic.

They were seated around the old oilcloth-covered kitchen table, Trixie eyeing her with no less affection than she ever did. Flies stuck to the used, sticky flytrap above their heads, and the old, worn turntable in the table's middle containing dozens of bottles of vitamins, prescription pills from the favorite druggist, the soiled sugar bowl, and a trail of sugar going from it to her father's coffee cup.

But it was warm, the cold November air kept at bay by the propane gas heater, the kitchen with its odors of fried mush and piecrust and high cholesterol.

Edna laughed outright, all by herself.

"What?" her mother asked, smiling.

"Oh. I was thinking how your kitchen always smells so good, like high cholesterol. You know, piecrust and fried mush."

Her mother laughed along with Edna, her round stomach shaking. She pointed to the pills on the turntable.

"That's what those are for."

Her father drank his coffee, scowling.

"Now, Edna, I thought sure you'd stop shaming us when you visited as a married woman. You're just nicer about it."

"I'm not shaming you, Dat. If you want to continue eating the old-fashioned way, then that's fine with me. Lard and fried mush and apple pie with lard in the crust . . ."

"Now you just hang on there, young lady," her mother said, shaking a finger. "I'm no dummy. I read an article on animal fats, and it wasn't all bad. In moderation, lard is better than Crisco."

"Oh, come on, Mam."

"I read it, Edna. In the *Reader's Digest*, I think it was."

Edna lifted her eyebrows.

"I don't use it for my piecrusts."

"But Orva has never tasted mine."

Edna's eyes sparkled. "I'll tell you what, Mam. I'll do Thanksgiving dinner at my house this year. You bring the pumpkin pie, and we'll see what Orva says."

"We'll do it!" her mother exclaimed, already excited about making her pies.

She grew neck pumpkins, peeled them, and cooked them on the stove, then mashed the pulp and cold packed it in jars, lined them on shelves downstairs in the basement. Her pies were custardy, rich with milk and eggs and spices, pies she was convinced were unbeatable.

"Sounds like a plan. The boys can get a driver and take us along. It's too far to drive old Dob," her father said, grinning.

The conversation turned back to Neil's birth and the objects in the attic. But her parents clearly had no remembrance of any of it, which convinced Edna that Sarah's family had not been from Indiana, but an Amish settlement in another state.

Her father said he couldn't remember Orva's marriage to Sarah, either, but then, it was understandable, given the size of the community.

Her mother thought it was strange that she still hadn't confided in Orva, but Edna shook her head.

"He'll think I was snooping."

"Which you were," her mother said shortly.

Edna cast her mother a look. "You're really full of yourself today."

Her mother socked a fist into an open palm.

"Feeling my oats," she said, laughing at her own joke.

"That's what lard does to you," her father said, finding his own joke absolutely hilarious.

"You two!" Edna said, shaking her head.

But she knew how good it was to be home. Home, where

you were accepted exactly the way you were, with no put-on, no airs, nothing.

You were loved, in spite of being imperfect: warts and all.

Jiggling hips and newly sprouted pimples or gray hair, uneven skirts or shoes that didn't look right didn't matter. You could be sassy or grouchy or burst into song, and it was all the same to them. You were Edna, their daughter, and daughters were held close to the heart. Always.

"So how're the girls?"

Edna frowned. "Marie is having serious problems at school. She's always been slow, but I don't know if she'll be able to complete fourth grade. Her teacher wants her to have a tutor three evenings a week, which I don't think will do any good, but I'll go along with whatever Orva thinks. Or the teacher."

"You will have to."

Edna smiled. "I am learning. I'm a married woman."

The tutor was a shy young girl dressed in a pale pink dress, her blond hair like spun gold, and her complexion the color of a faded yellow rose.

Completely smitten with Marie and Emmylou, she barely noticed Edna after a polite greeting, and settled into the living room around the folding table and proceeded with arithmetic, the hardest of Marie's subjects.

Her soft voice was punctuated by laughs, little bursts of sound that were followed by Marie's giggles and Emmylou's raucous snorts. Edna watched, enchanted, from the doorway, then turned away to complete her ironing.

She heard Neil come down the stairs, on his way out the door when his friend came to pick him up. But she also heard him pause at the living room door, only for a moment. Edna caught the quick glance, the second sidelong look, before he hurried out through the laundry room, slamming the door with much more force than was absolutely necessary.

The tutor stayed until eight, then had a driver pick her up. Edna walked out with her to pay the driver, intrigued by this wisp of a girl who was so ill at ease around adults, but perfectly confident with children.

Her name was Carla. Carla Yoder. Edna knew her Uncle Daniel and Aunt Linda but was not acquainted with her immediate family.

She would be back Thursday, she said.

Orva said he was glad Marie was getting the extra help she needed. Then stuck his head behind his daily paper and continued with his reading.

Edna put the girls to bed and listened to Marie's complaints about having a tutor.

"But you seemed to enjoy her. She was laughing, and so were you. And Emmylou."

Emmylou nodded, giggling.

"I was not laughing," Marie insisted, the customary pout put into place.

"Alright," Edna agreed.

With that, Marie seemed satisfied to have the upper hand, to have put Edna back into the place she belonged. But Edna was learning how important it was to Marie, that she stayed one step behind her, and things went smoothly. Needing to be in control of any given situation was perhaps the result of having been thrust into the pain and fear of her mother's passing at such a young age. At any rate, Edna was learning about stepping back, letting go.

Tonight, however, she had a plan for Orva and that newspaper. She smiled to herself, then put the plan into action.

Neil strolled nonchalantly into the kitchen where Edna was washing dishes and leaned against the counter with his arms crossed, one foot slung over the other. He had kicked his sneakers into a corner of the laundry room, and his white crew socks seemed almost endearing, like a schoolboy's.

He went to the pantry when no one acknowledged his presence, brought out the chocolate cake and cut a huge square, placed it in a cereal dish, and poured milk over it. The piece he put in his mouth was so big he had to angle it sideways to get it in, and then chewed like a chipmunk with both cheeks full.

Edna shook her head.

"What?"

"You have all evening to finish the cake."

"It's better this way."

Edna smiled. She wished he would meet her eyes, smile back, but she had to be content with a dip of his head and another load of chocolate cake going into his mouth.

When he came up for air, he looked at Marie.

"Who's your girl?"

"What girl?"

"That girl that was here."

"You mean Carla?"

"Who is she?"

"I don't know. Carla. She's my tutor."

Emmylou looked up from her coloring book.

"Her name is Carla Yoder. Marie can't do arithmetic, so she's helping."

Edna told him her parents' names, from over around Nappanee.

Neil acted as if he hadn't heard a word she said, so she left it at that. For him to be hanging out in the kitchen with her was miraculous enough, so if he chose to ignore her, it was fine with her.

She cast him a glance of appraisal. He was no longer the skinny lank-haired adolescent she had met before she married Orva. He was developing into a tall young man, widening in the chest and shoulders, his hair cut short, with well-shaped eyebrows. If the hooded eyes and perpetual pout were replaced with an open, happy expression, he would be quite a good-looking young man.

She found herself vouching for him, hoping he would be able to rise above everything God had handed him from the moment of his birth to the loss of his mother, and now, the acceptance of stepmother. Adding to that, there was the accident that had scarred him, the peer pressure of the company he kept, and working with a father he could barely tolerate.

It was a full load for one so young.

Neil needed a change of heart. A spiritual awakening with Christ knocking on the door of his conscience. Perhaps she was barred from his confidence, but she could pray. She could beg God to spare him the way Hannah had carried on in the temple, begging God to give her a son.

Since she'd found the origin of his birth in the chest in the attic, she felt a deep connection to this motherless young man, with a father he might never meet. He'd been forced to accept Orva as a stand-in, and now her to take the place of his beloved Mam.

Well, she would do her best. A visit to the kitchen was a giant step in the right direction. The chocolate cake disappearing at that speed was nothing short of astounding.

CHAPTER 22

SOMETHING WAS MISSING IN HER RELATIONSHIP WITH ORVA, EDNA decided. She no longer felt as close to him, not wanted to tell him everything, feeling free to express herself on every subject she chose, or anything that worried her.

It was Neil, that chest in the attic. It was Orva's disapproval of him and the fact that he was unwilling or unable to talk to him. All of the inappropriate connections snowballed in Edna's mind until she could think of nothing else.

It was time to talk.

She waited till the children were in bed, the way she always did, then simply sat beside him on the sofa and began to talk. She told him about the chest in the attic, nervously toying with the belt on her robe.

"I was snooping, I suppose. A locked chest was simply more than I could stay away from. I hope you won't be upset."

For a long moment, Orva was silent, staring at the opposite wall with a white, stricken face. The clock on the wall ticked away the seconds, the pendulum swinging inside the glass door, catching the light as it swung from left to right.

"So now you think less of me for marrying a single mother," he ground out, his voice gravelly with emotion.

"No. I don't."

"Why did you do it?" he asked, still staring at the opposite wall.

"Orva, believe me. I had no idea. I was curious, is all it was. I know I shouldn't have done it. I'm sorry."

He shifted his weight, adjusted a pillow. Still, he would not look at her.

"No need to be sorry. It's done now."

Edna did not know how to answer to this, so she stayed silent.

Orva breathed deeply, shook his head, and began.

"Alright, Edna. We've come this far; I'll just go ahead and tell you everything. If you're willing to hear."

Now he did look at her, with a veil drawn across his normally expressive eyes.

"I am. Just tell me all of it," Edna answered, searching to find an expression of love or approval.

"It all started when I was a small boy. I guess."

Here he hesitated, leaned forward and put his head in his hands, his elbows on his knees. Edna waited, then reached out to put a hand on his shoulder, gently rubbing in a soothing motion.

"I don't know if I can tell you this."

"I'm willing to listen."

Still he would not say what was on his mind. Edna simply waited. He sat up, leaned against the back of the couch, slumped against it as if the weight of what he had to say pressed him, folded him in half.

"When I was probably seven or eight, I had an uncle who . . . Well, he did things to me. This went on for many years."

He drew in a deep breath, then leaned forward, his shoulders heaving as rough, painful sobs came from his throat.

Horrified, Edna was shocked into silence. She could not move, could not touch him or comfort him.

"It's a long story, Edna," he said softly, between sobs.

She waited again.

"My father was a workaholic. You know, the type of person

who is driven from early in the morning till late at night, so he was an absent father. I don't remember very much about him when I was growing up.

"My mother was close to this uncle, her favorite brother. So I didn't think there was anyone who would believe me or care about me, so I had to be strong enough to stand on my own two feet. I fought with every ounce of my strength and remained free. But I was never free.

"Not for one minute of my life."

Here Orva stopped. A shudder passed through him.

"The only reason I grew up to be a normal person on the outside was on account of my upbringing. You gave yourself up, and did what you had to do, and went through your days working, going to church.

"By the time I started the *rumschpringa* years I knew I was not worthy to ask any girl to be my wife. God seemed very far away, almost like an afterthought, a fierce being in the sky that would strike me to hell when I died. You know. Have you ever felt so awful about yourself that there was no mercy, no forgiveness? So if I pushed God away, He wasn't really there. It's an awful way to live, but that's what I went through for years.

"The hardest part was being with my family at Christmastime and other holidays and events. He was so friendly, so well-liked and popular, especially by my mother, so I just quit going. I turned against my own mother, hating her for . . . sometimes I don't know why. Perhaps it was the love and respect she had for my uncle. I felt as if she betrayed me. I don't know. I only know I was so messed up I couldn't live with myself or anyone that knew him.

"So I left.

"Here is where it gets hard, Edna. I don't want to tell you everything I went through those few years. But I did meet Sarah. We started seeing each other, then agreed to return to our respective homes, return to the fold, and give our hearts

and lives to God. We were married, and had a good relationship, except for Neil. I felt as if he was her first love, her special
love, and I was merely a necessity.

"Now that I'm married to you I often wonder if she loved me
at all. I think this Shawn, Shawn Bickel was his name, was her
one and only true love, and that's why she loved Neil with an
almost unreasonable love. I would often come into the house to
find her in tears, and if I tried to comfort her, ask her to share
her feelings with me, she pushed me away. She didn't like to be
held and only slept in the same bed out of her adherence to her
Christian duty.

"I did love her very much, she was my beloved wife, but after
a while, I stayed afloat on that raft of my own making, by my
own will.

"The arguments about Neil became worse, and this is to
my shame, until I could hardly stand him sometimes, he was so
spoiled.

"Part of me pardons Sarah completely. Can we really help
who we are and who we loved with all our heart? It wasn't me,
that's for sure.

"When she became sick, I saw the willingness to give herself
up, the patience and . . . you know, Edna, if I think back, it was
almost as if she harbored a certain joy to think of leaving this
earth. She was not happy so much of the time. You know how
they say people with cancer fight the disease? They're battling
cancer?"

He looked at Edna, to affirm his statement, and ask her to
understand.

She nodded, afraid to break his chain of speech.

"She never fought. Wasn't interested in treatments."

He shook his head as if to clear it of debris.

"You know, to tell you this brings an even clearer picture to
me. It was probably worse than I knew, her desperate unhappiness, her refusal to see a doctor, just everything. I realize all

of this much more now since I'm married to you, to a normal woman like you."

Edna refused to meet Orva's eyes and felt herself blushing.

He reached for her, drew her close. She wrapped her arms around him, laid her head on his chest and sighed.

"It only makes me love you more, Orva. But there is one question. How are you as well-adjusted as you are? I mean, children are often damaged for life, and you don't seem to be, other than being absentminded, you know, sort of like you're in another world at times."

"I'll tell you how. It is only through the healing power of Christ that I have come this far. If we're sick enough, despairing of our own strength, He steps in, and it's amazing how He can take over our life when the bad feelings torment a person. I guess you realize, though, that I don't have much to do with my own family."

"I did realize that."

"It's just better that way."

Edna's thoughts raced. She wanted to ask a hundred questions but knew it was a part of his past that was best left untouched, an old decaying horrible thing that could not be dug out and examined. She imagined the power of Christ rolling a stone on top of a burial plot, which was all Orva would need, as long as he lived.

"Did you ever meet this Shawn?"

"No. Sarah was a single mother when we met, living in a second-story apartment above a garage in a squalid little town beside a heavily traveled interstate highway. She worked at the desk, and kept Neil in a playpen behind it."

"Poor thing. I guarantee she was so scared. So alone."

"She was."

"And too proud to return to her home."

Orva nodded.

"She had a lot of spunk, back then."

He shook his head, a wistful expression in his eyes.

"But a year into our marriage she was like a sputtering candle. The flame eventually died, for me, and for her two baby girls. It was only lit for Neil.

"But Marie and Emmylou seem like well-adjusted girls. They don't really give me more hassle than any normal little girls would.

"I tried to give what Sarah wouldn't. Or couldn't. I'm never sure which one it was."

He spread his hands, shrugged his shoulders.

"There was so much helplessness, at that point. Sometimes I would come home to find her on the floor, playing with Neil, while Marie screamed and cried in her little swing. I could tell by her red face, the heat in her tiny body, that the crying had been going on far too long. That first time, we had an awful row. I'm not proud of how angry I was. She never breastfed Marie, so I changed her diaper, fed her, and cuddled her most of the evening.

"That was pretty much the order of my days. So if I protect those two girls, that's the reason. I was their mother and father both.

"But . . . they loved their mother."

"Of course they did. Children will always seek for love in their parents, no matter how those parents mistreat them. It's a natural sense we all have. Without the love and approval of a mother and father, there will always be a missing link to your emotional well-being."

Edna was confused. Was the portrayal of a nearly perfect marriage all a hoax? He had her believe everything had been healthy, above normal.

His beloved wife.

"Why did you never let on? When . . . well, before we were married, you gave me the sense that your marriage was just perfect. You did love Sarah."

For a long moment, he said nothing.

"You know, Edna, it's in our culture. It's our way of hiding the raw deals that come along. I don't know if it's pride or simply Amish etiquette, but we present a shining picture of normalcy to those around us. It's the way we are raised."

Edna thought of Sadie and Fannie, the constant drama, the well-voiced opinions that reverberated through the community and bounced back to bite them again and again. They took no offense. Life was real, it held disappointment and plenty of folks who rubbed them the wrong way, and they both had no qualms about airing their assessment of any given situation.

Edna burst out laughing.

"I know two people who don't fit into that category at all."

"Who?"

"My sisters."

"And you."

Edna boxed Orva's shoulder. He laughed, grabbed her hand.

"I have been through plenty of trials this year, so I've quieted down quite a bit."

"I hope you don't, Edna. I enjoy your outspokenness; you know that."

After the talk they had, Edna had an easier time with the children. She understood Orva's lack of discipline with the girls when she thought it necessary, and she was also patient with his view of Neil's arrogant ways.

Edna realized he wasn't always arrogant.

Like this morning.

Neil was usually late to make an appearance, and Orva was pacing the floor, watching the clock, knowing the driver would show up any minute, and that Neil still had not donned his three or four sweatshirts or his work shoes that needed to be laced. His bacon, egg, and cheese sandwich that Edna had wrapped in aluminum foil was often eaten in three bites or grabbed to take along.

Why couldn't this boy hurry upstairs? How long did it take to use the bathroom, brush teeth, and get dressed? And so Orva paced, watched the driveway and fumed, like a hissing radiator.

When Neil finally made his appearance, his eyes hooded, and his mouth in a perpetual scowl, Orva had to say something, anything, to remind Neil that he was late and why couldn't he get down sooner?

Edna gritted her teeth, busied herself at the sink, and thought Orva would never get it.

Neil didn't bother answering, but merely slumped through the kitchen, grabbed his shoes and brought them in to sit on the recliner to put them on his feet. After he laced them, he left chunks of dried mud and a trail of residue to the counter, where he picked up his lunch. He clutched the sandwich between the palm of his hand and the handle of his lunchbox and slammed sloppily out the door.

Edna had learned early on to withhold the good morning or the "Bye" as he went out the door. It was like bouncing a foam ball against an iceberg. It was only a waste of a perfectly good foam ball, and if this was the way he wanted it, then this is how it would be.

On Tuesday evening of the following week, Carla Yoder arrived in her own cart and horse, which was nothing short of breathtaking. The cart itself was a masterpiece, with outsized wheels, natural wood polished to a glossy sheen, the seat high, and a sturdy back upholstered in red. The horse was unlike anything Edna had ever seen.

Very unusual, she thought. Like a miniature workhorse with the black and white markings of a paint. He was gorgeous, this compact animal with a heavy, arched neck, a mane and tail so thick and flowing it was like poetry when he moved, his knees lifted high. Carla was dressed warmly, with a lap robe across her legs, but when she brought the horse to a stop, she leaped out to calm him as the garage door was lifted from the inside and set up the usual clatter on its way up the steel tracks.

The horse stood, but his head was held high, his feet prancing as he obeyed.

It was Neil.

Edna watched, peered closely to see what he would do, confronted with this shy young girl driving her own rig, something he'd never attempted. Neil had never even shown an interest in a horse or a buggy.

He stepped aside, then spoke to her. She looped the reins in the ring attached to the harness, and with Neil on one side and Carla on the other, they unhitched together. It was Carla who led the horse out of the shafts, but it was Neil who took him to the stable.

She stood till he reappeared. They spoke a few words, then Carla walked up to the house and Neil closed the garage door.

Edna hurried to the door, drying her hands on a dish towel.

"Come in, Carla. It is too cold to be riding around in a cart," she said, laughing.

"He needs driving," Carla replied, in the soft lispy voice that Edna had thought so endearing.

"Well, he's a beauty."

"Gypsy Vanner. A foreign breed. He's my project, and quite a handful."

Edna shook her head.

"Never heard of them."

"They're not that common."

She had hung her coat on an empty hook, then draped her scarf across it, before checking her hair and covering in the mirror above the washbowl. Satisfied, she turned, gave Edna the full benefit of her smile, a dazzling display of white teeth in an almost perfect face.

Real natural beauty, something Edna had never possessed. For an instant, she wondered how it would feel to look in a mirror and be aware of your own good looks, to know you were presentable, beautiful.

Carla did not seem to be the type of girl to be vain in a *grosfeelich* way. She was only fifteen, had not entered the maelstrom of *rumschpringa,* so perhaps that was why she appeared untouched, unaware of the impact she would have as she grew older.

"How is Marie doing for you?" Edna asked.

"It's a bit soon to tell, but she seems willing. Her attention span is like a six-year-old. Really short. She's easily distracted, and I think it's hard for her to focus on her work."

Edna nodded. "Well, I'm so glad you agreed to do this. It will mean a lot to her, as she grows older, to be able to keep up with her class."

Carla looked around.

"They're upstairs. I'll get them."

"Marie!" Edna called, as Carla got out her books on the folding table in the living room.

The girls clattered down the stairs, eager to spend the evening with Carla. Edna smiled at them, then ushered them into the living room, before leaving quietly to resume her work in the kitchen.

It wasn't long before she heard someone in the laundry room. She smiled to herself and looked up to find Neil in the doorway, his hair combed a certain way, his hands in his pockets, and his shoulders hunched self-consciously.

"Any of that chocolate cake left?" he asked gruffly.

"No. Actually, there isn't. But I made chocolate chip cookies today."

He nodded, headed to the refrigerator for milk, set the gallon jug on the table and reached into the cupboard for a glass.

Edna almost asked him why wasn't he in his room the way he normally was, then thought better of it.

No use in scaring him off.

The kitchen was quiet, with only the sound of Carla's soft voice breaking the silence.

Neil dipped three cookies in his glass of milk, leaning forward over it as he wolfed them down in two bites, and turned his eyes repeatedly to the living room before casting covert glances in Edna's direction. She could sense his indecision, both wanting to stay and to disappear up the stairs to his room at the same time.

He reached for another cookie.

Carla's low melodious voice rose and fell.

Neil got up, went to the laundry room and returned with the DeWalt battery lamp. He walked through the kitchen without looking at Edna, and set it on the bureau by the couch.

"Thought you might need some light in here," he said gruffly.

Carla had been leaning over Marie's work, but she straightened, smiled at Neil, and thanked him before returning to her work.

He walked away slowly.

Carla watched him go. Neil reached the stairway and hesitated before making his way slowly up the stairs.

Hmm, Edna thought. Very interesting. He couldn't sit in the living room the way he wanted to, and the kitchen meant eating more cookies and putting up with her. Her shoulders shook as she turned her back to hide the laughter. Ah, young love. Only once were you smitten, never again slain by Cupid's arrow in quite the same way. Well, this was the cutest thing she'd ever seen, and she felt privileged to be a spectator. She would have to keep very tight control of her verbal observances.

She heard Carla tell Marie that she'd done well, but it was time for her to leave, driving her horse the way she had.

Marie said it was dark, how was she going to get home?

"I have lights, Marie. Bright ones," Carla answered.

"Oh, good. 'Cause I was going to tell you to stay here for the night. You could sleep with me and Emmylou. We have twin beds, but you could sleep in the middle on a pile of blankets."

"I could, couldn't I? That would be fun. O.K., Marie, one more time. Let's say the six times tables. Ready?"

Marie began, haltingly, stumbling already over six times three. Emmylou bounced up and down in her chair, broke in and recited the whole set without skipping a beat.

Marie's face crumpled, and she began to cry. Suddenly she balled her fists, drew in a deep breath, and her face turned red with rage before she attacked Emmylou, hitting and scratching.

Edna hurried to the living room, amid Emmylou's yells of protest.

Carla lifted a pale, worried face to Edna, who peeled Marie off her sister, with a firm hand on each shoulder.

"Stop it, Marie. That's not fair to Emmylou."

"Let go of me!" Marie shrieked.

Edna only grasped harder, and Marie's shrieks turned to yells of frustration and anger, till Edna hustled her away out to the kitchen and pushed her firmly into a chair, telling her to stay there till she calmed down.

"Everybody loves Emmylou. Nobody loves me. You're not my mother. You can't boss me around. I wish you wouldn't live here," she yelled.

Emmylou was lying on the couch with her back turned, hiding her face as Marie's words roared through the house. Carla was busying herself in the living room, without as much as glancing in Marie's direction, obviously a stranger to outbursts such as this.

Edna stood firm, her arms crossed, waiting for the storm to pass. When the yelling turned to screams, she reached for the distraught little girl, lifted her up, and carried her to the laundry room. Marie's eyes opened wide, and the screams stopped immediately.

"You're . . . you're not going to paddle me, are you?" she whimpered.

Edna set her down, hard, pushed her face close to hers and said, "No, I'm not going to. But you will be punished properly for this behavior. I don't care if you tell your father or Neil. I am your mother now, and throwing a fit like that is unacceptable. You know we love you, and that fit you threw was only being mad that Emmylou knows the six times tables. She studied with you. You didn't care if you learned them or not, because that's how you are. It's time you straighten up.

"You will wash dishes for a week, every single evening."

"I don't want to," Marie whimpered.

"I don't care if you want to or not, you're going to. Maybe till Friday or when you'll know your times tables. Now get in there and tell Carla and Emmylou you're sorry."

Marie refused to apologize. She sat down on the floor, hid her face in her hands, shook her head from side to side.

Edna did not coax or force her, but allowed her to sit alone while she told Carla how bad she felt. Carla assured Edna in her breathy voice that everything was fine, she was just upset, and that things would be different at the next session, but her face appeared pinched and drawn.

Edna accompanied her to the laundry room for her coat, watched as she bent to pat Marie's shoulder, and was ready to help her out the door when Neil appeared, got down his coat, and told Edna he'd do it.

Carla told him she could hitch up by herself, she was quite used to it, but Neil wouldn't allow it. Carla became quite flustered, didn't tell Edna good night, and fumbled with the buttons on her coat before following Neil out into the night.

Edna made a mental note to teach Neil to open a door for girls, to stand back and allow them to go first, the way Orva had always done.

She gritted her teeth when Orva came into the laundry room, his eyes red-rimmed with fatigue, took one look at the pouting Marie, and bent to console her. He coaxed her to his recliner, where he sat her on his lap and spoke to her in quiet tones of understanding, polishing and smoothing all of life's rough edges for his precious, neglected daughter, while Edna was left to fume, thinking how gladly she would have administered a sound "paddling," the way she had been disciplined at home.

But Orva thought of Marie as a helpless, unloved infant.

How immeasurable was communication between a man and a woman? Had she never known of the children and their first mother, she would be devastated, unable to understand Orva's way.

He would always feel responsible for the little girl's longing for their mother, but it was to be understood, of course.

And Edna loved him even more, for all he had endured as a child and all the trials of adulthood, yet he carried on bravely.

CHAPTER 23

IT WAS SUNDAY MORNING, WITH ITS USUAL SENSE OF URGENCY TO COMB the girls' hair, get them dressed in the best dresses and pinafore-style aprons, and prepare a good, hot breakfast, the way her mother had always done. Her mam said it was important to feed the body as well as the soul before and during church services.

She would take time to sit down and read the text for that day's Scripture, a sight Edna would always cherish. Her mother was not the neatest, most fashionable woman in church, but the heart inside was filled with a love, a curiosity, and caring for those around her.

Edna thought perhaps that was why she worked as a *maud* for so many different people; she had inherited her Mam's curiosity about people's lives.

Upstairs, Marie was arguing loudly with Emmylou. Her strident voice broke into Edna's thoughts, and she gazed upward, heaving a sigh of resignation.

Here we go again.

"Alright. Marie, what's going on?" she called from the foot of the stairway.

Emmylou's worried little face appeared, her hair sticking out in every direction. "She's mad!" she informed her.

What else is new? Edna thought, a weariness creeping across her shoulders.

"Marie!"

"What?"

"What's wrong?"

"Emmylou wants to wear green, and I don't. I want to wear my lavender dress."

"Well, go ahead and wear it."

"No, we have to wear the same. She's my sister."

So of course, as usual, Emmylou gave in, and they both appeared in the lavender dresses. Edna praised Emmylou, telling her how nice it was that she gave in and did what her sister wanted.

Marie sniffed and said she should have, Emmylou was younger than she was.

Edna gritted her teeth again. *With that attitude, young lady, you're going to have a hard row to hoe,* she wanted to tell her, but turned her back to start breakfast.

Orva came in from the barn, then sat at the kitchen table drinking his coffee as Edna made scrambled eggs, toast, and sausages.

"Cold this morning," he observed.

Edna didn't answer. She was still seething, thinking how Marie would always be a handful and that father of hers would always take her part, no matter what. Marie would vent her frustrations, never giving in, and he would come along with the Band-Aid of compliance, cajoling and wheedling her into a better mood. She did nothing wrong in her father's eyes.

Edna tried to picture this helpless baby, crying on and on, with her father being the one who would rescue her from the neglect.

Did she still feel the unreasonable disinterest of her mother? Why else was a child so unlovable?

Orva watched Edna's face as they ate, then got up to dress in his Sunday clothes. Edna washed dishes, and listened to Emmylou tell Marie that her gray bunny was going to have baby bunnies and all of them would be gray.

Marie scoffed at Emmylou, saying that gray bunny was a boy, so how could he have baby bunnies? As sweet-natured as ever, Emmylou agreed immediately, nodding her head and giggling at her own mistake. Edna found herself hoping the gray bunny would have babies to prove Marie wrong.

Marie yelled, clutched her head, and told Edna to stop yanking on the brush; she was pulling out all her hair. Edna told her she wasn't pulling hard, and to stop right this minute.

Orva came out of the bedroom in his white shirt and black trousers, his vest and coat in his hand, freshly shaved and showered. Edna always thought he was the best-looking man in church.

In any church.

"Edna, perhaps her head is a bit sensitive," he said softly.

"Perhaps it's not," Edna ground out, getting a surprised look from Orva, and a flash of righteous indignation from Marie.

"You know, I pull on the hairbrush just the same as I do for Emmylou, and she never makes a sound, Marie. So what does that tell you?"

"She's your pet. You love her, and you don't love me."

In exasperation, Edna sought Orva's approval, a bit of support to help with this difficult child, but found his eyes accusing her instead.

But Emmylou was so much easier to love. Whatever Edna required of her was fine, she sang or hummed under her breath as she played alone, ate what was on the table, and never complained about anything.

Edna turned away and finished Marie's hair before starting on Emmylou. She felt the lump rise in her throat, the separation from Orva already painful, manipulated by his willful daughter.

The ride to church was icy, and Edna's words frosted with resentment. She hadn't bargained for this the day she married him. Could not have known. The image of a neglected newborn was wearing thin with the way Marie bucked her for every reason imaginable, especially when Orva was in the house. And furthermore, where was Neil? Orva never attempted to get that boy to church. He merely stayed at a friend's house or lay in bed with the comfort of knowing his father would go to church and never bother him at all.

Edna was subdued as she greeted the women she had come to know as her own church people. Since moving into Orva's district, she felt welcomed, honored.

Here was the poor widower with a new wife, and by all accounts a capable one, a talented older girl who loved the whole family as her own.

They were such a sweet couple, so obviously in love. The children accepted Edna as their own mother, now didn't they?

Whatever Edna appeared, a rosy glow surrounded her, the other married ladies in awe of the newcomer. And friendly. Edna was so happy and talkative.

But this morning covert glances were directed her way. What was wrong with Edna? She seemed distant, battered down.

She cried as the minister talked, cried when they knelt to pray, wiped tears when they stood to hear Scripture being read. What had gone on, they wondered, casting inquisitive glances.

The white-haired grandmothers in the front row, the ones with bowed heads and hands with heavy blue veins threaded across the tops of their hands like rivers and tributaries on a road map, took notice.

They saw Edna and knew. They sent silent prayers.

It was the way of it. You couldn't expect anything else. Any girl, no matter their age, who stepped into another mother's territory, was bound to have days where she knew she was in over her head.

The children weren't hers. They were Orva's. That biological tie was missing. And so there was work, struggling, a path that turned unexpectedly to steep, treacherous climbing.

After services, when Edna sat alone, waiting till Orva made an appearance to ask if she was ready to go, Sylvia Burkholder, Paul Burkholder's wife, made her way across the kitchen to sit beside her.

Perched like a small bird, Edna thought. Sylvia, who was in her eighties, couldn't have weighed more than ninety pounds. Maybe a hundred.

Tiredly, Edna turned to acknowledge her. During services, she'd felt as if she was underwater, the congregation and the speaker swimming in circles. She was deflated now, exhausted, longing for home and a quiet place to rest.

"How is everything with your family?" Sylvia asked.

Just peachy. It's none of your business, Edna thought, but counted to ten, and turned to smile at the tiny little lady, hoping her smile was not too crocodilian.

"Good. Good. Everything's fine."

The curious eye sparkled behind the round frames of her eyeglasses, which she reached up to adjust, a small smile spreading across her face.

"Well, that's strange," she quipped.

"What?"

"That everything is good."

"Well, it is."

"You know, I married a widower with two children. We had ten of our own, after that. So I feel as if I know what you're going through. It's not always good. The children and their father have a special bond, and no matter how much you tell yourself you love them as your own, you don't quite manage it."

She lifted an arthritic finger with knobs like acorns beneath the skin. Her hands were a testament to pain and hard work, for sure.

"After I had a newborn of my own, I realized the difference. The irritation that came so easily with Paul's little ones simply vanished with my own. Do you find yourself resenting his protection of them?"

Edna nodded, ashamed to have her deepest struggle brought to light.

Sylvia wagged the knobby finger.

"Don't feel bad. It's a circle. He protects the children because he feels you're too hard on them, and you're too hard on them because you know he won't help you with discipline. You feel alone against your husband and children, and you think you're the only person in the world who has ever been quite as much of a failure."

The old gnarled hand was placed on her knee.

"Take heart. It's only normal. This, too, shall pass. If you need a listening ear, come pay me a visit. I have a quilt in frame."

At that moment, Marie ran over, told her Orva had sent her to let her know it was time to go. Edna nodded, placed her hand on the old one, and whispered, "*Denke*" before getting up and leaving Sylvia. With tears threatening again, there was no use trying to say more.

Orva was concerned, tentative. He searched her face, made small, cheerful talk, which Edna acknowledged with monosyllables of her own. Her throat felt as if an apple had taken up residence somewhere in her esophagus, the endless amount of water in her tear ducts threatening to squeeze out like the nozzle of a hose.

"Philip Yoder was interesting today. I always enjoy hearing him talk about Thanksgiving. He's a history buff. But you know, he totally has a point, how being ungrateful is one of the major sins. I think God wants our gratitude, our *dankbar* feelings, and to always mention this in our prayers."

Yeah well, Philip was underwater with everyone else, so I don't know what he bubbled on about, Edna thought.

"What's wrong, Edna?"

"Nothing."

"You don't seem very happy."

From the back seat, a loud throat clearing was followed by an emphatic "She's always grouchy. Nothing different today."

Orva turned around, "That's enough, Marie."

Emmylou began singing "When the Roll Is Called up Yonder" in her high piping little voice, as she tapped out the tune in time with her fingers. The unexpected sweetness of Emmylou's voice, coupled with one smidgen of support from Orva, sent the tear ducts full steam ahead. Edna wailed and snarfed into her handkerchief, coughed and choked and heaved with sobs.

Orva became alarmed, put an arm around her to draw her close, but Edna pulled away, snapped at him with unreasonable words, then went on with her hiccup and nose blowing.

"Edna, it's alright. Whatever I might have done to hurt your feelings, I'm sorry."

"You take up for the girls and you never make Neil go to church. You care much more about your children than you do about me." The "me" was extended to a long high wail, followed by more snuffling and nose blowing.

Orva brought the reins down on the horse's back, and they traveled home with record speed. Even Marie was quiet in the back seat, having never experienced an unraveling quite like this. Edna sank into the corner of the buggy, drew the lap robe tightly around her legs, and crossed her arms to pull the thin black shawl around her shivering body. She was cold and miserable and felt dreadful.

Now what?

All she could think of was that awful ham they had served at the lunch table. Grayish, slippery, and with a band of white fat circling it, completely unfit for human consumption. She swallowed and felt the saliva rush into her mouth.

Well, marriage was certainly interesting. Here she was, face splotchy with red and white patches from crying, eyes red and swollen, speaking in an unkind tone, and letting her husband get a glimpse of the real person he married.

Relieved to see the large house and shop come into view, Edna took a deep, cleansing breath, kept her face averted, climbed off the buggy as quickly as possible and hurried into the house without saying another word. She clawed at the strings of the bonnet and threw off her shawl before making a mad dash to the bathroom, with the smell of that awful ham clinging to her throat.

She had not vomited for many years, and she found the experience as horribly unpleasant as ever. She wiped her mouth, washed her face, peered into the mirror through whale's eyes, and thought how much she resembled Shrek, the green ogre. She loosened her cape and apron, sank into the deep cushions of the living room couch, drew up a soft blanket and closed her eyes. The room spun, tilted the couch sideways, then spun to the right again. She groaned.

Marie and Emmylou raced up the stairs, chattering like anxious birds. She heard Orva come in and listened to the bathroom door open. When he returned, he stopped and stood by the couch till she'd opened her eyes.

"You O.K.?" he asked quietly.

"Yes," she said weakly. "But there was something wrong with that ham they served at church. It was so gross."

"I didn't notice."

"Men don't. They eat anything." Edna huffed, then flopped onto her side and closed her eyes, shutting Orva out of her miserable existence.

Orva reached down to pat her shoulder, but Edna shrugged his hand away. He sighed, headed to the kitchen to make popcorn and put the coffee on.

He couldn't help but feel a jolt of panic, remembering his times with Sarah. To have Edna turn into this bear was a bit puzzling. This was not his beloved wife he knew and loved. He filled the coffeepot with water, mused about the fit she'd taken this morning already when combing the girls' hair. Well, nothing was perfect in life. Nothing.

Edna slept well that night, and awoke refreshed and full of energy, her good humor returned like the tide, sure and strong as always.

She filled the wringer washer with hot water and laundry detergent, sorted clothes, and got a load going before waking the girls. She bent to get out the plastic container of sausage to make their breakfast sandwich, opened the lid, and sniffed.

Ugh. What in the world was wrong with this stuff?

It smelled positively spoiled. It was gray and slippery. Seriously.

"Marie, do you mind having toast and cereal this morning? I'm sorry, but I think this stuff is not fit to eat."

"What?"

Marie peered into the container of sausage, sniffed, said it was O.K. She wanted a sausage, egg, and cheese sandwich.

"You sure, Marie? I bought Cinnamon Toast Crunch. Your favorite."

"Nope. I'm hungrier than cereal."

All her good humor asserted, Edna steeled herself and shaped the slimy sausage into patties and fried them, made eggs, put a slice of white American cheese on top and put everything on a toasted roll, then wrapped them in aluminum foil and got out a pitcher of grape juice. She sat down at the table with the girls, teased them about their love of arithmetic, and laughed along with them about the teacher's lack of patience.

They went off to school with a good warm breakfast in their stomach, and a mother who had bounced back from being in ill humor all day Sunday. In Marie's descriptive whispered words to Emmylou, Edna was like one of those fruit bats that hung in a cave, upside down, somewhere in Africa.

She was, and they did, those bats, she'd seen it in her geography book. Emmylou laughed so hard she had to put her head under the covers last night.

Halfway through doing laundry, Edna felt light-headedness coming on but thought it was only from the sickness the day before. She'd hurry up and get everything pegged to the line, then have a huge, very hot cup of coffee with her favorite creamer. Today she'd need all her strength planning this Thanksgiving dinner and calling relatives to let them know what to bring.

The coffee was terrible. Edna got out the blue bottle of creamer, shook it, turned it on its side to check the date, shrugged her shoulders and replaced it.

Ah, well. Must have caught a virus. Stomach bug of some kind. She ate her Bran Flakes with banana slices and a bagel with butter and Season-All, then felt wonderful and got down to business.

Turkey and stuffing.

Potatoes.

Sweet potatoes.

She felt energized, ready to seize the day. Nothing could take away her zest for life now; nothing could remind her of the cloud of gloom that had hidden everything all day yesterday. A good cry was healthy, she reasoned.

She called Sadie and Fannie, and left them hilarious messages in a squeaky Mickey Mouse voice, shaking and laughing as she did so.

She brought fresh hay for the bunnies, thinking they looked cold and lonely, and talked to the horses in the barn as she swept the forebay for Orva. Life was good. Absolutely nothing as satisfying as being married, a mother to children who'd lost their own dear mother. Her nose burned as the tears formed in her eyes. Poor little girls. They did their best, just like herself.

By late afternoon, she was cold, shivering, exhausted. She

turned up the thermostat on the gas heater, leaned over it as it rumbled to life, but chills raced up her spine and across her shoulders the moment she turned away. Nothing to do but wear a sweater in the house.

She told Orva at supper that he needed to check the windows, Neil, too. The house was drafty. Cold. Neil leaned sullenly over his plate of mashed potatoes and meatloaf and sniffed, but kept his opinion to himself. So Orva went around checking for loose windows and doors that weren't properly latched, but told Edna it really was warm in the house, that he saw no reason to repair anything.

Carla arrived in a cloud of pale blue and a fragrance that smelled like youth and sun and dreams. She was so gorgeous, so innocent and unaware.

Edna's nose burned as tears welled in her eyes. She cried in her dishwater because Carla was so lovely and God was so good that He sent this beautiful girl to help Maria with her lessons.

She sniffed, wiped her eyes and watched Neil fold himself into the kitchen recliner just a few feet away from the living room door, opening a magazine she was sure he didn't find interesting at all. Then she got goosebumps and more tears thinking about Neil falling in love with Carla, giving his life to God, and joining the church.

The thought was more than she could handle. Her shoulders heaved as short, hard hiccups of sound came from her throat.

Orva found her crying in the pantry, a bag of potato chips clutched in one hand.

"Edna, my love. What is going on? I'm so worried about you. I want you to see a doctor as soon as possible. I'm afraid you're depressed. I can't help it; I am so afraid you'll be like Sarah was, just a mere shadow of her usual energetic, happy self."

Edna nodded and tried to calm herself, but ended up in his arms, the bag of chips crackling between them.

He bent over her, kissing her forehead as if to comfort a

child, smoothing her hair away from her face, ruining her covering in the process.

He pulled away, lifted her chin to search her eyes, begged her to tell him what was wrong, why she kept bursting into tears.

"I don't know. Or yes I do. It's Carla and Neil and how innocent and how beautiful they both are and God spared his life, maybe, so he can experience a good life with a special girl, and the whole thing is so unbearably sweet how Neil acts so gruff and grownup when all he is, is a little boy. He's scared of life and how he's going to get through it and now he's falling in love with Carla and I can't take it."

Her words ended in a wail, subdued against his shoulder.

Orva pressed her head to his chest, the beginning of a small smile spreading across his face.

Carla's tutoring proved to be priceless. Marie looked forward to every session, responded to her patience and technique of teaching numbers in ways that were understandable. Slowly, the numbers that were jumbled in her head became orderly, with the division and multiplication making sense.

They spent weeks learning to borrow numbers for subtraction, resulting in Emmylou's climb to the head of her class and beyond, as she sat with Carla and absorbed everything she taught Marie.

Edna observed Neil's continued interest in Carla, her whole world collapsing around her with nausea and fatigue.

The Thanksgiving dinner was a disaster, with Edna plowing ahead in spite of being lost in a world she didn't understand, the debilitating sickness and utter weariness beyond anything she could have imagined.

Her sisters told her they couldn't believe she was so dumb and proceeded to tell her she would likely be a mother to her own child in approximately eight months, and why didn't she think of that?

Edna, wide-eyed and shocked, sat at the messy kitchen table and stared at them.

"No, I don't believe it."

"Get used to it, darling," Fannie laughed.

Sadie was clearing the table, shaking her head and laughing. The sisters-in-law all nodded, agreed, washed dishes and chased after children, then left the house in a state of chaos. There was food on the floor, leftovers all over the sink and countertop, stained tablecloths to be washed, along with a mountain of tea towels.

Edna made her way grimly through the day, pinched misbehaving children behind their mother's backs, cried when one sister-in-law said the stuffing was over-salted and got in an argument with her father about senseless politics she knew nothing about.

Her mother watched her and shook her head, thinking about the road Edna would be traveling. A mixed family, for sure. Well, she'd simply have to get the prayer wheels turning, knowing Edna's tendencies to become ruffled at the slightest upheaval of her orderly world. Babies were just that. An upheaval.

Orva got down on his hands and knees, wiped the kitchen floor with methodical strokes, scrubbing the same spot over and over, until Edna told him he'd wipe the shine right off the linoleum if he cleaned it like that. He sat back, grinned up at her, and asked her about appreciation.

"I mean, come on, Edna. A guy needs some admiration for doing a job like this."

She looked into his upturned face and thought, *This is my husband. This is my love, and just look at him.* Every appreciative thought she could summon crowded into her mind, and she got down on the floor and kissed him thoroughly.

"How's that for appreciation?" she asked him, returning his starstruck gaze.

"Edna, I love you. You are everything any man could ever ask for. The day I married you, I became the owner of a rare and precious jewel."

They sat together in the middle of the kitchen floor and talked about their day, laughing at Edna's description of the lumpy potatoes, the thickened gravy that curdled like sour milk, and the creamed corn that had no salt and tasted like a tin can.

"Orva, you know why, don't you?" Edna asked.

"I was hoping that's what was wrong with you a few Sundays ago when you were so cranky."

"Definitely cranky. But, with your love, I can handle anything. Seriously, if I ever feel better, I'll be thrilled."

CHAPTER 24

IT WAS A LONG WINTER.

Edna got through it in a haze of nausea and fatigue. She listened patiently to a bevy of friends, each one with a sure-fire remedy for her morning sickness, which turned into dinner, supper, and evening sickness as well. She bought ginger root and chlorophyll and quit drinking coffee. She went to the chiropractor and went to the Wellness Clinic, made sheep's eyes at the unsympathetic doctor and begged him for a pill, any kind of pill to take away this crippling nausea.

Marie and Emmylou took to staying in their room, doing crossword puzzles or playing with their dolls and toys upstairs, while Edna groaned inwardly as she washed dishes and folded laundry. She eventually flopped on the recliner to hang her arms down the sides, turn her face to the wall, and heave a sigh of self-pity and righteous suffering.

The only bright spot was Carla's tutoring and Neil's ongoing interest. After the first snowfall, she heard him walk into the living room and ask her to stay later; he'd hitch up his riding horse to a tractor tube and take them all for a ride. He accompanied her to the phone to call her parents, and Edna hurried to the window to watch them walk past the porch light and into the dim gray whiteness of a winter evening. The girls were in the laundry room chattering with excitement as they pulled on sweaters, coats, scarves, and boots.

A wail came from Emmylou.

"Now what?" Edna thought with exasperation.

"Wait, Marie! Wait!"

Edna heaved herself from the recliner and hurried to the door of the laundry room. The DeWalt battery lamp revealed the puddles of melted snow, the basket piled with laundry, and the boots strewn everywhere.

"Marie, what now?" she asked.

"She doesn't hurry up," Marie announced staunchly, her bearing like someone in the military, her eyes challenging Edna to do something about it.

"But I can't get my boots on!" Emmylou wailed.

Edna knew if she bent over, she'd lose her supper, the way she had struggled all evening to keep the bit of protein she'd managed to ingest.

"Marie, come back and help Emmylou, please."

"You can do it."

With that, Marie flung herself out the door and down the steps.

Emmylou set up a shriek of denial, then flopped back against the closet and howled. Edna ground her teeth in frustration, went to the door and called out into the gray-white winter evening.

"Marie!"

The dark form was moving into the barn, a mere dot in the swirling landscape.

From behind, Emmylou set up another volley of wails and loud cries of indignation.

Well, she was not going out into that snow and cold to retrieve the disobedient Marie, that was sure. She turned, told Emmylou to hush, she'd help her, then got down on the floor, leaned over, and tugged the boots up over her feet, willing herself to keep her supper from rising in her throat.

"There, Emmy. How's that?"

Emmylou swiped at her tears with the back of her hand, a smile breaking through her despair. Her sunny disposition was her norm, so it was always hard to see her disappointed or hurt.

She lifted herself off the floor, gathered up her mittens, then looked at Edna.

"I don't want to go alone in the dark."

Oh boy, Edna thought.

But she threw on a coat, grabbed her hand, and headed out to the barn in the cold.

She found Neil and Carla standing together under the light of the battery lamp, deep in conversation, with Marie hovering between them, listening to every word. Edna couldn't help the stab of irritation.

Now why couldn't she have enough manners to stay in the background at a time like this? She was the nosiest child.

"Marie, come here."

Reluctantly, Marie tore herself away.

Neil looked up, and a shadow of annoyance crossed his face as he stepped back and turned toward the gate to the horse's stall. Marie was in a huff, Edna could tell by the look on her face and the way she walked.

She gave her clear instructions to care for her younger sister, then turned and walked back to the house.

Was this the way it would always be?

She wasn't always obeyed, and was an annoyance in the life of these children. She was still an unwelcome stand-in for Sarah, and would likely always be. No matter how hard she tried to be a mother, she would always remain a step away. Perhaps that was where the "step" in stepmother came from.

It was a duty, this mothering of Orva's children. Yes, she loved Orva, there was no doubt, never a regret for having married him.

It was the children.

How many stepmothers before her could identify with the pressing responsibility of loving children who weren't particularly crazy about having a replacement? The whole thing weighed down on Edna's shoulders for the hundredth time.

She took to reading a morning devotional, to praying alone with a plea for help in loving these children. She knew a higher power than what she possessed would have to give her the strength to carry on, knowing she could not do it all alone. Neil was irritated when Carla said Marie was able to keep up in her grade, and no longer came to the house to spend her evenings as a tutor.

For some reason or other, he blamed Edna, and returned to his sullen ways, which Orva seemed to ignore. Marie brought homework with heavy red marks. "Do Over." When Edna tried to get Marie to tell her what was going on, she lashed out at her with forceful words of denial, ending in the usual, "You're not my mother."

This time, though, she completely overstepped her boundaries with an emphatic "I hate you." which left Edna no choice but to punish her with an old-fashioned method of discipline.

Orva was told, by his unrepentant daughter, who had omitted her outburst against Edna. When Orva gently questioned Edna's motive in punishing Marie, she told him the reason she had done it, watching his face for signs of support.

But he shook his head, told her Marie was only struggling with her schoolwork, and why had she let Carla go?

"She was the one who said Marie was doing well enough to return to school without tutoring. Not me."

Orva lifted an eyebrow.

"Really? Well, that sheds a different light on the subject."

"Who told you it was me that let her go?"

"Neil."

There you go, Edna thought. It was a sabotage, engineered

by all of them. How was she ever supposed to survive with her neck in the ever-tightening rope?

She went around in a cloud of self-pity for days on end. She didn't speak unless someone spoke to her, and then addressed them all in a clipped tone of voice that bore no sunny disposition toward anyone. Neil slunk upstairs and basically disappeared from her life. Marie glared at her at first, then circled warily, steadily becoming more respectful as time went on.

Orva was exactly the same.

He kept his distance but became increasingly concerned when Edna drew away from them all. Little Emmylou was the brightest star in Edna's darkened universe, never fully absorbing the ill feelings.

Edna did some soul-searching in that time. She decided she was already losing her identity, the zest for life, the quick decision-making, the spoken opinion, it was already falling away like crumbs. She was no longer the independent, outspoken person she had always been.

But was it a good thing?

She wasn't sure. But there was one thing she did know. It was her own fault if she turned into a doormat, with everyone walking all over her, constantly belittling her, saying she was not their mother, and Orva only half agreeing with her when she complained.

The baby came on a blistering day in August, a sweet, dark-haired little boy named Zachary. Edna fell into the role of motherhood as if she had lived her entire life to be crowned with this glory. She dressed him in the softest, dearest little sleepers and onesies, changed diapers, and marveled at God's gift.

She never allowed Orva to take a turn at night, even if he was fussy, saying that was her job, and one she enjoyed.

She did. The house was quiet, shadowed, the wind sighing its night song through the screened windows, the rest of the household in deep slumber while she nestled on the recliner with her precious miracle, who would always be a wonderful present to an undeserving human like her.

She thought of Sarah and Neil, alone in the world, the photographs in the attic paying homage to this kind of love. She felt a new connection to Orva's past since little Zachary came into her life. Was there any bond stronger than the bond between a mother and her first born?

Love came in waves of emotion, a natural tie that took no effort. It was amazing, an awesome gift straight from a loving God.

This was her son. Her's and Orva's. Their genes ran in this child's veins, strong and sure, the traits of their own DNA passed down to another generation.

She had never experienced this miracle with Neil, Marie, or Emmylou. This natural phase had never occurred for her. It was Sarah who had given birth to them, who had spent precious nights caring for her helpless infants. With Neil, it had been like this for Sarah. Perhaps not the same with girls.

And so Edna learned the difference and stopped being quite so hard on herself about her lack of true feeling for Orva's children. The more she relaxed and accepted the ever-present irritation that rose unbidden, the less it happened. To accept these stepchildren was like climbing a flight of stairs. You took one step at a time, waited on God's mercy before you attempted the next step, realizing you might never have the bond you had with children of your own.

And it was alright.

God knew her heart, her mind, her soul. He knew how she struggled to accept Neil's sullen attitude, Marie's selfishness, and Orva's lack of discipline for both of them.

She would not be able to change this natural process. They were his flesh and blood, Marie and Emmylou. Neil was not.

No matter how hard Orva hid this fact, he wore his lack of true parental love on his sleeve. So easily she saw this in Orva, and he saw the same thing in her where Marie and Emmylou were concerned.

But it was alright, she told herself over and over. They were doing the best they could, both of them. As time went on, they would all grow closer.

Wouldn't they?

It was on a warm September evening when the family was spending time on the back patio, a scene that would not have occurred before now. They lounged in patio chairs with their feet propped up on the braces of the table legs, glasses of iced tea scattered among plates with corncobs and half-eaten tomato sandwiches.

Carla and Neil were dating now, and Zachary was already two years old. Orva had put on weight, his neatly trimmed beard showing signs of white and gray along the sides. Edna was round as a mother hen, but it suited her, Orva told her. Motherhood made her face glow and her eyes shine with the happiness of her new role, he said, which Edna took as a compliment.

Carla was an asset to the mixed family structure, the connecting piece that held them closer, her enthusiasm and sunny disposition a boon to Neil's tendencies to be surly. He had changed, in spite of trying hard to remain cool and aloof.

"So, Neil, how many ears of corn was that?" Orva asked, peering around the iced tea pitcher.

"One, two, three. My word, Neil, eight of them," he exclaimed.

Carla giggled, her slender fingers held over her mouth.

"Two are mine. I snuck two over so no one would know I ate six."

"Oh, come on, Carla. You didn't eat six ears of corn," Orva said.

"Sure did! You got a problem with that?"

Edna laughed and reached over to wipe Zachary's mouth.

He was a dark-haired, dark-eyed boy, carrying Edna's traits, which secretly pleased her immensely. Short and muscular for a two-year-old, he was a barrel of energy, running and climbing, always moving at dizzying speed.

He loved Neil, which was much of the reason Neil was warming to Edna. He had largely ignored Zachary as an infant, watching him as he tried to sit by himself, but by the time he was crawling, Neil was bending to pick him up, with the promise of taking him to see the bunnies.

The two years had held a fair share of pain, of family quarrels and hard feelings, with Edna being driven to her knees on numerous occasions, begging God to instill the serenity prayer in all that she had on her plate. A stepmother's role was unbelievably hard so much of the time, and Orva was not always supportive.

But on this evening, when the heat of summer lingered, the promise of colorful leaves and crisp days and nights, Edna felt the hope rise within her, a calm assurance that God had helped her so far, and would continue to do just that. He would bless her with strength and wisdom, even if life felt far from perfect.

We are a family, she thought. *A real honest family. Neil has an absent father, none of them have their mother, except Zachary, but does any of that really matter? We have grown together, and our ties are strong. Perhaps not as cemented as a biological one, but a bond nevertheless.* She could look back and realize that each month brought some small victory, some gain in the ease with which they co-existed.

She watched as Neil reached over to scoop up Zachary, laughing as he howled in protest. Carla leaned over to take him, tugging on his leg, telling Zachary that Neil was mean.

"Komm, Zach. Doppa Komm."

Neil caught Carla's eye and relented. She smiled at him, and he smiled back, his face changed so unbelievably from the surly, unhappy youth of a few years ago. Carla was like an angel, sent from God to give Neil's life a purpose, and as their relationship grew, his confidence grew along with it, and the smiles became more frequent as time went on. Marie was still the one who seemed to be the thorn of Edna's existence. Prickly, outspoken, bossy Marie, with Emmylou bouncing happily in her wake, unaware of being the one who always gave in.

Was it the nature Marie was given, or did she harbor some known thought of never having received her mother's love?

Who could know?

There were, however, signs of Marie's growth. Marie no longer made smart retorts every time something was asked of her, since Edna simply didn't tolerate it.

So there were blessings along the way, small improvements and days when things went smoothly for everyone. Orva's love was constant, a deep and abiding gift that smoothed everything, taking the sharpest edge off the hurtful incidents.

Edna watched Orva help Zachary with his chocolate cupcake, his large stubby fingers carefully peeling the paper away from the cake, his eyes intent on what he was doing, with Zachary waiting, his hands clasped behind his back, as if to control the urge to grab it from his father.

This is my son, she thought.

She watched Neil slide an arm across Carla's shoulder, and thought, *he is my son, too.*

Neil caught her eye, opened his mouth to speak, then closed it again. Suddenly he spoke quickly.

"Edna, you remember when I was in the hospital?"

Edna nodded, smiled her encouragement.

"Remember how you used to knock on my door and say good night? Every evening, no matter what."

Edna laughed. "You mean no matter how much you disliked me?"

"Well, yeah. That, too. But you would always knock and say that. So when I sort of began to realize where I was, and that there were others around me, I wanted to wake up, to let people know I could hear them but I couldn't. And somehow, I listened for that tapping, the sound I was used to hearing. Actually, I looked forward to that sound.

"Every time you did that, it seemed as if you weren't mad at me, no matter how hard I tried to tell myself you should be. I treated you badly those first years. But that knocking is what woke me up."

Edna's face took on all kinds of strange contortions, trying to keep her emotions in check. Carla gazed at Neil with an expression of wonder. Orva caught Edna's eye, tears welling in his own.

Edna took a deep breath to steady her voice.

"Oh Neil, thank you for saying that."

The sun cast a golden evening glow on the surrounding trees, the rock garden illuminated like a shrine, her place of refuge in the first difficult years. God's glory surrounded them, this mixed, imperfect family that would all walk together down the path of life, for better or for worse.

For sure.

THE END

GLOSSARY

ach—Oh, oh dear, or oh my
Ausbund—the book of German songs
bupp or *buppa*—babies who are fussy, anxious
"Das bisht glay, gel?"— You are little, right?
denke—thank you/*Denkbar*—thankful
dichly—kerchief
essa—meal
fa-schticking—suffocating
freundshaft—family
griddlich—unhappy
grosfeelich—full of yourself
house-butza—housecleaning, a twice-yearly, thorough house-
    cleaning.
maud—maid
maud schoffing—working as a maid
ordnung—a set of rules for the community
rumschpringa—the time of youth
schliffa—splinter
shoe lumpa—shoe rag
ungehorsam—disobedient
verboten—forbidden

OTHER BOOKS BY
LINDA BYLER

LIZZIE SEARCHES FOR LOVE SERIES

BOOK ONE

BOOK TWO

BOOK THREE

TRILOGY

COOKBOOK

SADIE'S MONTANA SERIES

BOOK ONE

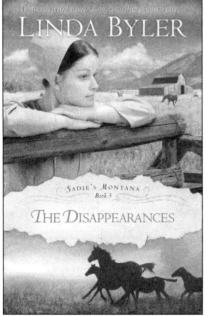

BOOK THREE

BOOK TWO

TRILOGY

LANCASTER BURNING SERIES

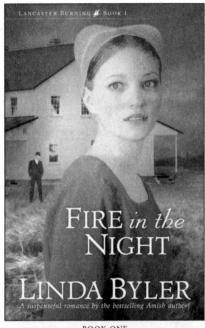

BOOK ONE

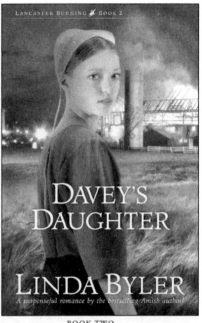

BOOK TWO

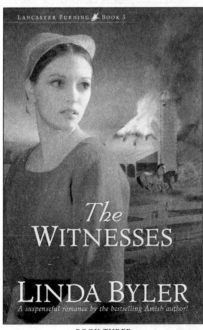

BOOK THREE

TRILOGY

HESTER'S HUNT FOR HOME SERIES

BOOK ONE

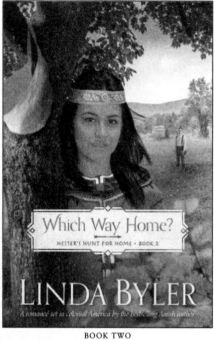

BOOK TWO

BOOK THREE

The Dakota Series

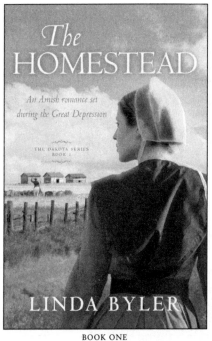

BOOK ONE

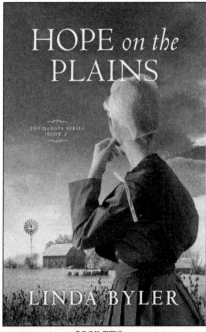

BOOK TWO

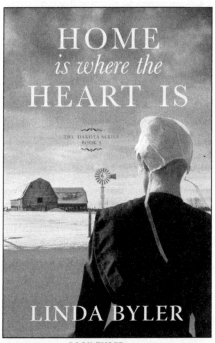

BOOK THREE

CHRISTMAS NOVELLAS

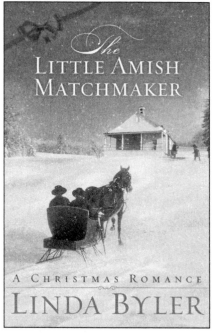

LINDA BYLER

BECKY
Meets Her
MATCH

Is Daniel Stoltzfus
really ready for Becky?

AN AMISH *Christmas* ROMANCE

A Dog for
CHRISTMAS

AN AMISH CHRISTMAS ROMANCE

LINDA BYLER

A Horse For
ELSIE

AN AMISH CHRISTMAS ROMANCE

LINDA BYLER

BUGGY SPOKE SERIES FOR YOUNG READERS

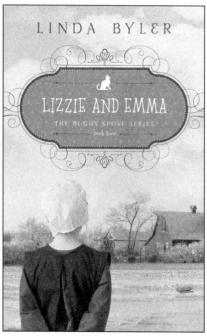

THE HEALING

ABOUT THE AUTHOR

LINDA BYLER WAS RAISED IN AN AMISH FAMILY AND IS AN ACTIVE member of the Amish church today. Growing up, Linda loved to read and write. In fact, she still does. Linda is well-known within the Amish community as a columnist for a weekly Amish newspaper. She writes all her novels by hand in notebooks.

Linda is the author of six series of novels, all set among the Amish communities of North America: Lizzie Searches for Love, Sadie's Montana, Lancaster Burning, Hester's Hunt for Home, The Dakota Series, and the Buggy Spoke Series for younger readers. Linda has also written six Christmas romances set among the Amish: *Mary's Christmas Goodbye*, *The Christmas Visitor*, *The Little Amish Matchmaker*, *Becky Meets Her Match*, *A Dog for Christmas*, and *A Horse for Elsie*. Linda has coauthored *Lizzie's Amish Cookbook: Favorite Recipes from Three Generations of Amish Cooks!*